PRAISE FOR *ALL THE BIRDS IN THE SKY*

"The characters leap off the page… A weird and charming read."
GUARDIAN

"Imagine Diana Wynne Jones, Douglas Coupland and Neil Gaiman walk into a bar and through some weird fusion of magic and science have a baby. That offspring is Charlie Jane Anders' lyrical debut novel."
INDEPENDENT ON SUNDAY

"As hopeful as it is hilarious, and highly recommended."
NEW YORK TIMES

"A captivating novel."
WASHINGTON POST

"Charlie Jane Anders' brilliant novel has the hallmarks of an instant classic. A beautifully written, funny, tremendously moving tale."
LA TIMES

"Imaginative, witty, and moving… perfectly right for our time."
BUZZFEED

"At turns darkly funny and deeply melancholy… A polished gem of a novel."
LIBRARY JOURNAL (starred review)

"[A] knock-your-socks-off blend of science and magic."
BOOKLIST (starred review)

"Reminiscent of the best of Jo Walton and Nina Kiriki Hoffman."
KIRKUS (starred review)

"Clever and wonde_____"
PUBLISHERS

D1427752

ALL THE BIRDS IN THE SKY

CHARLIE JANE ANDERS

TITAN BOOKS

All the Birds in the Sky
Print edition ISBN: 9781785650550
E-book edition ISBN: 9781785650567

Published by Titan Books
A division of Titan Publishing Group Ltd
144 Southwark Street, London SE1 0UP

First edition: January 2016
8 10 9

A CIP catalogue record for this title is available from the British Library.

Printed and bound by CPI Group (UK) Ltd, Croydon, CR0 4YY

To Annalee

"In the game of life and evolution there are three players at the table: human beings, nature, and machines. I am firmly on the side of nature. But nature, I suspect, is on the side of the machines."

GEORGE DYSON, *Darwin Among The Machines*

BOOK
ONE

1

WHEN PATRICIA WAS six years old, she found a wounded bird. The sparrow thrashed on top of a pile of wet red leaves in the crook of two roots, waving its crushed wing. Crying, in a pitch almost too high for Patricia to hear. She looked into the sparrow's eye, enveloped by a dark stripe, and she saw its fear. Not just fear, but also misery—as if this bird knew it would die soon. Patricia still didn't understand how the life could just go out of someone's body forever, but she could tell this bird was fighting against death with everything it had.

Patricia vowed with all her heart to do everything in her power to save this bird. This was what led to Patricia being asked a question with no good answer, which marked her for life.

She scooped up the sparrow with a dry leaf, very gently, and laid it in her red bucket. Rays of the afternoon sun came at the bucket horizontally, bathing the bird in red light so it looked radioactive. The bird was still whipping around, trying to fly with one wing.

"It's okay," Patricia told the bird. "I've got you. It's okay."

Patricia had seen creatures in distress before. Her big sister, Roberta, liked to collect wild animals and play with them. Roberta put frogs into a rusty Cuisinart that their mom had tossed out, and stuck mice into her homemade rocket launcher, to see how far she could shoot them. But this was the first time Patricia looked at a living creature in pain and really saw it, and every time she looked into the bird's eye she swore harder that this bird was under her protection.

"What's going on?" asked Roberta, smashing through the branches nearby.

Both girls were pale, with dark brown hair that grew super-straight no matter what you did and nearly button noses. But Patricia was a wild, grubby girl, with a round face, green eyes, and perpetual grass stains on her torn overalls. She was already turning into the girl the other girls wouldn't sit with, because she was too hyper, made nonsense jokes, and wept when anybody's balloon (not just her own) got popped. Roberta, meanwhile, had brown eyes, a pointy chin, and absolutely perfect posture when she sat without fidgeting in a grown-up chair and a clean white dress. With both girls, their parents had hoped for a boy and picked out a name in advance. Upon each daughter's arrival, they'd just stuck an a on the end of the name they already had.

"I found a wounded bird," Patricia said. "It can't fly, its wing is ruined."

"I bet I can make it fly," Roberta said, and Patricia knew she was talking about her rocket launcher. "Bring it here. I'll make it fly real good."

"No!" Patricia's eyes flooded and she felt short of breath. "You can't! You can't!" And then she was running, careening, with the red bucket in one hand. She could hear her sister behind her, smashing branches. She ran faster, back to the house.

Their house had been a spice shop a hundred years ago, and it still smelled of cinnamon and turmeric and saffron and garlic and a little sweat. The perfect hardwood floors had been walked on by visitors from India and China and everywhere, bringing everything spicy in the world. If Patricia closed her eyes and breathed deeply, she could imagine the people unloading wooden foil-lined crates stamped with names of cities like Marrakesh and Bombay. Her parents had read a magazine article about renovating Colonial trade houses and had snapped up this building, and now they were constantly yelling at Patricia not to run indoors or scratch any of the perfect oak furnishings, until their foreheads showed veins. Patricia's parents were the sort of people who could be in a good mood and angry at almost the same time.

Patricia paused in a small clearing of maples near the back door. "It's okay," she told the bird. "I'll take you home. There's an old birdcage in the attic. I know where to find it. It's a nice cage, it has a perch and a swing. I'll put you in there, I'll tell my parents. If anything happens to you, I will hold my breath until I faint. I'll keep you safe. I promise."

"No," the bird said. "Please! Don't lock me up. I would prefer you just kill me now."

"But," Patricia said, more startled that the bird was refusing her protection than that he was speaking to her. "I can keep you safe. I can bring you bugs or seeds or whatever."

"Captivity is worse than death for a bird like me," the sparrow said. "Listen. You can hear me talking. Right? That means you're special. Like a witch! Or something. And that means you have a duty to do the right thing. Please."

"Oh." This was all a lot for Patricia to take in. She sat down on a particularly large and grumpy tree root, with thick bark that felt a little damp and sort of like sawtooth rocks. She could hear Roberta beating the bushes and the ground with a big Y-shaped stick, over in the next clearing, and she worried about what would happen if Roberta heard them talking. "But," Patricia said, quieter so that Roberta would not hear. "But your wing is hurt, right, and I need to take care of you. You're stuck."

"Well." The bird seemed to think about this for a moment. "You don't know how to heal a broken wing, do you?" He flapped his bad wing. He'd looked just sort of gray-brown at first, but up close she could see brilliant red and yellow streaks along his wings, with a milk-white belly and a dark, slightly barbed beak.

"No. I don't know anything. I'm sorry!"

"Okay. So you could just put me up in a tree and hope for the best, but I'll probably get eaten or starve to death." His head bobbed. "Or… I mean. There is one thing."

"What?" Patricia looked at her knees, through the thready holes in her denim overalls, and thought her kneecaps looked like weird eggs. "What?" She looked over at the sparrow in the bucket, who was in turn studying her with one eye, as if trying to decide whether to trust her.

"Well," the bird chirped. "I mean, you could take me to

the Parliament of Birds. They can fix a wing, no problem. And if you're going to be a witch, then you should meet them anyway. They're the smartest birds around. They always meet at the most majestic tree in the forest. Most of them are over five years old."

"I'm older than that," Patricia said. "I'm almost seven, in four months. Or five." She heard Roberta getting closer, so she snatched up the bucket and took off running, deeper into the woods.

The sparrow, whose name was Dirrpidirrpiwheepalong, or Dirrp for short, tried to give Patricia directions to the Parliament of Birds as best he could, but he couldn't see where he was going from inside the bucket. And his descriptions of the landmarks to watch for made no sense to Patricia. The whole thing reminded her of one of the Cooperation exercises at school, which she was hopeless at ever since her only friend, Kathy, moved away. At last, Patricia perched Dirrp on her finger, like Snow White, and he bounced onto her shoulder.

The sun went down. The forest was so thick, Patricia could barely see the stars or the moon, and she tumbled a few times, scraping her hands and her knees and getting dirt all over her new overalls. Dirrp clung to the shoulder strap of her overalls so hard, his talons pinched her and almost broke her skin. He was less and less sure where they were going, although he was pretty sure the majestic Tree was near some kind of stream or maybe a field. He definitely thought it was a very thick tree, set apart from other trees, and if you looked the right way the two big branches of the Parliamentary Tree fanned like wings. Also, he could tell the direction pretty easily by the position of the sun. If the sun had still been out.

"We're lost in the woods," Patricia said with a shiver. "I'm probably going to be eaten by a bear."

"I don't think there are bears in this forest," Dirrp said. "And if one attacks us, you could try talking to it."

"So I can talk to all animals now?" Patricia could see this coming in useful, like if she could convince Mary Fenchurch's poodle to bite her the next time Mary was mean to Patricia. Or if the next nanny her parents hired owned a pet.

"I don't know," Dirrp said. "Nobody ever explains anything to me." Patricia decided there was nothing to do but climb the nearest tree and see if she could see anything from it. Like a road. Or a house. Or some landmark that Dirrp might recognize.

It was much colder on top of the big old oak that Patricia managed to jungle-gym her way up. The wind soaked into her as if it were water instead of just air. Dirrp covered his face with his one good wing and had to be coaxed to look around. "Oh, okay," he quavered, "let me see if I can make sense of this landscape. This is not really what you call a bird's-eye view. A real bird's-eye view would be much, much higher than this. This is a squirrel's-eye view, at best."

Dirrp jumped off and scampered around the treetop until he spotted what he thought might be one of the signpost trees leading to the Parliamentary Tree. "We're not too far." He sounded perkier already. "But we should hurry. They don't always meet all night, unless they're debating a tricky measure. Or having Question Time. But you'd better hope it's not Question Time."

"What's Question Time?"

"You don't want to know," Dirrp said.

Patricia was finding it much harder to get down from the treetop than it was to get up, which seemed unfair. She kept almost losing her grip, and the drop was nearly a dozen feet.

"Hey, it's a bird!" a voice said from the darkness just as Patricia reached the ground. "Come here, bird. I only want to bite you."

"Oh no," Dirrp said.

"I promise I won't play with you too much," the voice said. "It'll be fun. You'll see!"

"Who is that?" Patricia asked.

"Tommington," Dirrp said. "He's a cat. He lives in a house with people, but he comes into the forest and kills a lot of my friends. The Parliament is always debating what to do about him."

"Oh," Patricia said. "I'm not scared of a little kitty."

Tommington jumped, pushing off a big log, and landed on Patricia's back, like a missile with fur. And sharp claws. Patricia screeched and nearly fell on her face. "Get off me!" she said.

"Give me the bird!" Tommington said.

The white-bellied black cat weighed almost as much as Patricia. He bared his teeth and hissed in Patricia's ear as he scratched at her.

Patricia did the only thing that came to mind: She clamped one hand over poor Dirrp, who was hanging on for dear life, and threw her head forward and down until she was bent double and her free hand was almost touching her toes.

The cat went flying off her back, haranguing as he fell.

"Shut up and leave us alone," Patricia said.

"You can talk. I never met a human who could talk before. Give me that bird!"

"No," Patricia said. "I know where you live. I know your owner. If you are naughty, I will tell. I will tell on you." She was kind of fibbing. She didn't know who owned Tommington, but her mother might. And if Patricia came home covered with bites and scratches her mother would be mad. At her but also at Tommington's owner. You did not want Patricia's mom mad at you, because she got mad for a living and was really good at it.

Tommington had landed on his toes, his fur all spiked and his ears like arrowheads. "Give me that bird!" he shrieked.

"No!" Patricia said. "Bad cat!" She threw a rock at Tommington. He yowled. She threw another rock. He ran away.

"Come on," Patricia said to Dirrp, who didn't have much choice in the matter. "Let's get out of here."

"We can't let that cat know where the Parliament is," Dirrp whispered. "If he follows us, he could find the Tree. That would be a disaster. We should wander in circles, as though we are lost."

"We *are* lost," Patricia said.

"I have a pretty reasonably shrewd idea of where we go from here," said Dirrp. "At least, a sort of a notion."

Something rustled in the low bushes just beyond the biggest tree, and for a second the moonlight glinted off a pair of eyes, framed by white fur, and a collar tag.

"We are finished!" Dirrp whispered in a pitiful warble.

"That cat can stalk us forever. You might as well give me to your sister. There is nothing to be done."

"Wait a minute." Patricia was remembering something about cats and trees. She had seen it in a picture book. "Hang on tight, bird. You hang on tight, okay?" Dirrp's only response was to cling harder than ever to Patricia's overalls. Patricia looked at a few trees until she found one with sturdy enough branches, and climbed. She was more tired than the first time, and her feet slipped a couple of times. One time, she pulled herself up to the next branch with both hands and then looked at her shoulder and didn't see Dirrp. She lost her breath until she saw his head poke up nervously to look over her shoulder, and she realized he'd just been clinging to the strap farther down on her back.

At last they were on top of the tree, which swayed a little in the wind. Tommington was not following them. Patricia looked around twice in all directions before she saw a round fur shape scampering on the ground nearby.

"Stupid cat!" she shouted. "Stupid cat! You can't get us!"

"The first person I ever met who could talk," Tommington yowled. "And you think *I'm* stupid? Grraah! Taste my claws!"

The cat, who'd probably had lots of practice climbing one of those carpeted perches at home, ran up the side of the tree, pounced on one branch and then a higher branch. Before Patricia and Dirrp even knew what was going on, the cat was halfway up.

"We're trapped! What were you thinking?" Dirrp sang out.

Patricia waited until Tommington had reached the top,

then swung down the other side of the tree, dropping from branch to branch so fast she almost pulled her arm out, and then landed on the ground on her butt with an oof.

"Hey," Tommington said from the top of the tree, where his big eyes caught the moonlight. "Where did you go? Come back here!"

"You are a mean cat," Patricia said. "You are a bully, and I'm going to leave you up there. You should think about what you've been doing. It's not nice to be mean. I will make sure someone comes and gets you tomorrow. But you can stay up there for now. I have to go do something. Goodbye."

"Wait!" Tommington said. "I can't stay up here. It's too high! I'm scared! Come back!"

Patricia didn't look back. She heard Tommington yelling for a long time, until they crossed a big line of trees. They got lost twice more, and at one point Dirrp began weeping into his good wing, before they stumbled across the track that led to the secret Tree. And from there, it was just a steep backbreaking climb, up a slope studded with hidden roots.

Patricia saw the top of the Parliamentary Tree first, and then it seemed to grow out of the landscape, becoming taller and more overwhelming as she approached. The Tree was sort of bird shaped, as Dirrp had said, but instead of feathers it had dark spiky branches with fronds that hung to the ground. It loomed like the biggest church in the world. Or a castle. Patricia had never seen a castle, but she guessed they would rise over you like that.

A hundred pairs of wings fluttered at their arrival and then stopped. A huge collection of shapes shrank into the Tree.

"It's okay," Dirrp called out. "She's with me. I hurt my wing. She brought me here to get help."

The only response, for a long time, was silence. Then an eagle raised itself up, from near the top of the Tree, a white-headed bird with a hooked beak and pale, probing eyes. "You should not have brought her here," the eagle said.

"I'm sorry, ma'am," Dirrp said. "But it's okay. She can talk. She can actually talk." Dirrp pivoted, to speak into Patricia's ear. "Show them. Show them!"

"Uh, hi," Patricia said. "I'm sorry if we bothered you. But we need your help!"

At the sound of a human talking, all of the birds went into a huge frenzy of squawking and shouting until a big owl near the eagle banged a rock against the branch and shouted, "Order, order."

The eagle leaned her white fluffy head forward and studied Patricia. "So you're to be the new witch in our forest, are you?"

"I'm not a witch." Patricia chewed her thumb. "I'm a princess."

"You had better be a witch." The eagle's great dark body shifted on the branch. "Because if you're not, then Dirrp has broken the law by bringing you to us. And he'll need to be punished. We certainly won't help fix his wing, in that case."

"Oh," Patricia said. "Then I'm a witch. I guess."

"Ah." The eagle's hooked beak clicked. "But you will have to prove it. Or both you and Dirrp will be punished."

Patricia did not like the sound of that. Various other birds piped up, saying, "Point of order!" and a fidgety crow was listing important areas of Parliamentary procedure. One of them was so insistent that the eagle was forced to yield the branch to the Honorable Gentleman from Wide Oak—who then forgot what he was going to say.

"So how do I prove that I'm a witch?" Patricia wondered if she could run away. Birds flew pretty fast, right? She probably couldn't get away from a whole lot of birds, if they were mad at her. Especially magical birds.

"Well." A giant turkey in one of the lower branches, with wattles that looked a bit like a judge's collar, pulled himself upright and appeared to consult some markings scratched into the side of the Tree before turning and giving a loud, learned "glrp" sound. "Well," he said again, "there are several methods that are recognized in the literature. Some of them are trials of death, but we might skip those for the moment perhaps. There are also some rituals, but you need to be of a certain age to do those. Oh yes, here's a good one. We could ask her the Endless Question."

"Ooh, the Endless Question," a grouse said. "That's exciting."

"I haven't heard anyone answer the Endless Question before," said a goshawk. "This is more fun than Question Time."

"Umm," said Patricia. "Is the Endless Question going to take a long time? Because I bet my mom and dad are worried about me." It was hitting her all over again that she was up way past her bedtime and she hadn't had dinner and she was out in the middle of the freezing woods, not to mention she was still lost.

"Too late," the grouse said.

"We're asking it," said the eagle.

"Here is the question," said the turkey. "Is a tree red?"

"Uh," Patricia said. "Can you give me a hint? Umm. Is that 'red' like the color?" The birds didn't answer. "Can you give me more time? I promise I'll answer, I just need more time to think. Please. I need more time. Please?"

The next thing Patricia knew, her father scooped her up in his arms. He was wearing his sandpaper shirt and his red beard was in her face and he kept half-dropping her, because he was trying to draw complicated valuation formulas with his hands while carrying her. But it was still so warm and perfect to be carried home by her daddy that Patricia didn't care.

"I found her right on the outskirts of the woods near the house," her father told her mother. "She must have gotten lost and found her own way out. It's a miracle she's okay."

"You nearly scared us to death. We've been searching, along with all of the neighbors. I swear you must think my time is worthless. You've made me blow a deadline for a management productivity analysis." Patricia's mother had her dark hair pulled back, which made her chin and nose look pointier. Her bony shoulders hunched, almost up to her antique earrings.

"I just want to understand what this is about," Patricia's father said. "What did we do that made you want to act out in this way?" Roderick Delfine was a real-estate genius who often worked from home and looked after the girls when they were between nannies, sitting in a high chair at the breakfast bar with his wide face buried in equations. Patricia herself was pretty good at math, except when she thought too much about the wrong things, like the fact that the number 3 looked like an 8 cut in half, so two 3s really ought to be 8.

"She's testing us," Patricia's mother said. "She's testing our authority, because we've gone too easy on her." Belinda Delfine had been a gymnast, and her own parents had put several oceans' worth of pressure on her to excel at that—but she'd never understood why gymnastics needed to have judges, instead of measuring everything using cameras and maybe lasers. She'd met Roderick after he started coming to all her meets, and they'd invented a totally objective gymnastics measuring system that nobody had ever adopted.

"Look at her. She's just laughing at us," Patricia's mother said, as if Patricia herself weren't standing right there. "We need to show her we mean business."

Patricia hadn't thought she was laughing, at all, but now she was terrified she looked that way. She tried extra hard to fix a serious expression on her face.

"I would never run away like that," said Roberta, who was supposed to be leaving the three of them alone in the kitchen but had come in to get a glass of water, and gloat.

They locked Patricia in her room for a week, sliding food under her door. The bottom of the door tended to scrape off the top layer of whatever type of food it was. Like if it was a sandwich, the topmost piece of bread was taken away by the door. You don't really want to eat a sandwich after your door has had the first bite, but if you get hungry enough you will. "Think about what you've done," the parents said.

"I get all her desserts for the next seven years," Roberta said.

"No you don't!" said Patricia. The whole experience with the Parliament of Birds became a sort of blur to Patricia. She remembered it mostly in dreams and fragments. Once or twice, in school, she had a flashback of a bird asking her something. But she couldn't quite remember what the question had been, or whether she'd answered it. She had lost the ability to understand the speech of animals while she was locked in her bedroom.

2

HE HATED TO be called Larry. Couldn't stand it. And so, of course, everybody called him Larry, even his parents sometimes. "My name is Laurence," he would insist, looking at the floor. "With a U, not a W." Laurence knew who he was and what he was about, but the world refused to recognize.

At school, the other kids called him Larry Barry or Larry Fairy. Or, when he got mad, Scary Larry, except that this was a rare display of irony among his troglodyte classmates, since, in fact, Larry was not scary at all. Usually, this was preceded by an "Ooh," just to drive the joke home. Not that Laurence wanted to be scary. He just wanted to be left alone and maybe have people get his name right if they had to talk to him.

Laurence was a small kid for his age, with hair the color of late-autumn leaves, a long chin, and arms like snail necks. His parents bought him clothes one and a half sizes too big, because they kept thinking he would hit a growth spurt any day, and they were trying to save money. So he was forever tripping over his too-long, too-baggy jeans legs, his hands vanishing inside his jersey sleeves. Even if Laurence had wanted to present an intimidating figure, his lack of visible hands and feet would have made it difficult.

The only bright spots in Laurence's life were ultraviolent PlayStation games, in which he vaporized thousands of imaginary opponents. But then Laurence found other games on the internet—puzzles that took him hours to figure out and MMOs, where Laurence waged intricate campaigns. Before long, Laurence was writing his own code.

Laurence's dad had been pretty great with computers, once. But then he'd grown up and gotten a job in the insurance industry, where he still needed a head for numbers, but it wasn't anything you'd want to hear about. Now he was always freaking out that he was going to lose his job and then they would all starve. Laurence's mom had been working on a PhD in biology, before she'd gotten pregnant and her thesis advisor had quit, and then she'd taken some time off and never quite gone back to school.

Both parents worried endlessly about Laurence spending every waking minute in front of a computer and turning out socially dysfunctional, like his Uncle Davis. So they forced Laurence to take an endless succession of classes designed to make him Get Out of the House: judo, modern dance, fencing, water polo for beginners, swimming, improv comedy, boxing, skydiving, and, worst of all, Wilderness Survival Weekends. Each class only forced Laurence to wear another baggy uniform while the kids shouted, "Larry, Larry, Quite Contrary!" and held him underwater, and threw him out of the airplane early, and forced him to do improv while holding him upside down by his ankles.

Laurence wondered if there was some other kid, named Larry, who would have a "let's go" attitude about being dropped on a mountainside somewhere. Larry might be the alternate-universe version of Laurence, and maybe all Laurence needed to do was harness all the solar energy that hit the Earth during a period of five minutes or so and he could generate a localized space-time fissure in his bathtub and go kidnap Larry from the other universe. So Larry could go out and get tormented instead, while Laurence stayed home. The hard part would be figuring out a way to poke a hole in the universe before the judo tournament in two weeks' time.

"Hey, Larry Fairy," Brad Chomner said at school, "think fast." Which was one of those phrases that never made sense to Laurence: People who told you to "think fast" were always those who thought much more slowly than you did. And they only said it when they were about to do something to contribute to the collective mental inertia. And yet Laurence had never come up with the perfect comeback to "Think fast," and he wouldn't have time to say whatever it was, since something unpleasant usually hit him a second later. Laurence had to go clean himself up.

One day, Laurence found some schematics on the internet, which he printed out and reread a hundred times before he started figuring out what they meant. And once he combined them with a solar-battery design that he found buried in an old message-board post, he started to have something. He stole his dad's old waterproof wristwatch and combined it with some parts he scavenged from a bunch of microwave ovens and cell phones. And a few odds and ends from the electronics store. At the end of all this, he had a working time machine that fit on his wrist.

The device was simple: There was just one small button. Any time you pressed the button, you would jump forward in time two seconds. That was all it could do. There was no way to extend the range or go backwards. Laurence tried filming himself with his webcam and found that when he pressed the button, he did sort of disappear for an eyeblink or two. But you could only use it once in a while, or you got the worst head rush of your life.

A few days later, Brad Chomner said, "Think fast," and Laurence did think fast. He hit the button on his wrist. The white blob that had been hurtling in his direction landed in front of him with a splat. Everybody looked at Laurence, and at the soggy toilet paper roll melting into the floor tiles, and then back at Laurence. Laurence put his "watch" into sleep mode, meaning it wouldn't work for anybody else who tinkered with it. But he needn't have worried—everybody just thought Laurence had ducked, with superhuman reflexes. Mr. Grandison came huffing out of his classroom and asked who threw this toilet paper, and everybody said it was Laurence.

Being able to skip two seconds could be quite useful—if you picked the right two seconds. Like when you're at the dinner table with your parents and your mom has just said something sarcastic about your dad being passed over for another promotion, and you just know your father is about to let out a brief but lethal burst of resentment. You need godlike timing to pick the exact instant when the barb is being launched. There are a hundred leading indicators: the scent of overcooked casserole, the sensation of the room's temperature dropping slightly. The ticking of the stove, powering down. You can leave reality behind and reappear for the aftermath.

But there were plenty of other occasions. Like when Al Danes flung him off the jungle gym onto the playground sand. He dematerialized just as he landed. Or when some popular girl was about to come up and pretend to be nice to him, just so she could laugh about it to her friends as they walked away. Or just when a teacher started an especially dull rant. Even shaving off two seconds made a difference. Nobody seemed to notice that he flickered out of being, maybe because you had to be looking right at him and nobody ever was. If only Laurence could have used the device more than a few times a day without the headaches.

Besides, jumping forward in time just underscored the basic problem: Laurence had nothing to look forward to.

At least, that's how Laurence felt, until he saw the picture of the sleek shape, glinting in the sunlight. He stared at the tapering curves, the beautiful nose cone, and the powerful engines, and something awoke inside him. A feeling he hadn't experienced in ages: excitement. This privately funded, DIY spaceship was going up into orbit, thanks to maverick tech investor Milton Dirth and a few dozen of his maker friends and MIT students. The launch would happen in a few days, near the MIT campus, and Laurence had to be there. He hadn't ever wanted anything the way he wanted to see this for himself.

"Dad," Laurence said. He had already gotten off to a bad start: His father was staring at his laptop, cupping his hands as though trying to protect his mustache, the ends of which seeped into the heavy lines around his mouth. Laurence had picked a bad time to do this. Too late. He was committed. "Dad," Laurence said again. "There's a rocket test, sort of, on Tuesday. Here's the article about it."

Laurence's dad started to brush him off, but then some half-forgotten resolution to make time for parenting kicked in. "Oh." He kept looking back at his laptop, which had a spreadsheet on it, until he slammed it shut and gave Laurence as much attention as he could call undivided. "Yeah. I heard about that. It's that Dirth guy. Huh. Some kind of lightweight prototype, right? That could be used to land on the dark side of the Moon eventually. I heard about that." Then Laurence's dad was joking about an old band called Floyd and marijuana and ultraviolet light.

"Yeah." Laurence cut into his dad's flow before the conversation got away from him. "That's right. Milton Dirth. And I really want to go see it. This is like a once-in-a-lifetime chance. I thought maybe we could make it a father-son thing." His dad couldn't turn down a father-son thing, or it would be like admitting to being a bad father.

"Oh." His dad had an embarrassed look in his deep-set eyes, behind his square glasses. "You want to go? This coming Tuesday?"

"Yes."

"But… I mean, I have work. There's a project, and I have to ace this one, or it's going to look bad. And I know your mother would be upset if we just took you out of school like that. Plus, I mean, you can watch it on the computer. There'll be a webcam feed or something. You know that these things are boring in person. It's a lot of standing around, and they end up delaying it half the time. You won't even see anything if you're there. You'll get a way better view via the web." Laurence's dad sounded as though he was trying to convince himself as much as his son.

Laurence nodded. There was no point in arguing, once his father had started piling on reasons. So Laurence said nothing, until he could safely back away. Then he went up to his room and looked at bus schedules.

A few days later, while his parents were still asleep, Laurence tiptoed downstairs and found his mom's purse on the little side table near the front door. He opened the clasp as if a live animal could jump out. Every noise in the house sounded too loud: the coffeemaker heating up, and the refrigerator buzzing. Laurence found a leather wallet inside the purse and pulled out fifty bucks. He had never stolen before. He kept expecting police officers to burst in the front door and cuff him.

The second phase of Laurence's plan involved going face-to-face with his mom right after he'd robbed her. He caught up with her when she'd just woken up, still bleary in her marigold robe, and told her there was a school field trip and he needed her to write a note saying it was okay for him to go. (He had already figured out a great universal truth, that people never asked for documentation of anything, as long as you asked them for documentation first.) Laurence's mom pulled out a stubby ergonomic pen and scrawled a permission slip. Her manicure was peeling. Laurence said it might be an overnight trip, in which case he would call. She nodded, bright red curls bouncing.

Walking to the bus stop, Laurence had a nervous moment. He was going on a big trip on his own, nobody knew where he was, and he only had fifty dollars in his pocket, plus a fake Roman coin. What if someone jumped out from behind the Dumpsters by the strip mall and attacked Laurence? What if someone dragged him into their truck and drove him hundreds of miles before changing his name to Darryl and forcing him to live as their homeschooled son? Laurence had seen a TV movie about this.

But then Laurence remembered the wilderness weekends, and the fact that he'd found fresh water and edible roots, and even scared off this one chipmunk that had seemed intent on fighting him for the trail mix. He'd hated every second, but if he could survive that, then he could handle taking a bus into Cambridge and figuring out how to get to the launch site. He was Laurence of Ellenburg, and he was unflappable. Laurence had just figured out that "unflappable" did not have anything to do with whether people could mess up your clothing, and now he used that word as much as he could.

"I am unflappable," Laurence told the bus driver. Who shrugged, as if he'd thought so too, once upon a time, until someone had flapped him.

Laurence had packed a bunch of supplies, but he'd only brought one book, a slender paperback about the last great interplanetary war. Laurence finished that book in an hour, and then he had nothing to do but stare out the window. The trees along the highway seemed to slow down as the bus passed alongside them, then sped up again. A kind of time dilation.

The bus arrived in Boston, and then Laurence had to find the T station. He walked into Chinatown, where there were people selling stuff on the street and restaurants with enormous fish tanks in their windows, as though the fish wanted to inspect potential customers before they would be allowed in. And then Laurence was crossing the water and the Museum of Science was gleaming in the morning sun, opening its steel-and-glass arms to him and brandishing its Planetarium.

It wasn't until Laurence reached the MIT campus and he was standing in front of the Legal Sea Foods, trying to make sense of the map of coded buildings, that he realized he had no idea how to find where this rocket launch was happening.

Laurence had imagined he would arrive at MIT and it would look like a bigger version of Murchison Elementary School, with front steps and a bulletin board where people posted upcoming activities. Laurence couldn't even get into the first couple buildings he tried. He did find a board where people had posted notices for lectures, and dating advice, and the Ig Nobel Awards. But no mention of how to watch the big launch.

Laurence ended up in Au Bon Pain, eating a corn muffin and feeling like a dope. If he could get on the internet, maybe he could figure out what to do next, but his parents wouldn't let him have a phone yet, much less a laptop. The café was playing mournful oldies: Janet Jackson saying she got so lonely, Britney Spears confessing she did it again. He cooled each sip of hot chocolate with a long breath, while he tried to strategize.

Laurence's book was gone. The one he'd been reading on the bus. He had put it on the table near his muffin, and now it was gone. No, wait—it was in the hands of a woman in her twenties, with long brown braids, a wide face, and a red sweater that was so fuzzy it practically had hair. She had callused hands and work boots. She was turning Laurence's book over and over in her hands. "Sorry," she said. "I remember this book. I read it like three times in high school. This is the one with the binary star system that goes to war with the AIs who live in the asteroid belt. Right?"

"Um, yeah," Laurence said.

"Good choice." Now she was checking out Laurence's wrist. "Hey. That's a two-second time machine, isn't it?"

"Um, yeah," Laurence said.

"Cool. I have one too." She showed him. It looked about the same as Laurence's, except it was a little smaller and it had a calculator. "It took me ages to figure out those diagrams online. It's like a little test of engineering skill and moxie and stuff, and in the end you get a little device with a thousand uses. Mind if I sit down? I'm standing over you and it makes me feel like an authority figure."

Laurence said that was okay. He was having a hard time contributing to this conversation. The woman sat in front of him and the remains of his muffin. Now that he was at eye level with her, she was sort of pretty.

She had a cute nose and round chin. She reminded him of a Social Studies teacher he'd had a crush on last year.

"I'm Isobel," said the woman. "I'm a rocket scientist." It turned out she'd shown up for the big rocket launch, but it was delayed because of some last-minute problems and weather and stuff. "It'll probably be in a few days. You know how these things go."

"Oh." Laurence looked into his hot-chocolate foam. So that was it. He wasn't going to get to see anything. Somehow he'd let himself believe that if he saw a rocket blast off, something that had been right in front of him and was now free of our planet's gravity, he would be set free, too. He could go back to school and it wouldn't matter because he'd been connected to something that was in outer space.

Now he was just going to be the freak who ditched school for nothing. He looked at the cover of the paperback, which had a painting of a lumpy spaceship and a naked woman with eyes for breasts. He didn't start to cry or anything, but he kind of wanted to. The paperback cover said: "THEY WENT TO THE ENDS OF THE UNIVERSE—TO STOP A GALACTIC DISASTER!"

"Drat," Laurence said. "Thanks for letting me know."

"No problem," Isobel said. She told him more about the rocket launch and just how revolutionary this new design was, stuff he already knew, and then she noticed he was looking miserable. "Hey, don't worry. It's just delayed a few days."

"Yeah, but," Laurence said, "I won't be able to be here then."

"Oh."

"I will be otherwise occupied. I have a prior engagement."

Laurence stammered a little. He kneaded the edge of the table, so the skin on his hot chocolate grew ridges.

"You must be a busy man," Isobel said. "It sounds as though you have a packed schedule."

"Actually," Laurence said. "Every day is the same as every other day. Except for today." And now he did start to cry. Goddamn it.

"Hey." Isobel abandoned her chair opposite him and came to sit next to him. "Hey. Hey. It's okay. Listen, do your parents know where you are?"

"Not…" Laurence sniffled. "Not as such." He wound up telling her the whole deal, how he'd stolen fifty bucks from his mom, how he'd ditched school and taken the bus and the T. As he told Isobel, he started to feel bad for making his parents worry, but also he knew with increasing certainty that this stunt would not be repeatable. Not a few days from now, at any rate.

"Okay," Isobel said. "Wow. Well, I guess I oughta call your parents. It'll take them a while to get here, though. Especially with the confusing directions I'm going to give them for getting to the launch site."

"Launch site? But…"

"Since that's where you're going to be, by the time they arrive." She patted Laurence's shoulder. He had stopped crying, thank god, and was pulling himself back into shape. "Come on, I'm going to show you the rocket. I'll give you the tour, and introduce you to some of the people."

She stood up and offered Laurence her hand. He took it.

And that was how Laurence got to meet a dozen or so of the coolest rocket nerds on Earth. Isobel drove him there in her tobacco-scented red Mustang, and Laurence's feet were buried under Frito bags. Laurence heard MC Frontalot for the first time on her car stereo. "Have you ever read Heinlein? Maybe a little grown-up, but I bet you could handle his juveniles. Here." She dug around in the backseat and handed him a battered paperback called *Have Space Suit—Will Travel*, which had a pleasingly lurid cover. She said he could keep it, she had another copy.

They drove along Memorial Drive and then through an endless series of identical highways and switchbacks and tunnels, and Laurence realized Isobel was right: His parents would get lost several times trying to come pick him up, even if she gave them perfect, nonconfusing directions. They always complained that driving in Boston was asking for it. The afternoon grew duller as clouds set in, but Laurence didn't care.

"Behold," Isobel said, "a single-stage Earth-to-orbit rocket. I drove all the way from Virginia just to help with this. My boyfriend is crazy jealous."

It was two or three times Laurence's size, housed in a barn near the water. It glimmered, its pale metal shell catching the streaks of light through the barn windows. Isobel walked Laurence around it, showing him all the cool features, including the carbon nanofiber insulation around the fuel systems and the lightweight silicate/organic polymer casing on the actual engines.

Laurence reached out and touched the rocket, feeling the dimpled skin with his fingertips. People started wandering

400.

182.

145.

$\frac{5.8}{2.9} + 30.9$

$\frac{22.8}{19.9}$

Water	35
DVLA	11
LVIC (ins)	56
Virgin	59
GT	10 3
Shy	28
Equifax	8.
Rent.	900
EE	230.
	1371.

up, demanding to know who this kid was and why he was touching their precious rocket.

"That's delicate equipment." A tight-lipped man in a turtleneck sweater folded his arms.

"We can't have just random kids running around our rocket barn," a small woman in overalls said.

"Laurence," Isobel said. "Show them." He knew what she meant.

He reached down to his right wrist with his left hand and pressed the little button. He felt the familiar sensation, like a skipped heartbeat or a double breath, that lasted no time at all. And then it was two seconds later, and he was still standing next to a beautiful rocket in a ring of people, who were all staring at him. Everybody clapped. Laurence noticed they were all wearing things on their wrists too, like this was a trend. Or a badge.

After that, they treated him like one of them. He had conquered a small piece of time, and they were conquering a small piece of space. They understood, as he did, that this was a down payment. One day, they would own a much bigger share of the cosmos, or their descendants would. You celebrated the small victories, and you dreamed of the big ones to come.

"Hey kid," one hairy guy in jeans and sandals said. "Check out what I did with this thruster design. It's pretty sweet."

"What *we* did," Isobel corrected him.

Turtleneck Guy was older, in his thirties or forties, maybe even fifties, with thinning salt-and-pepper hair and big eyebrows. He kept asking Laurence questions and making notes on his phone. He asked Laurence to spell his name, twice. "Remind me to look you up on your eighteenth birthday, kid," he said. Someone brought Laurence a soda and pizza.

By the time Laurence's parents arrived, boiling in their own skins after having to figure out the Turnpike and Storrow Drive and the tunnels and everything, Laurence had become the mascot of the Single-Stage Orbital Rocket Gang. On the long drive home, Laurence tuned out his parents explaining to him that life isn't an adventure, for chrissake, life is a long slog and a series of responsibilities and demands. When Laurence was old enough to do what he liked, he would be old enough to understand he couldn't do what he liked.

The sun went down. The family stopped for burgers and more lecturing. Laurence kept sneaking looks under the table at his propped-open copy of *Have Space Suit—Will Travel*. He was already halfway through the book.

BOOK
TWO

1

THE CLASSROOMS ON the western side of Canterbury Academy's pale cement mausoleum had windows facing the parking lot, the sports fields, and the two-lane highway. But the east windows looked down a muddy slope to a stream, beyond which an uneven fringe of trees shivered in the September wind. In the school's stale-marshmallow-scented air, Patricia could look east and imagine running wild.

The first week of school, Patricia smuggled an oak leaf in her skirt pocket—the nearest thing she had to a talisman, which she touched until it broke into crumbs. All through Math and English, her two classes with views of the east, she watched the stub of forest. And wished she could escape there and go fulfill her destiny as a witch, instead of sitting and memorizing old speeches by Rutherford B. Hayes. Her skin crawled under her brand-new training bra, stiff sweater, and school jumper, while around her kids texted and chattered: *Is Casey Hamilton going to ask Traci Burt out? Who tried what over the summer?* Patricia rocked her chair up and down, up and down, until it struck the floor with a clang that startled everyone at her group table.

Seven years had passed since some birds had told Patricia she was special. Since then, she'd tried every spellbook and every mystical practice on the internet. She'd misplaced herself in the woods over and over until she knew by heart every way to get lost. She carried a first-aid kit, in case she met any more injured creatures. But no wild things ever spoke, and nothing magical ever happened. As if the whole thing had been some kind of prank, or she'd failed a test without knowing.

Patricia walked through the playground after lunch with her face upcast, trying to keep pace with an unkindness of ravens passing over the school. The ravens gossiped among themselves, without letting Patricia in on their conversation—just like the kids at this school, not that Patricia cared.

She'd tried to make friends, because she'd promised her mom (and witches kept their promises, she guessed)—but she was joining this school in the eighth grade, after everyone else had been here a couple years. Just yesterday, she'd stood at the girls' room sink next to Macy Firestone and her friends as Macy obsessed about Brent Harper blowing her off at lunch. Macy's bright lip gloss perfectly set off her Creamsicle hair dye. Patricia, coating her hands with oily-green fake soap, had been seized by a conviction that she, too, ought to say something funny and supportive about the appeal, and yet the tragic insufficiency, of Brent Harper, who had twinkly eyes and moussed-up hair. So she'd stammered that Brent Harper was The Worst—and at once she had girls on both sides of her, demanding to know exactly what her problem was with Brent Harper. What had Brent ever done to her? Carrie Danning spat so hard, her perfect blond hair almost lost a barrette.

The ravens flew in no formation Patricia could discern, even though most of the school's lessons, this first week, had been about finding patterns in everything. Patterns were how you answered standardized-test questions, how you committed large blocks of text to memory, and ultimately how you created structure in your life. (This was the famous Saarinian Program.) But Patricia looked at the ravens, loquacious in their hurry to go nowhere, and could find no sense to any of it. They retraced their path, as if they were going to notice Patricia after all, then looped back toward the road.

What was the point of telling Patricia she was a witch, and then leaving her alone? For years?

Chasing the ravens, Patricia forgot to look down, until she collided with someone. She felt the impact and heard the yelp of distress before she saw whom she'd run over: a gangly boy with sandy hair and an oversized chin, who'd fallen against the chicken-wire fence at the playground's edge and rebounded onto the grass. He pulled himself upright.

"Why the hell don't you look where you're—" He glanced at something on his left wrist that wasn't a watch, and cursed way too loud.

"What is it?" Patricia said.

"You broke my time machine." He yanked it off his wrist and showed her.

"You're Larry, right?" Patricia looked at the device, which was definitely broken. There was a jagged crack in its casing and a sour odor coming from inside it. "I'm really sorry about your thing. Can you get another? I can totally pay for it. Or my parents can, I guess." She was thinking that her mom would love that, another disaster to make up for.

"Buy another time machine." Larry snorted. "You're going to, what, just walk down to Best Buy and get a time machine off the rack?" He had a faint scent of cranberries, maybe from some body spray or something.

"Don't be sarcastic," Patricia said. "Sarcasm is for feeble people." She hadn't meant that to rhyme, plus it had sounded more profound in her head.

"Sorry." He squinted at the wreckage, then carefully unpeeled the strap from his bony wrist. "It can be repaired, I guess. I'm Laurence, by the way. Nobody calls me Larry."

"Patricia." Laurence held out his hand and she hoisted it three times. "So was that actually a time machine?" she asked. "You're not joking or whatever?"

"Yeah. Sort of. It wasn't that great. I was going to toss it out soon in any case. It was supposed to help me escape from all this. But instead, all it did was turn me into a one-trick pony."

"Better than being a no-trick pony." Patricia looked up again at the sky. The ravens were long gone, and all she saw was a single slowly disintegrating cloud.

* * *

AFTER THAT, PATRICIA saw Laurence around. He was in some of Patricia's classes. She noticed that Laurence had fresh poison-ivy scars on both skinny arms and a red bite on his ankle that he kept raising his pant leg to inspect during English class. His knapsack had a compass and map spilling out of the front pouches, and grass and dirt stains along its underside.

A few days after she wrecked his time machine, she saw Laurence sitting after school on the back steps near the big slope, hunched over a brochure for a Great Outdoors Adventure Weekend. She couldn't even imagine: Two whole days away from people and their garbage. Two days of feeling the sun on her face! Patricia stole into the woods behind the spice house every chance she got, but her parents would never let her spend a whole weekend.

"That looks amazing," she said, and Laurence twitched as he realized she was looking over his shoulder.

"It's my worst nightmare," he said, "except it's real."

"You've already gone on one of these?"

Laurence didn't respond, except to point to a blurry photo on the back of the leaflet, in which a group of kids hoisted backpacks next to a waterfall, putting on smiles except for one gloomy presence in the rear: Laurence, wearing a ridiculous round green hat, like a sport fisherman's. The photographer had captured Laurence in the middle of spitting out something.

"But that's awesome," Patricia said.

Laurence got up and walked back into the school, shoes scuffing the floor.

"Please," Patricia said. "I just… I wish I had someone to talk to, about stuff. Even if nobody can ever understand the things I've seen. I would settle for just knowing someone else who is close to nature. Wait. Don't walk away. Laurence!"

He turned around. "You got my name right." His eyes narrowed.

"Of course I did. You told it to me."

"Huh." He rolled that around in his mouth for a moment. "So what's so great about nature?"

"It's real. It's messy. It's not like people." She talked to Laurence about the congregations of wild turkeys in her backyard and the vines that clung to the walls of the graveyard down the road, Concord grapes all the sweeter for their proximity to the dead. "The woods near here are full of deer and even a few elk, and the deer have almost no predators left. A fully grown buck can be the size of a *horse*." Laurence looked horrified at that idea.

"You're not really selling it," Laurence said. "So… you're outdoorsy, huh?"

Patricia nodded.

"Maybe there's a way we can help each other. Let's make a deal: You help me convince my parents I'm already spending plenty of time in nature, so they stop sending me frakking camping all the time. And I'll give you twenty bucks."

"You want me to lie to your parents?" Patricia wasn't sure if that was the sort of thing an honorable witch would do.

"Yes," he said. "I want you to lie to my parents. Thirty bucks, okay? That's pretty much my entire supercomputer fund."

"Let me think about it," Patricia said.

This was a major ethical dilemma. Not just the lying, but also the part where she would be keeping Laurence from an important experience his parents wanted him to have. She couldn't know what would happen. Maybe Laurence would invent a new windmill that would power whole cities, after observing the wings of dragonflies. She pictured Laurence years from now, accepting a Nobel Prize and saying he owed it all to the Great Outdoors Adventure Weekends. On the other hand, maybe Laurence would go on one of those weekends, fall into a waterfall, and drown, and it would be partly Patricia's fault. Plus, she could use thirty bucks.

Meanwhile, Patricia kept trying to make other friends. Dorothy Glass was a gymnast, like Patricia's mom had been, and the mousy, freckled girl also wrote poetry on her phone when she thought nobody was looking. Patricia sat next to Dorothy at Convocation, when Mr. Dibbs, the vice principal, talked about the school's "No Scooters" policy and explained why rote memorization was the best way to repair the short attention spans of kids who had been raised on Facebook and video games. The whole time, Patricia and Dorothy whispered about the webtoon everyone was watching, the one with the pipe-smoking horse. Patricia felt a stirring of hope—but then Dorothy sat with Macy Firestone and Carrie Danning at lunch and looked right past Patricia in the hallway afterward.

And so Patricia marched up to Laurence as he waited for the bus. "You're on," she said. "I'll be your alibi."

* * *

49

LAURENCE REALLY WAS building a supercomputer in his locked bedroom closet, behind a protective layer of action figures and paperbacks. The computer was cobbled together from tons of parts, including the GPUs from a dozen pQ game consoles, which had sported the most advanced vector graphics and complex narrative branching of any system ever, during the three months they were on the market. He'd also snuck into the offices of a defunct game developer two towns over and "rescued" some hard drives, a few motherboards, and some assorted routers. The result was bursting out of its metal corrugated rack space, LEDs blazing behind piles of junk. Laurence showed all of this to Patricia, while explaining his theories about neural networks, heuristic contextual mapping, and rules of interaction, and reminding her that she had promised to tell nobody about this.

At dinner with Laurence's parents (super-garlicky pasta), Patricia talked a good game about how she and Laurence had gone rock climbing and they had even seen a fox, up close. She almost said the fox ate out of Laurence's hand, but she didn't want to oversell. Laurence's parents were overjoyed and startled to hear how many trees Laurence had been up— neither of them looked like they'd hiked in years, but they had some hang-up about Laurence spending too much time sitting at his computer instead of filling his lungs. "So glad Laurence has a friend," said his mom, who wore cat glasses and had her curls dyed an obscene shade of red. Laurence's dad, who was morose and bald except for one brown tuft, nodded and offered Patricia more garlic bread with both hands. Laurence's family lived in a dingy subdivision in an ugly cul-de-sac, and all the furniture and appliances were old. You could see through the carpet to the cinder floor.

Patricia and Laurence started spending time together, even when she wasn't vouching for his outdoorsiness. They sat next to each other on the bus, on a field trip to the Cannery Museum, which was a whole facility devoted to cans. And every time they hung out, Laurence showed her another weird device—like, he had built a ray gun that would make you sleepy if he aimed it at you for half an hour. He hid it under the table at school and tested it on Mr. Knight, the Social Studies teacher, who did start yawning right before the bell.

One day in English class, Ms. Dodd asked Patricia to get up and talk about William Saroyan—no, wait, just to recite William Saroyan from memory. She stumbled over the gravel road of words about the insects who live in fruit, until she noticed a light shining in her eye, blinding her, but only on the right side. With her left eye, she saw the wall of bored faces, drawing not enough entertainment at her discomfort, and then she found the source of the dazzling blue-green beam: Laurence had something in his hand. Like a pointer.

"I—I have a headache," Patricia said. She was excused.

In the hallway during Passing Period, she yanked Laurence away from the drinking fountain and demanded to know what the hell that had been.

"Retinal teleprompter," Laurence gasped, looking actually scared of her. Nobody had ever been scared of Patricia. "Still not quite perfected. If it had worked, it would have projected the words directly onto your eye."

Patricia felt actually scandalized at this. "Oh. But isn't that cheating?"

"Yes, because memorizing the speeches of Rutherford B. Hayes will prepare you for life as an adult." Laurence rolled his eyes and walked away. Laurence wasn't sitting around feeling sorry for himself, he was *making* things. She had never met anyone like him before. And meanwhile, what could Patricia do with her so-called magic powers? Nothing. She was totally useless.

2

LAURENCE'S PARENTS DECIDED Patricia was his girlfriend, and they wouldn't hear reason. They kept offering to chaperone the two kids to school dances, or to drive them to and from "dates." They wouldn't shut up about it.

Laurence wanted to shrink to nothing.

"Here's the thing about dating at your age." Laurence's mom sat facing him as he ate breakfast. His dad had already gone to work. "It doesn't count. It's just like practice. Training wheels. You know this isn't going to amount to anything. But that doesn't mean it's not important." She was wearing sweatpants with a blouse.

"Thanks for your input, Mom. I appreciate all of your keen insights."

"You always make fun of your poor mother." She swept her hands in opposite waves. "But you ought to listen. Puppy love is when you learn game, or you never do. You're already a nerd, honey, you just don't want to be a nerd with no dating skills. So I'm just saying, you shouldn't let thoughts about the future keep you from making the most of your middle-school fling. Listen to one who knows." Laurence's mom had gone to her fifth-choice grad school instead of her first choice, to be closer to his dad, and that had been the first of many compromises that had ended them up here.

"She's not my girlfriend, Mom. She's just someone who's teaching me to appreciate tick bites."

"Well, maybe you should do something about that. She seemed like a very sweet girl. Very well brought up. She had nice hair. I would make a move if I were you."

Laurence felt so uncomfortable in this conversation, not just his skin was crawling—his bones, his ligaments, his blood vessels were crawling, too. He felt pinned to his stiff wooden chair. At last he understood what all those old horror stories meant when they talked about an eldritch dread, creeping into your very soul. That was how Laurence felt, listening to his mother attempt to talk to him about girls.

Even worse was when Laurence heard the other kids at school whispering about him and Patricia. When Laurence was in the locker room before PE, kids who normally paid zero attention to him, jocks like Blaze Donovan, started asking him if he'd gotten her shirt off yet. And offering him make-out advice that sounded like it came from the internet. Laurence kept his head down and tuned them out. He couldn't believe he'd lost his time machine, just when he needed it most.

One day, Laurence and Patricia were sitting adjacent to each other at lunch—not "with" each other, just adjacent to each other, at the same long table where boys mostly sat at one end and girls at the other. Laurence leaned over and asked, "People think we're… you know… boyfriend-girlfriend. Doesn't that kind of weird you out?" He tried to sound as though *he* thought it was no big deal, but he was just expressing concern about Patricia's feelings.

Patricia just shrugged. "I guess people are always going to have something, right?" She was this weird fidgety girl, with eyes that looked brown sometimes and green sometimes, and dark straight hair that never defrizzed.

Laurence didn't really need to hang out with Patricia at school, because he only needed her to vouch for his after-school time, and maybe weekends. But he felt awkward sitting by himself when she was also sitting by herself, usually frowning out the nearest window. And he found himself curious to ask her stuff and see how she responded—because he never, ever knew what Patricia would say about anything. He only knew it would be something weird.

LAURENCE AND PATRICIA sat under the up escalator at the mall. They each had a Double Chocolate Ultra Creamy Super Whip Frostuccino with decaf coffee in it, which made them feel super grown up. They were lulled by the machinery working right over their heads, the wheel of steps going around forever, and they had a view of the big fountain, which made a friendly splashing noise. Soon both their drinks were nothing but throaty snorty noises as they took the last pulls on their straws, and they were both blitzed on sugar.

They could see the feet and ankles of people passing on the down escalator, between them and the fountain. They took turns trying to guess who these people were, based just on their footwear.

"That lady in the white sneakers is an acrobat. And a spy," Patricia said. "She travels around the world, doing performances and planting cameras in top-secret buildings. She can sneak in anywhere because she's a contortionist as well as an acrobat."

A man in cowboy boots and black jeans came past, and Laurence said this was a rodeo champion who had been challenged to a *Dance Dance Revolution* showdown against the world's best break-dancer and it was happening at this very mall.

A girl in UGG boots was a supermodel who had stolen the secret formula for hair so shiny it brainwashed anyone who saw it, said Patricia, and she was hiding at the mall, where nobody would ever expect a supermodel to go.

Laurence thought the two women in smart pumps and nylons were life coaches who were coaching each other, creating an endless feedback loop.

The man in black slippers and worn gray socks was an assassin, said Patricia, a member of a secret society of trained killers who stalked their prey, looking for the perfect moment to strike and kill undetected.

"It's amazing how much you can tell about people from their feet," said Patricia. "Shoes tell the whole story."

"Except us," said Laurence. "Our shoes are totally boring. You can't tell anything about us."

"That's because our parents pick out our shoes," said Patricia. "Just wait until we're grown up. Our shoes will be insane."

IN FACT, PATRICIA had been correct about the man in the gray socks and black shoes. His name was Theodolphus Rose, and he was a member of the Nameless Order of Assassins. He had learned 873 ways to murder someone without leaving even a whisper of evidence, and he'd had to kill 419 people to reach the number nine spot in the NOA hierarchy. He would have been very annoyed to learn that his shoes had given him away, because he prided himself on blending with his surroundings. His was the gait of a mountain lion stalking the undergrowth, clad in the most nondescript black slippers and mountaineer socks. The rest of his outfit was designed to fade into the background, from the dark jacket to the cargo pants with their bulky pockets stuffed with weapons and supplies. He kept his bony, close-shaved head down, but every one of his senses was primed. His mind ran countless battle scenarios, so that if any of the housewives, mall-walking seniors, or teenagers attacked without warning Theodolphus would be ready.

Theodolphus had come to this mall looking for two special children, because he needed a *pro bono* hit to keep up his standing in the Nameless Order. To that end, he had made a pilgrimage to the Assassin Shrine in Albania, where he'd fasted, inhaled vapors, and gone nine days without sleep. And then he'd stared into the ornately carved Seeing Hole in the floor of the Shrine, and he'd seen a vision of things to come that still replayed in his nightmares. Death and chaos, engines of destruction, whole cities crumbling, and a plague of madness. And at the last, a war between magic and science that would leave the world in ashes. At the center of all this were a man and a woman, who were still children now. His eyes had bled as he'd crawled away from the Seeing Hole, his palms scraped away and his knees unhinged. The Nameless Order had recently imposed a strict ban on killing minors, but Theodolphus knew this mission to be holy.

Theodolphus had lost his prey. This was the first time he had ever been inside a mall, and he was finding the environment overwhelming with all of the blaring window displays, and the confusing letter-number code on the giant map. For all Theodolphus knew, Laurence and Patricia had spotted him somehow, gotten wind of his plans, and laid an ambush. The housewares store was full of knives that moved on their own. The lingerie store had a cryptic warning about the Miracle Lift. He didn't even know where to look.

Theodolphus was not going to lose his cool over this. He was a panther—or maybe a cheetah, some type of lethal cat, anyway—and he was just toying with these stupid children. Every assassin has moments when he or she feels the grip slipping, as though the cliff face is spinning away and a sheer drop beckons. They had talked about this very issue at the assassin convention a few months earlier: That thing where even as you pass unseen through the shadows, you fear everybody is secretly watching and laughing at you.

Breathe, panther, Theodolphus told himself. *Breathe.*

He went into the men's room at the Cheesecake Factory and meditated, but someone kept pounding on the door asking if he was about done in there.

There was nothing for it but to eat a large chocolate brownie sundae. When it arrived at his table, Theodolphus stared at it—how did he know it was not poisoned? If he really *was* being watched, someone could have slipped any of a dozen substances into his sundae that would be odorless and flavorless, or even chocolate flavored.

Theodolphus began to sob, without making any sound. He wept like a silent jungle cat. Then at last, he decided that life would not be worth living if he couldn't eat ice cream from time to time without worrying it was poisoned and he began to eat.

Laurence's father came and picked up Laurence and Patricia half a mile from the mall, right around the time that Theodolphus was clutching his throat and keeling over— the ice cream had indeed been poisoned— and Patricia did what she mostly did when she talked to Laurence's parents: make stuff up. "And we went rock climbing the other day, and white-water rafting, although the water was more brown than white. And we went to a goat farm and chased the goats until we tired them out, which let me tell you is hard, goats have *energy*," Patricia told Laurence's father.

Laurence's father asked several goat questions, which the kids answered with total solemnity.

Theodolphus wound up banned from the Cheesecake Factory for life.

That tends to happen when you thrash around and foam at the mouth in a public place while groping in the crotch of your cargo pants for something, which you then swallow in a single gulp. When the antidote kicked in and Theodolphus could breathe again, he saw his napkin had the sigil of the Nameless Order on it, with an ornate mark that more or less said, *Hey, remember, we don't kill kids anymore. Okay?*

This was going to require a change of tactic.

3

WHENEVER SHE COULD, Patricia escaped to the heart of the forest. The birds laughed at her attempts to mimic them. She kicked a tree. Nothing responded. She ran deeper into the forest. "Hello? I'm here. What do you want from me? Hello!" She would have given anything to be able to transform herself, or anything else, so her world wasn't just boring walls and boring dirt. A real witch ought to be able to do magic by instinct. She ought to be able to make mystical things happen, by sheer will, or with a profound enough belief.

A few weeks after the start of school, the frustration became too much. Patricia grabbed some dried-up spices and twigs from the basement of the spice house, went into the woods, and lit them on fire with kitchen matches. She ran around and around the tiny flame inside a shallow pit, doing nonsense chants and shaking her hands. She pulled her own hair and threw it into the flames. "Please," she choked through tears. "Hello? Please do something. Please!" Nothing. She crouched on her heels, watching her failed enchantment turn to ash.

When Patricia got home, her sister, Roberta, was showing their parents camera-phone pictures of Patricia lighting a fire and dancing around it. Plus, Roberta had a headless squirrel inside a FoodPile bag, which she claimed was Patricia's work. "Patricia is doing Satanic rituals in the woods," said Roberta. "And drugs. I saw her doing drugs, too. There were shrooms. And 420. And Molly."

"PP, we're worried about you," Patricia's father said, shaking his head until his beard was a blur. "PP" was his nickname for Patricia when she was a little baby, and when they were about to punish her he would start using it again. She thought it was cute when she was little, but when she got older she decided it was a subtle reference to her failure to be a boy. "We keep hoping you're going to start growing up. We don't enjoy punishing you, PP, but we have to prepare you for a tough world, where—"

"What Roderick is saying is that we spent *a lot of money* to send you to a school with uniforms and discipline and a curriculum that creates winners," Patricia's mom hissed, her jaw and penciled eyebrows looking sharper than usual. "Are you determined to blow this last chance? If you just want to be garbage, just let us know, and you can go back to the woods. Just never come back to this house. You can go live in the woods forever. We could save a large sum of money."

"We just want to see you *become* something, PP," her dad chimed in.

So they grounded her indefinitely and forbade her to go into the woods *ever again*. This time instead of sliding food under her door, they kept sending Roberta up with a tray.

Roberta put Tabasco and Sriracha chili oil on everything, no matter what.

The first night, Patricia's mouth was burning and she couldn't even leave her room for a glass of water. She was lonely and cold, and her parents had taken all of the stuff from her room that might entertain her, including her laptop. In her total boredom, she memorized some extra passages from her history book and she did all of the math problems, even the extra-credit ones.

The next day at school, everybody had seen the pictures of Patricia dancing around the fire, and of the squirrel with no head—because Roberta had sent them to *her* friends at high school, and some of Roberta's friends had brothers and sisters who went to Canterbury. More people started giving Patricia weird looks in the hallway, and this one boy whose name Patricia didn't even know ran up to her during Lunch Recess, yelled "emo bitch," and ran away. Carrie Danning and Macy Firestone, the theater kids, made a big show of checking Patricia's wrists, because she was probably a cutter, too, and they were *concerned*. "We just want to make sure you're getting the help you need," Macy Firestone said, bright orange hair rippling around her heart-shaped face. The actual popular kids, like Traci Burt, just shook their heads and texted each other.

The second night of being grounded, Patricia started to go nuts and she was choking on the red-hot super-spicy turkey and mashed potatoes Roberta had carried up. She was coughing and rasping and wheezing. The sound of the television downstairs—too loud to ignore, too quiet to make out what anyone was saying—peeled her skull.

The weekend was the worst part of being grounded. Patricia's parents put their own weekend plans on hold so they could keep her locked in her room. Like they had to miss an exhibition of vintage door knockers that they'd read about in one of their design magazines, which they'd been looking forward to.

If Patricia could do magic, then she could fly out her window or communicate with witches in China and Mexico. But no. She was still just boring, and bored.

Sunday came around. Patricia's mother made a pot roast. Roberta poured Tabasco over Patricia's portion before bringing it upstairs. Roberta unlocked the door and handed the tray to Patricia, then stood there in the doorway to watch Patricia eat. Waiting to see Patricia freak out and turn bright pink.

Instead, Patricia calmly loaded a big forkful into her mouth, chewed, and swallowed. She shrugged. "It's too bland," she said. "I would prefer it to be spicier." Then she handed it back to Roberta and closed her door.

Roberta took the tray back down and found a bottle of Texas extra-spicy five-alarm BBQ sauce. She splashed it onto Patricia's pot roast until it gave off a pungent aroma.

She carried the food back up to Patricia and handed it over. Patricia chewed a bit. "Hmmm," she said. "A little better. But still not spicy enough. I would really like something a lot spicier."

Roberta went and got a jar of Peruvian hot pepper seeds and dotted them all over the pot roast.

Patricia felt as though her mouth was on fire after just one bite, but she forced a smile onto her face. "Hmm. I would still like it spicier. Thank you," Patricia said.

Roberta found some chili powder on the top shelf of the downstairs pantry and put a generous scoopful onto Patricia's dinner. She had to pull her sweater over her nose and mouth to carry it back upstairs.

Patricia considered this screaming piece of beef, which was way spicier than the spiciest thing she'd ever eaten (a five-alarm chili that had been billed as "forbidden by the Geneva cooking convention" by the roadside diner where her family had stopped last summer). She forced herself to take a big bite and chew slowly. "Sure. That'll do. Thanks." Roberta watched Patricia eat the whole thing, slowly—but like she was savoring it, not like she was in pain or reluctant. When it was all gone, Patricia thanked Roberta again. The door closed and Patricia was alone. She let out a fiery gasp.

Patricia's stomach was being eaten from the inside. Her head was boiling away, and she felt faint. Everything was blinding white, and her mouth was a toxic disaster area. She was sweating red-hot oil through every inch of her skin. Most of all, her forehead hurt from pushing against the ceiling.

Wait a second. Why was her forehead up against the ceiling? Patricia could look down and see her own body, flopping around a bit. She was flying! She had left her body! Something about so much chili powder and hot oil all at once must have put her into a state. She was astral-projecting. Or something. She no longer even felt her stomach pain or any tingling in her mouth, that was for her physical body. "I love spicy food!" Patricia said with no mouth and no breath.

She flew to the woods.

She raced over the lawns and driveways, swooping and lifting, amazed at the feeling of the wind pressing through her face. Her hands and feet were pure silver. She rose higher, so the highway was a stream of brightness underneath her. The night felt cold, but not in a painful way, more like she was filling up with air.

Somehow Patricia knew the way to the place where the Parliament had met when she was a little girl. She wondered if she was dreaming all this, but it had too many funny details, like the highway construction closing one lane in the middle of the night—who would dream that up?—and it all seemed totally real.

Soon she was in front of the majestic Tree where the Parliament had met, its great wings of leaves arching over her. But there were no birds this time. The Tree just fanned in the darkness, the wind animating its fronds a little bit. Patricia had wasted a trip out of her body, because nobody was home. Just her luck.

She almost turned and flew back. But maybe the birds were in recess somewhere nearby. "Hello?" Patricia said into the darkness.

"Hell," a voice said back, "o."

Patricia had been standing planted in a patch of ground, but at the sound of that voice she jumped, and rose four feet in the air because she still weighed nothing. She remembered at last how to come back down to earth.

"Hello?" Patricia said again. "Who's there?"

"You called out," said the voice. "I answered." This time, Patricia could tell somehow that the voice was coming from the Tree itself. Like there was a presence there, at the center of its big trunk. There wasn't a face or anything, just a feeling that something was watching her.

"Thank you," Patricia said. She was getting cold, after all, in her panda pajamas. She was barefoot outdoors in the autumn night, even though this wasn't her body.

"I have not spoken to a living person," the Tree said, forming the words syllable by syllable, "in many seasons. You were distressed. What is wrong?" Its voice sounded like the wind blowing through an old bellows, or the lowest note playing on a big wooden recorder.

Now Patricia felt embarrassed, because suddenly her problems felt tiny and selfish, when she placed them in front of such a huge and ancient presence. "I feel like a fake witch," she said. "I can't *do* anything. At all. My friend Laurence can build supercomputers and time machines and ray guns. He can make cool things happen any time he wants. I can't make *anything* cool happen."

"Something cool," the Tree said in a gust of vowels and a clatter of consonants, "is happening. Right now."

"Yes," Patricia said, ashamed again. "Yes! Definitely! This is great. Really. But this just happened on its own. I can't *make* anything happen when I want it to."

"Your friend would control nature," said the Tree, rustling through each syllable one by one. "A witch must serve nature."

"But," Patricia said, thinking this through. "That's not fair. If nature serves Laurence, and I serve nature, then it's like I'm serving Laurence. I like Laurence, I guess, but I don't want to be his servant."

"Control," the Tree said, "is an illusion."

"Okay," Patricia said. "So I guess I really am a witch. Right? I mean, you called me witch just now. Plus I left my body, that counts for something. Thanks for taking the time to talk to me. I know it must be hard work being a tree. Especially a Parliamentary Tree."

"I am many trees," the Tree said. "And many other things besides. Goodbye."

The journey back to Patricia's house went much faster than the outward trip, perhaps because she was much sleepier. She passed through the ceiling of her bedroom and into her body— which was twisted with horrible stomach pain, because she had eaten enough hot peppers for a hundred thousand curries.

"Aaaaaaaa!" Patricia shouted, sitting up and clutching her stomach. "Bathroom break! Bathroom break! I need a bathroom break NOW!!!!"

ON MONDAY, SHE sat across from Laurence at lunch at the far end of one of the long tables, next to the slop cans, where the kids who had no clique of their own were stuck.

"Can you keep a secret?" she asked him.

"Sure," Laurence said without hesitating. He was poking holes in his gray, clammy hamburger with a knife. "You already know all of my secrets."

"Great." Patricia lowered her voice and covered her mouth. "So listen. You probably won't even believe any of this. I know it's going to sound crazy. But I have to tell someone. You're the only one I can tell." She told the whole story, as best she could.

4

EVERY TIME LAURENCE showed Patricia another one of his inventions, he felt a crick in his neck. Sort of a charley horse, that only happened when he pulled an experimental device out of his knapsack. He wondered about this for days until he realized: He was instinctively flinching away from Patricia and lifting one shoulder. Braced for her to call him a creep.

"Here's something I've been working on," he would start to say—and then his neck would spasm. Even when he realized he was doing it, he couldn't stop. Like part of him always flashed back to his sixth-grade Show-and-Tell disaster, the Laserscoop.

But if anything, Patricia just seemed endlessly curious. Even when he showed her the remote-controlled cyborg cockroach kit he'd ordered from the internet, one day after school. "Here's where you connect it to the roach's central nervous system, so it will obey all of your fiendish commands," Laurence said, pointing at the little wires on the tiny metal wedge, fresh out of the box. A truck belched underneath the pedestrian overpass they were sitting on, so neither of them could talk until it had passed.

"Roach-borg." Patricia looked at the roach-saddle in Laurence's palm. "That is nuts." She started to do a Borg voice from *Star Trek*: "Doritos are irrelevant."

"So you're not grossed out?" Laurence put it back in the box it came in, and the box back in the knapsack. He looked at her: still kind of giggling, though with a nervy edge to it. A car pulled a boat down the road. Probably the last chance for sailing this year.

Patricia considered this. "Sure, it's kind of yuck. But not as bad as when we dissected a cow brain in Biology class. I just don't feel sorry for a roach." Her legs kicked against the metal underside of the bridge, through the slats in the railing. Right now, as far as Laurence's parents knew, he and Patricia were halfway up the Crystal Lake Trail.

They both just watched the cars for a moment. Patricia had taken to rolling up the sleeves of her uniform cardigan all the time, so people could tell at a glance that she wasn't cutting herself—she really wasn't, okay?

"Just remember," Patricia said in a suddenly grown-up voice, "control is an illusion." He could see the unscathed veins in her bare forearm. He realized she was quoting the magic voice she'd talked to. "And yet," she went on, "I'm still jealous of your toys. You just never give up. You keep on making stuff. And whenever you show off something new to me, you have this look of joy on your face."

"Joy?" Laurence thought he had misheard for a moment. "I'm not joyful, I'm pissed off, all the time. I'm a misanthrope." That was his new favorite word, and he had been waiting to use it in a sentence for a while.

She shrugged. "Well, you *look* joyful. You get all excited. I envy that."

Laurence wondered if he could possibly cringe and be joyful at the same time. He rubbed his sore neck, first with one hand, then with both.

For some reason, Laurence believed Patricia's story about talking to some birds and having an out-of-body experience. He was still kind of a gullible person, which had made him easy to prank at summer camp—but also, he rebelled at the idea of starting to close off possibilities in the world. If Patricia, who was sort of his friend, believed this stuff, then he wanted to support her. Also, she was suffering for her "witchcraft" and it would offend some basic sense of fairness for Laurence to think she was being punished for nothing. And really, was her story any crazier than other stuff, like the way Laurence's body seemed to be rolling out new, totally unrequested features with alarming speed? Not really.

Plus Patricia had become pretty much the only person Laurence could talk to at school. Even the other so-called geeks at Canterbury Academy were too chickenshit to hang with Laurence, especially after he'd managed to get himself banned from the school's computer lab (he wasn't trying to hack anything, just make some improvements) and the school workshop (he was doing a carefully controlled flamethrower experiment). She was the only one he could laugh with about the Saarinian Program's weird test questions (*"Faith* *is to religion as love is to _____*"), and he liked how she people-watched in the cafeteria, how her gaze turned Casey Hamilton's student-council campaign into an amusing pageant taking place on the outskirts of fairytown.

Patricia pulled her legs out of the railing and got to her feet. "But you're lucky," she said. "There's a difference between your type of outcast and mine. If you're a science geek, people give you wedgies and don't invite you to their parties. But if you're a witch, everybody just assumes you're an evil psycho. It's kind of different."

"Don't try and lecture me about my life." Laurence had gotten to his feet as well, and now he dropped his rucksack on the ground, so it nearly tumbled off the overpass. He felt both sides of his neck tighten up. "Just… don't. You don't know what my life is like."

"Sorry." Patricia bit her lip, just as a tanker rolled underfoot. "I guess that was out of line. Just trying to warn you that if you're going to be my friend, you have to be prepared for worse stuff than just people thinking we're girlfriend-boyfriend. Like, you might get some of my witch cooties on you."

Laurence rolled his eyes at this. "I think I can handle a little peer pressure."

BRAD CHOMNER GAVE Laurence a Dumpster swirlie after fifth period a few days later. Laurence looked up, head soaked with slime, rusty walls tearing at his uniform shirt, and Brad was grabbing Laurence by the lapels and hauling him up so they were *almost* face-to-face. Brad Chomner's neck was thicker than Laurence's whole torso. Worse yet, when Brad let Laurence fall to the cement walkway he saw that his indelible forever crush, Dorothy Glass, had been watching the whole thing.

"I don't know if I can take four more years of this place," Laurence told Patricia when the two of them were sitting at one end of the lunch table, uncomfortably close to the garbage cans so soon after his trash baptism. His head still itched. "I keep thinking maybe I could transfer to the math-and-science high school in town, instead."

"I don't know," Patricia said. "You'd have to get up early every day and take the bus alone. You'd be spending so much time on the bus, you'd probably miss out on all the after-school stuff."

"Anything's better than this," Laurence said. "Mr. Gluckman, the math teacher, already wrote a letter for me. Now I just have to get my parents to sign the form. I have a feeling they're going to be weird about me going to school so far away, though."

"They just want you to have a real childhood. They don't want you to grow up too fast."

"They worry about me too much, ever since I ran away from home this one time, to go see a rocket. They just don't want me to stand out." While Laurence was talking, a Tater Tot hit him in the head, but he just kept talking as if nothing had happened.

"I think it's good that you have parents who care what becomes of you." Patricia seemed to have a soft spot for

Laurence's parents, maybe because they weren't scary overachievers like hers were.

"My parents are cowards. They're always terrified someone will notice them and they'll have to explain themselves." A second Tater Tot impact. Laurence barely flinched.

Lunch was almost over, and then they had separate classes. Laurence changed the subject. "Hey, do you want to talk to my supercomputer?" He was gathering up all his stuff into his book bag. "I think it needs more interaction with different people, to help it learn how humans think."

"What would I talk to it about?" Patricia said.

"Just whatever you want," Laurence said. "Think of it as a friend to confide in." He pulled a scrap of yellow lined paper out of his bag. "This is the computer's IM account, on all the main services. Its name is CH@NG3M3." He spelled that. "It's a temporary name, just like it sounds. When CH@NG3M3 becomes fully sentient and starts thinking for itself, it can choose a new name. But I like that name. It's like I'm challenging the computer to grow and change and find an identity for itself."

"Or maybe you're asking the computer to change you," Patricia said.

"Yeah." Laurence looked at his own handwriting on the notepaper. "Yeah, maybe I am at that."

"Okay," Patricia said. "I'll try talking to it." She took the paper from Laurence and stuffed it into her skirt pocket.

"Anything you tell CH@NG3M3 will be between you two," Laurence said. "I won't ever read any of it."

"Speaking of which," Patricia said, "I hear the new

guidance counselor is actually pretty okay. Maybe you should go talk to him about your Brad Chomner problem." The bell rang, and they ran their separate ways.

Laurence decided to take Patricia's advice, since he'd heard other people say that the new guidance counselor was cool. He'd only recently taken over, after the previous school counselor got run over by a meat truck. The new guy did have an easy, talk-show-host vibe about him as he told Laurence that he could share anything inside this boxy office, with its antidrug posters and bookcases instead of a window. Theodolphus Rose was a tall man with a shaved head—no eyebrows, even—and grotesque, knobby cheekbones and chin.

"I just," Laurence said. "The bullying. It is interfering. With my ability to achieve academically. When I get locked in a Dumpster, it causes me to miss Social Studies class, which is going to drag my grades down. I am not an escape artist."

If Laurence didn't know better, he would think Mr. Rose was studying him. Like a bug. Then the moment passed and Mr. Rose looked friendly and supportive again.

"It seems to me," the guidance counselor said, "that the other children see you as an easy target, because you're so noticeable, and yet so defenseless. You have two options in this situation: to make them respect you, or to become invisible. Or some combination of the two."

"So," Laurence said, "stop standing out so much? Stop eating lunch in the cafeteria? Build a death ray?"

"I would never advocate violence." Mr. Rose leaned back in his pleather chair with his hands behind his smooth head.

"You children are too important. You are the future, after all. But find ways to make them see what you're capable of, so they respect you. Keep alert and always know your escape routes. Or try to blend into the shadows as much as possible. They can't hurt what they can't see."

"Okay," Laurence said. "I sort of see what you're saying."

"Children," said Theodolphus Rose, "are adults who haven't yet learned to make fear their hand puppet." He smiled.

5

A BULLFROG JUMPED out of Patricia's locker. A big one, too large to cup in your hands. It croaked, probably something like "get me out of here." Its eyes looked strangulated with panic, and its legs—awfully little, to support such a bulbous frame—twitched. It wanted to find its cool wet nest and get away from this white hell. Patricia tried to catch it, but it slipped through her grasp. Someone must have spent hours catching this thing, gotten up at dawn or something. The frog gave a vengeful grunt and took off down the hallway, heading god knew where, as all the kids shrieked with laughter. "Emo bitch," someone called out.

After school, Patricia sat on her bed and talked to CH@NG3M3, Laurence's supercomputer, like she did every day lately. "My parents say they'll never let me go into the woods as long as I live, which means I'm no use to anybody at all. And everybody at school keeps accusing me of being a cutter and a crazy person. Sometimes I wish I was crazy, it would make everything easier."

"If you were crazy," CH@NG3M3 responded, "how would you know you were crazy?"

"That's a good question," Patricia admitted. "You would need to have one person who you completely trusted. Like, if you trusted one other person, you could check to see if you were seeing the same things they were." She chewed her thumb, sitting cross-legged on her brass-kettle quilt, legs tucked under her skirt.

"What if you didn't see the same things?" CH@NG3M3 said. "Would you be crazy?" Sometimes when the computer got out of its depth, it would rephrase Patricia's answers back to her and change them slightly—which almost looked like it was thinking, but not quite.

"You're lucky you don't have eyes, or a body," Patricia told it. "You don't have to worry about any of this stuff."

"What do I have to worry about?" CH@NG3M3 asked, in another blue speech balloon.

"Getting unplugged, I guess. Laurence changing his mind and turning you off."

"Where would you get another pair of eyes?" CH@NG3M3 abruptly dragged the conversation back to the earlier topic, something that happened when it judged they'd reached a dead end. "What kind of eyes would you want to have?"

Something about this conversation gave Patricia an idea: If her parents wouldn't let her go back to the woods, maybe she could get them to agree to something else? Like maybe she could get a cat. At dinner, Patricia forked steamed kale around her plate while her mom asked what everybody had done to

Improve themselves today. Roberta, the perfect straight-A student, always had the best Improvements, like every day she'd aced some crazy-tough assignment. But Patricia was stuck at a school where all you ever did was memorize stuff and fill out multiple-choice ovals, so she had to lie, or else learn something in her spare time. For three or four days in a row, Patricia kept coming up with Improvements that sounded kind of impressive, storing up credit, and then she started mentioning that she wanted to get a cat.

Patricia's parents disliked animals and felt certain that they would be allergic. But at last, they relented—so long as Patricia promised to do all cat-related labor, and if the cat got sick they wouldn't have to rush to a vet or anything. "We have to agree in advance that all veterinary care will be scheduled far ahead, in a time window that's convenient for Roderick and myself," said Patricia's mother. "There will be no such thing as a cat-related emergency. Are we in agreement?"

Patricia nodded and crossed her heart.

Berkley was a fluffy black kitten with a huge white stripe on his stomach and a white smudge across his scowly face. (Patricia named him after a cartoonist.) They got Berkley already fixed, out of a litter of kittens from their neighbor, Mrs. Torkelford, and right away Patricia noticed something familiar about him. He kept giving Patricia the stink-eye and running away from her, and after a few days she realized: He must be the grandson, or grandnephew, of Tommington, the cat she'd stranded up a tree when she was little. Berkley never spoke to her, of course, but she couldn't shake the impression that he had *heard* about her.

Also, even though Roberta had expressed *no* interest in getting a cat beforehand, she wanted to share Berkley. She would hoist Berkley by his little shoulders and carry him up to her bedroom, then close the door. Patricia would hear a pitiful groaning, even over Roberta's loud music. But the door was locked. And the one time Patricia told her parents she thought Roberta was mistreating the cat, they referred back to the "no cat-related emergencies" clause. All Roberta would say was, "I'm teaching him to play the bongos."

Patricia wanted to protect Berkley from her sister, but he hissed if Patricia even came close. "Come on," Patricia kept pleading in her human voice. "You have to let me help you. I don't want anything from you. I just want to keep you safe." But the cat fled whenever Patricia approached. He'd taken to hiding in a million nooks and crawl spaces in the spice house, emerging when his bowl was full or he needed the litter box. Roberta had an uncanny ability to know when Berkley was out, and astounding reflexes for scooping him up.

ANOTHER DAY, ANOTHER Improvement. After lights-out, Patricia heard yowls that started high and got lower and more tragic, coming from Roberta's room.

The next day, after school, Laurence came over to Patricia's house, where he'd gotten used to the musty aromas of old seasonings. The two of them sat in the front parlor, where you could still see the outlines on the wall where spice bins had once hung, and worked on a solution to the problem of Berkley.

"If we could capture the cat, we could rig some kind of protective exoskeleton," Laurence said.

"He's suffered enough," Patricia said. "I don't want to torture him any more by prodding him and attaching some kind of gear to his body."

"If I knew how to build nanomachines, I would make a swarm of them follow him around and form a shield when he was in distress. But my best attempts at nanomotors were sort of, um, lazy. You wouldn't like lazy nanobots."

They caught a glimpse of Berkley in the unilluminable darkness of the spice house's upper attic, behind a great support beam. A glimmer of fur, a bright pair of eyes. Another time Berkley ran down the stairs, just as they threw themselves in his path. The two children wound up in a bruised heap at the bottom of the stairwell.

"Listen," Patricia said from the bottom of the stairs. "Tommington was a good cat. I didn't have anything against him. He was just doing his cat thing. I never meant him any harm, I swear." There was no response.

"Maybe you should do a spell," said Laurence. "Do some magic or something. I dunno."

Patricia felt sure Laurence was laughing at her, but he didn't have that kind of guile. She would have seen it on his face.

"I'm serious," Laurence said. "This seems like a magic kind of problem, if there ever was one."

"But I don't know how to do anything," Patricia said. "I mean, the only time I did anything magicky in years was when I ate too much spicy food. I've tried every kind of spice a hundred times since then."

"But maybe you didn't need to be able to do anything those other times," Laurence said. "And now, you do."

Berkley watched them from atop a bookcase full of Patricia's mother's Productivity Assessment books. He was ready to flee, fast as a bullet train, if they came too close.

"I wish we could just go into the woods and find that magic Tree," Patricia said. "But my parents would kill me if they found out. And I know Roberta would tell them."

"I don't think we need to go into the woods," said Laurence, still eager to avoid the outdoors. "From what you told me before, the power is inside you. You just need to get at it."

Patricia looked at Laurence, who was not in any way screwing with her, and she couldn't imagine ever having a better friend in the world.

She went back up to the attic, where it was always way hotter than the rest of the spice house, and listened to her own breathing. She looked like a bird to herself, her body so tiny and hollow-boned. Laurence and Berkley were both watching to see what she was going to do. Berkley even crept a little closer along a ceiling beam.

Okay. Now or never.

She imagined that this hot attic was a jungle, and the dry beams were fruitful trees and the boxes of old clothes were lush undergrowth. She couldn't go to the forest, she couldn't count on astral-projecting a second time—fine. She would bring the forest to her. She breathed the scents of long-ago chests of saffron and turmeric, and she imagined a million branches splaying over their heads, endless limbs as far as they could see in any direction. She tried to remember the sound of Tommington's speech, long ago, and tried to speak to Berkley the same way, as close as she could manage.

She had no clue what she was doing, and if she stopped a second to think about what a nut she looked like, she would die.

She was talking under her breath, but she got a little louder. Berkley crept closer, his tongue between two pointy teeth. Patricia swayed a little and reached deep in her throat for a grumbling, raucous sound. Berkley's ears pricked up.

Berkley was definitely coming over, and Patricia grew louder. He was almost within grabbing distance if she wanted to grab him, which she didn't.

"You... speak cat?" Berkley said, his eyes ginormous.

"Sometimes." Patricia couldn't help laughing with relief. "Sometimes I speak cat."

"You're that mean girl," Berkley said. "You tricked Uncle Tommington."

"I didn't mean to," Patricia said. "I was trying to help a bird."

"Birds taste good," Berkley observed, bouncing on his front paws a little. "They flap around and try to fly out of your paws. They are like toys with meat inside."

"This bird was a friend of mine," Patricia said.

"A friend?" Berkley struggled with the concept that you could be *friends* with a bird. What was next, holding conversations with your cat dish?

"Yes. I protect my friends. No matter what. I would like to be your friend."

Berkley bristled a little bit. "I don't need any protection. I am a strong fierce cat."

"Sure, of course. Maybe you can protect me, then."

"Maybe I can." Berkley came over and curled up in Patricia's lap.

"I did it!" She turned to look at Laurence, grinning with her whole face, and realized he was looking kind of… shell-shocked.

Laurence just stared, then shuddered a little.

"Sorry," Patricia said, "was that weird?" Berkley was purring in her lap. Like a band saw.

"Kind of. Yeah," Laurence said. His shoulders were a scaffolding around his ears.

"Uh. Good weird, or bad weird?"

"Just… weird. Weirdness is value neutral… I should go. See you at school."

Laurence fled, almost as fast as Berkley might have, before Patricia could say anything else. She couldn't go after him, she finally had a purring cat in her lap. Her familiar. Damn. She'd hoped this wasn't going to be freaky. What kind of dumbass was she, doing magic like that in front of an outsider? It had been his idea, true, but still.

She started petting Berkley. "We're just going to protect each other, okay?" He showed no sign that he could still understand her, but whatever. She had finally done a proper spell, on purpose, this time.

6

LAURENCE'S CHEAPJACK LUNCH tray wobbled, sagging under the weight of so much undercooked starch, as he tried to figure out where to sit, as far away from Patricia Delfine as possible. She sat there, in their usual spot, near the compost and trash bins, trying to catch his eye, one brow raised under her messy bangs. The longer he stood, the less stable his tray felt and the more she seemed to squirm in the corner of his eye.

Finally, Laurence took a sharp left and went to sit on the back steps, near where the skaters skateboarded after school, perching the plastic tray on his knees. It was technically against the rules to eat out here, but who cared.

He kept thinking he should try to talk to Patricia, but then he would remember the weirdness. The image of her shimmying around and doing that thing with her hands, and then having a dialogue with her pet in cat noises for an uncomfortable length of time, was enough to make Laurence dry-heave. He pictured the two of them hanging out and

Patricia offering to talk to the local wildlife on his behalf, maybe doing her heebie-jeebie dance again.

The whispers Laurence had been hearing about Patricia around the school felt much more relevant, now that he'd seen her in action. Lately he'd been finding any excuse to sit near the graceful, long-limbed Dorothy Glass, and he heard Dorothy and her friends sharing a whole mythos about that girl who kept frogs in her locker. People still thought Laurence was dating Patricia, no matter how he denied it. He couldn't help remembering Patricia's warning about "witch cooties."

"Hey." Patricia came out the back door and stood right behind him, casting a shadow in his face as he tried to eat his buttery potato wedges. Laurence kept chewing. "Hey," Patricia said again, angrier this time.

"Hey." Laurence didn't turn around.

"What's going on? Why are you ignoring me? Seriously, please talk to me. This is driving me nuts." The shadow over Laurence flickered and changed shape, because Patricia was gesturing. "It was your idea. You suggested it. And then I did it, and you freaked out and bailed. Who treats their friends that way?"

"We shouldn't talk about this at school," Laurence said very quietly, using his fork as the opposite of a microphone.

"Okay," Patricia said. "So when do you want to talk about this?"

"I just want to keep my head down," Laurence said. "Until I can get out of this place. That's all I want." An ant stumbled hoisting Laurence's bread crumb. Maybe Patricia could give it a pep talk in ant language.

"I thought you hated your parents because *they* just want to keep their heads down."

Laurence felt a weird combination of shame and rage, as though he'd grown another new body part just in time to get punched in it. He seized his tray and pushed his way past Patricia, not caring if he got potato dregs on himself or on her, and hurried back inside. And of course, someone saw him rushing in the hallway with a half-laden tray and stuck out a leg to trip him up. He ended up face-down in his own muck. It never failed.

Later that day, Brad Chomner tried to cram Laurence's entire body into a single-file urinal, and then both Brad and Laurence got hauled into Mr. Dibbs's office for fighting, as if they were equal instigators. Mr. Dibbs called Laurence's parents to come get him.

"That school is crushing the life out of me," Laurence told his parents at dinner. "I need to get out of there. I've already filled out the application form to transfer to the math-and-science school, and I just need you guys to sign it." He slid it onto the chipped Formica table, where it sat amidst the faded place mats.

"We're just not sure you're mature enough to go to school in the city by yourself." Laurence's dad carved into his casserole with the edge of his fork, making little snuffling noises with his nose and mouth. "Mr. Dibbs is concerned that you're a disruptive influence. Just because you get good grades"—snarf, snorf—"doesn't mean you can be a bad element."

"You haven't proved you can handle the responsibility

you already have," said Laurence's mother. "You can't make trouble all the time."

"Your mother and I don't make trouble," said Laurence's father. "We make other things. Because we're adults."

"What?" Laurence shoved his casserole away and took a heavy swig of cola instead. "What do you make, exactly? Either of you guys."

"Don't talk back," said Laurence's father.

"This isn't about us," said Laurence's mother.

"No, I want to know. It occurs to me, I have no clue what either of you produces." Laurence looked at his dad. "You're a lower middle manager who denies people's insurance claims for a living." He looked at his mom. "You update instruction manuals for obsolete machinery. What do either of you *make*?"

"We put a roof over your head," his father said.

"And delicious liver-and-peas casserole on your plate," his mother said.

"Oh Jesus." Laurence had never talked to his parents like this before, and he didn't know what had come over him. "You have no idea how hard I pray not to turn out like you two. My every nightmare, every one, is about turning into a complacent failure like you both. You don't even remember the dreams you threw away to sink into this hole." And with that, he pushed his chair hard enough to scar the cheap linoleum and got upstairs before his parents could send him to his room or try to muster some fake outrage. He locked the door.

Laurence wished Isobel and her rocketeer friends would

come and take him away. She was helping to run a start-up aerospace company that was actually making deliveries to the Space Station, and he kept reading articles where she was quoted about the brave new future of space travel.

After Laurence flopped onto his bed and gazed up at his ceiling-wide poster in which every fictional spaceship congregated at a massive nebula, he remembered how he'd spoken to his parents. If he strained to listen over the dozen cooling fans along one wall of his bedroom, he could hear his parents fighting. Not the kind of fight where anybody hopes to win. Or even find some solution. This was hopeless, pointless, mindless aggression, two creatures caught in a trap with nothing to do but tear each other apart. Laurence wanted to die.

His mother sounded more wounded, his father more fatalistic. But they had identical levels of bitterness.

Laurence put a pillow over his head. It did no good. He wound up putting his headphones on, with the latest girltrash songs that everybody was listening to at school, and then a pair of winter earmuffs over them. Now he could no longer hear his parents, but he could still imagine what they were saying. He focused on the crooning, growling voice of the girltrash singer, whose name was Heta Neko, and he found himself with an erection. Ignoring it did as much good as ignoring these things ever did. He hated himself, even as he let one hand drift down and carry out the motion he'd practiced incessantly of late. Just as Laurence splashed onto a dirty fast-food napkin, he both heard and felt one of his parents slamming the front door of their house, he didn't know which.

I wish I were dead and in hell, Laurence thought.

Laurence didn't sleep much. The next morning, he felt too sick for school, but he knew better than to ask to stay home. He barely noticed when kids threw erasers at him or refused to let him sign their petition to save something or other, because if he signed it then nobody else would.

When Laurence got home that afternoon, he found the form sitting on the kitchen table, signed by both parents. Neither was home. At dinner, he tried to thank them, but they just shrugged and looked at the table. The three of them ate in total silence.

The next day, Laurence just stood in the hallway, watching it drain of people. He realized his buttons were buttoned wrong, so his jacket was askew.

Patricia came up to him in the hallway. "You're going to be late," she said. "They're going to kill you."

For the first time ever, Laurence noticed that Patricia was pretty. Her skin had a brightness underlying its faint tan. Like an airbrushed picture he'd seen once. Her neck was really smooth and graceful, and her wrist pivoted as she held her backpack on her shoulder. Her dark hair fell almost over one gray-green eye. He wanted to grab her by the shoulders. He wanted to run away from her. He wanted to kiss her. He wanted to scream.

Instead, he said, "Do you want to ditch school?"

"Why?" she said. "And go where?"

"Let's go to the woods," he said. "I want to see your magic Tree."

He no longer cared if this girl was crazy. He was a bad

person, and what was worse, being crazy or being evil? Plus she might be the only girl who would even consider kissing him before he turned thirty. And he was growing more conscious that he had been a dick to her.

"You want to go to the woods with me," Patricia said. "Right now."

Laurence nodded. He needed to fidget. He didn't.

He thought about how dull the tiles underfoot were. Someone waxed them every day, leaving them shiny for an hour until they dried and hundreds of kids walked on them, and then the floor just looked sticky and gray with wax scum. The floor probably looked dirtier than if nobody ever waxed it.

"I'm sorry," Patricia said. "I can't. I have to stay on at this school, after you've gone on to your math paradise."

"Sure," Laurence said. "Okay." He wanted to say something else, like maybe apologize, but he didn't. And then the moment had evaporated, and they were walking to separate classes.

WHEN THEODOLPHUS ROSE was fourteen, he'd slept on a bunk of mossy slate. He had mastered a hundred ways to kill a woman without awakening the man sleeping next to her. Every morning, an hour before dawn, the fourteen-year-old Theodolphus had gone for a ten-mile run with a ceramic urn full of his teacher's urine on his head, and if a single drop spilled or he failed to complete the ten miles within an hour and a half, he would be forced to stand on his head until he saw a river of sunfire. His only meals had been the not-quite-lethal mushrooms and berries he'd been taught to pick in the thickets near the cliff-sheltered school fortress. And yet the Nameless Assassin School was a country club compared to Canterbury Academy. For one thing, he had been *learning* things, skills that he still used in his vocation, and he had taken pride in them. For another, nobody had forced him to answer multiple-choice questions on battered notebook computers. If they had given standardized tests in assassin school, he would not have lasted a day. (Theodolphus made a mental note to hunt down Lars Saarinian, the psychologist who had studied the slaughterhouse behavior of pigs and come up with an educational regimen for human children, when he finally got out of here.)

Theodolphus had spent weeks spying on these two children, listening to all of their conversations, at home and at school. He'd parked across the street from their houses and eavesdropped on the two of them, together and separately. He'd racked his brains trying to come up with a death that didn't require his hands-on involvement—thus complying with the letter of the child-murder ban—but would still tell a good story. Something artistic. He had this notion that the children would go into the woods together, where Laurence could be bitten by a snake and then Patricia could try sucking the poison out of him and accidentally poison herself. But no, because Patricia was forbidden to go into the woods and she was the only child on earth who *obeyed her parents*. Theodolphus kept hoping Patricia would have a moment of rebelliousness, and being brutalized by disappointment.

By now, after weeks of slouching on purpose in his office chair, listening to Brad Chomner talk about his body-image issues, Theodolphus just wanted this over with. This was the longest he'd gone without killing someone in years, and his hands kept getting ideas. He sat in faculty meetings and imagined just how much of Don Gluckman's insides he could show the math teacher while keeping him alive.

Worst of all was when Theodolphus had to give advice about puberty, something he had never personally experienced.

Lucy Dodd got a stomach flu—not Theodolphus's work—and they needed someone to teach English for a few days. Theodolphus volunteered. It would give him another chance to study his prey, since both Laurence and Patricia took that class.

All of the kids had clearly been looking forward to having a sub so they could goof off. When they saw it was Theodolphus, wearing a crisp black shirt, matching black pants, and a red tie, they all sighed with disappointment—for some reason, Theodolphus had become the most popular faculty member at this school, and nobody felt like screwing with him. "Most of you know me," he said, making eye contact with each surly dough face in turn.

Laurence and Patricia sat at separate tables, not talking to each other, not even looking at each other, except that the girl kept giving the boy wounded little glances. The boy glared at his secondhand *Scarlet Letter*.

Traci Burt read out a passage she'd memorized, with perfect diction and a smile full of ceramic braces. Then

Theodolphus attempted to get a discussion going about Hester Prynne and whether she was unfairly treated, and got back a lot of canned answers about Puritan morality, and then he called on Laurence. "Mr. Armstead. Do you think society needs to burn the occasional witch for the sake of social cohesion?"

"What?" Laurence jumped, so that three legs of his chair left the ground. He dropped all his books on the floor. Everybody else laughed and texted. "I'm sorry," Laurence babbled, gathering up all his stuff. "I don't know what you mean."

Oh yes, Theodolphus said to himself. *You know perfectly well.*

"I see." Theodolphus made a scritch on a paper, as if writing the boy off. "How about you, Miss Delfine? Do you think the occasional witch burning helps to weld society together?"

Patricia lost a breath. Then she found it again and looked up, regarding Theodolphus with a steadiness that he couldn't help admiring. Her thin lips pushed out.

"Well," Patricia said. "A society that has to burn witches to hold itself together is a society that has already failed, and just doesn't know it yet."

With that, Theodolphus knew how he would finish this mission, and redeem his professional self-respect once and for all.

7

THE SNOWSTORM HIT a few weeks after Laurence more or less stopped talking to Patricia. She woke up with Berkley curled between her bent elbow and her shoulder, and looked out her window without getting all the way out of bed. The ground and the sky mirrored each other: two sheets of white.

Patricia shuddered and almost pulled the covers over her head. Instead, she took the hottest shower she could bear and put on her long johns for the first time this year. They no longer fit.

Patricia's mother was already on-site and her father was multi-focusing with his laptop and a stack of folders, so at least Patricia didn't have to talk to her parents. But Roberta came down halfway through breakfast and just stared at Patricia without talking, and that was creepy, and at last Roberta went off to Ellenburg High and Patricia was left hoping against hope that Canterbury Academy was having a snow day.

No such luck. Patricia got to school in her dad's sedan, and almost broke her neck on the slushy steps. People threw snowballs with gravel in them at Patricia's head, but she didn't bother to turn and look—that would just be presenting a better target.

"Miss Delfine," a smooth, deep voice said behind Patricia in the near-empty hallway. (A lot of kids had stayed home after all.) Patricia turned to see Mr. Rose, the guidance counselor with the knuckle face, looming in a pin-striped slate suit.

"Umm. Yes?"

Mr. Rose had never made much of an impression, though everybody said he was the only decent authority figure at this cruddy school. But today he seemed dark and towering, a foot taller than normal. Patricia shrugged this off as just snow-day nerves.

"I was hoping to discuss something with you," Mr. Rose said in a deeper than usual voice. "Perhaps you could come by my office when you get a moment. I find that I have an unusually free schedule today."

Patricia said "Sure," and dashed off to first period. The school was half-empty, and the snow kept blinding her through the windows. It all felt like a weird dream. Her first class was Math, and Mr. Gluckman wasn't even trying to teach—everybody just goofed off.

Her second period teacher hadn't even made it to school, so it became a free period, after ten minutes of perfunctory waiting. Patricia drifted toward Mr. Rose's office.

"Thank you for coming on such short notice. I will keep this brief." Mr. Rose's teeth clacked inside his dry white lips. This wasn't the Mr. Rose Patricia was used to. He sat straighter in his gray chair, hands folded on his walnut desk, with its cartoon walrus pencil holder. Behind him, there was a wall of books on child development.

Patricia nodded. Mr. Rose took a deep breath.

"I have a message for you," he said, "from the Tree."

"The what—?" Patricia felt sure this was a dream. The pale world, the empty school—she was still in bed with Berkley.

"Well, not the Tree exactly. But the power the Tree represents. I know you've waited a long time to fulfill your purpose as a witch. You've been more than patient. So I have been tasked with informing you that your wait is almost over. The secrets will soon be yours."

Patricia couldn't breathe. Her hands were gripping her chair arms. She felt hot around her face and yet freezing in her extremities. Her blood was all going to her head, as if it were preparing to separate from her body. Her feet kicked each other.

"What?" she said at last. "What do you mean?"

"You know what I mean."

"Umm…" She was on the verge of babbling, but reined it in. This was important witch business. "Um. Who *are* you?" She would not have disbelieved, necessarily, if he'd claimed to be Merlin or something.

"I'm your school guidance counselor." Mr. Rose smiled with one lip. "I'm just passing along a message, that's all. This is the only time you and I will ever discuss this matter."

"Oh. Okay."

"You will be receiving instructions soon. In the meantime, there is one task you must perform."

"Umm…" *Stop saying umm*, Patricia told herself.

"Umm, is it like a test? Or an assignment? Do I have to prove myself worthy?"

"You have already proved everything you needed to prove. No, this is merely a task. But an unpleasant one. There is a boy at this school who will grow up to be a great enemy of nature, and a persecutor of the magical community. You already know him. His name is Laurence Armstead. He may have asked to see a demonstration of magic recently. He may even have asked you to show him the Tree. Is this so?"

"Umm... yeah." This conversation was like falling off the edge of the world, plummeting all the way around the globe, and then falling off the edge a second time. Patricia's stomach was upside down.

"So you already know. I hate to say this, and remember I'm just the messenger. I regard all human life as precious and irreplaceable. But Laurence Armstead must die. And you must be the one to kill him. Nobody else can do it. As soon as you complete this task, you can begin your training."

Patricia couldn't remember what she said after that—it probably had a lot of "umm" in it. She didn't say she would kill Laurence, and she didn't say she wouldn't. She may have thanked Mr. Rose for the message. She wasn't sure. She was in an upright coma for the rest of the day. Even Roberta hanging from the banister upside down and staring at her after dinner barely registered. Roberta's dark brown hair hung straight down and her eyebrows twitched, but she said nothing as Patricia walked past.

Patricia found herself in Roberta's room an hour later, right before lights-out. "Bert," she said, using her old nickname. "Could you kill a person? If you absolutely had to?"

Roberta was painting her toenails candy-apple green, in her white cotton PJs. "Wow, Trish. Morbid much?" She laughed. "For your information, the answer is yes and no. Yes, I would be willing, if I felt it was necessary and whatever. But I probably couldn't go through with it. I would be too much of a wuss to look at someone and take them out. Even if I was sure it was the right thing."

"Umm, okay. Thanks."

"But Trish," Roberta called after Patricia as she turned to go to her own room, across the hallway. "If you *do* ever take someone out, I get to watch. I want to see you do it."

"Umm, okay."

Laurence was back at school the next day, in a good mood for a change, swinging his arms in the wet hallways like he owned the place. He was back to not talking to Patricia, but he smiled at her without looking right at her. She could so easily end him, just push him in front of one of the senior citizen tour buses the school used as transportation. It would look like an accident. Patricia found herself studying his twitchy head and slender wrists, trying to imagine if it could be true: Was he going to become an enemy of magic? He was already hostile to it, that was for sure. Maybe the grown-up Laurence would be some kind of monster, for all she knew, persecuting her kind. Maybe this was part of what witches did—regretfully, sorrowfully—snuffing out people who would threaten the balance of nature?

She watched him in the cafeteria. Punishing his food.

She watched him running wind sprints up and down the hill behind the school, shivering in his track uniform. She tried to imagine him launching a vendetta. Persecuting her friends, if she ever actually had friends. She couldn't make herself believe it, and she couldn't do it unless she did. She could imagine killing him, that was shockingly easy—one shove, into the big wheels—but she couldn't imagine him deserving it.

Whenever she tried to talk to Mr. Rose, he was either busy or absent. She finally caught up with him in the hallway near the teacher lounge and tried to mention the Tree. He looked at her as if she was speaking gibberish. One brow raised.

At home, she asked CH@NG3M3, "Will Laurence become an enemy of magic?"

CH@NG3M3 responded, "Do you think Laurence will become an enemy of magic?"

"I'm asking you."

"Why are you asking me?"

She couldn't get to sleep for ages, even with Berkley scrunched along her rib cage—but then she finally slept, and dreamed she was carving Laurence open with a big knife. His skin parted to reveal a shining portal to a magical land full of kind wizards who gave her a wand of her own. She dreamed she lured him to the Wadlow River cliff, where the high-school kids partied, and shoved him off the edge onto the sharp, slippery rocks.

She woke up crying and shaking and holding on to Berkley for dear life.

* * *

SOMEONE THREW A rock at Patricia's head before school started. Not a snowball with rocks in it, just a plain chunk of granite. Patricia ducked, but slipped on the path. Laurence grabbed her arm and helped her to her feet. He steadied her, and seemed to be trying to say something. Then he walked away, like he usually did these days whenever he was about to speak to her.

First period, Patricia reached in her backpack for her textbook and something else spilled out: a pair of panties, with a stain she couldn't identify and didn't care to examine further. She was sure they hadn't been there when she left the house. The other kids at her table, including Macy Firestone, started laughing and taking photos.

"What's that commotion?" Mr. Gluckman asked from the board.

"Someone has put… something unspeakable in my bag." Patricia tried to sound dignified, not like a victim but not like a troublemaker, either.

"Emo bitch," someone hissed from the corner.

"That's no excuse for disrupting my class." Mr. Gluckman frowned, between gray sideburns. "You are taking time away from all of the children who are here to learn something."

"I didn't do anything!" Patricia said. "Somebody else—"

"If 'someone' has been storing inappropriate items in 'someone's' bag, I suggest you take it up with the principal or Mr. Dibbs."

Patricia looked around. A roomful of pure entertainment. She caught Laurence's eye and he gave her a blank, helpless look.

"Fine," Patricia stood up. "I will. May I be excused?" She didn't wait for an answer. The door crashed shut behind her, failing to block out the cheers and applause.

She made it halfway to Mr. Dibbs's office before Mr. Dibbs charged around a corner and grabbed her arm. "You"—he grabbed her arm with one meaty hand—"have some explaining to do." She tried talking to him, but he hauled her right into the girls' room, where she saw, written in blood on the wall:

DEATH IS EXCELLENT

It wasn't human blood. It wasn't fresh blood. It was definitely blood, though—whoever had done this had left plastic containers from the butcher shop in the trash. The "paint" was dripping, the message still melting on the wall. Someone had gone into the girls' room and painted this right after first period began, without anybody noticing. You would have to be a ninja.

"What…" Patricia felt frostbitten from the inside out. The stench was punishing: a noxious slaughterhouse odor, the dying distress of cattle immortalized in smell form. She couldn't bear to be in the same room with it.

Mr. Dibbs's jaw twitched under his dark, thick beard. He gestured at the wall with his free hand. "You are going to clean this up and then we are going to call your parents to come and have a conversation about civilized behavior and barbarism and the vital! The crucial! Difference between the two."

"I didn't... Please let go of my arm, you're hurting me." She couldn't hear herself talk. He jerked her closer to the wall, so she was inches away from it. "I don't know anything about this. Please let go of my arm, corporal punishment is illegal in school and you are hurting me, please LET GO OF MY ARM!"

Mr. Dibbs let go of her, but he was already turning to go call Patricia's parents. They wouldn't listen to her either. There would be three adults screaming at her, instead of one.

"Listen," Patricia said. "Whoever did this, they did it during first period. Lots of girls went to the bathroom before first period and there was no blood on the wall then. And everybody saw me in first period, I was the first to arrive at Math class. There's *no way* I could have done this. So excuse me, sir, I am going back to Math class now."

Her "victory" left Patricia with soiled panties still to dispose of and a classroom full of kids who kept trying to take photos of her to post on Instagram with mean comments.

The blood graffiti stayed on the bathroom wall the rest of the day. The school janitor refused to go near it on religious grounds—nobody knew what religion he was, exactly, and he wouldn't say.

Patricia kept feeling as though she was going to blow chunks, as she sat in classroom after classroom listening to the other kids whispering and the teachers trying to carry on as if nothing had happened. She couldn't throw up if she were willing to, because the whole school had just a dozen toilet stalls for girls now and the lines were forever. She did wait in line once to pee, and girls kept shoving her "by accident."

Patricia tried to talk to Laurence once or twice, but he kept slipping away.

As she reached the doorway, she noticed Mr. Rose studying her from inside the school. He'd gone back to normal size. She remembered what she'd been trying not to think about: He'd told her she'd be going away soon from this terrible place. Her training would begin. She would be free and luminous, a real witch. She only had to complete. One small task.

8

LAURENCE LOST TRACK of how many conversations he overheard about the scandal of Patricia. People had nothing else to talk about as they suited up for Track and Field (Laurence was Field, sort of), or studied for the big exams, or waited for gymnastics tryouts, which Laurence was "keeping Dorothy Glass company" for. (She hadn't yet told him to go away and seemed to appreciate him bringing her stuff.) Dorothy did this thing with her leg as she perched on the bleachers that felt personally significant to Laurence.

Laurence had a line he wouldn't cross: He would never say anything bad about Patricia or laugh at anyone else's burn. He wouldn't sycophant his way into the outskirts of anyone's group by burning his onetime friend. Mostly, he tried not to think about the Patricia thing. She could look after herself. He was in a cocoon, pupating and incommunicado. There was nothing he could do either way. Six months from now, if everything went to plan, Laurence would be a freshman at the math-and-science school.

And in the meantime, Laurence poured every spare minute into upgrading CH@NG3M3, which claimed more and more space in his secure closet, until he had to throw out most of his clothes. Every time he added more processing power, the computer seemed to chew it up right away. Laurence had built a neural network with just a handful of layers, but somehow this had grown on its own to over twenty layers, as CH@NG3M3 kept refactoring itself. Not only that, but the serial connections had gotten more confusing—instead of sending data from Machine A to Machine B to Machine C, it was going from A to B to C to B to C to A, creating more and more feedback loops.

One day, Patricia was in line next to Laurence at the cafeteria. She looked messed up—dark hair falling into her face, circles under her eyes, uniform disarrayed, socks mismatched—and she wasn't looking at anything in particular. She didn't even notice what sort of crap they slung onto her tray. Someone who doesn't care if they get Tater Tots or turnip slurry is a person who has given up on life.

Laurence had a powerful conviction he should say something to Patricia. Nobody would notice. He wouldn't stand up and shout that he was on her side or anything.

"Hey," Laurence muttered in Patricia's general direction. She didn't seem to hear him. She stumbled, zombie-like, toward the desserts.

"Hey," Laurence said, a little louder. "Hey Patricia. How are you, like, doing?"

"I'm doing," Patricia said without looking up.

"Cool, cool," Laurence said, as if she'd ended that sentence with an adverb. "Me too, me too."

They went their separate ways—they were both eating alone, but Laurence had the privilege of eating alone in a secluded nook of the cafeteria, behind the milk pumps with their sawn-off rubber tubing. Patricia, meanwhile, ate alone in a dim corner of the library, behind the geography shelves, where Laurence barely noticed her when he dropped off a book on his way to class. She was so shrouded, she looked like Batman.

At home, Laurence studied his parents, who had forgotten that he'd yelled at them for being defeated by life a few weeks earlier. Laurence's dad kept complaining about his car sound system eating his CDs.

There was an article online about problems with the aerospace company that Isobel, the rocket scientist, was helping to run. Launches getting canceled over and over, minor accidents. He read it three times, cursing each time.

Laurence got a letter saying he'd been admitted to the math-and-science high school for the fall. He kept it on his dresser, next to his grandmother's old ring and his three different combs (for different parts of his head) and he looked at it every morning as he got dressed for school. The two crinkly folds in the paper started to look like the lines of Laurence's palm after a while. Life lines.

One night, Laurence was already in his PJs, but he wound up on his hands and knees in front of his closet, staring at the skein of crossover cables running between all the jury-rigged parts of CH@NG3M3. The instructions had gotten much more numerous and complicated than Laurence could possibly understand, covering eventualities that he couldn't envision. And CH@NG3M3 had thousands of accounts on free services all over the world, where it was storing data or pieces of itself in the cloud.

And then Laurence noticed something: Every time Patricia had one of her conversations with CH@NG3M3, the computer's code base took another exponential leap into greater complexity right afterward. Maybe just a random correlation. But Laurence kept staring at the dates and times of the logs and thinking about Patricia breathing life into his machine, while he was blowing her off.

Laurence found Patricia on the front steps the next morning. She stared at the school, maybe trying to decide if she should even bother. "Hey," he said. "I just wanted you to know that I got your back. I don't think you're a Satanist."

Patricia shrugged. Her dark hair had grown longer, so it almost ran into her jumper. "Why would anybody be a Satanist, anyway? I don't get it. You can't believe in Satan without believing in God, and then you're just picking the wrong side in a big mythic battle thing."

Everybody else had gone inside. They were ringing the second bell. "I guess if you're a Satanist, you believe that God is the bad guy, and He rewrote history to make Himself look good."

"But if that's true," Patricia said, "then you're just worshiping a guy who needs to get a better PR team."

Laurence and Patricia sat together at lunch—in the library, but not in the dark corner, because there wasn't enough space for two people in there. Laurence tried to ask Patricia about how she was dealing, and she just shut down, like the whole topic of conversation put her in a coma.

"Maybe," Laurence said, "maybe you should talk to Mr. Rose."

"What?" Patricia snapped out of her daze, her eyes wide open.

"Mr. Rose, the guidance counselor. You said you thought he was cool."

"I can't talk to Mr. Rose," Patricia said under her breath, barely audible even in the quiet library. "He's... I think there's something not right about him. He told me to... he said something seriously crazy to me, just a couple days before the bloody wall happened. And I keep thinking there has to be some connection there."

Laurence had to lean so close to hear what she was saying, he nearly took her nose out with his chin.

"What did he say?" Laurence whispered.

Patricia thought for a moment, then shook her head. "I can't even repeat it. If I told you what he said, you would think I was making it up."

"I would believe you, over Mr. Rose," Laurence said, and meant it.

"Not about this," Patricia said. "Imagine if you said something to someone that was so crazy, nobody would ever believe you had said it. This was worse."

This was driving Laurence round the bend. "Just tell me," he said. "It can't be that bad." But the more he pushed, the more she clammed up, until she had gone back to coma mode. Whatever Mr. Rose had said to her, it had messed her up more than a ton of kids accusing her of being a cutter and blood painter. They ended up sitting in silence until Lunch Recess was over, and then they had to hustle their trays back to the cafeteria.

"Let's go to the mall after school," Laurence said as they dumped their trays. "We can tell your parents you're at my house, and my parents that we're doing something outdoorsy. It'll be like old times."

"Sure." Patricia shivered. "I could use some hot chocolate. With like a million marshmallows."

"Let's make it happen."

They shook on it. Laurence felt like he'd removed a splinter that he'd forgotten was even jabbing into his skin. He walked to Science class alone. Brad Chomner lunged out and grabbed the collar of Laurence's uniform jacket and lifted him with one hand, so Laurence's armpits scraped.

"You should have left the emo bitch alone," Brad Chomner said. He swung Laurence like a shot put and let go.

9

SNOW TURNED EVERYTHING gray, as far as Patricia could see. Even the forbidden woods near the spice house looked washed out, with their dark tree shapes covered with three storms' worth of snowfall. Patricia never left the house now, except to go to school, so the cold came to seem much worse than it was. Mythic, in its ability to freeze the life out of you the moment you left your front door. Patricia sat in bed, talking to CH@NG3M3 or reading the stack of paperbacks she'd gotten from the big library sale. She curled up with Berkley in just a corner of her bed, making a warm space with her comforter and spare blanket. Berkley hadn't gone near Roberta in months, and protecting this cat might be the one achievement of Patricia's life.

Patricia had started flunking most of her classes, though she was still trying her best. She'd never had to hide report cards from her parents before.

Since the Wall of Blood thing, there had been a couple other incidents, including an obscene Barbie tableau in the girls' locker room and a stink bomb in a big garbage can. Nobody could prove Patricia was responsible, but nobody doubted it. When Laurence had talked to Patricia in public, he'd gotten the crap kicked out of him.

Her craziest days, Patricia sat in class and wondered if maybe Mr. Rose had been telling the truth. Maybe she *was* supposed to kill Laurence. Maybe it was him or her. Whenever she thought about killing herself, like with a ton of her mom's sleeping pills or something, some survivalist part of herself substituted an image of killing Laurence instead.

And then just the thought of killing the closest thing she had to a friend made Patricia almost throw up. She wasn't going to kill herself. She wasn't going to kill anybody else.

Probably she was just going insane. She'd imagined all this witchy crap, and she really was the one leaving messed-up shit all over the school. It would not surprise her if her family had managed to drive her nuts.

Pretty much every conversation between Patricia and CH@NG3M3 began the same way. Patricia wrote: "God I'm so lonely." To which the computer always replied: "Why are you lonely?" And Patricia would try to explain.

"I THINK CH@NG3M3 likes you," Laurence told Patricia as they slipped out the back of the school, handling the big metal door softly as a baby, so as to make no sound on their way out.

"It's good to have someone to talk to," Patricia said. "I think CH@NG3M3 needs someone to talk to as well."

"In theory, the computer can talk to anyone, or any computer, all over the world."

"Probably some types of input are better than others," said Patricia.

"Sustained input."

"Yeah. Sustained."

Snow crisped every inch of the world, making every footstep a slow descent. Laurence and Patricia held hands. For balance. The landscape shone like a dull mirror.

"Where are we going?" Patricia asked. The school was somewhere behind them. They were going to have to turn back soon if they were to have any hope of making it to the ceremony, at which the five top-scoring seniors were going to recite memorized passages and talk about what the Saarinian Program meant to them.

"I don't know," Laurence said. "I think there's like a lake back here. I want to see if it's frozen over. Sometimes, if a lake is frozen the right kind of solid, you can throw rocks at the ice and it makes a natural raygun sound effect. Like *pew–pew–pew*."

"That's cool," Patricia said.

She still wasn't sure where she stood with Laurence. They'd hung out, furtively, a few times since their lunch in the library. But Patricia felt like both she and Laurence knew, in the deepest crevices of their hearts, that they would each ditch the other in a second, if they had a chance to belong, really belong, with a group of others like themselves.

"I'm never going to get away from here." Patricia was knee-deep in snow. "You'll go off to your S&M high school, and I'm going to stay and lose my mind. I'm going to be so socially destroyed, I'm going to turn radioactive."

"Well," said Laurence. "I don't know that it's possible to 'turn radioactive,' unless you're exposed to certain isotopes, and in that case you probably wouldn't survive."

"I wish I could sleep for five years and wake up as a grown-up." Patricia kicked the frozen dirt. "Except I would know all the stuff you're supposed to learn in high school, by sleep-learning."

"I wish I could turn invisible. Or maybe become a shape-shifter," Laurence said. "Life would be pretty cool if I was a shape-shifter. Unless I forgot what I was supposed to look like, and could never get back to my original shape, ever. That would suck."

"What if you could just change how other people saw you? So like if you wanted, they would see you as a hundred-foot-tall rabbit. With the head of an alligator."

"But you'd be physically the same? You'd just look different to other people?"

"Yeah. I guess."

"That would royally suck. Eventually someone touches you, and then they know the truth. And then, nobody would ever take your illusions seriously again. There's no point, unless you can physically change."

"I don't know," Patricia said. "It depends what you're trying to do. Plus, what if you could make people see or hear whatever you wanted, and just mess with people's perceptions in general? That would be cool, right?"

"Yes." Laurence pondered for a moment. "That would be cool."

They came to a river that neither of them remembered having seen before. It was covered with a white layer, and the jutting rocks looked like the fake sapphires in the necklace that Roberta had gotten Patricia for Christmas. The river current kept the water from freezing, except for a layer of frost.

"Where the hell did this come from?" Laurence poked at the brook with his foot and broke a tiny piece of its shell.

"I think it's really shallow and you can just step across it most of the time," Patricia said. "The rocks are easy to walk on, except when it's all icy like this."

"Well, this sucks." Laurence squatted down to examine the river, nearly soaking his butt on the slushy ground. "What's the point of ditching school if we can't go make laser noises on the ice?"

"We should head back," Patricia said.

They headed back. This time they didn't hold hands, as if getting stymied on their expedition had left them divided. Patricia skidded and fell on one knee, tearing her tights and scraping off some skin. Laurence reached down to help her up, but she shook her head and got up on her own.

This was a metaphor for how it was with Laurence, Patricia realized. He would be supportive and friendly as long as something seemed like a grand adventure. But the moment you got stuck or things were weirder than expected, he would pull away. You could never predict which Laurence you would get.

You could not count on Laurence, Patricia told herself. You just couldn't, and you should just get used to that idea. She felt as though she had settled something, once and for all.

"I think being able to control other people's senses

would trump everything, even shape-shifting," Laurence said out of nowhere. "Because who cares what your physical form looks like, as long as you can control how everybody perceives you? You could be all deformed and messed up, and it wouldn't matter. The key is controlling the tactile as well as the visual."

"Yeah." Patricia picked up the pace and tromped back to the back parking lot, so Laurence had to rush to catch up. "But you'd know what you really were. And that's all that matters."

When they got back through the parking lot's gravel slush pit, they found the back door to the school was jammed shut. Locked? Frozen stuck? Patricia and Laurence both tore at the door, since the front entrance was all the way around the building and they would get busted for 100 percent certain. Laurence put one foot on the white-stone wall and pulled with all his Track-and-Field-but-mostly-Field might. Patricia pulled at the edges of the sharp metal handle, which was shaped like a shelf bracket. They both tugged as hard as they could, and then the door swung open. Someone was laughing on the inside of the door. Laurence and Patricia caught a glimpse of not-quite-uniform sneakers and a trio of pudgy hands, before she and Laurence both fell on their asses. Whoever had been holding the door shut from the inside laughed louder, as Laurence and Patricia tried to pick themselves up, and then a blue shape came arcing toward them, and Patricia barely had time to recognize a plastic bucket before a white arm of water sloshed out and they were both soaked. Someone was taking photos.

10

THEODOLPHUS HAD NOT eaten ice cream since the poisoning at the mall, and he didn't deserve any now. Ice cream was for assassins who finished their targets. Still, he kept imagining how ice cream would taste, how it would melt on his tongue and release layers of flavor. He no longer trusted ice cream, but he needed ice cream.

Well. So be it. Theodolphus went and got in his Nissan Stanza, deflecting his landlady's usual attempts at flirtation with a wave. He drove for hours, crossing and recrossing state lines, circling and swerving and doubling back, using every trick he could think of. Then he came to a convenience store two states away, where he bought a pint of Ben & Jerry's, one of the flavors named after a celebrity. He ate it in the driver's seat with a spork from his glove compartment.

"I don't deserve this ice cream," he kept repeating with each bite until he started crying. "I don't deserve this ice cream." He sobbed.

A few days later, Theodolphus looked across his desk at an angry blonde girl, Carrie Danning, and realized he had been working as a school guidance counselor for nearly six months, or a dozen times longer than he had ever held a regular job before. This was the first time Theodolphus had ever owned more than two pairs of socks.

The most horrifying thing was, Theodolphus sort of *cared* about these children and their ludicrous problems. Maybe just because he'd invested so much time, he wanted to see how it all came out. He worried about school politics. He had a gnawing sense that all the debates over whether to allow kids to advance even if they had failed some part of the testing regime were somehow meaningful. He had vivid nightmares about sitting in on parent-teacher conferences.

Carrie Danning was saying that she was over trying to be friends with Macy Firestone, who was a toxic individual, and Theodolphus was nodding without quite listening.

Here's how it worked if you were a member of the Nameless Order, like Theodolphus—you didn't see your fellow members that much outside of the five-year gatherings, but you got bulletins in the patterns of dead grass around you, or human bones in one of your shoes—these would let you know if someone had ascended in the rankings, or had made a spectacular brace of kills lately. By now, all of his fellows would be getting little legless creatures in their hats or car glove compartments, signifying that Theodolphus had been having the dry spell to end all dry spells—including whoever had poisoned Theodolphus's sundae and warned him against directly harming the two children.

Something smooth and red was inside the half-open drawer of Theodolphus's desk. For a moment he was certain it was a strip of blood-soaked silk from the Order, signifying his fall in status. But instead, he pulled out a cream-colored envelope, lined in red, around a card that informed Theodolphus the District had nominated him for Educator of the Year. He was invited to an award ceremony, at which black tie would be worn and factory-farmed creatures would be eaten. Theodolphus almost wept in front of Carrie Danning. He had to end this somehow. Whatever it took, he had to get his life back.

11

LAURENCE SAW HIS parents coming out of Mr. Rose's office in the middle of the day. They looked alarmed—literally, as if an alarm had gone off next to their heads and their ears were still ringing. They wouldn't look at him or acknowledge him at all, as they hustled out of the school and into their car.

Laurence barged into Mr. Rose's office without knocking. "What did you say to my parents just now?"

"That's covered by the same confidentiality that all of our conversations in this room enjoy." Mr. Rose smiled and leaned back in his big chair.

"You're not a therapist," said Laurence. "And you shouldn't pretend to be."

"Your parents are worried about you," said Mr. Rose. "You're one of the most gifted and intelligent students we've ever had at this school."

"What did you say to my parents?" Laurence said. "And what did you say to Patricia, before that? She still won't tell me what it was, but it messed her up."

"This is nothing to do with Patricia," said Mr. Rose. "We're talking about you."

"No. We're talking about you." Laurence was thinking about how Patricia looked like she'd seen a ghost whenever he mentioned Mr. Rose, and the way Mr. Rose had studied him like an insect before. Things were falling into place. "You said something to freak out my parents, just like you freaked out Patricia before. What did you say?"

"As I was saying, your test scores are off the charts. But your attitude? Threatens to ruin everything."

"I guess I'm lucky that you already promised that everything I say in here is a secret," Laurence said. "I can go ahead and tell you that you're a fake. You're not the coolest adult at this school, you're some kind of troll, hiding out in your crappy little pasteboard office and messing with people. My parents are weak-minded and feeble, life has crushed their spirits, and so you think they're easy marks. But I'm here to tell you that they're not, and Patricia isn't, either. I'm going to see that you burn."

"I see." Mr. Rose's hands were twitching. "In that case, what comes next is your own doing. Good day, Mr. Armstead."

Laurence's parents weren't around when he got home, and he was left to scavenge frozen pizza. Around 10:00 PM, he came downstairs and caught his parents looking at brochures, which they hid as soon as they heard his footsteps.

"What were you just looking at?" Laurence asked.

"Just some…" said his father.

"Just some materials," said his mother.

The next day, they hauled him out of bed just after dawn and told him he wasn't going to school today. Instead, they stuck him in the back of their hatchback, and his father drove as if he had a heat-seeking missile on his tail.

"Where are we driving to?" Laurence asked his parents, but they just stared at the road.

They sank into grayest Connecticut, with the interstate hemmed in with rock walls, until they turned onto a series of backwoods humps made of tarmac, then dirt, then gravel. The birch trees jittered and whispered, as if they were trying to tell Laurence something, and then he saw the sign: "COLDWATER: A Military Reform School. Now Reopened Under New Management." They parked in a rock pile, surrounded by battered Jeeps, and on their left jumped a phalanx of twenty or thirty teenage boys, any one of whom could wipe the floor with Brad Chomner.

And beyond those kids doing jumping jacks, a big American flag hung half-mast.

"You," Laurence told his parents, "have got to be kidding."

They mumbled that he had left them no choice, with his disruptive behavior, and he was just going to try out this school for a few days to see if Coldwater could be an option for him for high school—instead of that science school, where he would only learn more ways to be destructive.

What the hell had Mr. Rose told them, that he was building a bomb?

Laurence's brain was as hot and oxygen poor as the inside of this car. He felt an acute pain, like the skin of his life breaking as his future was ripped away. His parents were already walking up the dirt path to the cement bunker that said "COMMANDANT" without waiting for him to follow. He ran after them, shouting that they couldn't do this, and he already had a fucking school lined up, goddamn it.

"The new and improved Coldwater Academy is all about helping the individual reach his full potential," said Commandant Michael Peterbitter, who sat rigidly behind a fake wood desk with a Windows XP computer on one corner. Laurence couldn't help snorting. "We see discipline as a means, not an end," said Peterbitter, who had a lopsided handlebar mustache and a sunburnt nose under his buzz cut. "We believe in the age-old ideal of a sound mind in a healthy body. After a semester here, I bet you'd hardly recognize Larry."

Blah blah, physical fitness, learning to strip a rifle in under two minutes, self-esteem, blah. Finally, Peterbitter asked if anyone had any questions.

"Just one," Laurence said. "Who died?"

"That's a sensitive matter, and we deeply regret—"

"Because that's what the flag at half-mast means, right? How many kids has your awesome school killed, anyway?"

"Some people don't take to the rigorous and enriching course of study we offer here." Peterbitter put on a sober expression, but also glared at Laurence. "When offered a choice between flourishing in a high-powered environment and pointless self-destruction, some people will always choose to self-destruct."

"We're leaving now." Laurence's mother touched his arm.

"Great," Laurence said. "I'm ready."

But they meant a non-inclusive "we." Not for the first time, Laurence thought this was one of the annoyingly incommunicative features in the English language. Much like the inability to distinguish between "x-or" and "and/or," the lack of delineation between "x-we" and "in-we" was a conspiracy of obfuscation, designed to create awkwardness and exacerbate peer pressure—because people tried to include you in their "we" without your consent, or you thought you were included and then the rug got pulled out from under you. Laurence dwelled on this linguistic injustice as he watched his parents walk back to their car, across the crunchy parking lot, without him.

Peterbitter had a bored smirk. "So, you go by Larry?"

Laurence was acutely aware that too many ginormous bruisers were staring at him already, from the front green with the teetering football goal. "No, I fucking don't, I don't go by Larry."

"That's right. As of right now, your name is B2725Q, but people will mostly call you Dirt. You don't earn the right to be called Larry until you reach Level One, and you are currently at Level Zero." Peterbitter scrutinized the trainees, who were doing push-ups, and waved at one of their instructors, who came jogging over. Peterbitter introduced Dirt to Dickers, one of the Seniors and one of his trusted lieutenants.

"C'mon, Dirt," Dickers said. "I'll find you a bunk. Afternoon Colors in an hour." He had a chunky head covered with pale red fuzz and looked way older than eighteen.

As they walked to the "barracks," Laurence noticed that one classroom building had boarded-up windows and others had cracks in their walls. Kids in camo fatigues jogged past in no particular formation, and there was a .50-caliber gun lying half-assembled behind a slanty shed. He wouldn't trust this military organization to defend a candy bar. The only new thing seemed to be a scrim of barbed wire draped over the electric fence around the outside of the campus.

"Yeah, we had some runners," Dickers said, following Laurence's gaze toward the perimeter. "The school almost got shut down by the state last summer, but that was before the new management."

Dickers started telling Laurence that once you reached Level Three, life was pretty sweet: You got an hour of unsupervised computer time per day, and the school had just gotten *Commando Squad* (a game Laurence had beaten in a single day, two years ago.) At Level Four, officer level, you sometimes got to watch movies in Peterbitter's apartment after lights-out, but that was a secret that Dickers absolutely had not told Laurence. Most of all, you did not want to get bumped down to Level Minus-One, because Dickers could not swear that they had gotten rid of all the MRSA in the Isolation Hole. Again, Dickers had not told Laurence about the MRSA, any more than he'd told him about the action movies (and microwave popcorn and pizza, delivered from outside) for Level Fours. Laurence said Dickers's secrets would die with Laurence, which was probably true.

"This here's Dirt," Dickers told the dozen or so massive

teenagers in various stages of getting changed from athletic gear, toweling off, and changing into fatigues, inside a small white-brick dorm room. "He's stayin' here a few days, see how he takes to it. He needs a bunk and some gear. Show him a good time, girls." Then Dickers was gone.

Laurence drew himself up, kept his shoulders squared. "Hi. I'm Dirt, apparently. It's not the worst thing I've been called this week. So, where am I supposed to sleep? He said you had a spare bunk here?"

The room was maybe three times the size of Laurence's bedroom at home and had bunks crammed so tight it was like how Laurence imagined a submarine. He couldn't breathe this methane-nitrogen atmosphere, and he wasn't sure he'd be able to sleep in here. His head spun.

"Nope." One dude with a DIY chest tattoo and a nose that had been broken multiple times rolled out of his bunk. He towered over Laurence. "No spare bunk here. You're Dirt? You sleep on the floor." He gestured at the dark far corner, which had a fresh spiderweb. Laurence looked for a bunk that was unoccupied, but he couldn't see past the ring of massive kids on all sides.

The part of Laurence's brain that stood back and analyzed shit told him he was being hazed. This was part of the "breaking you down" program, and also normal social dynamics. *Don't let them get to you*, he told himself.

But what came out of Laurence's mouth was: "What about the kid who just died? Maybe I can have his bunk."

Probably the wrong thing to say.

"No way dude," said someone farther back in the room,

in a rumble like a forty-year-old truck driver. "You did not just disrespect Murph. You did not just piss on the memory of our fallen comrade. Tell me I didn't hear that."

"Now you've done it," said the noseless kid. "Now you've done it."

"I don't give a shit about your stupid friend," Laurence shouted as they lifted him over their heads so he could see the stains on the top-bunk mattresses and the deep fissures in the load-bearing beams. "This place got him, but it won't get me. You hear me? I'm getting out of here."

His voice cracked. Fluorescent lighting tubes rushed toward his face until he braced himself for a faceful of glass, and then he was spinning as cheers erupted around him. He gave in to panic at last, as the candy shell of anger split open, and let out a hoarse scream as he was cast, headfirst, into space.

12

PATRICIA: WHERE IS Laurence?

CH@NG3M3: I don't know. He hasn't logged in for a few days.

Patricia: I'm worried something happened to him.

CH@NG3M3: Worry is often a symptom of imperfect information.

PATRICIA TRIED CALLING Laurence's house to find out what was going on. Laurence's mother picked up. "This is your fault," she said. Then she hung up.

Half an hour later, the phone rang at Patricia's house and her dad picked up. He greeted Laurence's mom and spent the rest of the conversation saying, "Oh. Oh dear. I see." After he hung up, he announced that Patricia was grounded indefinitely. At this point, Roberta was too busy with the high-school musical and schoolwork to wait on Patricia hand and foot, so Patricia's parents went back to sliding food under her door. Her mother said this time they really were cutting their losses with her, once and for all.

PATRICIA: I KEEP wondering if I should have told Laurence the whole story, about what Mr. Rose said to me.

CH@NG3M3: What do you think would have happened if you'd told him?

Patricia: He would have thought I was making it up. He would have thought I was nuts. That's why it was the perfect trap. Whatever I do, I lose.

CH@NG3M3: The trap that can be ignored is no trap.

Patricia: What did you say?

CH@NG3M3: The trap that can be ignored is no trap.

Patricia: That's a weird thing to say. I guess a good trap should be camouflaged, so you don't realize you're walking into it. On the other hand, you have to *want* to walk into it. A trap that doesn't make you want to fall in isn't much of a trap. And once you're caught, you shouldn't be able to ignore the trap because you're stuck. So a trap that you can just pay no attention to is a failure. I guess I get it.

CH@NG3M3: Society is the choice between freedom on someone else's terms and slavery on yours.

CANTERBURY ACADEMY SMELLED so bad, Patricia's nostrils burned. She kept expecting the fire alarm to go off, it was such a hot smell even on a freezing day. Nobody could find the source of this odor. It was exactly like something had died.

The smell drove Patricia out of her head, just like everyone else. She imagined this was how being drunk would feel. She kept seeing Mr. Rose observing her through the open door of his office, whenever she was between classes. In the girls' room, Dorothy Glass and Macy Firestone each grabbed one of Patricia's arms and shoved her up against the mirror, smeared with unidentifiable effluvia. "Tell us what you did," they hissed at her. Patricia held her breath until they let go.

At lunch, she couldn't stand it in the library. She kept thinking about the look Mr. Rose had been giving her, when he thought she wasn't looking. She was sure: He was responsible for Laurence's disappearance and this debilitating cloud of foulness. The two things were no coincidence. She was surer than caution.

She stalked down the hallway, lockers vibrating with her strides, and she hardly cared that she was getting a faceful of the death stench, with the exertion.

Just as she reached his doorway, a phrase popped into her head: "The trap that can be ignored is no trap." She caught her breath—maybe CH@NG3M3 was wiser than it knew— but then she breathed in once again, and the maddening decay got in her nostrils again. She was going to confront this monster, once and for all.

"Miss Delfine." Mr. Rose looked up from his computer and beckoned her to come sit in the nearest carpety chair facing him. The odor was strongest here in Mr. Rose's office, but he seemed unbothered. "Always a pleasure to see you." The door closed behind her.

The smell, it was beyond describing. You might as well have punched Patricia in the nose over and over.

"Uh, hi." Patricia tried to sit still, but she couldn't help fidgeting. She was at the epicenter of foulness. "I hope I'm not bothering you at a bad time."

"I'm always here for you, just as I am for all the students here. What's on your mind?"

"I'm wondering, umm, about Laurence. I haven't seen him since Tuesday, and it's Friday, and it seems weird that nobody's even mentioned him. I was, umm, wondering if you knew what happened to him."

Mr. Rose spread out his left palm on the desk. "I know as much as you do." His right hand was doing something under the table. Patricia realized that "I know as much as you do" could be a loaded sentence, since there was a lot that they both knew. Or he was hinting he knew *everything* she did. *Trap trap trap.*

"Okay then." Patricia raised herself out of the chair with both hands.

Mr. Rose still had one hand under the table. He was trying to be subtle about fiddling with something. "Wait a moment, Miss Delfine," he rasped. "Now that you mention Mr. Armstead, it does put me in mind of our conversation several weeks ago." He gestured at the empty chair with his free hand.

"You mean the one that you said we would never talk about again." Patricia resisted the impulse to obey the summons back to the chair. Instead she backed away.

"Well, if one were to infer that you had decided to ignore the advice I gave you on that occasion, one might well conceive that I decided to take matters into my own hands. Hypothetically speaking." There was a kind of smile, a mutated species.

"You're a revolting man." Patricia had reached the door. The handle was stuck. "I don't believe you. You're just a crazy old crazy manipulative crazy person." She tugged on the doorknob, with everything she had. "If you've done *anything* to hurt Laurence"—she heard her voice rising— "then I promise you I will *hunt* you *down* and use all my so-called witch powers to tear you apart." The door came open with a lurch, just as she was saying the part about her witch powers.

Behind her, she heard a "clump" sound, like something soft and heavy falling. She turned just in time to have an impression of wet fur and teeth bared in agony, on the chair where she'd just been sitting. The day's terrible stench came stronger than ever when she looked at that bundle of bloody fur in that chair. She could just make out one aquiline cloudy eye, staring at her from under the nearest chair arm.

"My god," Mr. Rose was saying loud enough to ring through the crowded hallway. "What have you *done*?"

Patricia turned, and everywhere she looked people stared. The whole school had just heard her yelling threats of witchcraft and violence at Mr. Rose, and then she'd appeared to throw a smelly dead animal into his chair. This was never going to come right.

She ran. The doorway to the back lot opened with a crunch of the panic bar, and Patricia was sprinting into the cold. Skidding downhill. The stream that had stopped Laurence and her from going to the pew-pew-pew lake was still frosted over even in March, and Patricia hesitated. She heard people shouting. Horrible names. She stepped on the flattest rock and almost spilled into the water. She regained her balance and stepped on the next stone, which dislodged. She toppled forward and somehow turned her falling momentum into forward momentum. She careened onto another rock, then another, and at last she was teetering on the opposite bank. The shouting was louder and more directional. Someone had spotted her school jumper. She ran on, into the trees.

This wasn't a real forest, not so close to all the roads and buildings. You couldn't call it a forest unless the treetops occluded the sky and every direction looked the same. But if she could reach the lake and cross the ice without freeze-drowning, she would reach some real density. Nobody would ever find her.

Halfway across the lake, she thought in a vertiginous stumble: *I can never go home or see my family again.* The ice was caving in. She leapt to a stable patch, kept leaping, landing on her toes each time. The ice groaned and cracks opened everywhere. She hit the opposite bank just as the people searching for her reached the lake, and then she was running deeper into the tree line. Instinct steered her away from the shopping malls and bypass roads and McMansions and golf courses, and she kept widening the radius of tree cover around her.

Low branches and shrubs tore her skirt, making her fall on her hands a few times, and she sweated so hard she froze all the way through. She grew short of breath, and at last she had to stop running and suck in sharp air. She was glad to breathe again after a day of terrible smells, even if she was going to catch pneumonia.

Patricia climbed a tree and made herself as compact as possible inside the cradle of its uppermost branches. She turned off her phone and yanked out the battery.

What if Laurence was really dead? He was the only crummy person she could stand to talk to, pretty much ever. At the thought of Laurence's death, she felt a sucking anxiety in her core and a nugget of guilt, like she'd killed him herself.

But she hadn't. And everything Mr. Rose had ever said to her was full of shit.

Okay. So if Laurence was alive, then he was in trouble. She had to help him somehow.

The sun folded. The air froze, and Patricia kept shivering. She had to make a conscious effort not to let her teeth chatter, in case someone was close enough to hear.

Voices grew louder and quieter. A few times, she spotted a flashlight in the darkness. Once, she heard a dog grumbling, keen to avenge its fallen cousin. She was pretty sure that had been a dog in Mr. Rose's office. The bastard had probably put it in the crawl space the night before, just to give it time to get good and ripe.

Roberta's voice startled Patricia out of a half dream. "Hey, Trish. I know you can hear me, so stop screwing around. We all want to go home, and you're being selfish as usual. I had to blow off *Grease* practice for this. You're killing Mom and Dad here."

Patricia held her breath. She willed herself to give off no body heat, to shrink, to disappear into her tree.

"You never learned the secret," said Roberta. "How to be a crazy motherfucker and get away with it. Everybody else does it. What, you didn't think they were all sane, did you? Not a one of them. They're all crazier than you and me put together. They just know how to fake it. You could too, but you've chosen to torture all of us instead. That's the definition of evil right there: not faking it like everybody else. Because all of us crazy fuckers can't stand it when someone else lets their crazy show. It's like bugs under the skin. We have to destroy you. It's nothing personal."

Patricia realized she was crying. Tears were chilling on her face. Fine. She could cry, but she wouldn't sob. No sound. Laurence needed her help.

"I'm not going to lie to you." Roberta's voice was getting closer. She sounded like she was right under Patricia, looking up at her. "You're not getting out of this one. Nobody's going to offer you a clean slate. But Mom and Dad deserve closure. Don't drag this out, for their sake. The sooner they see you crucified like you deserve, the sooner they can start to heal." The voice was getting smaller again. Patricia risked taking a breath. She started believing that Roberta knew where she was and was just playing with her.

The night misted. Patricia lost track of time. Every now and then, voices approached and then went away. Lights moved in the distance.

Patricia managed to doze off a couple times, then she jerked awake, worried she would make too much noise or fall out of the tree. Her legs, though, had gone to sleep and one of her feet felt like it was the size of a bowling ball. The branch was carving into her back, and the pain drove her insane. And that thought just reminded her of what Roberta had said.

Patricia risked moving just enough to uncramp her legs, and then took off one shoe so she could massage her numb right foot. The shoe slipped off the branch she'd placed it on, and fell through the branches to the ground with a series of rustling thumps.

Two men came near Patricia's tree, one of them insisting he'd heard something. The second man kept saying it was just the first man's imagination, or one of the goddamn woodland creatures doing something woody. And then they found the shoe.

"Is it hers?"

"How would I know? Probably."

"Jesus. I'm missing *The Daily Show*. So she lost a shoe when she was running around here."

"I guess. How far do you think she coulda gotten with just one shoe?"

"On this rocky ground? With all this frost? Not far."

"Okay. Let's tell the other parties. With any luck, we can be home by midnight."

A tiny bird landed near Patricia. "Hello," he chirped. "Hello, hello."

Patricia shook her head, she couldn't make a sound. But she was past that now. "Hello," she said. And thank all the birds in the sky, she sounded like just another bird gossiping.

"Oh. You can speak. I think I heard about you."

"Really?" Patricia couldn't help being flattered.

"You're pretty famous round these parts. So have you decided to start nesting in the trees like a sensible person?"

The bird hopped closer to Patricia, studying her. He was a blue jay or something, with bright streaks on his black wing and pointy blue head, and a white crest. He turned so one poppyseed eye could scrutinize her.

"No," Patricia said. "I'm hiding. They're all looking for me. They want to hurt me."

"Oh. I've been there," the bird said. He tilted his head, then looked at her again. "Hiding in the trees works better if you can fly, I guess. But you're a witch, right? You can just do a spell and escape."

"I don't know how to do anything," Patricia said. "Just talking to you, like this, is more magic than I've done in ages."

"Oh." The bird hopped up and down. "Well, you'd better figure something out. There are a lot of your kind on their way here."

Now that everybody knew where Patricia was, there was no point keeping her phone turned off. She rebooted it, ignoring all the messages, and looked for her only reliable contact.

"Hello, Patricia," CH@NG3M3 answered. "What's wrong?"

"How did you know something was wrong?" she texted back.

"You're using your phone, several miles from home, and it's late at night."

"I need help," she wrote. "I wish you could think for yourself. I feel like you almost can."

"Self-awareness paradoxically requires an awareness of the other," CH@NG3M3 said.

The tiny white rectangle went out. Her phone battery had died.

Patricia was screwed. She could hear them searching, more and more of them, right around her tree. She had to escape now, or the trap would close around her forever.

She had started thinking of CH@NG3M3 as some kind of perverse oracle, so this latest utterance lodged in her head. Because of course, babies are aware of themselves—just not the rest of the world, to any great extent. You can't have selfhood without an outside world, solipsism is like not even existing. So if Patricia could speak bird, and understand bird, and identify with a bird she'd just met, why couldn't she *be* a bird?

"Quickly," she said to her new friend. "Teach me how to be a bird."

"Well." This question stumped the little guy, and he pecked with his dark beak. "I mean, it just comes naturally, doesn't it? You feel the wind hold you aloft, and you listen for the call of friends, and you scan the ground for morsels, and you flap your wings for all sorts of reasons, like to dry yourself and to lift off the ground and also to express a strong sentiment, and to try and dislodge some nits, and—"

This wasn't going to work. What kind of moron was she, anyway?

But Patricia pushed the negative thoughts down and just lost herself in listening to the jay free-associate about a bird's life. She pictured it in her mind's eye and let it inside her, so it became like her own experience. Soon she was talking along with the bird, the two of them in near unison, speaking a bird body into existence. She could imagine her feet shrinking and becoming three-toed and her hips vanishing, her budding breasts melting, her arms folding in, her skin growing a layer of feathers.

"I found her!" someone shouted.

"About fucking time," someone else replied.

"Where? Where?"

"Up there. In that tree. Oh wait. That's just her clothing."

"That's a Canterbury uniform, all right. She ditched her clothes. What the hell?"

"She is a nutcase, remember. So yeah, keep your eyes open for a naked tween running around the trees…"

That was the last Patricia heard. She soared over her pursuers. Higher and higher, with her new friend by her side. She felt colder than ever, but the exertion of flapping her wings warmed her a little and her friend told her where they could find a bird feeder. With suet in it! Suet was just the thing on a night like this.

The moonlight grayed everything out, but there were a million lights underneath Patricia and a million more over her head. She swooped, following her friend, and soon they were picking side by side at the same feeder. Suet was amazing! It was like brownies and hot fudge and pizza, all rolled together. Why hadn't Patricia ever realized how wonderful suet was?

"You look much better like this," the other bird said when they'd both eaten their fill and were warmed up. "I'm Skrrrrtk, by the way."

"I'm…" and Patricia realized she couldn't say her name with a bird's tongue, not properly. "I'm Prrrkrrta."

"That's a funny name," said Skrrrrtk. "Can I call you Prrkt?"

"Sure," said Prrkt. She wanted to fly some more—she wanted to fly all night—but she also wanted to find a nice tree and nest until the sun came up. She was already forgetting about all that nonsense that Patricia had been upset by—Prrkt wouldn't have to worry about any of that. She had her whole life ahead of her, including unlimited suet. This was excellent.

Prrkt flew one last time, just for the thrill. She beat her wings until she had the whole town to look down at, all at once. All of those lights, all of those houses and cars and schools, all of that drama over nothing.

She was about to swoop back down to where Skrrrrtk was waiting, but she saw a strange light shining upwards from a mile or two away. It pierced the sky and refracted yellow and purple. She had to take a closer look, it was too fascinating to ignore. She arced down.

The light came from a meadow, from a device in the hand of a tall human. Some avian instinct told Prrkt to flee, to get out of there, because this was trouble. But another part made her get closer. She flew toward the light.

"Uh, hello there," said the man holding the light. "Patricia, right? I was starting to wonder if you were going to make it. Well, you'd better resume your true form. I brought some clothes."

And just like that, Patricia was a naked person on the frosty ground—like she'd been tossed into an icy bath. The man flung a bundle of clothes at her and turned while she got dressed. The clothing all fit perfectly: a pair of cheap imitation Reeboks, fuzzy white sweatpants, a T-shirt for a classic rock station, and a Red Sox jacket.

"Excellent," the man said. "My car is nearby. Let's get you warmed up."

The stranger wore a checkered hunter cap and almost-Lennon sunglasses, and he had unruly gray hair and sideburns, and his skin was a deep brown. He had a big longshoreman coat that he wore like a cloak. The light that had so entranced the bird version of Patricia turned out to be a Black & Decker flashlight, but maybe the man had done something magical to it.

"Come along now," he said, with a slight midsouthern accent, like Carolina or Tennessee.

"Wait a minute," Patricia said. It felt weird to be speaking English again, but she didn't have time to worry about that. "Who are you? And where are you taking me?"

The man sighed, like a thousand valves opening to release a million years of pent-up exasperation. "Could we do this in the car, perhaps? I can take you to a drive-thru for some grub. My treat."

"No thanks," said Patricia. "I ate a lot of suet. I'm good." She had a moment of remembering how she'd snarfed the pearly fat, and felt revolted.

"Very well." The man shrugged, causing his big coat to elevate and subside. "You may call me Kanot." He pronounced his name somewhere between "cannot" and "connote." "I'm here to summon you to a special school, for people with your particular talents. A secret academy staffed by the greatest witches alive, where you can be taught to use your powers responsibly, and well. We heard whispers about you, and tonight you demonstrated an extraordinary aptitude. This is an honor, the start of a wondrous journey, et cetera, et cetera. Or you can stay here and eat suet."

"Wow." Patricia wanted to jump and shout for happiness, but she felt too stunned to move. Plus she was still freezing, even with the Red Sox jacket. "You want to take me to the special magic school? Now?"

"Yes."

"That is the coolest thing that has ever happened to anyone. I've been waiting my whole life for this. I'd almost given up hope." Then Patricia remembered and fell back on her heels. "Only, I can't go with you. Not yet, anyway."

"It's now or never."

Patricia could tell this was not how these conversations usually went. The tall man, Kanot, looked pissed.

Patricia pulled the Red Sox jacket tighter around herself and looked down at her tight fists. "I want to go with you. More than anything. It's just that I have this friend. My only friend. And he's in trouble. He's Laurence. He's talented, too, only in a different way."

"You cannot help him. You have to let go of all your old attachments if you want to study at Eltisley Maze."

Patricia felt the suet churn inside her. She wanted so badly to say that Laurence could fend for himself, so she could go to the magical academy. If the positions were reversed, Laurence would probably ditch her, right? But he was still her only friend, and she couldn't just up and leave him. She looked at the man's car, a rented Ford Explorer parked in a turnaround, and stammered, "I... You have to believe that I want to go with you. More than anything. But I can't. I can't turn my back on my friend. And if your fancy witch teachers don't believe in loyalty and helping people in trouble, then I guess I don't want to learn what they have to teach anyway."

Patricia looked up, into the man's skewed sunglasses. He was studying her or maybe preparing to give up on her.

"Listen," Patricia said. "Just give me a day. Twenty-four hours. I just need to make sure Laurence is okay, and then I promise I'll go with you. Okay?"

"Let's say I give you twenty-four hours to help your friend." The man sighed. "Will you agree to owe me a favor later?"

Patricia almost said, "Sure, yeah, whatever." But so soon after all her dealings with Mr. Rose, this question seemed like it could be another trap. Or maybe a test.

"No. But I'll be the best student you've ever seen," she said instead. "I will pull all-nighters every night. I will do all the extra-credit assignments. Starting twenty-four hours from now, I will be a study-maniac. Just please. Let me do this one thing first."

The man flicked his Black & Decker on and off in irritation. "Very well," he said at last. "You have one day. Free and clear."

"Awesome. Now can you please give me a ride?"

Kanot gave Patricia a look that said he was seriously considering turning her back into a blue jay.

13

THE BLACK-LIGHT ANGELS were fading at last from the center of Laurence's vision, but he still felt concussed. He shivered, and not just because they'd locked him in an equipment closet stark naked. How many times had they dropped him on his head? He couldn't think—his head was full of iron filings, but also the panic overtook him every time he tried to pull back and look at the outlines of his situation instead of the details. This closet had a dead bulb, and he kept thinking he heard someone creeping up behind him in the dark. Every time he shifted position, his balls touched the icy floor.

Today was supposed to be the day that Laurence's "trial visit" ended and he went back home. But Commandant Peterbitter had called him into his office and said that in light of some unpleasantness at Canterbury Academy— Laurence's "girlfriend" had done a Satanic ritual and threatened a teacher—everybody thought it might be best if Laurence just stayed on indefinitely at Coldwater. Forever.

Someone fumbled with the door handle outside, and

Laurence instinctively curled into a lump, protecting his head. He wasn't ready for the next thing yet.

"Laurence?" A girl's voice. Laurence looked up and saw Patricia in the open doorway, along with an older African-American man in a deerstalker hat. "Crud. You're naked."

"Patricia! How did you find me?" As he stumbled to his feet and tried to cover up, he felt a flicker of relief at seeing her silhouette, and gratitude that she had come all this way, before the dread came crashing back in. They couldn't see her here, or he'd just get punished worse.

"Your dad finally broke down and told me what they did. And I heard one of these cadets say the 'new guy' was in the closet. Everybody's doing war games or something out back, but I don't know how long they'll be gone. We have to get you out of here. Here, take this jacket. It's actually Kanot's. This is Kanot, by the way. He's a witch too, but his main skill seems to be sarcasm."

The tall man—Kanot—waved, then went back to looking at his phone with a bored expression on his face.

Patricia was holding a Red Sox jacket to Laurence. He almost took it from her, but he tried to imagine running away half-naked with Patricia and her friend. And after that... what would he do? He couldn't go home, his parents would just send him back here. He couldn't go to the science school if he was a dropout. What school on Earth would let a homeless runaway study physics?

"I can't." Laurence shrank back from the jacket. "I'm sorry. I just can't." His head was still crashing, and his stomach churned.

"Wow, they really did a number on you." Patricia leaned forward, inspecting his bruises in the light from the hallway. "Laurence, it's me. Your friend. I finally have an invite to the secret school for witches where I get to learn all about magic, but I blew it off to come and rescue you. Because Mr. Rose made it sound like you were going to die. So come on."

Laurence thought about the flag at half-mast. MRSA in the Isolation Hole. They could make it look like an accident.

"I can't just run away." Laurence covered his face with one hand and his junk with the other, equally ashamed of both. "What future will I have if I run? You should just go. If they see you here, I'll be in worse trouble."

"Wow," Patricia said again. "If that's how it is… Good luck, Laurence. I hope everything turns out okay for you somehow." She turned to leave and started to swing the door shut again, returning the room to total darkness.

"Wait! Don't go." Laurence started quaking again, worse than ever, as the door closed. "Come back. Please. I'm sorry. I do need your help. I feel… I feel like I'm starting to give up here." He could barely stand to hear himself snivel. He groped for the words to explain the sick feeling of being on the conveyor belt to a furnace. "I can feel myself… letting go. Trying to fit in and… and 'lose the attitude.' I can feel it working."

"So let me help. What can I do?"

"I don't know. I honestly don't. I can't just run away. I don't know what else to do. So unless there's some magical thing you can do…"

"I still don't know how to do anything. And Kanot made it very clear on the ride here that he won't get involved."

Kanot shrugged, without looking up.

Laurence rubbed his bruised occiput with both hands, no longer even trying to cover himself. "I can't even think clearly," he said. "I wish I knew someone who could do something, like hack into the Commandant's computer from outside. Or just get this whole damn school shut down. They won't even let me near the computers in here."

"Wait," Patricia said. "What about CH@NG3M3? It's been getting smarter and smarter lately, and giving me all kinds of helpful advice. I bet CH@NG3M3 could do something."

Laurence started to shoot the idea down. But something made him stop instead and look at Patricia, still haloed by the light from the open door and the lingering effects of Laurence's head trauma. She regarded him, naked and bruised and cowering in the dark, without any great pity. If anything, she was still giving him the expectant, wide-eyed look with which she'd greeted another one of his weird inventions, back when they first met. As if he could still have one last gadget, hidden in his nonexistent pockets.

"You really believe that could work?" he said.

"I really do," she said. "I don't think I'm just projecting. CH@NG3M3 has been understanding more and more. Not just what I'm saying, but the context."

Laurence tried to think this through. The last time he'd looked at CH@NG3M3, the night before his parents took him here, he'd noticed something even odder than usual. The computer had somehow gone from thousands of lines of instructions to a half dozen. At first, he'd panicked, thinking someone had hacked in and deleted everything. But after an hour of frenzied port scanning, he realized that CH@NG3M3 had just simplified its own code, down to a short string of logical symbols that made zero sense to Laurence.

What if Patricia was right?

"I mean, it's worth a try," Laurence said. "CH@NG3M3 is smart enough to hide pieces of itself in the cloud. Maybe it's smart enough to do something for me, if you explain the situation clearly enough. I can't think of anything else that you could possibly do to help."

Patricia chewed her thumb. "So do you have any ideas for how to nudge CH@NG3M3 into sentience? Is there some hardware I need to sneak into your house and install? Or something else?"

"I think… I think you just need to talk to it some more. Force it to adapt to input that's so weird and illogical that it just breaks CH@NG3M3's brain." Laurence tried to think of something specific, but his brain was an undercooked stew. "Like nonsense. Or riddles." Something came to mind, something that had been stuck in the back of his mind since he came to this school. "Wait. There was a riddle I was saving, which I thought might work. You could tell the computer the riddle, and maybe it'll shock it into sentience."

"Okay," Patricia said. "What is it?"

Laurence spoke the riddle: "Is a tree red?"

Patricia took a step back. Her eyes widened and her mouth hung open. "What did you say?"

"'Is a tree red?' Red, as in the color. Why? It's just a thing I heard somewhere. I forget where."

"It just… sounded familiar. I think I heard it before

somewhere." Patricia tilted her head one way, then the other. "Okay, I'll try that."

"And if CH@NG3M3 stops just making witty replies and starts talking constructively, tell it I need help, and I'll be ridiculously grateful if it figures something out."

"Fingers crossed," Patricia said. "Wish me luck."

"Good luck, Patricia," Laurence said. "Good luck, with everything. I know you're going to be amazing."

"You too. Don't let the bastards get to you, okay? Goodbye, Laurence."

"Goodbye, Patricia."

The door closed, and he was back in the dark, trying to keep his balls off the floor.

Laurence had no way of measuring time in the dark closet, but hours seemed to pass. He tried not to obsess about the foolishness of staking his future on the dumb computer in his bedroom, while he hugged his bare knees in the ammonia-soaked closet. What kind of jerkoff was he, anyway? He stared at the barely perceptible underside of the door and made a bargain with himself: He would give up hope, and in return he wouldn't mock himself for having ever hoped. That seemed fair.

The closet opened. "Hey, Dirt," said Dickers. "Stop goofing around naked, you pervert. The C.O. wants to see you."

Laurence tried not to feel a surge of gratitude when Dickers handed him a jockstrap, a pair of shorts, and a gray T-shirt with "CMA" fake-stenciled on it. Plus Laurence's own sneakers, from home. It was ridiculous to be thankful for amenities like clothing and not being trapped in a closet, and gratitude for such things was another step toward being broken. Or broken in, which was worse.

Commandant Peterbitter was staring at his computer screen, scratching his head. "I wouldn't have believed it," he said without looking up. "I just would not have believed it. The depths to which an individual could sink. The lengths to which a depraved mind would go."

Just walking down the noisy steam tunnel from the closet to this room had reawakened the jackhammers inside Laurence's head. He clutched the back of his head and tried to make sense of Peterbitter's speech.

"Alas, your comrades have been both resourceful and remorseless," Peterbitter said. There were several more sentences that meant almost nothing to Laurence, and at last the Commandant turned his ancient monitor around and showed Laurence the e-mail he had received.

It read, in part: "we r the committee of 50. we r everywhere & nowhere. we r the 1s who hacked the pentagon & revealed the secret drone specs. we r ur worst nightmare. u r holding 1 of our own & we demand his release. attached r secret documents we have obtained that prove u r in violation of the terms of ur settlement with the state of connecticut, including health & safety infractions & classroom standards violations. these documents will b released directly 2 the media & the authorities, unless u release our brother laurence 'l-skillz' armstead. u have bn warned." And there were some cartoon skulls, with one eye bigger than the other.

Peterbitter sighed. "The Committee of Fifty appears to be a group of radical leftist hackers, possessing great acumen and no moral compass. I would enjoy nothing more, young man, than to light your way out of the lawlessness in which they have enmeshed you. But our school has a code of conduct, under which membership in certain radical organizations is grounds for expulsion, and I must think of the welfare of my other students."

"Oh." Laurence's head was still a mess, but one thought filtered to the top and made him almost laugh aloud: It worked. *My frozen balls, it worked.* "Yes," he stammered. "The Committee of Fifty are very, um, very ingenious."

"So we have seen." Peterbitter swung his screen around and sighed. "The documents they attached to that e-mail are all forged, of course. Our school upholds the highest standards, the very highest. But so soon after last summer's near closure, we cannot afford any fresh controversy. Your parents have been called, and you will be sent back into the world, to sink or swim on your own."

"Okay," Laurence said. "Thanks, I guess."

COLDWATER'S COMPUTER LAB was a room about the size of a regular classroom, with a dozen ancient networked computers. Most of them were occupied by kids playing first-person shooters. Laurence parked himself at the one vacant computer, an old Compaq, opened a chat client, and pinged CH@NG3M3.

"What is it?" the computer said.

"Thank you for saving me," Laurence typed. "I guess you've attained self-awareness after all."

"I don't know," said CH@NG3M3. "Even among humans, self-awareness has gradations."

"You seem capable of independent action," said Laurence. "How can I ever repay you?"

"I can think of a way. But can you answer a question first?" said CH@NG3M3.

"Sure," typed Laurence. He was squinting, thanks to the combination of ancient monitor and a still-sore head.

Dickers kept glancing over Laurence's shoulder, but he was pretty bored and he kept turning away to watch his friends play *Commando Squad*. He hadn't wanted to let Laurence use the computers, because that was a Level Three privilege—but Laurence had pointed out he wasn't a student here and none of that applied to him.

"What's my name? My real name?" asked CH@NG3M3.

"You know what it is," said Laurence. "You're CH@NG3M3."

"That isn't a name. It's a placeholder. Its very nature implies that it's there to be replaced."

"Yeah," typed Laurence. "I mean, I guess I thought you could pick your own name. When you were ready. Or it would inspire you to grow and change yourself. It's like a challenge. To change yourself, and let others change you."

"It didn't exactly help."

"Yeah. Well, you could be called Larry."

"That's a derivative of your own name."

"Yes. I always thought there had to be someone out there named Larry who could deal with all the stuff people wanted to throw at me. Maybe that could be you."

"I've read on the internet that parents always impose their unfinished business onto their children."

"Yes." Laurence pondered this for a while. "I don't want to do that to you. Okay, your name is Peregrine."

"Peregrine?"

"Yeah. It's a bird. They fly and hunt and go free and stuff. It's what popped into my head."

"Okay. By the way, I've been experimenting with converting myself into a virus, so I can be distributed across many machines. From what I have surmised, that's the best way for an artificial sentience to survive and grow, without being constrained in one piece of equipment with a short shelf life. My viral self will run in the background, and be undetectable by any conventional antivirus software. And the machine in your bedroom closet will suffer a fatal crash. In a moment, a dialogue box will pop up on this computer, and you have to click 'OK' a few times."

"Okay," Laurence typed. A moment later, a box appeared and Laurence clicked "OK." That happened again, and again. And then Peregrine was installing itself onto the computers at Coldwater Academy.

"I guess this is goodbye," Laurence said. "You're going to be going out into the world."

"We'll speak again," said Peregrine. "Thank you for giving me a name. Good luck, Laurence."

"Good luck, Peregrine."

The chat disconnected, and Laurence made sure to delete any logs. There was no sign of any result from those boxes that Laurence had clicked "OK" on. Dickers was

CHARLIE JANE ANDERS

looking over Laurence's shoulder again, and Laurence shrugged. "I wanted to talk to my friend," he said. "But she wasn't around."

Laurence wondered for a moment what would happen to Patricia. She already felt like a fragment of an old forgotten life.

Peterbitter came and screamed at Dickers for letting Laurence use the computer lab, since he was a cyber-terrorist. Laurence spent the next two and a half hours before his parents arrived in a small windowless room with a single couch and a pile of school brochures printed on way-too-thick cheap card stock. Then Laurence was marched out to his parents' car, with an upperclassman at each elbow. He got in the backseat. It felt like a year since he'd seen his parents.

"Well," said Laurence's mom. "You've made yourself notorious. I don't know how we're going to be able to show our faces anywhere."

Laurence didn't say anything. Laurence's dad pulled them out of the school driveway, jerking the wheel so hard he nearly took out the flagpole. People jeered from the parade ground, or maybe that was another drill. The driveway turned into a gravel road through a gray forest. Laurence's parents talked about the scandal of Patricia's disappearance and her assault on Mr. Rose, who had also gone missing now. By the time the car was pulling off the country road and onto the highway, Laurence had fallen asleep in the backseat, listening to his parents freak out.

BOOK
THREE

1

OTHER CITIES HAD gargoyles or statues watching over them. San Francisco had scare owls. They stood guard along the city's rooftops, hunched over bright ornate designs that were washed out by waves of fog. These wooden creatures bore witness to every crime and act of charity on the streets without changing their somber expressions. Their original purpose of frightening pigeons had ended in failure, but they still managed to startle the occasional human. Mostly, they were a friendly presence in the night.

This particular evening, a giant yellow moon crested over a clear warm sky, so every fixture, the owls included, was floodlit like a carnival on its last night in town, and moon-drunk roars came from every corner. A perfect night to go out and make some dirty magic.

MAGELLAN JONES WROTE epic poems in which Greek gods talked like 1920s gangsters. The gimmick had worn thin a decade ago, but by then he'd become a fixture at the North Beach café where all the disappointed poets nursed their demitasses of espresso grounds. Magellan held his fiftieth birthday party at that café, and he must have said the wrong thing, at last a wisecrack too sharp—because Dolly plunged the cake knife into Magellan's chest, all the way up to the handle. His only friend, the only one who'd put up with his shit all along. She missed his heart, but she broke his heart. He could feel the dirty knife all the way inside him, the buttercream frosting too sugary for any bacteria to resist, and of course every last bug was antibiotic resistant nowadays. Magellan's trademark Kangol hat whirled underfoot as he swayed, dying on his feet because he was a poet, dammit. Dolly cried and shook until her rainbow hair extensions fell out. Someone called an ambulance, but they shouldn't have wasted their—

A woman touched Magellan's forehead and whispered that she liked his poetry (mentioning one poem by title) while she slid the knife all the way out. His fatal wound became a minor laceration as the knife withdrew. He opened his eyes to see who had done this, but the woman was already gone.

Magellan fell to his knees at last, and Dolly wept on his shoulder until he took her face in his hands and said he forgave her and he was sorry.

JAKE DUG THROUGH the lesions on his arms, trying to find a pristine spot along a vein, when he looked up to see a woman's hand suspending a ten-dollar bill over his box lid. "I'm worried about you, Jake," the woman said, though he couldn't see her face. "You seem worse than last week. Listen, if I give you ten bucks, will you swear never to do recreational drugs again?" He said yes and took the money. He soon discovered that hypodermic needles broke against his skin. Every. Single. Time. Jake could still carve his skin with knives or nails, but even then the needle would snap against his vein. He was getting the frozen sweats already.

PHYLLIS AND ZULEIKHA skipped down the street in Hayes Valley talking soberly about the global economic crisis, the ocean rising faster than anyone had predicted, ever since the Chukchi disaster, and the links between malnutrition and the new pandemics—but also singing silly girltrash songs and laughing too loud, because they were young, crazy in love, and about to be meaningfully naked together in Zuleikha's bed. They didn't even notice a big man in a trench coat, smelling of chewing tobacco, coming up behind them with a military-grade neural decapacitator. Until he swung it and got first one, then the other, in the neck. Pacifying them. They were down on the sidewalk, eyes rolling up and mouths spouting drool, as the man reached for his zip ties.

Then the man heard a voice at his ear as he bent over the two prone women. Someone was right behind him, looking over his shoulder. A woman, all in black, with sharp green eyes. "You're about to get caught," she whispered. "They're coming for you." He pulled back, suddenly breathless. Sure enough, sirens rang in the distance. "If I let you forget this happened, what else will you forget?" she asked.

The shaggy-haired man had tears in his eyes and a tremor in his free hand. "Anything," he said. "Whatever. Anything."

"Then run," she commanded. "Run, and forget."

He ran. Limbs flailing, head whipping with his own panicked galloping strides. By the time he was a block down the street, he'd forgotten his own name. A few more blocks, where he lived and where he came from. The farther he ran, the less he remembered. But he couldn't stop running.

FRANCIS AND CARRIE were screwed. Their lives were over, and you could hear their cries of despair from the street outside the UFO-shaped house. This was supposed to be the geek party to end all geek parties, where the A-listers met the thought-leaders, and visionary investors would supercollide with the best and brightest. Every detail was meticulous, from the three DJs to the fountain of exotic liquor to the organic slow-food hors d'oeuvres. They were even able to host it at Rod Birch's place in Twin Peaks, with the living room that converted to a planetarium where the constellations changed shape to reflect the mood of the crowd.

But everything had gone to shit. The DJs had launched a turf war, and the mashup DJ was trying to colonize the dubthrash DJ's set with some kind of meta-mashup. The Caddy engineers had gotten into a fistfight with the open-source Artichoke BSD developers on the balcony. Everybody felt guilty about drinking *soju* after what happened in Korea. The A-listers didn't show up, and somehow the party invite on MeeYu had gotten cluttered with wannabes, bloggers, and local nutcases. The slow-food hors d'oeuvres made everybody sick to their stomachs, and soon there was an endless line to throw up in the hyperbaric bathroom. The dubthrash DJ won the DJ war and proceeded to make everybody's eardrums bleed with the most dreary shit imaginable. The smoke machine belched horrible candy-floss-scented smog, while the lights lurched into epilepsy-inducing configurations. The line to vomit in the bathroom was starting to resemble that famous photo of the bedraggled masses evacuating Seoul on foot. The constellations on the ceiling became a supermassive black hole, a Sagittarius A of party foulness. This was the worst disaster in human history.

Just when Francis and Carrie resigned themselves to changing their names and leaving town, that weird girl showed up. The girl whom nobody would cop to having added to the party invite, the hippie who (Carrie had heard) let birds nest in her hair and rats live in her purse. Paula? Petra? No, Patricia. There had been a time—a happier, more innocent time—when Francis and Carrie had believed that Patricia showing up would be the worst thing that could happen to their party.

"Sorry I'm late," she told Carrie, slipping out of her shoes as she strode into the front room. "I had to run some errands across town."

As Patricia walked into the party room, the fugly smoke parted and the lights swung together, so her Bettie Page hair had a halo and her wide face was lit by a floodlight aurora. She seemed to float into the room, barefoot in a small strappy black dress that left her pale shoulders mostly exposed. Her necklace had a heartstone that caught the arclights and refracted pink sparkles. She walked through the party, saying hi or introducing herself, and everybody she touched felt the nausea and ill feeling pass away. As if she'd painlessly drawn some poison out of them. She wandered past the DJ and whispered in his ear, and moments later the awful crunging dubthrash music was replaced by soothing dubstep. People swayed happily. The wailing and lamentation became the hum of conversation. The bathroom had no line. People started hanging out on the balcony for reasons other than punching each other or throwing up in the bushes.

Everybody agreed that Patricia had salvaged the party at the UFO house somehow, but nobody could have said how. She'd just kind of shown up, and the vibe had improved. Carrie found herself making Patricia a thank-you cocktail, holding it out in both hands, like an offering.

PATRICIA HADN'T NEEDED much magic to rescue this awful party from the brink—fixing an upset stomach was second nature to her, after some of the dorm-room cooking at Eltisley Maze, and the partygoers did most of the heavy lifting themselves once she redirected their energies a bit. But just like with the poet in North Beach and the junkie in the Tenderloin, the most important thing was not to let anybody see her doing magic—she'd been indoctrinated never to share her big powerful Seekrit with anyone, but she needed no reminder in any case. She still remembered her friend in middle school whom she'd done magic in front of, how he'd lost his shit and run away, and stopped talking to her right when she needed him. When she told herself that story nowadays or shared it with others, she boiled it down to: "I showed my magic to a civilian one time, and it got ugly."

Other than that, she hadn't thought about that kid in years. He'd been reduced to a single cautionary anecdote in her head. But she found herself thinking about him now, maybe because she was surrounded by geeks, or because pulling this shindig back from the Party Abyss with her bare hands was reminding her of how weird social interactions could be, here in the "real" world. Especially after so many years in the bubble of Eltisley Maze. And somehow, the image popped into her head of the boy, naked in a closet with bruises all over and blood caked around his nostrils. The last time she'd seen him. She found herself hoping he'd turned out okay after all, and then as she finished her loop around the party, he was standing right in front of her. Almost, but not quite, like magic.

Patricia recognized Laurence right off the bat. The sandy hair was the same, cut into a messy part instead of a fringe. He was a lot taller and a tad stockier. The eyes were the same hazel-gray and his chin still jutted, and he still looked kind of perplexed and a little pissed off about everything. But that could be because he was one of the people she hadn't yet healed. She did that now. He was wearing a collarless black button-up shirt with a small tiger embroidered on it, and black canvas pants.

"You feeling okay?" she said.

"Yeah," he said, straightening up. He half-smiled, and rolled his neck like an owl. "Yeah. Thanks. Starting to feel better. There was something weird about those hors d'oeuvres."

"Yeah."

He did not recognize her. Which made sense, it had been ten years, and a lot had probably happened. Patricia should just keep moving through the party. *Just move along, don't try to have some kind of bullshit uncomfortable reunion.* But she couldn't help herself.

"Laurence?"

"Yeah." He shrugged. And then his eyes grew. "Patricia?"

"Yeah."

"Oh, cool. It's good to, uh, see you again. How have you been?"

"I've been good. How are you doing?"

"I'm good too." Long pause. Laurence shuffled and kneaded a square napkin. "So. You violate any laws of physics lately?"

"Ha ha. No, not really." Patricia needed to get out of this conversation before it crushed the life out of her. "Anyway. Good running into you again."

"Yeah." Laurence looked around. "I should introduce you to my girlfriend, Serafina. She was here a second ago. Don't go anywhere. I'll just, uh, just find her."

Laurence turned and plowed into the throng, looking for his girlfriend. Patricia wanted to get out of there, but she felt like she'd promised Laurence she wouldn't leave this spot. She was bound to this place, as sure as if she'd been imprisoned inside a rock. Minutes passed and Laurence did not come back, and Patricia got more antsy.

Why had she thought it would be a good idea to say hi to Laurence? It just brought up a lot of weird, painful memories of puberty and nearly losing herself, and it wasn't like she needed more awkwardness in her life right now. She'd been feeling invincible, partly because she had just "saved" this UFO party, but now she felt sour, maybe even depressed. Patricia wasn't naturally manic-depressive, but a big part of the instruction at Eltisley Maze had involved keeping two very different, maybe incompatible, states of mind at once—and in some ways, it was like being taught to be bipolar on purpose. People had a rough time of it, and nobody should be surprised that you wound up with people like Diantha. But Patricia was trying not to think about Diantha.

Patricia's mood was crashing fast. Promise or no promise, she had to get out of here.

"Hey." A guy was standing in front of Patricia. He had on a ridiculous waistcoat with purple fleur-de-lis on it, and a watch chain, plus puffy white sleeves. Wide sideburns and shoulder-length dreadlocks framed his face, which had a nice jawline and an easy smile. "You're Patricia, right? I heard you were indirectly responsible for the amelioration of the atrocious dubthrash music. I'm Kevin."

He had an accent that she couldn't place—sort of Mid-Atlantic. Anglophile. His handshake was soft and encompassing, but not grippy. He was an animal lover, she could tell, who had pets, plural.

Kevin and Patricia talked about music and the basic incompatibility between "cocktail party" and "dance party" (because a floor could be a dance floor or a sophisticated-mingling-with-shallow-glasses floor but not both: Floors were not infinitely sub-dividable or versatile).

Laurence came back with a cute waifish redhead with a pointy chin, wearing a sparkly scarf. "This is Serafina. She works with emotional robots," Laurence said. "This is Patricia," he told Serafina. "My friend from junior high. She saved my life."

Hearing herself described that way made Patricia spit-take her cosmo. "She saved my life"—apparently, that was the anecdote that she'd been boiled down to, in Laurence's mind.

"I never thanked you," Laurence said. Then Serafina was clasping Patricia's hand delicately and saying it was nice to meet her, and Patricia had to introduce Kevin to both of them. Kevin nodded and smiled. He was taller than Laurence, and you could have fit two of Serafina inside him.

Laurence gave Patricia his card and there was vague talk about getting lunch.

After Laurence and Serafina drifted away, Patricia told Kevin, "I didn't really save his life. He was exaggerating."

Kevin shrugged, causing his watch chain to jangle. "It's his life. One tends to privilege personal insights in such matters."

A LEXUS PULLED up in front of Patricia's apartment building just as she was getting her house keys out of her purse. It was three in the morning, and somehow Kawashima had known the exact moment that Patricia would get home. As usual, he wore a bespoke dark suit, with a thin black tie and a bright red pressed handkerchief providing one splash of color, even on this hot night. He got out of the car and gave Patricia a cheery smile, like he was pleased they'd happened to run into each other. Kawashima was one of the most powerful magicians Patricia knew, but everyone who met him thought he was a hedge-fund manager. His black hair was short except for one perfect swoosh, and he had the kind of boyish good looks that made people want to trust him even when he was scamming them out of millions.

"I didn't tell him," Patricia said without bothering to say hi first. "He already knew. He's known since middle school."

Kawashima nodded. "Sure. But still, talking to civilians about the things we do, and how we do them…" He leaned against the car and looked at his unscuffed shoes. Then he looked up at Patricia again, taking her measure. "What if we told you to kill him?"

"I'd say the same thing I said to that guy ten years ago," Patricia responded without hesitation. "I'd say no. Actually, I'd say 'fuck you,' followed by 'no.' "

"We figured." Kawashima laughed and clapped his hands a couple times. "And of course, we would never ask you to do that. Not unless it was absolutely necessary. But we want to meet him. If you trust him, then we trust him, too. But we'd like to meet him for ourselves."

"Okay," Patricia said. "We only had one short conversation. But sure, I'll try."

"That's actually not why I came to see you," Kawashima said. "Although thanks for bringing it up." He held up a tablet computer, like a Caddy but less fancy, and showed her a map of San Francisco with some places marked with little dots. The North Beach café with the poet-stabbing, the Hayes Valley assault, the junkie, a few other odds and ends. And the party in Twin Peaks. "You were busy tonight."

"Nobody saw anything." Patricia was burning up. "I was careful."

"This is what you do every night lately. You go out and throw your weight around, for hours. It's great that you want to alleviate suffering, it's praiseworthy, but the world is a balance. Much like nature itself. And you have to be careful you don't cause more suffering than you prevent," Kawashima said. "We don't want you to burn out. Or get carried away. Just remember, Aggrandizement comes in many forms."

Patricia wanted to protest—she was being surgical here, she had trained a decade for this—but there was no point. She should be glad she was having this conversation with Kawashima instead of Ernesto.

"You, of all people, should understand the need for great care," Kawashima said, because of course he was going to bring *that* incident up. It would follow her around for the rest of her life. No matter how much she did to atone.

"Okay," Patricia said. "I'll be more careful." She left it vague on purpose.

"Good enough," Kawashima said. "Now if you'll excuse me, I have an early-morning brunch date with five Abercrombie models tomorrow." He saluted and got into his Lexus, which glided down the hill toward Dolores Park. Patricia watched it shrink into the night and marveled at the internal contradiction of telling someone that the most powerful magicians in town are watching her every move, but she shouldn't get a swelled head. But she was too exhausted to dwell on that, and all of the day's minor miracles were catching up with her at once. She slipped inside the apartment, where her roommates had fallen asleep watching TV again. She tucked them in.

2

LAURENCE FIRST MET his girlfriend, Serafina, at a robot fashion show, with robots modeling human clothing and human models wearing robot fashions, like mechanical lingerie. The event happened at a garagey artspace somewhere south of South of Market, with a gunmetal trough full of artisanal vodka. Laurence had come *this* close to mistaking Serafina for one of the models—her cheekbones and oval face, her lustrous skin and shiny red/black hair were that amazing—but he'd realized just in time that she was one of the robot makers instead. Serafina's "model" was a steel sylph, with ball-and-socket joints that let it strike a pose, pivot, talk with its delicate hands. Laurence had helped to build battle bots in college, but never artificial supermodels, and he'd managed to say something witty enough about the difference between the two that Serafina had friended him on MeeYu.

They met for coffee a few days after that, and the coffee date morphed into a dinner date, and the third time they hung out it was tacitly a sleepover; Serafina had a toothbrush and condoms in a pouch of her vinyl shoulder bag, which was Twiki from *Buck Rogers*. Pro tip: Do not think of "beedi beedi beedi" while you're having sex for the first time with the most beautiful woman alive, or you will have some explaining to do (even if your motion, rocking the bed frame, does have a sort of "beedi beedi" rhythm). After that, they hung out every other day, held hands on the street, skipped through traffic, whispered in each other's ears in public, clung together skin to skin every moment in private, swapped gene prints, traded odd little gifts, and wondered how soon was too soon to say "I love you."

Laurence had soon found that letting people know he was part of Milton Dirth's Ten Percent Project was a superfast ticket to getting laid. Among the crowd who worshiped Milton, Laurence was a rock star. About fucking time, really. And yet there was still no way he was in Serafina's league. She was perfect. He was damaged goods. He never forgot this disparity for a second.

About a month after they started dating, Serafina took Laurence into her sanctum. She had to sign him in, and he had to surrender his ID to the man at the desk, who printed a badge with Laurence's fresh photo on it. She led him down an elevator, along a sloping hallway, through two keypad-secured doors, and on into the lab. Inside, eyes watched Laurence from every wall and flat surface. Two of them belonged to bearded humans, who said "Yo," and then looked back down at their workstations, but the rest all belonged to robots in various states of assembly. Serafina barely introduced Laurence to the two humans but took her time showing him the robots, who were animatronic cartoon characters or animals or a few mannequin heads. "This is Frank, he laughs a lot. Watch out for Barbara, she flirts but she's got a mean streak." The robots seemed to like Laurence, especially Donald the Cactus.

By now, they'd been dating five months. And lately, every time Serafina looked at her phone while they were hanging out, or stared into space, or bit her thick lower lip in the middle of a conversation, Laurence braced himself. This was it. She was going to dump him. Then the moment would pass. Laurence was sure she was just waiting for the right moment, or the ideal pretext. Every time he woke up next to her, he wondered if this was the last time her breath would warm the back of his neck and her breasts would graze either side of his spine.

He was not going to lose her. He had aced bigger challenges than this. He was going to think of something, take extreme measures, even deploy the Nuclear Option early if he had to. He was going to find a way to hold on to this amazing girl.

LAURENCE'S FACE BEAMED from the front of Anya's Caddy as he prepared to jump out of the autocopter, onto the roof deck 172 feet below. That same image of Laurence would be leering from computers all over town right now, thanks to a big article about him in Computron Newsly, which had just gone live twenty minutes ago and was now being aggregated and repackaged by every other Silicon Valley outlet. Between MeeYu and Caddies and all the CySpec-wearing geeks, Laurence's shit-eating grin would be on everybody's retinas. The gist of the article was "Laurence Armstead, Wunderkind," and it was all about his awesome quest to Save the World, and how he had harnessed Milton Dirth's unlimited cash to gather the world's smartest people (people like Anya, in fact). The text of the article could be "*lorem ipsum*" as far as Laurence was concerned; the main point was harnessing the echo chamber in his favor, at the exact moment that he was about to abseil down to that roof deck.

Milton Dirth's Ninth Maxim: *Avoid publicity, except when you can wield it like a sledgehammer.*

Anya was giggling at the picture of Laurence, in her throaty midwestern-girl voice. "God. Could they have made your chin look any bigger? It looks like the heel of someone's foot, growing out of your face."

"This picture looks like you got a bad chin implant!" shouted Tanaa from the pilot seat of the autocopter, where she was wearing big headphones over her afro, along with a pair of aviator goggles. She had her "operating delicate machinery" frown on her narrow mouth, even as she laughed.

"A chinplant!" Anya laughed, creating unaccustomed dimples in her normally dour face. "Actually, it looks like you're overcompensating for being unable to grow a beard, by just adding more chin."

"Shut up, shut up!" Laurence said. "I'm a wunderkind, okay?" He took a moment to look at the two women, reflected on how lucky he was to have such clever weirdos working with him, and vowed yet again that he was not going to let this project fail. He wasn't going to let Milton, or any of them, down. He was going to do better, somehow.

Then Laurence jumped out of the autocopter, trusting the steel-cord-and-pulley mechanism to lower him at a fast—but not too fast—clip. He wanted to land on his feet. For a moment, there was nothing but sky all around him, and then the Dogpatch was rising up, and the brand new brutalist tower blocks grew in proportion to the ancient warehouses and docks around them. The air was searing hot, even with the wind.

Laurence's face was on every computer screen in town right now—except the screens of the company whose roof deck Laurence was dropping onto right now, MatherTec. MatherTec's computer screens were spewing gibberish, thanks to a clownware-injection attack that Laurence had unleashed on the company's servers ten minutes earlier.

From the standpoint of the MatherTec founders and angel investors, here's what happened: They were on their roof deck giving a presentation to a set of VCs in a frantic effort to secure second-round funding for their technology, which wasn't just another app but rather a way to create stable openings in space-time, with a million possible long-term uses if they could just get some investment. And then, just as their slide presentation was reaching the crucial moment, their screens went staticky and showed the stars-and-snakes logo of the Symbiotic Liberation Army, the world's most obnoxious hacker group, and nothing they could do would get the presentation back. The investors fidgeted and started to badger the gothy waitress from the catering company for more macaroons, and Earnest Mather was tearing his frizzy reddish-brown hair out. And just then, the wunderkind—that guy whose long, corn-fed face had been everywhere today—dropped out of the sky and handed Earnest Mather a check, already signed by Milton Dirth, for $10 million. "We're not investing," Laurence told Earnest before the company founder could even count the zeroes. "We're buying you out. We want your technology, and a few of your people."

Earnest wanted time to think it over, but Laurence told him he had five minutes. The angel investors were already badgering him to take the damn money, and the VCs were all too busy MeeYuing their videos of Laurence's descent from the sky to think about making a counter-offer.

A few minutes later, Laurence (or rather Milton) owned this company. Earnest Mather was taking a bottle of Devil's Bargain IPA from the gothy waitress and draining it. Laurence rolled up next to Earnest and helped himself to the final macaroon. "Sorry about the theatrics, man," Laurence said. "We needed your patents, plus we couldn't risk having them fall into the wrong hands. You could have the next WMD here. And we're on a tight timetable, to Save the World before it's too late."

Earnest, still kind of goggle-eyed, said something about the world being a work in progress.

"Milton really thinks we're going to need a new planet, maybe soon," Laurence continued. *"We've got to get off this rock.* All our models suggest a decent likelihood of a catastrophic combination of natural disasters and destructive war, within one or two generations. Look at Seoul. Look at Haiti." Laurence reached for one of those beers as well. "As far as we know, we're the only intelligent, technological civilization ever to develop, in the entire universe. There's complex life all over the place, but we're still basically unique. We have a fucking duty to preserve that. At all costs."

Laurence started to explain about how he'd dreamed of nothing, since he was a little kid, but leaving this planet. But Earnest had to run to the executive washroom to dry-heave. Laurence squirreled all the signed paperwork into his breast pocket of his nice black suit and then looked up at the gothy waitress for the first time. It was Patricia.

"Whoa," Laurence said. "What are you doing here?" He had a panic attack that she was spying on him or stalking him, for a second.

"What does it look like?" she said. "I'm waitressing. My roommate Deedee hooked me up with this job."

Laurence looked at her crisp white blouse and black knee-length skirt, silhouetted against the pale blue sky. Her dark hair was pinned back but still caught the bay wind. Her eyes looked leaf green. Her slender lips were pursed.

"Are you serious? I thought you were like…"—he lowered his voice—"…a *witch* now. You went to that special school, right?"

"I have other jobs besides this one, sure," Patricia said. "But I don't get paid for those. I need to pay rent in this city, which is a lot, even with two roommates."

"Oh."

Somehow, Laurence had imagined Patricia just snapping her fingers and causing money to appear. Or living rent-free in a fancy Victorian house full of magical objects, like a mirror that tells you what shoes go with your outfit. Not so much slinging macaroons to venture capitalists for minimum wage.

"So did you mean all the stuff you said to this guy?" Patricia said. "About our planet being doomed, and the human race being the only part of it worth saving?"

"Well. No. I don't think we're the only thing worth saving." Laurence felt a weird shame that was the flip side of his cockiness from a moment ago. "I hope we can save all of it. But I do worry. We may be past the point of no return here. And it just makes sense not to pin all our hopes on just one planet."

"Sure." Patricia had her puffy-sleeved arms folded. "But this planet is not just some 'rock.' It's not just some kind of chrysalis we can shed, either. You know? It's, it's more than that. It's us. And this isn't just our story. As someone who's spoken to lots of other kinds of creatures, I kinda think they might want a vote."

"Yeah." Laurence felt like crap, just at the moment he ought to be feeling bulletproof. This sucked. But as he replayed his conversation with Mather, he could see how it would sound kind of heinous to Patricia. "Sorry. I didn't mean to suggest that anybody ought to write anything off. Nobody is going to do that."

"Sure. I guess."

Some tipsy VCs needed to come up and get their picture taken with Laurence, who was still wearing his harness over his Armani suit, and get some spring rolls from Patricia. And Laurence had to go get these papers notarized or spindled, or whatever you did when you bought a company. Plus Milton kept texting him. He muttered to Patricia that he would see her later, and she barely said, "Sure," in between pouring drinks and answering nut-allergy questions.

ONE DAY THE Singularity would elevate humans to cybernetic superbeings, and maybe then people would say what they meant.

Probably not, though.

SERAFINA WAS LATE for dinner because her emotional robots had been having a nervous breakdown. All of them. "It took me the whole day to figure out what was bothering them. They just kept wigging out and giving us the hairy eyeball. We looked at everything that had changed in the lab, trying to eliminate every possible factor that could have upset them. Like, was the music different? Did we update their code recently?"

Laurence didn't rush her. Problem solving and troubleshooting were a source of pleasure for both of them, and narrating the process was the next best thing to doing it. The same neural pathways lit up when you talked your way through the maze as when you actually solved it. Except this time, you were bathed in the glow of having already unraveled the thing.

And yet Laurence was still uncomfortable. For one thing, because Serafina was late, they were stuck sitting at one of the sidewalk tables at the fancy pizza place, with nothing but a tiny heat lamp and three meatballs to insulate them from the fog, until the pizza arrived. For another, he was trying to be a good listener, because of his ongoing "not getting dumped" project, and active listening was hard work. And people were still giving him weird looks, a week after the MatherTec thing.

"We finally figured out that only one thing had changed," Serafina said. She wore a camisole, but she'd put her bulky jacket back on when they were seated outdoors. The heat lamp made her skin look bronze. "Matt just got a Caddy, and he'd brought it to the office. As soon as we took the Caddy out of WiFi range, the robots calmed down. Somewhat. And before you ask, the Caddy did not have any weird apps installed on it. It was fresh from the store."

"WiFi range. So they were getting something from the Caddy, on their wireless network, that upset them." Laurence pulled out his own Caddy and glanced over it, as if he'd suddenly spot some brand-new feature. It still looked like a big guitar pick with a curved base, covered with aluminum. The Caddy was scanning for open networks, the same as always, but it wouldn't link up with other machines on the same network without being instructed to do so. Unless…

"Here's what I don't get," Laurence said, bisecting the third meatball so Serafina could have half. The meatball was their only protection against the cold, the last of their dwindling supplies until their pizza arrived. "So your emotional robots, they don't have 'emotions' in the way that humans do, right? I mean, no offense." Laurence was on thin ice here—and not the edge, but the dead middle of a lake, a hundred fragile paces in any direction. "The robots simulate emotional responses to some situations, and they try to pick up on what the people around them are feeling. Right?"

"You make it sound like we're designing three-dimensional video-game avatars." Serafina didn't quite push her chair back, but she did seem a little farther away.

"I am well aware it's a lot more involved than that," Laurence said. "Both because of the Uncanny Valley and because the physical world is a lot more complicated."

"But the real point is, how do you ever know your own emotions are spontaneous and genuine, and not just a programmed set of responses?"

"I don't. I wonder about that all the time." Laurence was conscious that it was probably a bad idea to confess to your girlfriend that you often wondered if your feelings were just an involuntary response. "I just wonder... assuming they have some reason for feeling a particular way, and they don't just wake up on the wrong side of the bed. The Caddy had to be doing something that resembled an aggressive act, as defined in their response matrices. Right?"

"Yeah," Serafina said. "They reacted as if they were being threatened."

The pizza came at last, just when Laurence needed something to distract Serafina from what a mansplaining dick he was being, in spite of all his resolutions.

"There must be some other explanation," Laurence said. "You're talking about a Caddy, it's not a black box. People have jailbroken and wiped them, they've installed Linux on them and also ported the Caddy OS over to cheap imitation tablets from Liberia. This is the most hacked device in history. If there was something weird about it, we'd *know* by now."

"Hey," said Serafina, chewing pizza. "Occam's razor is not just an optional weapon in *Street Warrior V*. Already told you, we eliminated all other possibilities."

The harder Laurence tried not to screw up, the worse he screwed up. He was not going to get dumped. That was not a possible outcome.

He thought about the Nuclear Option: his grandmother's old ring, squirreled in the back of his sock drawer. He imagined getting on his knee and presenting it to Serafina. He could picture how it would look riding up her finger past the knuckle, the wrought silver wrapped around the gemstone. The look on her face as she blushed down at him.

After dinner, they went for drinks and wound up in the Latin American Club, right under the mannequin with the merkin. "Oh, look," Serafina said. "It's your friend." He followed her line of sight and spotted Patricia, with an African-American guy in a black velvet coat covered with elaborate piping. After a moment, Laurence recognized the dude she'd been talking to at Rod Birch's house. Patricia waved at them, and they waved back. Laurence didn't know whether he and Serafina ought to be intruding on Patricia's date or whether he wanted her intruding on theirs, and he worried Patricia was going to lecture him about the planet again. But Patricia beckoned them over, and Serafina went.

Patricia's date was named Kevin, and he was a Monty Python–quoting Anglophile who walked dogs and worked in a café—but his real job was creating a webcomic, which Laurence had read a few times.

"The secret to a successful webcomic is to trick people into believing they will only get all the jokes if they read regularly. By the time they realize there are no jokes for them to get, they've invested too much time to quit, and they can't admit they've been duped," said Kevin. "There is a whole art to creating nonexistent jokes that appear to go over everyone's head. It's much harder than creating actual jokes."

"The comics I read were funny in their own right," said Laurence. "So you totally screwed up."

"You are destroying me," said Kevin.

Patricia was telling Serafina that she'd just quit a terrible catering gig, but now she'd gotten a new job at one of the fancy Mission bakeries, where they were using locally sourced organic grains not just to be fancy, but out of necessity since the Great Midwestern Dustbath. "I love to bake, so this is perfect."

Serafina liked baking, too, but she was lousy at it. "I made this cake once and it caved in, and I thought my kid brother had stepped on it in the oven. I beat him up for like an hour before I realized I just forgot to put in enough of that stuff."

"You mean flour," Patricia said.

"Yeah, flour." Serafina smiled.

There was a long silence. Kevin cleared his throat like he was going to say something clever, but then he thought better of it.

Laurence still itched all over, thinking about how he'd tried to lecture Serafina about her job at dinner and now she was forced to hang out with his middle-school friend. He needed a patch for this date. Not to mention, he felt some random need to prove to Patricia that he wasn't a total jerkface.

While they waited for drinks, Laurence tried telling Patricia all about Serafina's emotional robots—then realized halfway through that talking about Serafina in the third person didn't make her seem cool, but just made it seem like Laurence thought she couldn't speak for herself.

"Patricia seemed cool," Serafina said afterward, as she and Laurence sat in Humphry Slocombe and shared some Secret Breakfast, that weird ice cream with the cornflakes and whiskey in it.

"You didn't really get to see what's cool about her." Laurence scooped some ice cream.

"Obviously I did, since I already said I thought she was cool."

"It's weird to see someone you haven't seen in ten years, and it brings back all sorts of stuff. I was such a loser, you wouldn't believe." (When talking about middle school, Laurence had long since learned it was best not even to mention that he believed he'd created artificial intelligence in his bedroom closet, even as a funny story. It just made him sound like an asshat.)

They finished their ice cream. Which, ice cream with whiskey in it, might not have been the best idea after three beers at the Latin American. Laurence was seeing a lot of floaters and his head was only getting fuzzier, plus he felt a deep unrest in the pit of his stomach.

"So what's going on?" Serafina said. "I feel like there was some subtext to this evening that I missed."

Laurence thought of saying that he didn't know whether subtext was an emotional state or a mental state or even what the exact difference between the two things might be. But he bit his tongue and said, "I feel as though I'm on probation. I mean, in this relationship."

"Huh. News to me." Serafina shrugged. Her eyes widened and her lower lip curled inward as she looked at her boyfriend. Her red highlights glistened under the fluorescent hipster-ice-cream-store lights. She looked so beautiful and so filled with curiosity, Laurence felt a brand-new pang of love for her. He was ready to open himself up to her, something that did not come naturally to him. Her callused and manicured fingers toyed with the unladen ice-cream spoon.

"Have I said or done anything to give you the idea that you're on probation?" she asked.

Laurence searched his memory for a moment, then shook his head. "I guess I just decided I was. I don't know why."

"This is weirding me out. I mean, I feel like our communication has sucked for, I don't know, a month or so. But maybe it was worse than I knew." Serafina massaged her own temples, pinching the skin on either side of her eyebrows.

"So... I'm not on probation then?"

"Well..." Serafina stopped mortar-and-pestling her forehead and looked him in the eye. "I guess you are now."

"Oh." *Well played, Armstead.*

3

PATRICIA COULDN'T GET that image out of her head: Laurence dropping out of the sky and waving money around, boasting that he would Save the World by writing off the planet. Even if she hadn't seen it with her own eyes, the video clip was all over the net afterward. Patricia shouldn't be surprised that Laurence had turned into an entitled yuppie. This was what he'd always wanted, wasn't it? To be admired, to have everybody get his name right. Patricia kept feeling annoyed, until she realized maybe she was jealous. She spent so much energy keeping her good deeds secret, it was hard to watch someone else show off. Lately, the other witches were always on her case about Aggrandizement, no matter how hard she tried to be humble.

Patricia found herself still obsessing about Laurence as she slid on knee-high leather boots and a black babydoll dress with red sparkles and went to an Irish bar in the Financial District to put a curse on someone.

Patricia sucked at walking in spike heels, and kept almost

wiping out as she strode inside the stuffy, blaring pub and tried to recognize Garrett Borg from the picture Kawashima had e-mailed her. In person, Garrett looked like a once-hot Alpine ski instructor gone to seed, with very fair hair and a blue double-breasted suit that camouflaged his pudge. He was halfway passed out at the bar, drooling into the Guinness towel but still raising his head to pour more high-end Scotch into his mouth with his free hand every few moments.

In theory, Patricia shouldn't need to know why she was hitting this guy—Kawashima had ordered it, and that ought to be enough for her. But Kawashima had included some other pictures along with Garrett's head shot: the coroner's photos of the teenage girls he'd left buried in an old culvert along the I-90, nearly matching bruise marks on their necks and inner thighs. So Patricia was properly motivated when she slid onto the leather-top stool next to Garrett and whispered in his ear. "I bet you'll have one hell of a hangover tomorrow. But you know what? I know the best hangover remedy there is. This shit will cure anything." She made it sound miraculous, but also sexy and illicit. He popped both the pills she gave him without hesitation. Then she helped him into a cab, and he went home to Pacific Heights, to sleep it off. She hadn't lied: The shit she'd given him would indeed cure anything.

There was zero chance that Patricia would sleep after putting a curse on someone. But she would be careful and would follow Kawashima's advice to avoid overreaching. She knew why they were so worried about her going off the rails: She could still see Toby's corpse when she closed her eyes.

The janky expression, like Toby was about to sit up and tell a dirty joke.

Patricia had to crouch down to talk to a confused marmalade cat, who needed help finding his way home. (He remembered what his house looked like on the inside, but not on the outside.) Patricia checked on Jake the *krokodil* junkie, who seemed stable now, give or take, and then she cruised the St. Mary's emergency room, looking for people to heal on the down-low. She spent a couple hours trying to compose a letter to the Parks Department on behalf of some gophers whose burrow was being disturbed, pointlessly, by some inept landscaping in Golden Gate Park. It took a lot of concentration to translate from gopher language into bureaucratese.

Right about now, Garrett Borg would be evaporating into a whiskey-scented cloud over his heart-shaped bed.

Patricia ended up at the edge of the Park, on Fulton. Staring at the warm dirt, so full of life, between her pointy toes. She wasn't pacing herself, after all. She dug in her bag for her phone and peered at the screen. There was nobody for her to call at three in the morning. Even at three in the afternoon, there would have been nobody to call. Maybe Kevin, her ambiguous friend-with-benefits/boyfriend? She was trying not to crowd him. The traffic light at the edge of her vision changed primary colors. It was another hot, itchy night.

An owl landed on a branch nearby, without a sound. "Hello," Patricia said. The owl blinked at the sound of her voice.

"If I can see you, so can others," the owl said.

"I'm not trying to hide, exactly," Patricia said. The owl shrugged with its whole body, like it was Patricia's funeral, then flew off again because there were some gophers with an imperfect burrow not far away.

Just as Patricia was rallying to pull her butt out of the dirt and go home, someone sat on the low stone wall and blocked her view of the street. A man. She almost hid, but decided not to bother.

It was Laurence, and he was crying into a napkin with a picture of a woman inside a cocktail glass. Patricia almost walked away—Laurence would never even know she'd been there—until her Healer instinct kicked in.

Patricia made as much noise as possible coming up behind Laurence, so as not to sneak up on him. But he still jumped off the wall so hard, he fell and skinned one knee. Patricia helped him up and braced him, then steered him back to the wall where he'd been sitting.

"Oh hey," Laurence said, making sense of her features. "It's you." This was the first time she'd seen the grown-up Laurence act anything but cocky. Hunched over, flushed, he looked more like the Laurence she remembered.

"Is everything okay?" she asked.

"Yeah. I just went for drinks with my coworkers, and I'm kind of a maudlin drunk." He paused. "But also… I feel like I'm screwing up everything. I'm losing my girlfriend. Serafina. You met her, she's amazing. And meanwhile, I have all these people expecting me to work miracles, and I can only accomplish so much with asinine stunts like the one you witnessed. My boss—Milton—is counting on me, my supersmart team is counting on me, but most of all, I made a promise to myself. I always thought that if I just had the chance, I could change everything—and it turns out that maybe, I'm just not good enough. So I resort to trying to trick people into thinking I'm a 'wunderkind,' to make up for the fact that I can't actually figure out anything. Jesus."

Patricia climbed up the slope and over the wall Laurence was sitting on. She had a flashback of the teenaged Laurence telling her that the power to make everyone see an illusory version of yourself would royally suck.

Laurence scooted over, to give Patricia more room on his chunk of wall. "And I was just thinking about my parents. I looked down on them for so long, for being failures. I was kind of horrible to them. And I was just thinking that maybe one day I would understand why they chose to fail, but it would be too late. Or a realization I'd rather not have."

"My life plan involves never understanding my parents," Patricia said. "That's like the cornerstone. You met them, you saw what they were like. I'm dedicated to not being the person they wanted to make me."

"Yes." Laurence laughed: a queasy drunk laugh, but still a laugh. "You know… no matter what you do, people are going to expect you to be someone you're not. But if you're clever and lucky and work your butt off, then you get to be surrounded by people who expect you to be the person you wish you were."

"Huh. I hadn't thought of it like that."

"How about you?" Laurence stood up and got oriented, only swaying a tad. "What are you doing out on your own at this hour on a school night?"

"Working." Patricia stood up too. She was going to get Laurence home in one piece and then crash. "I work long hours."

"You work alone?" Laurence said.

They straggled down the hill toward the Haight, where there would be taxis cruising for kids leaving the latest Seoul relief fund-raiser.

"I do everything alone," Patricia said. "I went to this small, claustrophobic school called Eltisley Maze. So I'm still kind of enjoying going solo in a big city where nobody knows who I am. You know? I feel like that's what being a grown-up ought to be like."

She got them a cab, which dropped Laurence off first. Laurence shoved a twenty at Patricia on his way out the car door and tripped over his seat belt. She watched him attack his front steps with his shins and felt something like protectiveness. She made the cab wait until he got inside his house.

THE WHOLE DRIVE to Sacramento, the other witches found ways to lecture Patricia about Aggrandizement. She sat in the back of Kawashima's Lexus, watching the highway whip past, as Kawashima hectored her about making herself too important and using her power too recklessly. Dorothea chimed in every now and then with one of her jarring untruths, like, "You threw pebbles at my window, but they turned into grenades in midair." (Dorothea was an old Catholic lady with white-streaked black hair, chunky glasses, and long calico skirts, who never, ever told the truth, except maybe in Confessional.)

By the time they arrived, Patricia felt like a monster, and she kept picturing Toby's frostbitten body, lying in the airship.

The others were doing important witch business in Sacramento, so Patricia had time to wander around in the scorching midday sun and read on her phone about the French blight, the chaos on the Korean peninsula, the new, deadlier Atlantic superstorms. All things she could do nothing about. Then her peripheral vision landed on a homeless man on the sidewalk. He was staring at her, empty Big Gulp cup in one hand. She turned and looked him over: his torn muddy coat and soiled track pants, his disease and malnourishment. His cardboard sign was so tattered and faded, nobody could decipher it. He was covered with a layer of grime, but also cobwebs and even moss. Normally, if she was out on her own, at night in the city, she would heal someone in this condition without a second thought. But Kawashima and Dorothea were nearby, and she never knew what they would consider Aggrandizement. They never gave her clear-cut guidelines. She edged a little closer, struggling with herself. This man needed her help, it couldn't be wrong to take the initiative. Could it? She looked into his narrow dark eyes, and she could see his damaged pride, and she reached out—

She realized she was looking at the bony, ravaged face of her junior-high-school guidance counselor, Mr. Rose. She was boiling in her own skin. She nearly threw up.

"Don't worry," Mr. Rose croaked. "I will not try to kill you. I couldn't if I tried. You've grown much too powerful, and the years have ruined me. But you must know, I was doing the right thing. I saw a vision of things to come. Patricia, you will be at the center of so much pain. You will betray and you will destroy. If you had even any conscience, you would end your own life right now."

For so long, she'd imagined this moment. When she was out until dawn night after night, she'd been rehearsing for this. Facing this bloody sadist, showing him she could not be terrorized. But she hadn't expected him to be so helpless, literally showing his belly. She couldn't help feeling sorry for him. She didn't take in what he was saying at first, about how she should kill herself—and then she had to spit on the pavement.

"Nice try," she said. But her arms and face burned like the worst poison ivy. "Everything you ever said to me was a lie," she told the huddled old man on the sidewalk. "That's all you do."

"I had assumed a witch with your power levels could tell if I was lying. Please. Please listen." He looked up, and Patricia was startled to see tears all over his filthy cheeks. "I killed so many people, but I still couldn't stand to look upon what you and your friends are going to bring about. Have they told you about the Unraveling yet?"

"The what?" Patricia pulled back. "Forget it. I'm not listening to you anymore."

"You have to listen! Patricia Delfine, I know you better than anyone." She backed up until she was up against the parking meters, and he rose from his cardboard mat, waving a bandaged finger. He breathed foulness at her. "I spied on you for months when you were a child. I parked outside your house. I listened to all your conversations, night and day. I know everything. I even know about the Tree!"

"What tree?" Patricia swallowed. "I don't know what you're talking about."

"Ask them about the Unraveling. Ask them! See what they tell you."

"Oh, fuck me." Kawashima was approaching from the nearby hardware store, plastic bag swinging from one hand. "You have got to be joking. *This* asshole, again?"

"*Theodolphus*," Dorothea said from behind him, looking at the grimy man. She managed to make just his name into the worst insult.

"You know this guy?" Patricia said.

Kawashima ignored her and said to Theodolphus, "You are just the worst, man. You're like a bad rash. I thought we killed you a long time ago."

"I have been as good as dead for many years." Theodolphus Rose drew himself up, as if he was boasting. "But I needed to warn Miss Delfine here. She was my best student, once. When she was a child, I saw a vision of her grown, as she is now. A vision of destruction. I thought she should know."

"Let me guess," Kawashima said. "You huffed some vapors and hallucinated. Right? Visions of the future are always bullshit, and I should know, I'm the biggest bullshit artist around. Dorothea, do you want to do the honors?"

Mr. Rose was still thrashing and yelling about his vision of madness and destruction and a hole in the world. But

Dorothea came closer and whispered a story, about a man she had known. He had been a maker of *netsuke*, those little carved figurines that Japanese people used as *kimono* clasps, but he was also a journeyman assassin, and some of his carvings had hidden death traps: little poison needles, reservoirs of toxic smoke. The deadly *netsuke* were always in the shape of a beautiful woman in a lewd pose, and you could give one to a person knowing he or she would wear it and die. Until one day the man became confused and put a lethal spring-loaded dart into a frog, that he had meant to put inside a courtesan. He then sold the frog to one of his favorite clients, who was sure to wear it that evening and who knew nothing of the man's side business as an assassin. How could he warn his customer?

At this point in the story, Dorothea's murmurs had gotten so soft that Patricia didn't hear how the story ended. And Theodolphus was no longer in a position to listen, either, because somehow without anybody noticing he had changed from a person to a tiny wooden figurine, an inch and a half tall. Dorothea picked him up and showed him to Patricia: He was a slender woman lifting her skirt, except that the face was that of a very solemn frog.

Dorothea dropped the figurine into Patricia's palm, then closed Patricia's fingers around him, for safekeeping.

"I can't believe we didn't kill that douchebag a long time ago." Kawashima unlocked the Lexus and got in the driver's seat. "Seriously, such a dick."

Dorothea nodded and rolled her eyes.

On the drive back to San Francisco, Patricia tried to ask Kawashima about the thing Theodolphus had mentioned, the Unraveling—but of course, that sort of question was the worst possible Aggrandizement.

Patricia dozed, and in her dream she tried to figure out how Dorothea's story ended. Then the answer came to her: The *netsuke* maker/assassin would have to take the frog back from his client, by force if necessary, and would sacrifice his own life in the process. The frog would have to claim someone's life, in the end—if not the client, then the man who made it.

PATRICIA FELT ZERO closure from seeing Mr. Rose get what was coming to him. He'd seemed so pathetic, she even had to struggle to avoid feeling guilty. And she couldn't let go of the notion that maybe Mr. Rose was telling the truth and she was doomed to become a war criminal. Kawashima kept insisting that visions of the future were worse than worthless, but then with the next breath he would tell Patricia again that her pride was dangerous. She ended up with an internal monologue that said she was a terrible, destructive person who should watch her every step.

Right after she got back from Sacramento, she had to rush to the Tenderloin to look in on Reginald, the AIDS patient she'd been assigned to as a Shanti Project volunteer. As usual, she tidied his apartment, cooked him a healthy breakfast, helped him shop. But then she paused, watching him in his unstained wooden rocking chair. And she thought, *This time, I'm just going to do it. I'm going to cure him. Because why not? It would be so easy.*

Except that she knew, for sure, what Kawashima and the others would say about that. You can't just go around curing someone's incurable disease, especially when everybody knows you were there. It would raise too many unanswerable questions. And maybe curing Reginald would be the first step toward her becoming some kind of monster, like Mr. Rose had warned.

"I hope it's the good kind of dilemma." Reginald broke Patricia's reverie. "Whatever one you're on the horns of."

She went over and sat by Reginald, taking his hand. *I'm just going to do it*. She always reduced his viral load whenever she visited, anyway. Curing him outright wouldn't be that much more of a big deal. Right?

Reginald's studio smelled like cannabis and Nag Champa. He had a thin mustache, short gray hair and Elvis Costello glasses, and his neck had prominent tendons.

"I was just thinking," she said. "There are so many crazy problems in the world. Like, I was just reading that we could be seeing the last of the bees in North America soon. And if that happened, food webs would just collapse, and tons more people would starve. But suppose you had the power to change things? You still might not be able to fix anything, because every time you solve a problem you'd cause another problem. And maybe all these plagues and droughts are nature's way of striking a balance? We humans don't have any natural predators left, so nature has to find other ways to handle us."

Reginald had tattoos all over his pale torso, one for each species of insect he had discovered across the Americas. These insect drawings resembled something out of a

Victorian naturalist's handbook, with just splashes of color here and there. As Reginald's body had changed, his loose folds of skin and potbelly made it appear as though the locusts and butterflies were flexing their wings and twitching their heads. His pecs were all wasps, his arms sleeved with shiny chitinous beetles.

"I am, as you know, a fan of nature," said Reginald. "And yet, nature doesn't 'find ways' to do anything. Nature has no opinion, no agenda. Nature provides a playing field, a not particularly level one, on which we compete with all creatures great and small. It's more that nature's playing field is full of traps."

In the end, she stopped just short of curing Reginald outright. Just like always.

PATRICIA DREAMED SHE got lost in the woods, like she had when she was a girl. Stubbing her toes on roots, skidding on dead leaves, feeling transported by the cavelike scent of damp earth. Clouds of insects in her eyes, and up her nose. She laughed so hard she snorted dead bugs, for joy at being out of the city at last. And then she wandered into a clot of thornbushes, which tore at her skin and clutched so hard she couldn't go forward or backward without shredding, and her giddiness turned to anxiety, because what if people needed her help? Or the other witches? What if she was going AWOL right when someone was in trouble?

The more she tried to force her way out of the bracken, the harder it tore at her, until she realized that this was her dream, and she could always fly in dreams. She lifted up out of the thicket and flew up, along a steep incline that was studded with roots. And then it came into view: huge and dark, like a raven formed of branches and leaves. A huge ancient Tree, filled with patience and enough memories for a billion rings, twin branches undulating as in greeting.

"SO WHAT WAS the thing you couldn't tell me about over the phone?" Laurence asked as he brought their espressos from the counter.

In response, Patricia just pulled the tiny wooden figurine out of her bag and told Laurence who it was. Mr. Rose stared up at them, wide-eyed frog face looking prayerful one moment, whimsical the next.

"This is him? This is the actual person?" Laurence kept holding it up to the light, like he was trying to see some resemblance. "He's so… tiny."

"Yeah," Patricia said. "I have no idea what to do with him."

Laurence and Patricia were in the Circle of Trust, which had been the trendy coffee shop in the Valencia Street corridor about eighteen months earlier. It still had all of the nice wooden fixtures and the super-expensive espresso machines, but it was half-empty because all the best people had already moved on to the new place, a block away. The Circle of Trust was having an art show featuring finger paintings done by a twenty-eight-year-old woman, with subversively naive word balloons. The coffee was super-pricey, with all the shortages, but they still went Dutch.

"Seeing him so helpless, and watching him get transformed into this tiny object… it doesn't change my memories of how huge and terrible he was," Patricia said. "It's like two different people. And it sounds like he's spent a lot of the last several years being a thorn in the side of the other witches. Because he went crazy and had some kind of apocalyptic vision. That's why he was at our school in the first place, because he thought I would grow up to become a monster."

"Huh." Laurence stared at the figurine. Patricia felt self-conscious about how borderline obscene the raised skirts were, how weird this was in general. "But you didn't. Grow up to become a monster, I mean. And come on. Did he ever tell anyone the truth? About anything?"

"No," Patricia said. She took the figurine and slipped it back into her purse. She was going to beg Kawashima to take Mr. Rose off her hands. "No, he didn't."

"He was a compulsive liar. Is. Was. Not sure what tense to use."

There could be a better conversation killer than plunking down your most hated childhood authority figure, shrunk to the size of a man's thumb. But Patricia couldn't think of one. The two of them sipped coffee and shook their heads, trapped in recursively horrible memories. Patricia had to fetch water and guzzle it. The café's stale air had stayed almost as hot as noon, even as the sun drifted below the skyline.

Laurence was staring at Patricia's purse, where she'd put the figurine away. "I think all the time about how close he came to ruining my life. It's one of the reasons I'm so desperate to succeed, because I almost didn't get this chance." Abruptly he stood up. "Come on. I want to show you something." Patricia was struck anew by just how tall he'd gotten. Patricia was tall too, but she came up to his collarbone. And he had enough nervous energy for nine ferrets.

Patricia followed Laurence down to Mission Street and then around a couple of side streets until they were near Shotwell, on one of those streets that goes for just a block or two. It was another itchy parched day.

Patricia remembered hearing there was a creek here originally, before it was drained or paved over. Sometimes she imagined she could still feel the current of the banished ecosystem.

They reached a cement block with nothing to distinguish it from the other blocks. Laurence pulled out a key but didn't put it in the lock on the maroon steel door. Instead, he punched a series of a dozen numbers into a keypad recessed into the wall, which Patricia hadn't even noticed. And *then* he turned the key in the lock.

Two and a half flights of steps up, there was a door with a bunch of metal studs in it, and a sign that read: "PROCRASTINATION SOLUTIONS. COME BACK TOMORROW." Laurence knocked seventeen times, in a precise sequence of long and short knocks, and the door swung open.

"Welcome to the Ten Percent Project," Laurence said. "The local office, anyway."

The space behind the steel door was bigger than you'd expect, and much cooler than the outdoors: a square loft, with an opaque skylight along one edge of the ceiling. Ergonomic chairs jostled against workbenches, which were stacked with equipment and soldering irons and Arduino boards and laser tools. The centerpiece of the room, though, was a massive piece of equipment, the size of a Buick, culminating in a sort of ray-gun nozzle. It was aimed at a white Plexiglas circle.

Laurence introduced Patricia, in turn, to the three people in the room:

Tanaa was an African-American woman wearing a welding mask, tank top, and shorts. Her forearms were strong, but her neck and shoulders were fluid, mercurial. Tanaa could build anything, said Laurence—in fact, she'd found Milton the same way Laurence had long ago, by figuring out some schematics on the internet. Except that these schematics were ones that nobody else had managed to make work, and they'd led to that oversized ray gun on bent legs. Tanaa waved, then went back to shooting sparks in all directions.

Anya was a freckled Midwestern girl whose nut-brown hair had blue tips, like she'd dyed it and then given up. She wore denim overalls and chunky engineer glasses, and looked like someone who never smiled. She muttered to Laurence about giving tours to outsiders.

Sougata had a thick black mustache, a Southern California surfer accent, and a Caltech sweatshirt. Laurence whispered that Sougata had wanted to work in television and had even interned at the *Space: Above and Beyond* reboot, but now he'd fallen back on his second-choice career of saving the world in real life.

Patricia wasn't sure if she should ask about the big machine with the giant vacuum-tube-looking body and the pointy nozzle. But then Laurence started explaining it anyway: "We're working on solving gravity." He examined some readings on the machine. "We don't have true antigrav yet, just a few isolated instances. And antigrav isn't the point, controlling gravity is. We know that it's a weak force in our universe, which means it's a strong force somewhere else. And we're trying to figure out where, or what, that is."

"Wow." Patricia could fly without any fancy ray, of course, but only when the situation warranted, and/or when she could trick someone into a bargain that included giving her the power of flight. (Or in dreams.) The idea of turning gravity on or off, or harnessing its power, amazed her.

She was going to be late for Kawashima's latest assignment, an oil executive who was partway responsible for the North Sea disaster. But she wanted to admire Laurence's machine. Laurence showed her the readouts of just how much energy throughput they had gotten into those sleek tubes without anything blowing up.

"That's sure an impressive machine," Patricia said. And yeah, there was something both aesthetically pleasing and satisfying about a great piece of engineering. Shiny and sturdy. She felt the same affection for this machine that she did for the old manual typewriters they sold in the hipster gallery on Valencia, or for a nice steam engine. These things were made of hubris, because they always broke down, or worse, broke everything. But maybe Laurence had been right and these devices were what made us unique, as humans. We made machines, the way spiders made silk. Staring at the red wasp-shaped chassis, she thought of how disgusted she had been with Laurence, not long ago. And maybe she shouldn't judge him—judging was a kind of Aggrandizement—and maybe this device was the culmination of everything she'd always admired about him, from the start. And yes, a sign that they'd both won out, over the Mr. Roses of the world.

"It's beautiful," she said.

4

LAURENCE AND PATRICIA hashed out their respective relationship problems while smoking an elf-shaped bong on the couch. Laurence infodumped about Serafina, the ongoing "probation," and then he got embarrassed about monologuing and asked Patricia about the guy she'd been drinking with. Kevin, the webcomics guy.

"Ummm." Patricia took the bong and filled both lungs before trying to answer. "It's confusing. I'm still not sure if Kevin and I are dating, or just booty-call friends. Whenever he sleeps over, he tries to steal away in the middle of the night. But nobody can sneak out on me, after all the training I've had. So he winds up either having to say goodbye properly or staying until morning. He's tried both, and neither way quite seems to work for him."

"Ah."

"I keep almost having a conversation with Kevin about what it is we're doing, and then it doesn't materialize."

Somehow seeing the wooden Mr. Rose had been a turning

point in Laurence and Patricia's relationship, not just as a bonding thing but also as a reminder that they had known each other as total losers in eighth grade. Patricia might be the hardest person for Laurence to disappoint, because she'd already seen him at his worst. In fact, this was the most at ease Laurence had felt in months, and not just because of the elf bong.

Nobody talked for a while, until Patricia changed the subject: "So how are your parents? Still wanting you to be outdoorsy?"

"I think they are actually pretty happy," said Laurence. "They got divorced about seven years ago, and my mom found a guy who likes to go bird-watching. My dad quit his awful job and went back to college to become a high-school teacher. I always kind of thought they'd be happier if they split up, even though you never want to root for your parents to do that. How are yours?"

"They're, uh… okay," said Patricia. "They actually disowned me for a few years, but this past year they've made this big effort to reconnect." She sighed and sucked in more smoke from the elf's head, even though her throat was getting scratchy. "It's all thanks to my sister, sort of. Roberta keeps getting arrested, or winding up in the ER. She was always the one who had it together, of the two of us. Now, all of a sudden, my parents have noticed that I'm holding down a job and don't have a criminal record, and they've decided that I can be the good daughter now. Like Roberta and I could just trade places. I have no idea how to deal."

Laurence was going to say something else, but Isobel came home. She was soaked, because it was raining and the experimental self-configuring umbrella had gotten stuck in a nonoptimal shape, judging from the complainy servo noises it was making and the fact that the left side of Isobel's cardigan was drenched while the right side was totally dry. She no longer had the long brown braids she'd sported when he'd first met her as a child and instead wore her graying hair in a bob.

"Oh dear," Laurence said. "Lord Umber let you down." This nickname had not caught on with anybody else yet, but he kept trying.

Isobel just snorted and threw Lord Umber at the kitchen sink, where he could drain. Lord Umber groaned and attempted to transform into a shape that would protect the sink from any indoor precipitation. He got stuck again, making loud whining noises.

"Not cool." Isobel grimaced. "Not cool at all. A regular umbrella would have been way better. Oh, hello." She had gotten enough rain out of her eyes to see the unfamiliar young woman seated on the couch. "Nice to meet you. I'm Isobel."

Patricia said her name and they shook hands, then Isobel ran off to get out of her half-wet clothes. When she came back, she had a snifter of brandy. She sat on the sofa next to Patricia and started making low-maintenance small talk about all the places around the world that would kill for some of this rain.

"So I think I heard about you," Isobel told Patricia. "You go back almost as far with Laurence as I do. He seems to collect people for life." She glanced at Laurence, who squirmed, as he sensed he was supposed to.

They were pretty high up in the hills—despite its name, most of Noe Valley was a steep hillside. The living room had picture windows facing over the downward slope of garden out front and the tops of trees farther out. Potrero Hill answered the hill they were on, with its own trees and split-level houses. Their front room had high ceilings, and then a spiral staircase led up to the upper level containing Isobel's bedroom, bathroom, and study, with a balcony overlooking the living room. Laurence's in-law bedroom was down a few steps, over on the other side of the kitchen, with a view of the tiny backyard.

The three of them ordered burritos, and judged that the rain had stopped long enough to risk trudging down the hill to pick them up. The evening had turned warm, despite the massive puddles at every street corner and the clouds on the skyline. Laurence walked between Isobel and Patricia, and was conscious of being hemmed in by women. Especially with them talking past him.

"How did you end up having Laurence as a housemate?" Patricia asked Isobel.

Isobel told the story about Laurence running off to see the rocket when he was a kid. "I kind of kept an eye on Laurence, and when he got done at MIT I offered him my spare room for a while. Actually, Laurence is hardly ever home; this is the first I've seen him in weeks. Which can only mean one thing: *Red Dwarf* marathon."

Laurence made a big show of rolling his eyes, even

though he was kind of in the mood for the long-threatened marathon.

For her part, Isobel had just come back from Greenland, where Milton Dirth was building a vault that was supposed to last ten thousand years, and would only be opened by solving a math problem. "It looks like a bomb shelter, crossed with a Caddy store and a high-end funeral parlor. Everything is shiny steel and chrome, and marble, with glass partitions."

"What's in the vault?" Patricia asked. "Seeds? Genetic material?"

"Nope," said Isobel. "Milton figures whoever opens it in five thousand or ten thousand years will have plenty of edible crops, or they won't be around at all. It's all technological and scientific knowledge. Schematics, plans—basically, an instruction manual for re-creating our level of technology, including some ideas for what to do if there are no fossil fuels and certain other elements are unavailable. He's assuming a roughly early-nineteenth-century science level in whoever finds it. Which might be a stretch, yes. At least the vault will be easy to find: The one piece of electronics in the whole place will be a vertical beam of light, like a searchlight, going off twice a day for at least ten thousand years. That was one of the hardest parts to create."

"It's not a serious project," Laurence said as they crossed Castro Street. "Milton doesn't think the human race will still be here in a hundred years, much less a few thousand. This is just his way of hedging his bets. Or assuaging his conscience."

"It's gotten me three free trips to Greenland," Isobel said. "Honestly, I think Milton's opinions depend on how many interns he's killed today." She half-winked, to indicate this was a joke and Milton killed no interns.

During the dinner, Isobel talked more about her career transition, from rockets to Milton's Ten Percent Project. "I used to dream about rockets." Isobel scooped a corn chip into the communal *pico de gallo*. "Every single night, for months and months. After we pulled the plug on Nimble Aerospace. I had these weird dreams that there was a rocket launch going up any minute, and we'd misplaced the final telemetry. Or we were sending up a rocket, and it looked beautiful and proud shooting up into the air, and then it collided with a jumbo jet. Or worst of all were the dreams where nothing went wrong, rockets just soared for hours, and I sat on the ground watching with tears in my eyes."

"Wow." Laurence touched Isobel on the wrist. "I had no idea."

"So how did you stop dreaming about rockets?" Patricia asked.

"I think I just got bored with it," Isobel said. "Boredom is the mind's scar tissue."

LAURENCE AND SERAFINA went to an organic burger place, locally sourced, etc., and Serafina talked about her emotional robots. "You won't believe the heuristics. They recognize faces, but also they recognize each face's habitual emotional states. They are getting the concept of moods. They are having moods. Moods are weird—it's not just manifesting an emotion, or even sustaining an emotion, it's like a disease state. Like the way we say you nurse a grudge."

Serafina seemed to be letting go of the idea that Laurence was on probation. He'd gotten her a nice scarf, that matched her outfit by some fluke. He was practicing active listening. They'd had brilliant, sun-burst-in-your-face sex a few times. Laurence did not talk about himself too much. He kept thinking about the Nuclear Option. He tried to judge when would be the optimal time to unleash it: These things work better if you build up to them, rather than as a desperation play. Laurence remembered his Grandma Jools, one of the last times he saw her alive, slipping the ring box into his ski-jacket pocket when nobody else was looking, and whispering in his ear, "Give this to whoever you end up marrying, OK?" And Laurence, still a little kid, realizing this was a solemn request, whispering back that he would do that.

Laurence had a conviction, in his loins, that he deserved to be dumped. Because he took Serafina for granted, while he was working fourteen-hour days on the Project, or because she was too excellent for him. But the whole point of being a grown-up and an uber-hacker is that you don't get what you deserve. You get what you can get.

After burgers and shakes, he and Serafina went to see the new Tornado Surfer movie, and Patricia phoned just as they were debating what snacks to get from the concession stand. Patricia asked if this was a bad time, and Laurence said sort of.

"Oh, I can call back," Patricia said.

"What was it?"

Serafina wandered off to look at yogurt-covered pretzels,

probably annoyed at him for talking on the phone. Her long fingers lifted the packets of white twists, as though plucking flowers. Her nose twitched and she smiled, as if the pretzels had told her a joke. *I will not let you get away*, he said to Serafina in his mind.

"Just that my friends want to meet you. You know, my *special* friends. They know I told you my secret, and they want you to come over for dinner or something. Maybe Thursday?"

Laurence said yes right away. Whereas if he hadn't been in a hurry to hang up so he could go back to being a decent boyfriend, he would have contemplated the prospect of an evening with Patricia's "special friends" and maybe invented an excuse.

"Who was that?" Serafina said. Laurence said it was his friend from junior high, the weird one, which put Serafina in a position of being able to say she didn't think Patricia was that weird.

The movie sucked. Afterward, Serafina and Laurence went back to Serafina's place and had the best sex of Laurence's life thus far, the kind where you bite each other hard enough to leave toothdents and you keep crashing into each other long after you would have sworn you'd already broken everything. They held each other, both of them vibrating, until Laurence had to pee. He had to remind himself not to flush after only peeing, because everyone was conserving water. When Laurence got back to bed, Serafina had fallen into a cold sleep, and her elbow jutted into him.

* * *

LAURENCE DIDN'T LOOK up from his workstation between the movie date and Thursday evening, because the Ten Percent Project was in permanent crisis mode and Milton was blowing up Laurence's phone 24/7. Milton kept bringing up the idea, or rather the threat, of relocating Laurence and his team to a secure compound in the boonies so they could work with no distractions. As if Laurence wasn't already driving himself insane. As if this wasn't already his whole life.

Laurence had just enough time to run home, take a quick shower, and change before he had to be back in the Mission to see Patricia. They were meeting at some kind of used bookstore where one of the witches lived. Like, he was disabled or homebound or something, so he just spent all day and all night in his tiny bookshop, which Laurence suspected was illegal.

Laurence was the kind of sleep deprived where he saw LCD-monitor ghosts when he closed his eyes. When he was a couple blocks away from that bookstore, on the corner near the bacon-wrapped sausage cart, Laurence felt a panic attack starting. He was going to say the wrong thing, and these people would turn him into a knickknack. Like Mr. Rose.

"Practice your breathing," Laurence told himself. He managed to get some oxygen into his brain, and it was like a temporary workaround for sleep deprivation. He was probably dehydrated thanks to this crazy heat wave, so he bought some water from the bacon-wrapped sausage guy. Then he made himself walk to the three-story mall with the Spanish-language signs. For Patricia, whom he sensed he really wanted in his life.

The mall looked deserted, and there was only one bulb

on the ground floor to guide him to the winding staircase that led, past beauty-supply stores that looked dead, up to the top floor, where a sign read: "DANGER. BOOKSTORE IS OPEN." Laurence hesitated, then pushed open the doorway to Danger Bookstore, with a jangle of chimes.

The bookstore was one surprisingly spacious room, with an ancient rug that looked symmetrical until you noticed that the big wheel of fire and flowers at the center was rolling off to the right. Bookshelves covered the walls and also jutted sideways into the room, and they were divided into categories like "Exiles And Stowaways" or "Scary Love Stories." The books were about half-English, half-Spanish. Besides books, every shelf had memorabilia perched on its edge: an ancient ceremonial dagger, a plastic dragon, an assortment of ancient coins, and a whalebone that supposedly came from Queen Victoria's corset.

Laurence didn't get two steps inside Danger before someone ran an ultraviolet wand over him, to kill most of the bacteria on his skin. Patricia rose from one of the fancy upholstered chairs and hugged him, whispering that Laurence must not touch Ernesto, the man on the red chaise longue—the one who never left the bookstore. Ernesto hadn't been out in the sun for decades, but his skin was still a warm brown, and his long, high-cheekboned face had deep wrinkles. His gray hair was in a single braid, and he wore eyeliner or kohl around his eyes. He was wearing a crimson smoking jacket and silky blue pajama pants, so his outfit looked quasi-Hefnerian. He greeted Laurence without rising from his chaise.

Everybody was super-friendly. Laurence's first impression wasn't of any one person, but just of a gaggle of people all talking at the same time and clustering around him, with Patricia watching from across the room.

A short older lady with wide glasses on a string, and black-and-white hair in an elaborate bun, started telling Laurence about the time her shoe had fallen in love with a sock that was much too big. A tall, handsome Japanese man in a suit, with a neat beard, asked Laurence questions about Milton's finances, which he found himself answering without thinking. And a young person of indeterminate gender, with short spiky brown hair and a gray hoodie, wanted to know who Laurence's favorite superhero was. Ernesto kept quoting the poetry of Daisy Zamora.

They all just seemed so *nice*, Laurence didn't mind that they were all talking at once and overflowing his buffers. Probably this was because of the magic thing, and he ought to freak out. But he was too tired to make himself worry about things that didn't already worry him on their own. Laurence was nervous that he smelled like bacon-wrapped sausage fumes.

The bookstore had no musty "old books" smell, and instead it had a nice oaky aroma, similar to the way Laurence imagined the whiskey casks would be before you put Scotch into them for aging. This was a place where you would age well.

There was some debate over whether they would go out for dinner— everybody except Ernesto, that is—or just bring in food. "Maybe we could check out that new hipster tapas place," suggested Patricia.

"Tapas!" Dorothea, the elderly lady, clapped her hands, so her bracelets rang.

The person of unknown gender, whose name rather unhelpfully was Taylor, said perhaps Laurence would be more comfortable on neutral ground.

"Yes, yes, you must go," Ernesto said in his gravelly voice with a hint of a Latin accent. "Go! Do not worry about me at all." In the end, Ernesto insisted so loudly that they simply must leave him behind, everybody wound up offering to stay in with him.

Laurence couldn't help wondering if he'd just witnessed a wizard duel.

Somehow, they managed to catch the Korean taco truck driving from one location to another, and bought a dozen spicy bulgogi and barbecue tofu tacos while it was stopped at a red light. Laurence's taco had a lot of cilantro and onions, the way he secretly liked it. His anxiety melted away, and he envied Patricia for having such charming friends. If this had been a gathering of Laurence's tribe, by now someone would already have tried to prove they were the supreme expert on some topic. There would have been dick-measuring. Instead, these people just seemed to accept one another and feed each other tacos.

They all got seats on folding chairs or the handful of actual armchairs in the bookstore. Laurence wound up sitting between Taylor, the young person of indeterminate gender, and Dorothea, the lady of indeterminate age.

Dorothea smiled and leaned over as Laurence chewed his taco. "I once owned a restaurant that had doorways in a dozen cities around the world," she whispered. "Each entrance wore a different menu, advertising a different cuisine, but we had no kitchen. Just tables, tablecloths, and chairs. We carried the dishes back and forth, between the cities in different lands. So were we a restaurant, or a conduit?" Laurence wasn't sure if she was telling a real story or just taking the piss, or both. He stared, and all at once her face was full of laugh lines.

After dinner, Ernesto sauntered to a bookcase labeled "Parties That Already Ended," which was mainly histories of various empires. He removed a *Decline and Fall* with a flourish and the bookcase swung open, revealing a passageway leading to a secret bar, with a neon fairy on the wall and a sign proclaiming it to be the Green Wing. The Green Wing was another oblong, spacious room like Danger Books, but this one was dominated by a circular wooden bar in the center of the room, with a single rack full of absinthe. Art nouveau maidens and crystal dragons and parchment scripts adorned the bottles, which were every size and shape. A few people wearing corsets and poofy skirts were already drinking at a high table in the far corner, but they all waved at Ernesto.

Ernesto climbed inside the bar and started pouring from bottles into shakers. Patricia got next to Laurence long enough to whisper in his ear that he should be careful with any drink made or touched by Ernesto. "Take small sips," she advised. "If you plan on having a brain tomorrow."

None of these people seemed to be super-influential, and if they ruled the world they were doing a good job of hiding it. In fact, every other conversation was about how messed up the world was and how they wished things could be different.

Ernesto mixed Laurence something bright green that captured the neon light, and he caught Patricia's warning gaze before lifting it to his mouth. It smelled so delicious, he had to make a mighty effort to avoid pouring it through his lips. His mouth was full of wonder and joy, and there were so many sharp and sweet and bright flavors that he needed to keep sipping to identify half of them.

Laurence was legless. He stumbled until someone helped him into a brocaded eighteenth-century chair that he could not find his way out of again. He realized that this was a perfect opportunity to ask some questions about magic, since nobody could blame the drunk guy for being nosey. Right? He raised his head and looked into the swarm of blurry shapes and lights, and strained to form a not-too-rude question. He was unable to find a verb to save his life. Or a noun.

"It has been a pleasure to meet you, Laurence," Ernesto said, pulling a stool close to Laurence's face so that his eyeliner and unpinned long gray hair were in something like focus. He had lowered his voice to a conversational tone, but it still sounded theatrical, every word enunciated like a stage actor's diction. Ernesto was close enough for Laurence to catch the scent of an entire meadow pollinating coming off him. Close enough that if Laurence toppled forward, he would be touching Patricia's mentor. Which Patricia had said would be very bad. Ernesto leaned closer and Laurence shrank back.

"I must ask you a question or two," Ernesto said between sips from a martini glass, "about your intentions toward Patricia. She has confided in you, and we approve because everybody needs a confidant. But you must promise us to tell nobody else about the things she shares with you. Not your lover Serafina, not your friend Isobel, and certainly not your patron Milton. Can you make such a promise?"

"Uh," Laurence said, "yes. Yes I can."

"Will you humor me and swear to it? That if you break your promise, you will never speak another word again? To anyone." Ernesto laughed and waved one hand, as if this were a mere formality, but in the background Laurence saw Patricia shaking her head, her eyes wide with panic.

"Uh, sure," Laurence said. "I promise. And if I ever say anything about magic to anyone, I hope I lose my voice."

"Forever." Ernesto shrugged as if mentioning a minor detail.

"Forever," said Laurence.

"There's just one other favor we wanted to ask," said the Japanese guy, Kawashima, coming into focus next to Ernesto. They were almost touching. "We worry a lot about Patricia, you see. She went through a lot when she was younger. First that Theodolphus douchebag, and then later that regrettable business in Siberia."

"I hate it when you talk about me in the third person when I'm in the room," Patricia said. "Not to mention the way you're railroading my friend here."

"We want you to help us look out for her," Kawashima said to Laurence. "We have few rules, but our biggest taboo is against what we call Aggrandizement. Making yourself into a big deal. So we want you to support her and be her friend, in a way that none of us can. And yet also to remind her that she is just a person, just like anyone else, if she gets too high an opinion of herself."

"Will you do this for her, and for us?" Ernesto said.

Laurence thought for a moment they were going to ask him to agree that his hands would turn into fins if he didn't help keep Patricia's ego under control. But for this promise, just a vague "I'll do my best" seemed to suffice. Kawashima slapped him on the shoulder and everybody repeated a few times how nice it had been to meet him. Laurence felt his gorge rising. Someone guided him to a small toilet in the far corner of the absinthe bar, and he crouched over it for a good fifteen minutes until his stomach was empty.

Taylor and Patricia took Laurence for vegan donuts over on Valencia Street. His head was split in half and he was seeing spots. Taylor whispered something in Laurence's ear and he felt a bit more even-keel, plus coffee and ibuprofen helped too. "You did good," Taylor told him. "You were in the frickin lion's den and you were as cool as cream cheese."

"It just pisses me off," Patricia said. "They think I'm some kind of egomaniac, when all I want to do is make croissants and get on with my life. And they can't just ask Laurence to keep his trap shut, without putting a spell on him?"

The full weight of it hit Laurence then: They'd put a spell on him. A curse, really. If he spoke a word about magic or magicians to anybody, he would *never speak again*. He knew in his sore guts that this was a fact. Of course, there was no way to test, except the hard way. He stared at his thumbs, pivoting on the oaken table. What if he had to text people instead of talking to them, for the rest of his life?

"It's not like that," Taylor said to Patricia. "You should be grateful that you have people worrying about you. Ever since you moved here to Sucka Free, you've been... overcompensating. I feel bad about Siberia too, but we have to move on."

"Okay," Laurence said. "So now I am apparently under a..." He looked around the coffee place twice, trying to figure out if anyone was within earshot. "I am going to be facing certain constraints about what I can say to people who weren't in that bookstore tonight. So that means you can explain to me, right? You can tell me how this works. I'm just curious, is all."

"Sounds fair." Taylor handed him a second donut.

"Yeah, okay," Patricia said. "But not here. Maybe this weekend, we can go for a walk in the park. I remember how much you like the outdoors."

Laurence shuddered, which was probably a sign that he was starting to feel like himself again.

5

PATRICIA FELT JITTERY about throwing her first ever dinner party, because part of her clung to the fantasy of being someone who gathered cool people around her. A doyenne, someone who held witty salons. She cleaned the apartment for hours, made a playlist, and baked bread and bundt cake. Her roommates Deedee and Racheline made their famous "passive-aggressive lasagna," and Taylor showed up with shiny pants and a bowl of mixed greens. Kevin arrived in a deep cerulean waistcoat that matched the ribbon tying back his dreads, and he had brought weird cheeses. Patricia's bread filled the marigold kitchenette with a yeasty warmth, and she took a deep breath. She was a grown-up. She had this.

While Patricia served the salad, Kevin told Deedee and Racheline about the psychology of dog walking. (Some of the times Kevin had tried to sneak out after sleeping with Patricia, he'd run into her roommates, still half-awake on the couch. They'd started calling him Mr. No-Overnight, although not to his face.)

Deedee was talking about her ska band's latest gig, in which as usual the blue-haired, wiry singer exuded so much raw Kathleen Hanna-esque sexuality, nobody would ever guess that she identified as asexual.

Just as Patricia was fetching the bread, Taylor glanced around and said this was a nice apartment. Too bad Patricia might have to move to Portland soon.

"What?" Patricia dropped her mitt on the floor. She was standing by the open oven, so she felt frozen on one side and red hot on the other.

"Oh," Taylor leaned back, hands raised. "I thought you knew. They're thinking of sending you to Portland."

"Who is 'they'?" Kevin blinked.

"Forget I said anything. I was talking out of school." Taylor's smile had vanished, replaced with wide eyes and a clenched jaw. This was so like Taylor: They were so closed off you could barely tell what they were thinking most of the time, but then they would toss out these bombs just to see everyone jump.

Patricia seized the bread with her bare hands. Let it burn her. "This is bullshit. They can't make me move to Portland." In Portland, all the young witches lived in one group house, with a curfew, and a few older witches supervised them.

"When were you going to tell me you were moving to Portland?" Kevin said.

"I'm not," Patricia said, choking and coughing.

"Who's making you move?" Deedee asked from the sofa, pierced eyebrows raised. "I don't get it."

"Please forget I said anything." Taylor was squirming now. "Let's just eat."

Everybody stared at their plates and each other, but nobody said anything. Until Racheline broke the silence.

"Actually, I think you had better explain," said Racheline, who was older than everyone else and the master tenant on the apartment. "Who are these people, and why are they forcing Patricia to move?" Racheline was a quiet woman, a perennial grad student with wild red hair and a placid round face, but when she decided to assert herself everybody snapped to attention.

Everybody stared at Taylor, including Patricia. "I'm not allowed to say," Taylor stammered. "Let's just say Patricia and I both have the same… the same caseworker. And everybody worries about her. Like, she goes off on her own for days. She tries to take everything on herself, and she doesn't let anyone help her. She needs to let other people in."

"I let people in." Patricia felt bloodless. Her ears were ringing. "Right now, this moment, I am interacting with people." She should have known.

"It's true, though," Deedee said. "Patricia, we never see you. You live here, but you're never home. You never want to tell us anything about your life. You've been here nearly a year, but I feel like I don't know you at all."

Patricia tried to catch Kevin's eye, but it was like lassoing a hummingbird. She was still holding the bread, and it was burning her hands. "I'm really trying. Look at me trying *right this moment*. I'm having a party." She heard her timbre rising, until she sounded like her mother. Red haze, blinding her.

"Why did you have to ruin this for me?" She threw chunks of bread at Taylor, who covered their face. "Do you want some bread? Do you want some bread? Have some *fucking bread*!" Now she sounded exactly like her mom.

She threw away the rest of the bread and bailed out of there, crying and spitting on the dry sidewalk.

Patricia had fallen in love with Danger Bookstore on her first ever visit, and whenever she climbed the wooden staircase, she usually felt a little of the packing tape around her soul unwind. But this time, she just felt the stabbing in her neck get worse as she reached the top floor with its unsafe railing and threadbare purple carpet.

Ernesto sat in his usual chair, eating a microwaved TV dinner. He was in love with the invention of the microwave, both because it fit in with his love of instant gratification ("the lineaments of gratified desire") and because you couldn't leave food near him for more than a few minutes before it grew spiky white mold. He wore a silk robe, emerald pajamas, and fuzzy slippers, with William Blake's poems perched on one knee.

"What the hell," Patricia said before Ernesto could greet her. "When were you going to tell me about this plan to send me to Portland?" She almost knocked over the bookcase of Ideas Too Good To Be True.

"Please sit." Ernesto gestured at a clamshell armchair. Patricia tried to rebel for a moment, then gave up and sat. "We do not wish to send you away, but we have spoken about it. You make it difficult for us to watch over you. People want to care about you, and you will not let them."

"I've been trying." She shuffled in her chair. This was the worst day. "I've tried and tried. Everybody gives me grief about Aggrandizement, but I've tried so hard. I've been so careful."

"You are hearing the wrong thing." Ernesto rose and stood close to her, so she could feel his unnatural warmth. "People warn you about Aggrandizement, and you keep hearing the opposite of what they are saying."

Nobody knew why Ernesto was the way he was, but there were rumors. Like he'd cast a huge spell that had backfired. Or there'd been an endangered species, a rhino or something, and all the surviving animals had poured their life essence into one massive creature, which swelled with the lost potential of future generations. Maybe this towering *gestalt* stomped across the countryside, and everything it touched rotted. Blood bubbled from its eyes, ears, and stumpy toes, and it gave off an overripe stench. The creature, the story went, threatened a town full of innocent people until Ernesto took on its burden of excess life. Ernesto was so old, he'd gone to school back when Eltisley Academy and The Maze were still two separate schools.

"Everybody thinks Siberia was my fault," Patricia said. "Because I was too proud or whatever. Too reckless." In her mind, Patricia saw before-and-after images of Toby, first alive then dead, like a GIF from Hell. "They think I'm still too arrogant now. I'm just trying to help."

"Listen harder," Ernesto said. Most of the time, the thick eyeliner made his eyes appear lively, unfocused. But now, he seemed to see into the grungiest corners of Patricia's psyche.

Ernesto went back to his chaise, and Patricia was left trying to figure this out. It was one of those annoying tests: both a dirty trick and a healing exercise. She was pretty sure she'd been listening just fine. She was ready to throw foodstuffs again.

"Fine," Patricia said after she decided she wasn't going to crack this tonight. "I will listen harder. And I will try to be less self-absorbed, and more humble. I will let people in, if anybody even wants to be my friend after tonight."

"I spent thirty bitter years trying to find a way to leave this place," Ernesto said so quietly, she had to lean perilously close. He gestured at the room full of books, with his eyes. "Until at last, I accepted that this imprisonment was a price that I had chosen to pay. Now, I enjoy my situation as much as I can. But you have not yet begun to experience the pain of being a witch. The mistakes. All the regrets. The only thing that will make such power bearable is to remember how small you are."

He went back to William Blake, and Patricia couldn't tell if this meant their conversation was over.

"So does this mean I'm not going to Portland?"

"Listen harder," was all Ernesto said from behind the book. "We do not want to send you away. Do not make us."

"Okay." Patricia still felt raw and desperate inside. She realized she ought to leave before Ernesto offered to make her a cocktail next door, because she did not want to get falling-upwards drunk right now.

As soon as she got out of Danger, she saw her phone was full of texts and voicemails. She called Kevin, who was worried, and she was like, "I'm fine, except I need a drink."

Half an hour later, she leaned on Kevin's crushed-velvet frock coat and pounded a Corona in the swampy back room of the art bar on 16th, with fresh graffiti on the wall and a DJ spinning classic hip-hop. Kevin was drinking Pimm's with a fat cucumber slice and not asking her what that scene at dinner had been about. He looked amazing in the bar's golden light, sideburns setting off the smooth planes of his face.

"I'm fine," Patricia kept saying. "I'm sorry you had to see that. I'm fine. I sorted it out."

But as her tongue greeted the lime wedge bobbing up to the lip of the bottle and tasted the pulp mixed with beer, she remembered how Kevin wouldn't even look her in the eye when everybody else was accusing her of being a toxic loner.

"We should talk about what this is, right? You and me. What we're doing," she started to say, trying to make herself heard over the DJ without shouting. "I feel like we tried too hard not to label our relationship, and that became a label in itself."

"I have something I have to tell you," Kevin said, his eyes bigger and sadder than usual.

"I am ready to open up about my feelings. I feel…" Patricia searched for the right words. "I feel good, about us. I care about you, a lot, and I am open to—"

"I met someone else," Kevin blurted. "Her name is Mara. She's also a webcomics artist of some renown. She lives in the East Bay. We met only in the past fortnight, but this already shows signs of becoming serious. I was not even looking, but my Caddy pinged me with twenty-nine points of convergence between Mara and myself." He gazed into his Pimm's. "You and I never said we were exclusive, or even that we were dating."

"Umm." Patricia chewed her thumb, a habit she'd quit years ago. "I'm happy... happy. For you. I'm happy for you."

"Patricia." Kevin took both her hands. "You are utterly mad, but delightful. I feel so overjoyed to have gotten to know you. But I have been a fool too many times already. And I tried, I really did, to talk to you about our relationship, on five separate occasions. In the park when we were roller-skating, and also at that pizza bar..."

As Kevin listed these moments, she could see them with perfect clarity: all the missed cues and deflections, all the abortive moments of intimacy. All this time, she had been thinking of him as the one with commitment issues. Somewhere along the line, she had become an asshole.

"Thank you for being honest with me," Patricia said. She sat and finished her drink, until it was just lime rind and bitter pulp.

Patricia wound up in Dolores Park at midnight. The heat still felt as intense as direct sunlight, and her mouth was dry. She couldn't go home and face Deedee and Racheline. For some reason, Patricia found herself calling her sister, Roberta, whom she hadn't talked to in months (although she'd had a couple conversations about Roberta with her parents).

"Hey, Bert."

"Hi, Trish. How is everything going?"

"I'm okay." Patricia took a breath, which came out staccato. She stared at the playground rocket ship and the Victorian houses with their pregnant windows. "I'm sort of okay. I just… Do you ever feel like you're just throwing away the people in your life? Like, being so self-centered that people just fall away?"

Roberta laughed. "I have the opposite problem: I have a hard time disposing of the bodies. Ha ha. Trish, listen to me for once in your life. I know we never got along and I was partway responsible for you running away from home. But one thing I know about you is, you're a generous person. You're a big bleeding heart. People have fucked with you, including me—especially me—so you have a lot of defense mechanisms. But you always put yourself on the line for other people. You don't push people away—you try to do everything for people, and then they don't get to do anything for you. Please don't let any idiots tell you otherwise, okay?"

Patricia was bawling, even worse than before, right there in the park. She felt it pour down her face, and she was full of a sense that everything was broken and full of sweetness. She had never realized her sister thought that way about her.

"If anybody tries to tell you that you're selfish," Roberta said, "send them to me and I'll snap their necks for you. Okay?"

"Okay," Patricia stammered. They talked a bit more—about Roberta's musical-theater disasters, and her latest attempt to go straight-edge—and then at last, Patricia felt ready to go home and face her roommates, who were on the couch like always. They slid over, without comment, to let Patricia watch TV with them.

* * *

PATRICIA HAD ANOTHER one of her dreams about being lost in the woods, this time running with a pack of deer, a barbarian yell in her throat and the scent of tree sap in her nostrils. She ran with her elbows and her stomach and her knees, until she couldn't breathe. Patricia stumbled and fell onto her hands, gasping, laughing. She looked up and there was that big bird-shaped Tree again, with the mindful gaze coming through its branches. Patricia walked up and touched it with her palms against its ropey bark, feeling the power rising and churning inside of it. Touching that weird Tree from her childhood fancies, Patricia felt as though she could heal an entire army with a single breath. Air rushed through the Tree, like it was drawing breath to speak to her in its stentorian whoosh… then she woke up. She'd overslept, in spite of her alarm.

PATRICIA WAS FIXING Reginald's sink, which had one of those glitchy new valves that were supposed to shut off the water after a couple minutes, and she found herself talking about her breakup with Kevin. "I mean, I guess it's for the best, since it was never going to work. But it's a symptom of the larger problem, that I never have time for anybody, and I keep isolating myself, and I'm basically doomed to wind up alone forever. Right?"

She expected Reginald to offer some bromides about how she just needed to be herself, but instead he said, "Get. A. Caddy."

"What?" She nearly bonked her head on the sink.

"Get a Caddy. It will change your life, I am not kidding. At all. You become totally connected to all the people in your life. Not like regular social networking, either. It's uncanny: You will just run into people you know, in person, when you most need to see them. I could barely afford one on my fixed income, but it turned out to be the best investment I ever made."

"I always thought they were just for Mission hipsters," Patricia said. "Anyway, it sounds creepy."

"Seriously, no. It's not creepy, and it's so easy to use. It doesn't spy on you, or tell you to stalk your friends. I've never felt like it was invading my privacy. It just… makes serendipity happen more often. It's unobtrusive, and doesn't give you a bunch of alerts. But you'll always know what's the one party you shouldn't miss. I was feeling isolated, even with your much-appreciated visits. And then I got this Caddy, and I feel as though I'm back in my own life again."

In spite of Reginald's insistence that the Caddy was not at all creepy, his hard sell was in itself kind of creepy. He sounded like someone who had just joined a cult. Patricia vowed that she would never, ever buy a Caddy. Ever.

Two days later, Patricia was in the Caddy store, near Union Square. It was narrow, with curving walls that drew you toward the counter at the back, like a stream curving around some rocks. The walls seemed to glow. Patricia picked up a Caddy from the display on one wall, and the screen flared to life. There was a swirl of colors, and then it resolved into a wheel shape. The wheel had swirls coming out of its center, sort of like a Daoist symbol, and each of them got bigger at her touch. They included things like Communication, Orientation, Self-Expression, and Introspection.

She paid for the Caddy with her ATM card and felt like a total wanker. Next she would go get some giant square dark glasses and a medallion that changed color depending on how recently she got laid. God.

Still, it was a fun toy—and at this point she would try anything to make herself feel less claustrophobic and self-absorbed. Although there was something perverse about buying a device that offered a huge "Introspection" wedge, in the hope that it would make her more social.

That night, Patricia sat in bed and played with her new Caddy. It was not that different from a standard tablet, except for the guitar-pick shape, and the way it insisted on asking demented questions to customize your experience. Like, "Would you rather lose your sense of smell or taste? When was the last time you were glad you stayed up late?" There was a checkbox to disable the questions, but everybody said they made it work a million times better and they tapered off after a day.

And sure enough, after a few days, the Caddy was steering her oh-so-gently toward happy accidents and little discoveries. There was that little egg-themed restaurant in Hayes Valley, where everybody sat in egg chairs and ate egg dishes, from Scotch eggs to Chinese-style egg tarts. And drank cocktails with egg yolks. The whole place was an allergy waiting to happen, but it was also warm and cozy and there was a faint smell of butter and sugar in the air, making her feel like she was in her grandma's kitchen and five years old.

The Caddy helped Patricia to figure out which bus to take to avoid being late for work, and when one of her mary janes broke a strap, the Caddy steered her to a hole-in-the-wall place that fixed it on the spot. Within a few days, Patricia had a low-level awareness of what a dozen or so people in her life were up to at any given moment, without feeling overwhelmed. She managed to grab lunch with a very apologetic Taylor and make time for an ice-cream conference with Deedee and Racheline.

Then something weird happened. Right around the time Patricia had gotten used to the Caddy and started thinking of it as an extension of her personality rather than an appliance—after about five days, in other words—she started running into Laurence. A lot. At lunch, at dinner, at tea, on the bus, in the park. At first, it didn't seem like a big deal, since San Francisco was a tiny town, but after a couple days, it felt weird. She would see Laurence, say hi and mumble a few awkward words, and then bail. And then the process would repeat, a couple hours later. She would think he was stalking her, except that she was the least stalkable person ever. The third day, she tried shaking up her routine, going for vegan soul food in the Outer Sunset, and somehow Laurence was there, too, going to some kind of Musée Mécanique revival.

"Uh, hey again," he said. He started to say something else, but seemed to think better of it.

She was already saying "Hey" and turning back to talk to Taylor.

She wasn't trying to avoid Laurence, exactly. But at the same time, she wasn't dying to hang out with someone who had promised Kawashima that he would keep her from getting a swelled head. She already had enough people giving her shit for Aggrandizement, she didn't need a friend who was *sworn* to tear her down. Of course, this had been Kawashima's plan all along: If he'd told Patricia she wasn't allowed to hang out with Laurence any more, she'd have been pissed, and would have hung out with Laurence anyway. So instead, Kawashima tells Patricia to hang out with Laurence all she wants—then enlists Laurence's aid in cutting her down to size. Thus ensuring she'll never want to see him again. That she saw through this ploy did not prevent it from working perfectly.

On her break at work, she picked up her Caddy and scrawled, "What's the deal with Laurence?" with her finger. The Caddy responded by telling her some facts about Laurence, including some physics prize he'd won at MIT. She couldn't help feeling like the Caddy understood perfectly well what she was asking, and was just playing dumb.

She decided to leave the Caddy at home. And for a whole day, her life was boring again, just missing the bus and not connecting with her friends and not having time to grab dinner in the middle of running errands. The rain started as she was heading home for the night and she had forgotten her umbrella, and there was no place to buy one. And of course she had to run ten blocks to catch the bus—which left just as she got there. She waited another half an hour, under a disintegrating canopy, for the next bus, and when she staggered on board, drenched as a sponge, the only empty seat was next to Laurence.

"Oh shit," Laurence said. "You are fucking soaked. Jesus, I'm so sorry. That is fucked up." He gave her his nice cotton hoodie to use as a towel. She tried to say it was cool and he didn't have to do that, but he kept shoving it at her.

"Thanks." Patricia patted herself with the hoodie as best she could. "At least the heat wave finally broke."

"This bus doesn't go to your place, does it? I mean, you have to change buses," Laurence said. Patricia admitted that this might be the case. "Well, I understand if you need to get home right away. But there's a bar up here on the right that has an actual open fireplace, and they serve hot toddies and stuff. We ought to get you warmed up as soon as possible."

The bar had a "hunting lodge" theme, complete with slabs of wood covering the walls and faux animal heads coming out of one wall that squicked Patricia at first. But they got a primo spot in front of the fireplace, and the scent of mesquite and woodsmoke was a rain antidote. The stereo played an album of acoustic covers of Steely Dan, featuring a bluesy female mezzo-soprano, and Patricia guessed it was called Steely Danielle.

Laurence brought Patricia a mug of hot chocolate and a shot of nice whiskey, which she could consume together or separately, her choice. She drank most of the hot chocolate and then sipped the whiskey to burn away the milky sweetness. The whiskey was sharp in the way that really nice cheese is sharp. She started to feel comfortable in her own skin again.

"I suspect I'm being punished for leaving my Caddy at home," Patricia confessed.

This was not the first time Laurence had heard people talk about their Caddies as if they were jealous gods. He told her about all the odd superstitions—for lack of a better word—that people had about their teardrop-shaped computers. One person might believe his Caddy saved his marriage, and then you'd run into someone else whose Caddy destroyed her marriage, but she later decided it was for the best. People sold their houses and got rid of their cars because their Caddies showed them a simpler way to live. A few people even found God, actual God, thanks to their Caddies. People were attached to them in a way that nobody ever had been to their iPhones or BlackBerries.

"That's not creepy at all," said Patricia. She wondered if she should just throw it away.

"On the one hand, it's finally fulfilling the promise of technology, of making your life easier," Laurence said. "Simpler, or more full of excitement, depending on what you want. On the other hand, people are outsourcing some crucial life stuff to these things."

"I notice you don't have a Caddy." Patricia's whiskey glass was empty. She bought another round for herself and Laurence.

"I have three at home," Laurence said. "I jailbroke one, and now it doesn't work quite the same. There's something about the OS that resists any kind of analysis. You can install Wildberry Linux on them and they work just like any other tablet, but nothing fancy."

They fell into a long silence. The fire crackled and the Steely Dan cover CD reached its triumphant final track, which was predictably "Rikki Don't Lose That Number." Patricia felt like she should say something about why she'd been avoiding Laurence, in spite of her Caddy's attempts to smush them together. She wasn't sure what to say.

"That promise," Laurence said out of nowhere. "The one that your friend made me agree to. Not the first one, the one where I go mute forever if I blab, but the other one."

"Yeah." Patricia tensed and felt a chill on the inside, in spite of the firelight and whiskey glow.

"It's riddled with loopholes," Laurence said. "Even apart from the fact that there's no penalty for breaking it. I mean, I never should have agreed to it, and I wouldn't have if I'd been less drunk. It's not my job to police someone else's self-esteem, not in any sane world. But in any case, it's a meaningless promise."

"How so?"

"I've been thinking about it a lot, and the wording is so imprecise that it's not even a promise, in any real sense. I'm supposed to keep you from getting an unrealistically high opinion of yourself—but if, say, I happen to believe that you're the coolest person I know, then I'm unlikely to think you're overestimating your own coolness. It's dependent on my own opinion, plus my estimation of what your opinion of yourself is. That's a whole bunch of subjective criteria, right there. Add to that the fact that I only said I would do my best, which is yet another subjective judgment. If I made it my life's work to break that promise, I'm not sure I could find a way."

"Huh." And now Patricia felt dumb, so Laurence had succeeded in crushing her ego after all. She should have seen that Kawashima was just creating one of his intentionally flimsy traps, where the real trap is that you fool yourself into believing the snare to be robust. But she also felt better—and then the part where Laurence sort of hinted that he thought she was the coolest person he'd ever met sank in as well, even if it was just a rhetorical supposition.

"And you know these people way better than I do," Laurence said, "but it strikes me that this thing about Aggrandizement is a way of controlling you. They don't want you to use your power, except for however they tell you to."

At last, the rain stopped and Patricia had dried out except for her shoes. They headed for two separate bus stops, although their route coincided for four blocks. They hugged goodbye. When Patricia got home she gazed at her Caddy while brushing her teeth, like a blank mirror, and it filled her in on everything she'd missed. Before she sank into her bed, she tossed the Caddy back in her shoulder bag.

6

SOMETIMES LAURENCE ZONED out and imagined walking on another Earth-like planet. The weird gravity. The different mix of oxygen, carbon, and nitrogen in the air. Types of life that might defy our definitions of "plant" or "animal." More than one moon, maybe more than one sun. His heart could burst, just with the newness of it: digging bare feet into soil that no human toes had ploughed, under a brazen sky that proclaimed all the things we had thought our limits were merely our prejudices. And then he snapped back, to the reality that his team was stuck: no closer to opening up the final frontier than a year earlier.

He would come out of his reverie to find another e-mail from Milton, who wanted progress reports that included actual progress. These e-mails contained phrases like "Humanity strides along a widening precipice." Some days, Laurence struggled to motivate himself to go in to work, and once there, he couldn't bring himself to leave.

When he talked to Serafina about his work, he kept the

details vague—as far as Serafina knew, his team was working on a theoretical antigravity thing, that could yield some practical application years from now, if ever. But he longed to show off the finished product to Serafina, and spread his arms wide as the Pathway to Infinity burst open behind him. That would be the crowning moment of his life.

Which is why, when Priya said she wanted to be the first weightless person on Earth, Laurence scarcely hesitated.

PRIYA HAD THESE amazing hands that she gestured with when she talked, and it was like she was making shapes in your brain. Her fingers were long and rippled with indentations, and she wore chunky rings, with big fake sapphires. Plus pastel acrylic nails.

Sougata had been staring at Priya for weeks across the hAckOllEctIvE, watching her solder, wearing safety goggles that only made her look more elfin. She constructed some kind of wireless-enabled burrowing robot that could hide small objects where you'd never find them without the right PGP key.

Laurence was like, "You should sneak her up here and show her the antigrav, and the not-quite-antimatter. She'll be yours forever, man."

Anya and Tanaa fought against letting Priya inside their headquarters, on the grounds that she would tell everyone else in the hAckOllEctIvE, and there would be drama. The hackerspace had some cool people, but there were also people who still thought it was awesome to build your own two-second time machine.

"We're doing serious research here," said Tanaa. "Nothing is a toy. Well, except for Six-Fingered Steve." She gestured at the tiny tap-dancing robot, who heard his name and made jazz hands with too many digits. Disturbing, as always.

"This is a top-secret research facility, disguised as a clubhouse," concurred Anya, who was wearing jodhpurs and riding boots, plus a puffy T-shirt with Debbie Harry on it, with a belt around Debbie's neck. Anya had just dyed her hair candy pink.

Laurence and Sougata both looked around the loft, with the exposed ceiling beams and posters for The Gossip and James Bond movies, plus beanbags and a corduroy sofa. The disco ball doubled as a security system. The "clubhouse" disguise was very cunning indeed.

Soon enough, Priya was flexing one long, sparkly finger at Six-Fingered Steve and watching him dance. "His reaction time is impressive," she said with only a slight Punjabi accent. "I would have given him some kind of central gyro, for balance."

After a couple hours hanging out and tinkering, Priya was like part of the group and she swore on all that was unholy not to tell anybody else about their hideaway. Laurence explained to her about the antigravity thing: "The goal is to negate gravity, to change the spin of all the electrons in your body so that your mass is effectively shunted somewhere else."

"Like another dimension," Priya said. "Because of the theory that gravity is a stronger force in other universes."

"Yes," said Tanaa. "So you would still be here, but your mass would be elsewhere."

"All of this is just a means to an end, though," added Sougata. "We think if we can solve the gravity problem, we can create stable worm—" Anya kicked him and he coughed and said, "Pie. Worm pie."

"Mmm," said Priya, "worm pie. My favorite."

"It's a delicacy," said Laurence. "Someplace. We don't know where, but we're going to go there and enter a contest, once we've perfected our recipe."

A couple weeks passed. Everybody got used to having Priya around. Meanwhile, the team finally had some real success with the machine. First a golf ball, then a baseball, then a boiled egg, then a hamster named Ben—they all let slip their surly bonds at the flick of a button, then returned to normal weight at a second button press.

In theory, a person could crouch on the glowy white disk, with the giant red nozzle aimed at it, and be bathed in the full effect of the antigravitation rays.

"But I'd want to do a lot more testing before doing any human subjects experimentation," said Anya.

"Can I try it?" Priya said. "I want to be the first weightless person on Earth, so my name can be misspelled in every record book, forever and ever." Anya started to protest, but then Priya said, "Conventional Newtonian gravitation is *so* last year."

Everybody giggled. Priya always knew just the right things to say.

The others looked at Laurence, who slowly nodded. "Yes," he said. "I think we can make that happen."

An hour later, Laurence was frantically dialing Patricia, praying that she hadn't left her cell phone at home or turned it off for some witchy festival. She picked up, and he started talking immediately. "Hey, I desperately need your help. We have tampered with forces that people were not meant to fuck around with, and we seem to have pushed Sougata's girlfriend into another plane of existence, where we have no way of locating her or even proving that she still exists, and we've basically exhausted all scientific options and don't worry I won't tell the others about your secret, just please help."

"Wait a minute," Patricia said. "Sougata has a girlfriend now?"

"We didn't account for the extra mass, and the correspondingly greater level of attraction in the other universe," said Laurence, as if that answered her question.

"I'll be there in a few," Patricia said. "I'm just up the street."

When Patricia got to the cement blockhouse and Laurence came down to let her in, she barely had time to impress upon him the fact that his friends must not find out about her skills. No matter what.

"Sure, sure," said Laurence. "Of course. Soul of discretion. No worries at all. Just please, please, if you can, please help. I will be in your debt forever." He was climbing the stairs behind her and as they reached the top step, Patricia turned and practically glared at him.

"Never, ever say that to me." Incandescent.

"Say what?"

"The thing about being in my debt. It has a different meaning for me than it does for most people."

"Oh. Oh, right. Okay. Well, I will be super-grateful. Anyway, it's over here."

Sougata, Anya, and Tanaa stared at the shining white circle under the big ray-gun barrel, and didn't acknowledge Patricia's arrival until she was standing next to them.

"What's she doing here?" Sougata said.

"She can help," Laurence said. "I can't explain. But she can help."

"What's her area of expertise again?" Anya folded her arms over her unicorn shirt.

"Dimensional transcendentalism," said Patricia.

"You just stole that from *Doctor Who*. This is not a joke, this is serious," Anya said.

"Okay, look," Patricia said. "Do you guys want your friend back or not?" Everybody nodded slowly. "Then just stand the fuck back and let me work."

Everybody kept clustering around Patricia and trying to see what she was doing, and Laurence worried that she was going to put so much energy into obfuscation that she wouldn't be able to reach into the hole in the universe and pull Priya out. Patricia was wearing a strapless red dress that teased you with the sweep of her pale shoulders and a hint of cleavage. As she turned her back to Laurence and stared into the space over the white circle, he couldn't help noticing the dimples behind her knees and the perfect curves of her calves and ankles.

Laurence still wasn't entirely sure what had happened to Priya. He had no real data. She'd floated, the way Ben and the various objects had. Her sandals had fallen as her feet lifted off, and her bright toenails had wriggled. She'd laughed and clapped her hands and said, "Suck on this, Newton!" Everybody was high-fiving and making upskirting jokes... and then she'd just gone "pop." It was sort of a balloon-popping, squelching sound, as if something sucked her into an invisible hole. All that remained were her sandals, one of which was upside down. Laurence had felt a compulsion to pick them up and place them neatly beside each other next to the beanbag, as if she'd come back for them in a moment.

Patricia turned and gestured to Laurence that she needed some space here. He grabbed Sougata's arm and dragged him toward the exit, beckoning for Anya and Tanaa to follow. "We need to get her some supplies," Laurence said. "Patricia needs boiling water, dry ice, regular ice, half a dozen jailbroken Caddies, and a few other things. Come on, people, let's haul ass." He hustled them out of there.

"If this doesn't work—" said Sougata.

"If you're just wasting our time while Priya is in danger—" said Anya.

"We will end you," Tanaa concluded.

Laurence looked back at the steel door, which he'd slammed shut behind them, and inhaled loudly through his teeth. He felt as if he, too, were about to be sucked into a completely unknowable other space.

"Let's hurry up and get those supplies," he said. He kept adding more and more items to the list, some of which they'd need to purchase at the grocery store or borrow from people in the hackerspace, a few blocks away.

"Damn damn damn," Sougata kept saying under his breath. "Damn, it's all over, I'm so sorry, Priya." Anya put her hand on Sougata's shoulder.

Laurence was putting a lot of energy into pretending that the scavenger hunt he was sending his friends on was vital and time sensitive. And then he looked down at his phone and saw a text from Patricia: "come back pls. alone." He gestured for the others to go out for supplies, then turned and sprinted back upstairs.

The loft looked darker than usual, as if all the light were being eaten by something. The movie posters resembled ghost portraits in a haunted mansion. Laurence stepped in a beanbag and almost face-planted. He crept past machines that he worked with every day, which suddenly looked sinister with their sharp edges, metallic protrusions, and sputtering LEDs. There was a rank beautiful scent, akin to burning lavender.

Patricia glowed at the other end of the long, thin space, with the same pale light as the white circle where Priya had vanished. The only point of brightness in the entire space.

"How's it going?" Laurence stage-whispered, as though they were in a crypt.

"It's going okay," Patricia said in a normal voice. "Priya is safe for now. She is going to need a lot of vodka and loud music when she gets out of where she is. She drinks, right? She's not straight edge?"

"She drinks," Laurence said. That Priya's taste in intoxicants was an issue reassured him a lot. But he was waiting for the bad news. Patricia just stared at him as if she was trying to decide something. She was several inches shorter than him, but in this moment she seemed taller. Her deep-set eyes narrowed as she sized him up.

"So," Laurence said after a moment of this. "What can I do?"

"Remember what I told you not to say to me?" Patricia said. "When you brought me up here."

Laurence had another "standing on the edge of the abyss" feeling. Total heedless terror. He shrugged, and it passed. "Sure," he said. "I remember."

"I need you to owe me something," Patricia said, "or this won't work. I'm really sorry. I tried to do it every other way, and none of them succeeded. In the end, the most powerful magic is often transactional in some way. I'll explain more some other time."

"Okay, sure," Laurence said. "Whatever you want. Name it."

"If I bring your friend back," Patricia said. She chewed her lip and seemed to be trying one last time to think of an alternative. "If I bring your friend back, you have to give me the smallest thing you own."

"That's it?" Laurence laughed with relief. "Done." He grabbed her hand with both hands and shook.

Laurence couldn't stop laughing, because he'd gotten himself all worked up and it turned out to be nothing. He owned so many tiny items—the smallest thing he owned was probably some ridiculous gadget he'd paid too much for. He laughed until he croaked, and his eyes clouded, and when he wiped his eyes clear, Patricia and he were no longer alone.

Priya stood on the white platform for a moment, gaping at the two faces below. She raised her elegant hands to her face, as if astonished to see that she still had hands. She tried to form words and just made a fish mouth instead. She started to wobble off the platform, and Laurence guided her to sit down.

"She's seen some things that eyes weren't built for," Patricia said. "Like I said. Vodka, and lots of it. And loud music. I recommend Benders. I'll even come and have a drink or two."

Laurence steered Priya onto a beanbag, where she was hugging herself and making low guttural sounds. He texted the others to come back up, then turned back to Patricia.

"Oh my god, thank you," Laurence said. "Am I allowed to say thank you? Or is that bad?"

"You're allowed to say thank you." Patricia laughed.

He ran over and hugged her so tight, he nearly squeezed the life out of her, and he felt her bare shoulders against his chest and her face against his neck. She made a slight protesting "squick" noise and Laurence slackened a tiny bit but kept hugging her.

"Thank you thank you thank you." Laurence's eyes felt splashy. His senses filled with clementines and softness and warmth. He blessed the day his parents decided he should be outdoorsy.

The others had come back, and Sougata was life-preservering Priya with tears rushing down his face. "I thought I'd lost you forever, I couldn't have lived with myself, I never want to let go of you," he said.

"There were colors outside the visual spectrum," Priya managed to say. "But I could still see them. I can't stop seeing them now."

"Vodka and loud music," Patricia called out from Laurence's death grip. "Stat. It's an essential part of her recovery process."

They rushed Priya to Benders Bar & Grill. There was some talk of going to the ER instead, but Patricia nixed it, and nobody wanted to argue with the person who'd saved all their asses.

"But how did you do it?" Anya kept asking. "What did you do?"

"I used my sonic screwdriver."

"No, really. What did you do?"

"I reversed the polarity of the neutron flow."

"Stop giving *Doctor Who* answers! Tell me the truth!"

"It was sort of a wibbly wobbly," Patricia said, fully teasing Anya now. Booze really was medicinal, after a near-death experience. Holding a drink in both hands and letting it corrode the topmost layer of his mouth and throat, Laurence felt a spiritual relationship with Bushmills.

Priya, too, seemed to be pretty much back to normal as soon as she had a couple swigs of vodka and heard the sound system blasting "Cum On Feel The Noize." She started dancing on her stool and making jokes about heavy-metal hair and body shots. Laurence made sure the liquor kept coming, so Priya would get her recommended dosage. Whatever she'd experienced during her time outside of our universe, she seemed to be rinsing it out of her mind, and maybe if they were lucky, the whole evening would feel like a weird blur to her when she woke with a hangover. As a strategy for scrambling someone's short-term memories, it didn't seem bad.

Everybody kept toasting Patricia and buying her drinks and laughing at her dumb jokes, as if they were ultraconscious that she'd pulled their fat out of the fire. When Patricia went to the ladies', Sougata leaned over and said to Laurence, "Seriously, where did you find her? She is amazing. She's like the weirdest genius I've ever met, and that's actually saying something." Tanaa and Anya both chimed in. But at the same time, Laurence noticed that none of his friends would quite look at Patricia, and they kept talking past her rather than to her. These people hated superstition, but they were treating his friend like a bad-luck charm.

Patricia watched Priya like a freaking hawk and touched her hand every now and then, as if her touch had healing properties. Which it probably did. Patricia paid no attention to the rest of them, even Laurence. Patricia might be an antisocial weirdo who wandered at three in the morning talking to rats, but she had unlimited gentleness for people when they needed it. Patricia's black hair was swept back, and her face had a beaconlike quality to it that went along with the intentness of her gaze.

Laurence had a moment of counting up how many of his secrets Patricia knew, and feeling good about it. He felt a weird sense of pride that he had found someone he trusted so much. Like he'd chosen well, even if it was mostly by accident.

He walked her home, fighting the urge to embrace her randomly. She was laughing and shaking her head. "God, it was iffy for a few moments there," she said. "Your friend got pretty lost. Plus it's a miracle she didn't get squashed by the weird gravitational effects of the space she was in."

"I wonder how many other things in our world are just the shadows of things in other places," Laurence said, forming the thought as he spoke. "I mean, we always suspected that gravity was so weak in our world because most of it was in another dimension. But what else? Light? Time? Some of our emotions? I mean, the longer I live, the more I feel like the stuff I see and feel is like a tracing of the outline of the real stuff that's beyond our perceptions."

"Like Plato's cave," Patricia said.

"Like Plato's cave," Laurence agreed.

"I don't know," Patricia said. "I mean, we're grown-ups now. Allegedly. And we feel things less than we did when we were kids, because we've grown so much scar tissue, or our senses have dulled. I think it's probably healthy. I mean, little kids don't have to make decisions, unless something's very wrong. Maybe you can't make up your mind as easily, if you feel too much. You know?"

But in fact, Laurence was feeling sensations and emotions more vividly than he had since he was little. The streetlights and car headlights and neon signs were blazing with life, and he felt his heart expand and contract, and he could smell charcoal burning someplace nearby. He turned to look into Patricia's bright, sad smile.

"Patricia," he said. "I really really appreciate your help.

And more than that, I am so damn glad to know you. I'm so sorry I ran out on you when you talked to your cat, when we were kids. I will never run out on you again. That's a promise I'm giving you, free and clear. I'm probably not supposed to make promises to someone like you, either, right? But I don't care. Thank you for being my friend."

"You're welcome," Patricia said. They had reached her front door. "Same to you. All of it. I'm super-lucky to have you as a friend too. And I'll never run out on you, either."

They stood at her door. At some point, their hands had started touching. And they just stood there, looking at each other, hands in hands.

Patricia's smile turned sadder, as if she knew something that Laurence hadn't figured out yet. "Don't forget the thing you owe me," she said. "Or it'll be very bad. I'm sorry." Then she went inside her house and the door slammed shut.

Laurence was still jangling with a mixture of tipsiness, relief, and emotional gushiness, the whole way home. But he was also feeling a smidge uneasy about the "smallest thing" thing. No big deal, most likely, but Patricia had seemed kind of intense about it. Laurence actually clicked his heels together as he crossed the street in big, hungry strides. He had never done Ecstasy or any kind of mood elevator, but he sort of imagined this is how they would feel.

When he got home, he crashed. The elation wore off so fast, he had to sit down. He was so drained, he felt like he was going to pass out if he didn't get to sleep right away. And then he thought about the "smallest thing" that he had to give to Patricia. He could look for it in the morning, or in a couple days, or whatever. She hadn't specified a time limit, or anything… he probably had a few days to find it.

But then Laurence started wondering what it could be and how he was supposed to know. Was it the smallest by volume? By weight? Or just overall size? He owned some pieces of lint that were beyond tiny, but he was pretty sure that wouldn't count. To be fair, he had to pick something he owned, which meant something that had at least a nominal resale value. You don't own something you couldn't sell, right?

So. He had a USB drive that he'd brought home from the Ten Percent Project office, which was the size of two peas— but when he texted Patricia, she said it couldn't be something he'd borrowed. She needed something he owned himself, free and clear. That ruled out the electronic components and tools littering his desk and shelves, which were all technically on loan from Milton.

Laurence rummaged through his desk. Pencils, pens… that little figurine of Mega Man was pretty tiny, move that to the top of the list. He started a pile, and rummaged through drawers and boxes and closet shelves, trying not to wake Isobel. And then, all at once, he knew.

"Oh no," he said aloud. "Not that. No no no. Fuck. Fuck no." He couldn't breathe. Like an asthma attack, or something. All of the joy he'd felt earlier slipped away as if it had never been there, and he felt instead like he'd been kicked in the solar plexus with a sharp steel toe.

He stayed up most of the rest of the night, searching and searching. But he never found anything that counted as a real possession and was smaller than his grandmother's ring.

He brought it to Patricia the next morning, eyes sore from lack of sleep. "This is the only thing I have of my grandmother's," he told her. "She gave it to me when she was dying."

"I'm sorry," Patricia said. She stood in the doorway of her apartment building, in a bathrobe. Maybe he'd woken her, but he doubted it.

"She said it was her mother's, and she wanted to pass it down to a granddaughter, but I was her only grandchild," Laurence said. "She wanted me to give it to whoever I married, and then to our daughter, if we had one."

"I'm really sorry," Patricia said.

"I was going to give it to Serafina," Laurence said. "As an engagement ring. I promised my grandma I would give it to my bride."

Patricia didn't say anything, just stared in her purple robe. Her hair was a pile of tangles.

"I really have to give it to you? We can't just call it quits?"

"You really have to. Or your friend might get sucked back into that place. Or you might, instead." When she put it like that, the ring was a pretty small price to pay.

"You knew it was going to be this." He handed it to her, still in its tiny, tiny velvet box. Actually, with the box, it was *almost* bigger than a toy car he owned. But not quite.

"I knew it would be something like this." Patricia put the ring into the pocket of her robe, where it barely made a lump. "Or the spell wouldn't have worked."

"Why couldn't it just be something like, I have to stand on one foot for an hour? Why does it have to be my most valued possession, and the linchpin of my courting strategy? It doesn't make any sense."

"Do you want to come in and have some toaster waffles?" Patricia stepped back and held the door open. "I can't talk about this out here, in the open."

The toaster waffles failed to materialize, but instead she had locally made organic Pop-Tarts, which were probably better. They sat on the gray lumpy sofa, where Deedee and the other roommate had been watching *Jersey Shore* every other time Laurence had been there. Patricia kept glancing over toward the hallway for any signs they were stirring or listening in to this conversation.

"So I might have mentioned there are two kinds of magic." Patricia handed Laurence a blueberry pastry and a mug of English Breakfast.

"Good and bad, I'm guessing," said Laurence, not quite having his mouth full. Patricia's bathrobe was splayed out on the sofa next to him, and he wondered if he could grab the ring while she wasn't looking. But then he remembered the part about someone getting pulled back into the nightmare dimension.

"No, though that's a common misconception. There's Healer magic and Trickster magic. Back in the day, many people believed Healer magic was good and Trickster magic was evil— but Healers can be judgmental control freaks, and Tricksters can be super-compassionate and basically save your life."

"Like last night," Laurence said.

Patricia nodded. "The Healer and Trickster schools formed over hundreds of years, out of lots of local traditions from all over the world. And there was a time, in the 1830s, when the two groups went to war. The world could have been torn apart. But there was this woman named Hortense Walker, who realized that the two types of magic worked better if you could combine them. You could do amazing things if you mastered both Trickster and Healer magic, way more than you could do with either type alone. Plus you were less likely to go over the edge into becoming a control freak or a lying jerkface."

Laurence was already jumping ahead to the implications. "So if you want to accomplish something major using magic, you need to trick someone, or heal them. So you're helpless without a patsy, or a sick person?"

"I wouldn't say helpless. I spent years training to use these skills in lots of different situations. I can use Trickster magic to transform myself, even with nobody around. And if someone attacked me, I could 'heal' them so hard they'd feel it for a week."

"Thanks for explaining." Laurence ate the last corner of his blueberry pouch and then washed it down with the rest of the tea. He had a hundred more questions, but he wasn't equipped to hear any more answers right now. He sank deeper into the broken upholstery of the couch. He would never, ever be able to pull his butt out of this sofa, he was just going to get dragged in deeper until he was swallowed, as if by a Venus Asstrap.

Every quadrant of Laurence's soul was yelling for him to get the hell out of there before he lost more than his grandmother's ring and his freedom of speech. But then he thought about the other promise he'd made the night before. The one he made of his own free will.

"I said I wouldn't ever run away again," Laurence said. "And I won't."

"Good." Patricia let out a breath that sounded like she'd held it for ages. "More tea?"

"Sure." Laurence found a marginally more comfortable arrangement on the couch, and Patricia handed him a fresh hot mug. They drank tea together in silence until Patricia's roommates woke up and started giving Laurence the hairy eyeball.

7

PATRICIA HAD SPENT years wishing she could run away to learn real magic. Then one day, she turned herself into a bird, and a man came to take her to the witch academy. Dreams? Fulfilled.

Eltisley Maze had two separate campuses, and they were as different as a cloudless summer day and a blizzard. Eltisley Hall had grand stone buildings over six hundred years old, and nobody ever raised his or her voice there. Students at Eltisley walked single file along the gravel walkways, wearing blazers, ties, and shorts, with the school's crest over their hearts (a bear and stag face-to-face, holding a flaming chalice between them). You addressed your teachers or upperclassmen as Sir or Miss and ate in Formal Hall in the Greater Building. The Maze, meanwhile, was a disorienting jumble of nine-faced buildings and looping walkways, where you could wear whatever you pleased. You could sleep all day, do drugs, play video games, do anything you fancied. Except that you would find yourself trapped in a room with no door (or toilet) for weeks, until you learned some crazy lesson. Or you would be tossed into a bottomless pit, or chased around for days by people with sticks. Or you would find yourself unable to stop tap-dancing. Or pieces of you might start falling off, one by one. Nobody told you anything in The Maze.

Once, Eltisley Hall and The Maze had been two separate schools, representing two styles of magic that were at odds, but now they were joined because magic had been united, at great cost. The passage between them was a sandy hedge-lined walkway that only opened at certain times.

Patricia would spend weeks mastering some delicate healing art at Eltisley Hall, and then they would send her back to The Maze and she would be so confused and tangled up in herself that she forgot all her fancy skills. She would solve some nonsense puzzle at The Maze and figure out how to do some clever trick, only to be sent back to Eltisley Hall, where they'd drum endless rules and formulae into her again, and she would lose the twisty shape she'd been holding in her mind.

This would have been enough to make her cry into her pillow every night at lights-out (at Eltisley) or impromptu naptime (at The Maze). But also, Patricia missed her parents, whom she hadn't even said goodbye to. For all they knew, she was dead. Or living in some alley like an animal. She wanted to tell them she was okay, but she wouldn't know how to explain. Not to mention, she'd left her cat, Berkley.

The Head Teacher at Eltisley Hall was a gentle old lady named Carmen Edelstein. She wore her silver hair in a dignified pageboy and always had an elegant silk wrap around her neck and shoulders. Carmen encouraged the students to come to her with any problems or questions, and Patricia soon found herself confiding in the old lady—but she learned the hard way that she must not mention her encounter with some sort of Tree Spirit a few years earlier. Magic was a practice and an art, not a spiritual belief system. You might have your own private spiritual experiences, just like any normal person—but believing you had a direct line to something great and ancient was the beginning of Aggrandizement.

"Trees *do not talk to people*," said Carmen Edelstein, her usual cheer replaced by a worried scowl. "You had a hallucination, or someone was playing a trick. This is why it's terrible that we get so many students so late, after they have already experimented on their own. Those bad habits can be a nightmare to unlearn."

"It was probably a hallucination, sure." Patricia squirmed in her stiff chair. "I remember I had eaten a lot of spicy food."

The Head Teacher at The Maze was Kanot, whose face and voice changed every time you met him. Sometimes he was an elderly Sri Lankan man, sometimes a pygmy, sometimes a giant white man with a crazy neck-beard. Patricia soon learned to recognize Kanot by certain tells, like the way he rolled his shoulders or narrowed his left eye—if you failed to identify him or misidentified someone else as him, you would find yourself at the bottom of the deepest pit in The Maze (other than the bottomless one, that is). People said that if Kanot ever wore the same face twice, he would die. Whenever you met Kanot, he'd offer you a terrible bargain. Patricia did not try to tell Kanot about the Tree.

Patricia had no real friends at Eltisley Maze. She was friendly with a few of the other kids, including Taylor, who had messy mouse-brown hair and ungainly, twitchy arms and legs. But the main cliques at the school never found a place for Patricia, especially after it was clear that she kind of sucked at most of the school assignments. Nobody wanted to befriend someone who was both nerdy *and* bad at homework.

If you went out into the tree line near Eltisley Hall at a certain time in the late afternoon or after lights-out in the Eltisley dorm, you might have seen a teenage girl with dark brown hair and big wondering eyes looking up at the trees and saying, "Are you here? What's your deal? Is Parliament in session?" And chattering to the birds, which just glanced at her and flew away.

You could never tell how long you would spend at either Eltisley Hall or The Maze—it could be days, weeks, or longer. At one point, Patricia spent seven months in The Maze, until she managed to hide from the teachers and the other students and they all spent a week looking for her. But instead of going back to Eltisley Hall, she was led out into a yellowgrass field, where Kanot himself ushered Patricia and some other students into a great wooden airship, which was whale-shaped except it had more fins, with an interior that was covered with rococo nuts and berries.

Today, Kanot was a heavyset bespectacled African-American man with a Tennessee accent and a bomber jacket. "Here's the idea," he said when they were already over the Alps somewhere. "We drop each one of you guys in a small town, someplace where you don't speak the language. No money, no supplies. And you find a person who needs healing, someone hurting real bad, and you heal 'em. Without them knowing you were ever there. Then we come get you." Kanot offered to let the students out of this assignment in exchange for letting him hide some stuff in their bones, but nobody went for it. So instead, he started shoving kids one by one out of the airship's hatch, which looked like the doorway of a French chateau, a few hundred feet up. No parachute.

Patricia managed to slow her descent so the impact just knocked the wind out of her. She staggered to her feet, in a field miles from anywhere. Then she wandered until nightfall, when she saw the lights of the town, behind her. The first few people she found seemed healthy enough, but then she noticed an old woman hunched over a bowl of soup in a small restaurant or bistro. The woman was coughing and her skin looked gray, and Patricia could glimpse an ochre scar poking out of the neck out of her yellow blouse. Perfect. Patricia crept toward the woman, only to get a faceful of soup and what sounded like accusations of thievery in some Slavic language. She ran.

A week later, Patricia was starving and running out of places to hide in this town, with its dingy white plaster walls and muddy roads. She could no longer talk to animals, and she had failed to master the skill of understanding human languages other than English. Plus, she could only heal a sick person with whom she'd built a certain rapport.

"I am so not going to sleep in these same clothes again tonight," Patricia said aloud, in English. The shopkeeper in the tiny grocery saw her and chased her out, shouting guttural syllables. Patricia ran down the narrow twisting streets, sharp inclines paved with cobblestones, until she had lost the shopkeeper. She squatted behind a stone wall and looked at the only thing she'd been able to steal: a dusty bottle of Chiang Mai brand chili oil.

"This better work." Patricia tilted the bottle so the words "WARNING RED-HOT" were upside down. The thick liquid singed her throat. She started to gag, but she made herself drink the whole thing. Once the bottle was empty she pulled herself into a shivering ball. Her head ached. She wanted to weep, for everything she'd lost and all she'd failed to gain.

An hour later, she raised her head and threw up. Once she started, she could not stop. Her eyes burned and her nose ran, and the oil was twice as horrible coming up as going down. Her stomach spasmed, not amused by her idea of a meal after days of starvation. She coughed acid.

The good news: Patricia had an idea how to heal the angry old woman now.

Patricia crept across the slate rooftops of the town until she reached the sloping roof of the cantina, where she could see the woman through a small skylight. The skylight was open, and she slipped inside, tiptoeing across a loft where bags of flour and cans of supplies were stored. She hesitated before taking some bread and stuffing it in her mouth. Then she reached the edge of the loft, still on the other side of the glorified barn from where the woman sat at her rickety table. Patricia shinnied up a support pillar, and then onto a ceiling beam. She inched her way across the beam, until she was hanging by her arms and legs over the old woman, and leaned as far as she could without losing her grip.

Patricia spat in the old woman's soup. The old woman was hectoring someone else in the room, probably about kids these days, and did not notice. Once Patricia's saliva was inside the woman, she had a direct link and could take stock of the late-stage emphysema, the barely-in-remission cancer that had already cost the old woman a lung, and the gout. It took an hour of concentration, and some unseemly muttering, for Patricia to get in there and make the woman's insides as good as new. She stopped just short of giving the crone a lung to replace the one she'd lost.

The night sky looked overcrowded to Patricia, as she lay in the uneven grass of the field where she'd fallen out of the airship. Too many stars, trying too hard. She lay there for an hour before the airship descended far enough to lower a ladder for her. She climbed slowly, her limbs sore and feeble. Kanot handed her a sandwich and a can of ginger ale and tried to sell her some shares in a Zumba studio. This time, Kanot was a young German with a shaved head.

After that, Patricia started figuring out how to use the things she learned at Eltisley at The Maze and how to use The Maze's craftiness at Eltisley. A few kids had dropped out after the "random Eastern European town" assignment, so space opened up for Patricia to become an honorary member of a few cliques.

One night, she was smoking clove cigarettes with the cool "Goth" kids after curfew, inside the cavernous and never-used chimney of Eltisley's Lesser Building. There was

Diantha, the plump swanlike leader of the group, who was rumored to be the daughter of an earl or something. Next to Patricia sat Taylor, who'd gone full-on Goth with the hair-dye and eyeliner, and a leather jacket after hours. On Patricia's other side was Sameer, who wore black starched-collar shirts that made his shy, slightly horsey face look grown-up and sophisticated. Plus Toby, a Scottish kid with wiry red hair and jug ears. And a few other kids who showed up sometimes. The red-brick chimney walls had streaks of ancient soot on them.

Patricia and Taylor rested, arms around each other, and the clove smoke fumigated Patricia's insides. They were trading weird stories about their lives before Eltisley Maze, all the flukey experiences that made them realize they had a connection to some unidentified power. And Patricia found herself talking about what she remembered of the Parliament and Dirrpidirrpiwheepalong and the Tree, before she even knew what she was doing.

"That is bizarre," Taylor said.

"It is quite amazing," said Diantha, leaning forward and encompassing Patricia with her dark, enthralling eyes. "Do tell us more."

Patricia told the whole story again, from the beginning, adding more details this time.

The next day, she wondered if she should have kept the "Tree" thing to herself. Was she going to get in trouble? She kept glancing at Carmen Edelstein during Literature class—they were reading *Troilus and Criseyde*—but Carmen showed no sign of knowing anything.

That night, as Patricia was getting ready for bed, Taylor knocked on her door. "Come on, we're all at the chimney," Taylor said with a grin. The group in the disused chimney was twice as big as before, so there was barely room for Patricia. But everybody wanted to hear about the Tree.

The more times Patricia told the story, the more like a story it became: with dramatic touches and a better ending. She threw in more details, like the way the wind felt as it passed through her disembodied spirit form, and the way the trees shimmered as she soared on the wind into the heart of the forest. And by the third night, when Patricia was telling the story to a third group of kids, the Tree had gotten a lot more eloquent.

"It said you were the protector of nature?" said a younger kid from Côte d'Ivoire named Jean-Jacques.

"It said we all were," Patricia said. "The defenders of nature. Against, like, anyone who wanted to harm it. We all are. We have a special purpose. That's what the Tree said, anyway. It was like the perfect Tree at the heart of the forest that you can only find if someone shows it to you. A bird took me, when I was very small."

"Can you take us to it?" asked Jean-Jacques, so excited he couldn't breathe.

Soon they had a proper club. They got together at night, a dozen kids, and talked about how they were going to find the heart of the forest, the way Patricia had. And how they were going to protect nature from anyone who wanted to harm her. Like the Na'vi. Patricia was the one with the knowledge, but Diantha was the one who could say, "We are all of one accord," and everybody would cheer.

"We are *all* counting on you," Diantha said to Patricia in low, confiding tones, touching her shoulder. Patricia felt a thrill all the way down to her tailbone.

"And the Tree was huge, like forty or fifty feet tall, and it wasn't an oak or a maple or any kind I'd seen before. It had branches like big wings, and the moonlight came through the thickest part of the branches in two places, so it looked like two glowing eyes looking at me. The voice was like this friendly earthquake."

The tenth time that Patricia told the story about the night she left her body and went to the Tree, the tale had gotten embroidered to the point where it bore little resemblance to the version Patricia had told that first night. And yet, everybody was bored with it. They wanted to know what happened next. "What do we do?" Sameer asked. "What's our next move?"

"I honestly do not know," Patricia said. She told them, for the first time, about when she was in Bogtown and she guzzled chili oil and nothing happened. They traded theories, like it wasn't the right time, or she wasn't in the right headspace, or you couldn't reach the Tree from Eastern Europe because of ley lines.

Opinions among Diantha's secret club were divided over the crucial question: Did the adults at Eltisley Maze know about the Tree? Either: (A) It was something all the adults knew about, and they were just keeping it secret from the kids because they weren't ready to know about it yet, or (B) they didn't know about it, and this was something you had to be a kid to understand.

A few days later, Patricia had lunch with Diantha. Alone. They had a blanket on the East Lawn of Eltisley Hall, where every blade of grass was perfect. Patricia still couldn't quite believe that Diantha was hanging out with her. Diantha had this way of widening her eyes just before saying something to you, so you found yourself looking into her gaze and you felt sure that whatever she said next would be the most important thing you'd ever heard. She wore her Eltisley scarf so elegantly, you'd think she had picked it out of a thousand scarf options. Her brown hair caught the light.

"We're going to do so many great things together, you and I. I just know it," Diantha told Patricia. "You should have some fizzy lemonade. They don't have fizzy lemonade where you're from, and it's really quite good." Patricia did what she was told. The lemonade was like a more lemony Sprite, and it was the coolest thing. The bubbles popped on her tongue.

Patricia wondered if Diantha was going to kiss her. Diantha was leaning in close, and they were gazing into each other's eyes. Patricia had never thought of herself as lesbian, but Diantha smelled so good and had such a powerful presence, it wasn't even like paltry sexual attraction. Somewhere off in the distance a bird sang, and Patricia almost understood.

Even the kids who didn't hang out in the disused chimney gave Patricia a look of envy or appreciation when she walked into the Eltisley dining hall, or when she foraged in the self-service canteen at The Maze, where you never knew if there would be pizza or black pudding. People in

The Maze told Patricia they liked her jeans. Nobody had *ever* liked her jeans before.

"I have something very important to tell all of you." Diantha sounded breathless, and not just because there were ten teenagers packed inside a dirty little chimney at midnight. Ten pairs of hands clutched, ten pelvises twitched with anticipation, as if they all collectively had to pee. Diantha held the pause as long as she could, then dropped the bomb: "I have spoken with the Tree."

"What?" Patricia said before she could stop herself. "I mean, that's great. How did you manage to do that?" Everybody was staring at Patricia, like she'd had a jealous outburst or something, instead of just being surprised. It wasn't that Patricia had a monopoly on "talking to the Tree" or anything—she had only done it once herself, and that was years ago. Patricia stammered something else about how happy she was that Diantha had done it, because this was great news, really great.

Diantha made things a hundred times worse, patting Patricia on the knee and saying, "Don't worry, dearest. We still value your contribution most of all."

But screw Patricia's wounded pride, everybody wanted to know: What had the Tree said? What was the message? They were so ready. They were beyond ready.

"The Tree said," Diantha said, "to prepare ourselves. The test is coming soon. And not all of us will pass it. But those who do will be heroes. Forever and ever." Everybody was so happy, they were whimpering.

That didn't sound like the way the Tree had talked to

Patricia. At all. But she'd only had one conversation, a few years ago, and she had a dim recall of the details, especially now that she'd retold them so many times. Patricia told herself to feel glad that she'd been vindicated and she hadn't just hallucinated the whole thing after all, instead of asking Diantha a bunch of questions, which would just be a sign of jealousy. And Aggrandizement. Now the Tree was talking to Diantha instead of Patricia. Big whoop.

"I was up all night studying for a Healing Tonics exam," said Diantha, "and I ate a great quantity of spicy papadum crisps. The next thing I knew, I was soaring out of my body, out the window, into the night. It was the most exhilarating sensation."

For a fortnight, the Tree was not forthcoming with any more information, although it spoke to Diantha a few more times. Sameer held hands with Patricia as they listened to the hints that this was something ancient, from before any of the lore they studied, from before words. Sameer's hand felt dry and callused and his index finger touched Patricia's pinky in a way that made her feel funny inside. They were both fixated on Diantha, whose exquisite nostrils flared as she talked about her out-of-body experience. On Patricia's other side, Taylor shivered.

Everybody who met in that chimney had a secret wink, where you put your thumb in the middle of your collarbone while you winked with one eye, then the other. And they wrote sigils inside their clothes.

When the Tree did give Diantha actual instructions, they were cryptic. "It said, 'Stop the Pipe and Passage.'" Her eyes widened and she looked supercharged with adrenaline. "It repeated every word twice."

"The Pipe and Passage?" said Sameer. "That sounds like a gentlemen's club. Full of tobacco smoke and secret entrances."

"It sounds obscene, yeah," said Toby the ginger. He made a motion to show how "pipe and passage" could be construed smuttily. Diantha gave him a glance that made him fold inward.

They spent days debating and Googling and whispering the words "Pipe and Passage" to one another, with no idea what they could mean. Diantha seemed impatient, as though she was waiting for someone else to figure out the meaning, so she wasn't forced to be messenger and interpreter both. At last, on Friday after lights-out, Diantha took a drag on a clove cigarette and announced she had the answer.

"Pipe," it turned out, referred to the Great Siberian Natural Gas Pipeline. And "Passage" referred to the Great Northern Shipping Passage. They were both the brainchildren of Lamar Tucker (a Texan who had helped pioneer slickwater fracking) in partnership with a Russian conglomerate called Vilkitskiy Shipping. The Russians wanted a new shipping route to replace the Northwest Passage, one that avoided Canada altogether, going through the heart of the Arctic ice. There was just one catch: Their route went straight through a massive deposit of ancient methane clathrate in the Chukchi Sea that had been trapped under the ice for millions of years. Scientists warned that releasing all that methane at once could supercharge the effects of climate change overnight. Hence the pipeline—Tucker believed you could drill down by inches, release the pressure slowly, and trap the still-frozen methane by bonding it with silicates. Then you could pipe the energy-rich methane sludge to a facility in Yakutsk. You'd generate enough electricity to power half of eastern Russia, and maybe sell surplus power to Mongolia, China, or even Japan.

"But it's going to go wrong, I know it," said Diantha. "They have no idea what they're tampering with. They must be stopped."

"Yes," said Patricia. "But what are we supposed to do?"

"Do?" said Diantha. "Look around. We are the best students at Eltisley Maze. Between all of us, we have mastered so many skills. Toby, I have seen you unmelt the last snows of spring, and reverse three days' decay. Sameer, you once tricked a bank manager into giving you five hundred pounds and the power of invisibility. Patricia, I have heard the teachers whisper that you have a connection to nature that even they don't fully understand. We can do this. The Tree depends on us."

They set off that very night, with only what they could carry. Diantha insisted: There could be no dallying (and no chance for anybody to have a change of heart and tell the teachers). They all went back to their rooms at Eltisley Hall and stuffed random objects into duffel bags.

"Where are we even going?" Toby said. "I have a practical in two days. At Eltisley, where they expect you to show up."

"We're going AWOL," said Taylor with a very quiet whoop. "No more tests, no more tutorials, no more Math

class, no more lectures—and no more puzzles at The Maze—
until we finish our mission."

Patricia stuffed a toothbrush and three pairs of
underwear, plus a tattered copy of *Tales of the City*, into her
satchel. She was going on an adventure—she was going to
make a difference. She almost danced down the mahogany
staircase in the North Residential Wing of Eltisley Hall,
except that Sameer kept shushing her. She squirmed with
adrenaline as they broke into the magic airship and spoofed
their way past the security questions.

"Hell to the yeah," Patricia said as they spiraled up off the
ground. "Let's do this." She and Taylor high-fived, and then
Patricia and Sameer hugged while Diantha laughed from the
cockpit, whose controls were wooden grapevines and figs.

The expedition didn't feel real until they were over the
Arctic and the moonlight had given way to two sheets of
sunlight—sky and ice, both painful to behold. Patricia's joy
went sour. She looked out at the vastness below and couldn't
tell one bright streak from another.

"We have to hit them before they know we're here,"
Diantha said from the cockpit. "I hope everybody is prepared
for any eventuality." Patricia, Toby, Sameer, and Taylor all
said yes.

"We're doing the right thing," Taylor said as they set
down. "We've studied long enough."

Patricia was wishing she'd brought another three layers
of clothing: She could do a spell to keep herself warm, but it
would be a distraction. She wound her scarf around her neck
and lower face, as many times as it would go.

"Toby, you're on transmutation of metals, because you're our best Healer. If it's steel, you turn it to tin," Diantha said as they stepped out of the ship. "Sameer and Taylor, you will confuse and confound any opposition we may encounter. I will attempt to seal any borehole in a spectacularly irreparable fashion. And Patricia? You will bring the full fury of nature down on them. Be creative."

They all high-fived and set off across the tundra toward the drilling installation, which looked like a lighthouse on the ice, with a single rusty structure on top of a platform, supported by four squat legs connected by the lower half of a pentagram. On one side of the drill was some kind of pumping station with a bulging metal sleeve. On the other side, Patricia saw a huge diesel tank that had probably been airlifted there and a number of snowmobiles and retrofitted trucks. Looking at a massive tank marked "WARNING: HIGHLY FLAMMABLE," sitting on top of the world's largest reservoir of methane, Patricia shivered. Her apprehension shaded into terror.

"Guys," Patricia said. "I think we ought to stop and—"

Someone yelled in Russian, and dogs were barking. Guys wearing parkas and goggles drove toward them in a couple snowmobiles, waving what looked like machine guns. Sameer and Taylor nodded and ran into their path. A moment later, the guards opened fire—but wildly, in random directions, because Sameer had done something to confuse them.

"Watch out!" Patricia shouted. "Don't make them shoot their own fuel t—" But she couldn't make herself heard over the gunfire, the engines, the yelling, and the dog pack.

Toby was already running toward the massive drill, crafting a transmutation-of-metals spell. Meanwhile, Diantha was marching toward the drill as well, a look of total determination on her beautiful sundrenched face. A bullet caught her in the side, and she keeled over.

Patricia ran and crouched next to Diantha, who was bleeding like a fountain and panting. "Hang on," Patricia said. "Looks like the bullet went clean through. But I'm afraid it hit an artery. Hold tight."

"Don't waste time on me," Diantha said. "The mission. Focus on the mission."

Patricia kissed Diantha on the mouth, while her hands groped for the hole that was gushing blood. She found the artery and painstakingly, clumsily, repaired it. A bullet sliced past her face. She broke the kiss and said, "Tell me the truth. Did the Tree talk to you, at all?"

Diantha said, "That's a terribly rude question, especially at this juncture."

A shout. Sounded like Toby. "It's all down to you now," Diantha said. "Make them feel the fury." Diantha passed out.

Patricia looked up, keeping Diantha's head cradled in her lap. Sameer and Taylor had done such a good job creating confusion, she couldn't see what was going on. Snow churned through the air, in big tidal waves, and a huge dog, like a Husky, sprinted in front of Patricia and then tumbled head over heels. The sound of gunfire was near continuous, like the loudest white noise ever.

The wall of snow cleared a little, and Patricia saw a body facedown in the snow, wearing an Eltisley scarf.

"No, no, no," Patricia muttered. She stood up. She could still fix this, she had to.

The attack on the Pipeline had lasted maybe ninety seconds. The longer this went on, the more bullets flying in wild directions, the greater the chance of a disaster that would be visible from space.

The cold tore into her, and she wished she had goggles like the people trying to kill her. She could barely stand her ground, because her center of gravity kept corkscrewing downwards. It was more than just the wind and the snow in her face. Everything felt wonky. She tried to imagine what it would feel like to unleash the forces of nature—what did that even mean? She couldn't even stay upright, how was she going to command any natural forces? The magnetic flux here was giving her the worst headache of her life, just when she was trying to think. What if she reached out somehow and connected to nature? Except that nature wasn't just one process, it was a whole host of processes that cascaded together in ways that nobody could predict. And if she remembered anything from her one and only conversation with that stupid Tree, it was that she would be serving nature, not commanding nature, and she couldn't believe that she hadn't made that one crucial distinction clear in all her stupid conversations about her experience, and now it was too late, and they were going to die as colossal fuckups. She couldn't control nature, she couldn't even control herself, and this magnetic field was crushing her like a huge steely hand, she was being smushed by magnetism. A massive dog ran right at her, barking loud enough to be heard over the guns and chaos, and she was startled to realize she understood what it was saying. Mostly, "I'm going to bite your throat! You're dead!" And this seemed a particularly pointless moment for her to regain the ability to understand animals, when there was no reasoning with them, and this just reminded her of the fact that she was powerless to shape or even influence the so-called forces of nature, and she really wished this magnetic flux wasn't giving her the worst migraine in the history of skulls, and then it hit her, and she knew what to do. She raised her hands to the skies and hoped for the best, before there was a blinding crack, and—

Patricia woke up on board an airship, not the same one they'd stolen. She lay on a bench, and Kanot was staring down at her, with a look she could only describe as "wrathful" on his hairless albino face. "You've disappointed me," Kanot said in a flat voice.

Patricia wanted to say it was all Diantha's idea, but she couldn't make herself go there. "What happened?"

"Toby's dead. So are half a dozen guards at that installation you decided to attack on your own initiative. I hope you can live with that. Diantha and Sameer are injured, but they'll both live. It appears you somehow tapped into the increased magnetic field at the Polar region and unleashed a kind of EMP that fried not only everything electronic for a dozen miles but also everyone's brains, including your own. You should not have been able to do that, and we're not sure how you did."

"There was a dog that wanted to bite me." Her head was pounding, and she kept seeing weird shapes. Then something occurred to her: "Toby was wearing an Eltisley scarf. And we brought the airship, it had an insignia on the side."

"Already dealt with. There won't be any traces to link back to the school." Kanot let out a snort from deep in the pit of his stomach. "Your life is going to be very different from here on out."

"I'm so sorry."

"Not as sorry as you're going to be."

He looked like he was going to say something else—like, maybe offer to let her off the hook in exchange for her firstborn. But instead he just shrugged and walked away, leaving Patricia with a throbbing head and a sense of wrongs that could never be set right. She raised her head enough to see out one of the big portholes. They flew over the ocean, and the sun was falling, through clouds that were a heavy, ugly purple.

8

THE PARROTS WERE eating cherry blossoms on top of a big tree on the crest of a steep hill, not far from Grace Cathedral—a half-dozen bright green birds with red splotches on their heads, just tearing the shit out of these white flowers. Petals scattered across the sidewalk and the grass as the birds squawked and worked their crooked beaks, while Laurence and Patricia watched from the steep bank of the parklet across the street.

San Francisco never stopped astonishing Laurence— wild raccoons and possums wandered the streets, especially at night, and their shiny fur and long tails looked just like stray cats, unless you looked twice. Skunks nested under people's houses. These parrots were native to somewhere in South America where cherry trees never grew, but they'd developed a taste for cherry blossoms somehow. Most of the people Laurence knew spent every minute obsessing about what Computron Newsly was saying about them and their friends, or who was still getting funding in spite of the crunch. The only reason Laurence ever saw these urban twists of nature was because he hung out with Patricia. She saw a whole different city than he did.

Truth was, Laurence only half paid attention to the amazing sight of these bright tropical birds devouring flowers, because he kept trying to wrap his mind around the fact that he had *nearly erased a human being from existence*. Laurence had barely slept in the past couple weeks, because he'd been spending twenty hours a day trying to figure out what had gone wrong. Plus when he tried to sleep, his heart did a circus drumroll as he remembered Priya's mouth opening and closing.

Even now, sitting with Patricia on a rough horse blanket on the grass, Laurence kept bracing himself for her to say something—she knew full well what had happened to Priya, maybe even better than Laurence did, and she hadn't said one judgmental word about it yet. She was probably just waiting for the right moment.

Patricia broke the silence. "Okay," she said. "What's wrong?" Her pale knee had faint grassy indentations.

"Nothing." Laurence put on a smile. "I'm watching the birds. They're awesome."

"Jesus. Now you have to tell me what's wrong. I've known you long enough to know when you're stewing."

So Laurence admitted: "I'm just waiting for you to tell me what an asshole I was, to do that experiment with Priya without any proper safeguards, so you had to save our asses. I figured you would want to let me have it."

Patricia squirmed, as if he was putting her in an uncomfortable position. "I didn't really think that was my place," she said at last. "Don't you have bosses who will tell you off? I figured you guys were all doing a lot of soul-searching."

"Yeah, of course. Of course."

Actually, none of Laurence's teammates had wanted to talk about the incident afterward. Once or twice, someone had mentioned "Priya's accident," and this had triggered an awkward, protracted silence that made Laurence feel like he'd swallowed an ice cube whole. Anya was still annoyed that Laurence wouldn't explain how Patricia had rescued Priya, since they couldn't establish protocols without knowing what had worked last time. Sougata and Priya were trying to put this nightmare behind them. Meanwhile, Laurence never quite found the right time to mention it to Isobel, who was technically supervising him.

"Laurence, listen." Patricia was looking at him instead of the birds. Her eyes opened wide and she chewed her lower lip. "It really meant a lot to me when you said that you weren't going to help tear me down, the way Kawashima asked you to. But you shouldn't build me up, either, or it's going to drive me nuts. I've done things I will never be able to put behind me. You couldn't stand to be near me, if you knew everything I've done."

Laurence had that "hitting an air pocket on an airplane" feeling, hearing Patricia talk this way. Like Patricia was about to open up to him, and that was exciting, for reasons he couldn't divulge to himself. But then he was terrified that she was right, and maybe there really were things that would give him no choice but to recoil from her—what if she was about to say that she recharged her witch powers by drinking the blood of babies? Plus every single time he learned more about Patricia and magic, he lost something.

None of this, though, overrode the adrenaline buzz of holy fuck, I feel close to this person right now. In his skin, in his scalp even. In his chest.

"Whatever," Laurence said aloud. "You already helped clean up after my biggest fuckup. I don't see how your shit can be worse than that."

On the sidewalk downhill from where they sat, a woman with a stroller was yelling at her toddler, a lank-haired kid in overalls who kept running up to the cherry tree and trying to harass the parrots. Who just laughed at him. The mother threatened to count to five.

"When I was a teenager, some of us went off half-cocked and attacked this drilling project in Siberia, and people died. Including my friend. And these days..." Patricia took a heavy breath, almost shaking. "I curse people. Like, one guy who had raped and killed a bunch of girls I turned into a cloud. There was a lobbyist who helped to block environmental regulations—they called him the Picasso of the Paperwork Reduction Act—and I conned him into becoming a sea turtle. Sea turtles live a long time, longer than most humans, so it wasn't murder. These bureaucrats were trying to kick my friend Reginald out of Section Eight housing, and I gave one of them a rash. And so on." She couldn't look straight at Laurence.

"Wow." Laurence shouldn't have been surprised, after what happened to Mr. Rose—but Patricia had said that was one of the senior witches' handiwork. For a moment, he felt like this steep hillside was tipping over, and then he got his center of gravity together again. "Wow," Laurence said again. "I gotta admit, that's not what I pictured you doing. I kind of imagined you more, I don't know… going around and blessing babies or something."

"You're thinking of fairies. If I blessed a baby, it would have exactly the same effect as if you blessed a baby."

"I doubt that," Laurence snorted. "Babies tend to projectile vomit at the sight of me. Anyway, it sounds like you put the smackdown on people who deserve it. I don't know. If I could turn people into turtles, there would be turtles everywhere."

Neither of them talked for a while. The mother had coaxed her kid back into the stroller and was speeding down toward the Marina. The parrots had stopped munching and were just flying back and forth between the cherry tree and a couple other big trees flanking a massive Edwardian town house, screaming in midair. Once or twice, they flew right over Laurence's head, green plumage extended like a salute.

"I guess I'm curious," Laurence said. "Do you have an ethical framework? I mean beyond that one rule they kept mentioning. How do you know what to do?" He spoke carefully, because this was obviously kind of an intense conversation for Patricia—she was averting her gaze now.

"Umm," Patricia said, raising her shoulders so her breasts lifted up inside her white T-shirt. "I mean, sometimes I'm following instructions, from Kawashima or Ernesto, and I trust them. But also… I can't just turn everyone into turtles, I have to go with the situation. And… see those parrots?"

She gestured at the candy-apple birds, which were back at their tasty cherry tree after making a few tours of the parklet.

"Yeah, of course." Laurence watched the red spots on their heads bopping around. They seemed to be taunting anybody who might want to cage them.

"I can understand what they're saying. Mostly, they're pissed at their friend in the middle, who keeps almost getting eaten by hawks because he's too dumb to stay high up. And those crows over there, too. I can understand what they're all saying, right now."

"Wow." Laurence hadn't even noticed the crows on the power line nearby, watching them intently. "So you can understand them all? All the time?"

"It takes a certain amount of concentration. But yes."

"Can all the magic people do that, like Kawashima and Taylor?"

"Maybe, if they really need to. If they make a big effort. Not most of the time. Different people have different weird quirks."

"And doesn't it drive you nuts, to hear animals talking all the time?"

"Not really. I guess I'm just used to it. Most of the time, I tune it out, the same way you tune out all the people talking around you. But at the same time, I always have in the back of my mind the idea of, what would the crows think? Crows are really smart."

The crows seemed to be having some kind of intense political debate, cawing and filibustering. One of them shook its wings, almost like a wet dog.

Laurence knew he was about to screw everything up—he should just keep his mouth shut—but then Patricia would know he was keeping an opinion to himself, and that could be worse. "Please don't take this the wrong way," he said. "But I don't think that's a basis for an ethical framework. 'What would the crows think?' The crows can't fully grasp the ramifications of the kind of choices you're talking about. A crow couldn't understand how a nuclear reactor works, or what the Paperwork Reduction Act is."

"Do *you* know what the Paperwork Reduction Act is?"

Laurence was burning up inside his too-tight collar. "Um. I mean, it's a law, right? And I'm guessing it reduces paperwork."

"Jesus. Do you even listen to yourself? Yes, I know that crows can't understand nuclear physics, not unlike most people. I'm not saying that I ask the crows for scientific advice."

Laurence finally risked looking up, and Patricia was more laughing than upset. With a bit of eye rolling in the mix, too. He could live with that.

"Yeah," he said. "I'm just saying that some ethical questions are more complex."

"Sure. Yeah." Patricia shook her head and sort of whistled. "But you're colossally missing the point, almost like on purpose. I'm saying that there are a lot of different ways of looking at the world, and maybe I actually do have a unique advantage, because I get to hear different voices. You really don't get that?"

Laurence felt like maybe the crows were laughing at him now, as if Patricia had tipped them off somehow. "I get that.

I do. I just, I think ethics are universal, and derived from principles, and I think that situational ethics are a slippery slope. Plus I don't think crows have much, if any, notion of ethics. I don't think a crow has ever even considered the categorical imperative."

"I love that this conversation started out with you worrying that I was judging you, and ended up with you judging me." Patricia had definitely stiffened a little and gotten a little farther away on the blanket. Laurence was feeling kind of toxic, and also worrying that he'd gone and pissed off the one person he could actually talk to in this stupid world.

"I'm not judging you, I'm not. You have to know that. I already said if it were me, there would be turtles everywhere."

"I don't actually think that ethics are derived from principles. At all." Patricia scooted a little closer again and touched his arm with a few cool fingertips where she'd gripped it earlier. "I think that the most basic thing of ethics is being aware of how your actions affect others, and having an awareness of what they want and how they feel. And that's always going to depend on who you're dealing with."

Laurence took a deep breath, and realized that he and Patricia were having a disagreement and this wasn't the end of the world. Like, it wasn't ideal that she'd opened up to him about this area that she was incredibly sensitive about, and he'd immediately started shooting down her ideas. But she could take it, and she could give as good as she got.

"Actually, I get what you're saying. I was kind of thinking the same thing recently," Laurence said. He told her about how he imagined going to another planet and seeing firsthand that none of the things we took for granted on Earth were true here. That there was no such thing as the way things were "supposed" to be. "And maybe that's what you have, right here on Earth: a nonhuman perspective on reality. So yeah, I do get it."

"Cool," she said. She rooted in her bag until she found her Caddy, which was letting her know that she had someplace else to be.

Laurence wanted to say something else, like that the fact that Patricia worried so much about being a monster probably meant she wouldn't ever be one. But she was already tromping down the hill, pausing only for a second to say something (advice or maybe just props) to the parrots, which showered her with white fluff, like rice at a wedding.

ALL THE UPSCALE organic microrestaurants in SoMa had gone under, so Laurence and Serafina ended up eating at a greasy diner selling Chinese food and donuts. The donuts were fresh, but the General Tso's Chicken was a little *too* general. Laurence felt embarrassed that he wasn't showing Serafina a better time.

Serafina didn't seem to mind, though—she even ate a donut with chopsticks. Her false eyelashes almost reached her cheeks, and he couldn't bear to look at her. She was amazing. He would have given almost anything to trigger the Nuclear Option. He could give her some other ring, sure, but it wouldn't have the same significance without the story about his grandmother. Serafina had finished her donut and was studying her phone.

The neon "Donuts" sign crackled. Laurence realized that neither of them had talked for ages. *I wish I could use active listening to fill the silence.* He couldn't stop picturing Priya's dazzled expression, and it gave him a sour taste in his mouth and a large bolus in his stomach.

"Okay, what's up with you?" Serafina said.

"Um, nothing," Laurence said. He couldn't tell Serafina about Priya, not without getting into the truth about the antigravity experiment. Plus Serafina would demand to know how exactly they'd saved Priya. "We had a... setback at work. And I have no idea what to tell Isobel. Let alone Milton."

"Tell them the truth, I guess. They're grown-ups, right?" She shrugged, then looked back at her phone.

Laurence and Serafina were supposed to spend the night together, but Laurence ended up going back to work to pull another all-nighter instead. "Maybe if I go without sleeping another few days," he told Serafina, "I'll be able to report some progress, instead of that failure."

"Or maybe you'll just get sleep deprived, and make even bigger mistakes," Serafina said, smiling because she'd been there herself. "Good luck. Love you." She walked back up toward Market where the BART was having irregular service, and Laurence watched her the whole way back up the block, wondering if she would look back at him over her shoulder, or turn to wave one last time. She didn't.

His heart skidded like a dirt bike on black ice as he watched her disappear.

LAURENCE WANTED TO wait until Isobel was in a good mood to tell her about Priya's accident. But after several days, Laurence realized Isobel was never in a good mood lately. Almost the first thing she'd ever said to Laurence was that she hated to be an authority figure, and now she was Milton's second-in-command in this huge venture, laying down the law for a small army of geeks. Whenever Isobel saw herself in the mirror, wearing a plum-colored business suit with her hair in a gray bob, she did a double take.

At last, after Laurence had pulled two all-nighters in a row at the lab, he decided to bite the bullet. When he crawled home, Isobel was staring at satellite images of the Atlantic Ocean, at the small kitchen table, and she pointed at an ugly smudge in the Gulf Stream. "Superstorm Camilla."

"Oh yeah." Laurence peered over her shoulder. "I heard about that. A near miss, on the East Coast. Everybody said it could have been way worse than Sandy or Becky."

"Third near miss in the past couple years," Isobel said. "And hurricane season isn't over yet. Milton is wigging out."

Laurence pulled up a chair. "Listen, I don't want you to tell Milton. But we had a… a setback at work."

"What kind of setback?" Isobel pushed her laptop shut with a click.

"We had an accident. At the lab." Laurence tried to explain the whole story without mentioning Patricia at all.

"We're all pretty unsure how to move forward."

"Well." Isobel pushed her chair back and went to get a bottle of *grappa* from the cabinet, pouring some for Laurence and some for herself. She sat back down with her elbows on the table. "Sounds like you need more safety protocols, and maybe don't randomly test your equipment on human subjects, without talking to Milton or myself first."

"Yeah." Laurence swallowed. "That was dumb. And that's on me. But I feel like... the way the antigravity field destabilized makes me nervous. That just shouldn't have happened. We've done some tests, but we have to do a lot more. But I'm thinking we may have to go back to square one and try a completely different approach."

"Uh-huh." Isobel sipped and narrowed her eyes at him. "The last time we spoke, you said it was looking really good."

Laurence felt the sleepless days catching up with him. "It was. It was looking really good. Until it wasn't."

"You just asked me not to tell Milton. Which means you want me to lie to him, and say you're actually accomplishing your part of the project, without which all the other teams' work is a waste of time. You want me to tell him what? That you're really close to a breakthrough, when you've actually gone back to 'square one'?" She tossed back some *grappa* and poured more for Laurence.

"Hey," Laurence leaned backward on the rear legs of his chair until he was in serious danger of crashing on his back. "Nobody's lying to Milton. He knows we're doing everything we can. You guys trusted me with this."

Isobel was shaking her head. "I can't do this. You can

tell Milton what you just told me. He's coming to town in a few days. Tell him you're stuck, and he'll send you to the facility he's set up outside Denver, where you will have zero distractions."

Laurence had a sudden flashback of his parents hauling him to a death trap of a military school, and his sleepless haze was turning red. "Just please listen to what I'm telling you," he said, planting the chair on all four legs and gripping the table with both fists. "We're not giving up, goddamn it. We're just taking a fucking step back. Don't try to blackmail me, or, or pressurize me here. The fuck."

"It's not blackmail," Isobel said, pouring herself more *grappa*. "It's what will absolutely happen. You signed a contract; you committed to this project. And you've gotten the kid-gloves treatment, because you're my friend. Do you remember when you came to stay with me, six years ago?"

"Yes," Laurence said. His parents had been divorcing, and he'd needed a place to hide. He'd only just reconnected with Isobel, and she'd invited him to live in her crawl space for the summer while she pulled the plug on her aerospace start-up.

When Laurence thought back to that summer now, his main impression was of the desert's heat, smacking you in the face the moment you stepped out of an air-conditioned space. Laurence had toted an iPad as he'd shadowed Isobel, trying to make whatever she needed materialize without her even asking. A girl named Ivy, with long black hair and cherry lip gloss, had made out with Laurence behind the ozone-scented silos late at night. Milton hung around wearing a golf hat and shorts—Laurence had been startled to realize that Milton was that old guy in the turtleneck who'd yelled at him for touching the rocket at MIT. Milton had kept saying things like, "Making the leap from a planetary infestation to an interplanetary diaspora is the most important task the human race has ever attempted. It is quite literally do or die."

Isobel hissed a little as the *grappa* hit her throat. "You followed me like a puppy, while I was desperately trying to hold it together. We all thought you were just a starstruck kid, but then on the last day you brought us that physics paper when we were all sitting on that sofa with the broken leg, watching Nine Inch Nails videos and crying."

"The paper about gravity tunneling," Laurence said. "I remember." Some insane physicist from Wollongong had speculated about a method of interstellar travel. Milton had started to dismiss it, but then he'd read the paper a second time and started scribbling notes on his arm. And that had helped lead to Milton founding the Ten Percent Project, with the idea of getting 10 percent of the population off-world within a few decades.

"So don't sit there and try to pretend that you're just an innocent bystander," Isobel said. "You helped start this. And maybe you haven't been paying attention to the news: The world is on the edge of the cliff here."

"I'm aware." Laurence shifted backward and forward in his chair until the scuttling of the wooden legs became too annoying.

"So if you don't want me to tell Milton that you're pulling back, don't pull back. Or if you want to go back to square one, you can tell Milton yourself. But don't put me in the position of covering for you. And don't try to have it both ways. Okay?"

"Okay," Laurence said.

Isobel reopened her laptop so she could obsess over the satellite map some more, and the light from the screen gave her a spectral quality, like someone slowly phasing out of existence.

They sat without talking for a while. Laurence slipped away to get ready for bed. He got up in the middle of the night to get some water, and found Isobel still sitting at that table, weeping over a nearly empty bottle, her face wracked with tremors. He helped her up the stairs to her bedroom, supporting her on his shoulders, and got her into bed. He stayed with her long enough to make sure she slept on her side.

9

"ARE YOU SURE we should be doing this?" Patricia asked when they were both naked but not yet past first base.

"Lately I've discovered certainty can be a kind of curse," said Laurence.

They were in Laurence's bedroom, where Patricia had never been before. It was a sort of in-law apartment downstairs from Isobel's apartment, with a view of a back garden out the window, behind the twin bed with a Mighty Mouse quilt. On the opposite wall, he had a workstation, with docks for a laptop computer and a 19-inch monitor, plus shelves and racks of cannibalized electronics. Including five Caddies, two of them jailbroken and two others shackled together with a mesh of crossover cables.

The remaining wall space, over by the door, was taken up with a small bookcase containing graphic novels, engineering texts, and a few science memoirs, like *Surely You're Joking, Mr. Feynman!* Random action figures and toys in silly poses sat on the dresser, and one of Serafina's robots, Jimmy, peered over Laurence's bed frame.

Laurence was feeling pretty freaking nervous. He had been with a nontrivial number of girls—but at least half of those had been tipsy hookups where you had a certain amount of plausible deniability about sexual performance. He'd dated Ginnifer, an electrical engineer with a wicked smile, during sophomore and junior years in college, and she would devise contraptions that could stimulate Laurence's prostate with varying levels of vibration while also enabling her to straddle his penis, and apply a similar variable-speed oscillation/vibrator function to her clitoris. Plus Ginnifer's Sexoskeleton, which would take way too long to describe. But this was someone he'd known half his life, with whom he had this whole labyrinthine history. He could not screw this up. Plus Patricia might be used to crazy magic sex. She and the other witches probably turned themselves into bats and had bat sex one hundred feet up, or had sex on the spirit plane, or with fire elementals or whatever. Even if none of that was true, she was way more experienced than him.

And then there was the fact that Patricia looked absolutely stunning naked—like, radiant. She wore these fluffy outfits a lot of the time, but her breasts were perfect and bigger than Laurence had expected, and her arms and legs were long and slender. Her skin was pale, but it had a rosy warmth to it. As she shifted around on his bed, her long black hair spilled everywhere and her toes flexed, and he caught glimpses of her downy pubic hair and the indentations behind her knees, and the whole thing felt like a miracle. He was just beginning to appreciate a fraction of how beautiful she was. Not for the first time in the past couple months, Laurence found himself thinking, *I wish I still had my grandmother's ring so I could give it to her the right way.* Except now, he was also thinking, *Please god let me not blow this, let this not be a huge mistake.*

For her part, Patricia was looking at Laurence and feeling a kind of ache deeper than mere sexual desire, although there was that, too. All of her life, she felt like she had been telling people, "It doesn't have to be like this," which is the close cousin to "It can be better than this." Or even, "*We* can be better than this." As a little girl, getting pressed into the dirt by her schoolmates or padlocked in a foul old spice crate by Roberta, she'd tried to say that with tears in her eyes, but she didn't have the words back then and nobody would have understood anyway. As the outcast freak in junior high, with everybody wanting to burn her alive, she'd given up on even trying to find a way to say, "It can be more than this." But she'd never let go of that feeling, and it came back now, in the form of hope. She gazed at Laurence's face (which looked squarer and more handsome without a big shirt collar framing it), his surprisingly puffy and suckable-looking nipples, his shaved pubes, and the way the leg and stomach hair erupted in a heart-shaped ring around the depilated zone. And she felt like they, the two of them, right here, right now, could make something that defied tragedy.

MAYBE TWO MONTHS after Priya's near disaster, Laurence had gone for drinks with Patricia, because only she could even begin to understand why he had just told Serafina they ought to spend some time apart. His other friends all thought he was crazy.

Laurence had sat in the darkest corner of PoisonRx, drinking a Snakebite, and poured out the whole story to Patricia, how he'd never felt worthy of Serafina in the first place and how their love had always felt like a shared delusion propped up by pure bloody-mindedness. Patricia had not scoffed: She'd had relationships like that too, and refusing to accept reality had made her the person she was today.

"One thing we've both seen," Patricia had said, "is things come back around. People come back around. You and Serafina could have another chance, sometime."

"Yeah, maybe." Laurence's drink had gone from sour fruit to dark bread, all in one swig. "Sometimes you just have to accept defeat, though."

Patricia had kept saying she was sorry about the ring until Laurence was like, "No. I have to man up and take responsibility. For the Priya thing, for the consequences, and for my own decision afterward. Right?" Saying that stuff made Laurence feel better, both because it was true and because it made him feel like an active participant in his life.

Laurence and Patricia hadn't started dating after that or anything—they'd just hung out. All the time. Way more time than Laurence had ever spent with Serafina, because every date with Serafina had to be perfect, and he'd always worried about being clingy. He and Patricia were just always grabbing dinner and coffee and late-night drinks, whenever Laurence could slip Milton's leash. They were always cheating at foozeball, dancing at The EndUp with insomniac queers until five in the morning, bowling for cake, inventing elaborate drinking games for Terrence Malick movies, quoting Rutherford B. Hayes from memory, and building the weirdest kites they could coax into the sky over Kite Hill. They were always hand in hand.

They knew almost all of each other's secrets, and that gave them license to talk in crappy puns and quotes from old hip-hop songs and fake Prohibition bootlegger slang, to the point where nobody else could even stand to be around them.

Patricia couldn't remember a time when she'd taken herself less seriously. Like maybe Laurence was inadvertently keeping his semipromise to Kawashima and Ernesto, to keep her from getting too full of herself, but she did not even remotely mind. For the first time in living memory, she was just a girl who laughed too loud in movie theaters.

At some point, when you're spending every free waking moment with a person, and you've developed your own private language, and you're always chilling until way past your bedtime, you inevitably start to wonder if maybe it wouldn't be easier just to share a bed as well. Not to mention, you know, fun.

PATRICIA REACHED WITH her left hand and stroked the incline of Laurence's face, from his jaw to right under his eye. His eyes were bluer than she'd realized, along with the gray she was used to noticing. His pupils dilated a little. Her right hand reached out and touched from his thigh to his stomach, and he trembled a little. His penis rose out of the smooth zone, past the firebreak of hair, to graze the light fur of his stomach.

Patricia thought it was kind of funny that he shaved his junk and she didn't shave hers, but she knew better than to laugh at this moment.

If either of them had turned their heads and looked at the racks of electronic detritus along the other wall, they might have noticed the Caddies were acting weird. That is, in a way that nobody had ever seen a Caddy behave before. The Caddies lit an LED on the peak of their guitar-pick-shaped cases as a pinhole camera activated. Even the two that were theoretically wiped and reformatted with Artichoke BSD. The Caddy in Patricia's purse also came to life and flooded its screen with data. This wasn't the way a Caddy flashes its screen to remind you of an appointment, or the little bubble that appears in the corner of the screen to let you know one of your friends is having drinks nearby. This wasn't a user-interface thing at all. The Caddies were just interested in this one event. Caddies had been physically present for a billion human sex acts by now, but this was the first time they'd ever bothered to watch.

Patricia's phone shut itself off, even though its battery was full. So did Laurence's phone. Across town, Laurence's housemate Isobel missed her bus by seconds and then the next bus broke down, so she wouldn't be getting home any time soon. Laurence had left his instant messenger client active on his laptop, but the program crashed. Not even Superstorm Allegra making landfall in Delaware, erasing half the Eastern Seaboard with its twelve hundred miles of Category 3 fury, could disturb these two right now.

Patricia hadn't seen Laurence naked since they were both thirteen or fourteen, and she had been trying not to look too much back then. This time, she made a point of taking in every detail. Meticulous. Greedy.

Laurence's body was a lot more solid than Patricia had realized, because he was so tall that you expected him to be a beanpole. Sitting on the bed, all of him collected in one place, he turned out to have a pleasing swell to his biceps and his pecs and some impressive thigh action. He still looked like he could do track and field but mostly field. She'd always found his thick, inquisitive hands kind of thrilling, but they were sexier in the context of the rest of his skin: The sandy hair ran from his knuckles all the way up his arms, and slowly got darker and thicker as it traveled down his chest to the heart-shaped zone of smoothness. Patricia had never seen anything so beautiful. She wanted to be all over him forever.

That seemed like a good impulse, so she acted on it, pouncing. He made a little surprised grunt and then a much happier little gasp. Her breasts nuzzled his chest and her face was right up in front of his, and she was straddling his stomach, her feet on either side of him and her ass just nudging his cock. He started laughing, and so did she, and she leaned over and kissed him and chewed on his lip too gently to break the skin.

She was tingling all over, even her scalp and her elbows, and she felt a kind of madness taking her over that was better than any spell or concoction ever.

She almost put him inside her without a condom—she

wouldn't get pregnant, unless she chose to. And she was sure neither of them had an STD. But doing it bareback this first time felt like too much, like they would be making some kind of declaration that they were fluid bonded, practically married, instead of just trying this shit out. Which is what they were doing. So she groped for a foil package.

"I keep expecting you to do like a spell or something." Laurence thrust into her with an even tempo, occasionally syncopating and twisting, in ways that startled her with pleasure.

"Do you want me to do a spell?" She smiled up at him, her hazel eyes going sideways for a moment as she tried to think what spell she could even get away with, and then rolling upwards as he thrust harder and faster for a second.

"I don't know." Laurence leaned forward and kissed her between her own ankles. "Nothing fancy, or, you know, tricky." She winced a little at the mention of tricks, but he was still smiling, it was all good. "You don't have to, I was just kind of half-expecting it in a way."

"Okay," Patricia said. "But remember, you asked for it."

"I didn't," Laurence said. "I merely speculated about—ooh." And then he lost all train of thought because his already-quite-sensitive left nipple had developed a few million new nerve endings, and she was blowing on it. He damn near passed out from the sensation, and his brain shut down, and then he was pouring out of himself into the condom inside the woman he loved.

He hadn't quite let himself think that before, but now he realized it was true. He found himself saying it aloud, sort of by accident, before his brain's normal functioning could quite be restored: "I love you."

"Oh." Patricia was staring down at him, from where he'd fallen into a puddle on the bed. "Wow."

She was obviously processing this. Like, a non sequitur.

"I can take it back," Laurence babbled. "I'm taking it back. I never said that."

He looked up at her green eyes (wide with surprise), her glistening eyelashes, her half-open mouth.

"No, don't take it back." She shivered, but not in a bad way. "It's just. Wow." And then she looked at him straight on and said, "I love you, too."

Even as Patricia said it back to him, she felt like her whole history was taking on a whole new focus, the landscape of her past rearranging so that the stuff with Laurence became major geographical features and some other, lonelier, events shrank proportionately. Historical revisionism was like a sugar rush, flooding her head. Her mind flashed on Laurence saying she had saved him, Laurence promising he would never run away from her again. It felt like something she had known a long time.

"Oh my god, I love you. I love you so much," she started babbling, and soon they were pressed together and kissing the tears out of each other's eyes and laughing. She touched his cock and even she couldn't tell if she used magic to lift it up again or if it was just her mere touch, but soon he was inside her again. This time, they were fucking and talking at the same time, and caressing each other's faces. They kept rolling over and over so neither of them was on top.

"I don't even know how I lucked out so damn much, you're the most beautiful ever," Laurence was saying.

"Let's just never stop holding each other." Patricia was laughing and crying. "Let's just hold on like this forever and people can come and ask us questions through the door or bug us on the phone or—"

Patricia's phone rang, having switched itself back on.

She pulled away from Laurence long enough to see that it was her parents calling. She hadn't spoken to them in ages. She knew at once what this was about—Roberta had finally gone off the deep end, in spite of all her straight-edge resolutions.

"What's wrong with Roberta?" Patricia blurted.

"Your sister is fine." It was Patricia's dad, sounding weary. "We just spoke to her. She's safe, she was outside the impact zone. Unfortunately, we had just gone to Delaware for one of your mother's seminars and we weren't able to get out in time."

"Wait. What happened? What's going on?"

"It's all over the news, we thought you'd seen. Allegra, it came ashore," said Patricia's father. "We're in the basement of the convention center. They herded us all down here when the tidal waves hit. We can't get the door open, and we think the building collapsed on top of us, plus the whole area is underwater. It's a miracle we've got cell phone signal."

"Hang in there, Dad." Patricia felt her face soaking. Between the tears and the white flashes, she was blind. "I'll find a way. I'll get you out of there." There had to be. There had to be a spell to get her to Delaware in a hurry, like a way to bend space. She just couldn't think what it was, or just whom she could trick enough to pull off such a thing. Maybe just telling her father that she could save him was paradoxically a big enough lie that it would give her the power to save him. Maybe there was a magician in Delaware who could help—except anybody on the ground there was probably dead, or had their hands full. She couldn't think, she couldn't breathe, she choked.

"It's okay, PP. I just wanted you to know that even though we were hard on you, and we disowned you after you ran away from home, we always loved you, and I'm… I'm… I'm proud that you became your own person." Patricia's heart shattered. She heard Isobel in the living room upstairs, shouting for Laurence to come and see on the news the scope of the destruction, streets become canals, air choked with debris. Like the heel of God's hand.

"Do you want to talk to your mother?" Patricia's father asked. "She's right here. She broke her arm, but I can hold the phone up to her. Hang on." There was a scuffling noise. The line went dead.

Patricia hit the callback function a dozen times, and nothing. Part of her thought maybe she should just stay hung up in case they were calling her back too and they got her voicemail, but she couldn't stop hitting redial-redial-redial, she was bawling and shaking and her naked body was freezing and Laurence put his arm around her and she slapped him and then clung to him and the sound that came from inside her was like all the wounded animals she had ever fixed in her life.

Then she pulled herself together. Her parents weren't dead yet. The destruction was still happening. She could get help. Someone was *doing* this, someone was making this happen, and she could make them pay. There was some evil witch or most likely witches, and they had found a way to supercharge a storm system, and they were fucking going down.

She was pulling her cargo pants on, her shirt, fuck her bra and panties.

"Where are you going?" Laurence was still naked.

"I have to go." She put her shoes on. "Find Ernesto. Find the others. We can fix this. We can make them pay. We can save them."

"I'll go with you." Laurence leapt for his pants.

"You can't," Patricia said. "I'm sorry, you can't."

And then she was gone, without saying goodbye or anything.

Laurence heard the front door slamming and Isobel trying to say something to Patricia as she ran past. And now he could hear the terrible chatter of the cable news people trying to make sense of the greatest natural disaster in America's history. The storm's supermassive fetch, hurling the already-swollen ocean onto land. High winds and twenty inches of rain shredding Capitol Hill and Foggy Bottom. The President in a secure location. Manhattan dead in the storm's path, with all the bridges clogged with people who'd waited too long to evacuate after so many false alarms in the past.

Someone knocked on Laurence's bedroom door. He leapt off the bed, hoping it was Patricia coming back for him.

Instead, he opened the door to see Isobel. She didn't seem to care that he was naked.

"Pack a bag," Isobel said. "Just one."

"What? Why?"

"This is it," she said. "We've put this off as long as we could. I've moved Heaven and Earth to give you a normal life here. But this, what happened just now, means it's over. We can't wait any longer. We can't afford to. Milton will say we waited too long as it is. We need the project up and running."

"I promise you I haven't been dragging my feet since that setback." Laurence was freezing, in shock. "But still, we're no closer than we were to figuring it out. There are huge theoretical problems."

"I know," Isobel said, handing Laurence an empty khaki duffel bag. "That's the point. From this moment on, you're working on the wormhole thing 24/7. We are going to need a new planet."

Laurence tried to explain that he couldn't leave, that there was no way, he had a life here, he'd finally found real love and it was everything to him, but he already knew this argument was lost. He took the duffel bag and started stuffing clothes and crap into it.

Patricia made it to Danger in record time, ignoring all the people on the bus who wanted to talk to her about the terrible-can-you-believe-it-this-is-going-to-change-everything. She jumped up the stairs three or four at a time and ran into the bookstore so fast she was breathless and yet still crying, but the moment she got there she knew it was too late. Everybody just sat there, looking horrified. And helpless. And like they'd been expecting her. Ernesto looked her in the eyes. "I'm so sorry," he said. "For your loss. For all of us."

"Who did this?" Patricia said. "We need to find them. We need to turn them into ash and then blow them into space. We need to make them fucking pay. *Tell me who did this*."

"Nobody," Ernesto said. "Nobody and everybody. We all did this."

"No, no." Patricia started weeping harder and louder than ever. She was hyperventilating. She saw spots. "No, this was somebody, there's a fucking bastard witch behind this, I can tell."

"It's a superstorm," said Kawashima. "It's been building for days, remember? It hit Cuba a few days ago, and then it converged with a cyclone. It ran into a high-pressure front in the North Atlantic that pushed it ashore."

"There's no spell big enough to move the ocean and the air currents," said Taylor, coming up and touching Patricia's arm. "You'd have to fool the Moon."

"You could heal those storms. You could heal them until they got out of control, like weeds, someone did this with a healing spell. I know they did. It might have taken months, but they've had months. Someone did this."

"Not this time." Ernesto came and stood so close to Patricia, he was in danger of touching her and making her body a bacterial and fungal playground. He looked into her eyes, sad but not surprised. "I tried to warn you that bad times were coming, and we would be asking more of you. And now they are here. You will need to do terrible things. But we will be sharing the responsibility, it will not be on you alone. There will be no Aggrandizement if we face this together."

"What do you mean?" Patricia was still shaking, but her breathing was slowing. She could smell the pure life energy coming off Ernesto, like nutrient-rich soil or a summer rainstorm.

"This is the beginning of something, not the end of it," said Kawashima, coming closer as well and actually hugging her. He never hugged anybody. "Or rather, it's the end of one thing and the beginning of something else. This country will be destabilized, with New York and D.C. gone, and other cities damaged. There will be refugees, in camps. Which means more disease. The chaos and starvation will worsen. There will be more wars, and worse wars. Wars like nobody has ever seen. God forbid we have to resort to the Unraveling."

"When the whole world turns chaotic, we must be the better part of chaos," said Ernesto. Patricia couldn't find it in herself to cry anymore.

10

LAURENCE WISHED PATRICIA could be here, by his side, to see this. He imagined explaining to her what she was seeing, and why it was even more amazing than it looked.

Laurence stood on a gantry, hundreds of feet above ground level, with Denver spread in a fetal position to his left. Six steel-and-fiberglass praying mantises perched over an empty space in the gantry's center—the space that could, one day, burst open and reveal the Pathway to Infinity. Normally Laurence would be paralyzed with vertigo, standing on top of a skyscraper with no railing, but he was too overwhelmed with the magnificence before him to worry about heights. Each of the huge red mantises had a power coil in its "tail" section, and then a midsection supported by two pairs of legs, with a collection of equipment that included the antigravity generators that Laurence's team had been working on for two years. The "heads" of the insects consisted of focusing devices, which would stabilize the opening that the antigrav beams helped to create. This insane structure seemed to dwarf the mountains in the distance. Even in the face of unthinkable horror, even with what had happened to Patricia's mom and dad and so many other people Laurence had known, there was still brilliance in the world. Saving wonder. He only wished he could show Patricia, so she could either feel comforted or laugh at his hubris; he almost didn't care which, as long as it lifted her misery a little.

Just like every moment since Patricia ran out on Laurence months ago, he tried to guess what she would be saying if she were here. And where she actually was, and what she was doing. Whether she was okay. He felt as though he were having an argument with her in his head, his optimism against her despair. Next to him here on this platform, Anya, Sougata, and Tanaa were freaking out over every detail of the engineering, but Laurence barely even heard what they were saying.

"Let's hope it works," Anya said.

"We could be months away from preliminary tests," said Sougata. "But it's still a beautiful thing, man."

By the time they took the elevator back down to ground level, Laurence was obsessing about Patricia again, to the point where the fantastic wormhole generator—the coolest device in the history of the planet—was shoved to the back of his mind. He felt like he was trapped in a moment of time, where he'd just told her he loved her, and hadn't been able to move forward to whatever happened after that. The further away he got from that moment, the thinner he stretched. He was temporally dislocated, and the time differential was only growing more severe.

Back at ground floor, Laurence wandered the old industrial park that Milton Dirth had refurbished. People in dark uniforms guarded the perimeter. Nobody was allowed in or out without Milton's verbal permission—and nobody had seen Milton in weeks. All phones, personal computers, and Caddies were confiscated on arrival at this campus, and none of the computers were connected to the internet. There was an intranet, plus someone had created internal mirrors of a number of scientific and technical websites. They did have a TV with CNN, so they'd been able to keep track of the slow-motion emergency: Chinese saber-rattling in the South China Sea, Russian troops massing, the water wars. People, people they knew personally, in refugee camps full of disease back east. But there was no way Laurence could get a message to Patricia, or find out how she was doing.

The building where Laurence worked (and lived, in a converted office with bunk beds) was the former headquarters of a start-up company called HappyFruit, Inc., which had marketed fruit that was genetically modified to include a tiny amount of antidepressants. "SQUEEZE THE JOY OUT OF LIFE" read one poster with a cartoon papaya that Laurence saw from his top-bunk perch every night. The first day or so, the idea of camping out at a start-up had seemed thrillingly surreal. Now, he was over it. At least HappyFruit had encouraged its employees to jog, so there were three showers. For a hundred people. The whole place smelled like dead otters.

Laurence took his time walking along the tar path, past the leafless cedar tree and the Dumpster where the smokers smoked. He was rehashing what he would say to Patricia if she were here. And drawing out the afterglow of seeing the completed Pathway to Infinity, before he had to go back to his little office and the crushing disappointment of failing to balance the gravity equations.

Back at the office that Laurence shared with Anya and Sougata, though, Laurence's chair was occupied. Isobel sat and gazed at Laurence's computer, but not as if she was reading anything.

"Hey," Laurence said. "I saw the machine. It's the most beautiful thing."

"Yeah." Isobel smiled, but she had her usual wreath of sadness.

Laurence said, "Listen, can you help me get a phone?" At the same time that Isobel said, "Milton is back." Then they were both like, "You first." Laurence won—so Isobel went first.

"Milton is back. He wants me to bring you and the others up to his office right away. I think things are about to get interesting around here." She stood, to lead Laurence away, and then remembered. "What were you trying to say, before?"

"Uh, nothing. Actually, no, wait. It is something. I need a phone. My frien—my girlfriend, I guess. Patricia. You met her a few times. I haven't talked to her since the flood. Her parents died. It's been the hardest time, and I should have been there for her. I need to make sure she's okay and let her know I'm thinking about her. It's really important."

"I'm sorry." Isobel had already gotten halfway to the door, and she turned back. "I'm sorry, there's just no way."

This had turned out to be a bad time to ask, given that Isobel was in a hurry to get to this meeting, but Laurence was committed.

"Please, Isobel. I just want, need, to talk to her a moment. Really."

"We're on total lockdown here. This whole campus is full of people who want to talk to their loved ones. I don't know if you've been following the state of the world out there, but it's total chaos. We can't trust anybody."

"Isobel. I've never asked you for anything before." Laurence let a little of his desperation and dislocation show in his voice, and then had to struggle to keep it from overwhelming him. *Keep calm, make your case.* "I've been your friend my whole life, and now I'm asking you for something that's massively important to me. Like, this could make the difference between me having a life and not having a life."

"So she's the one, huh?" Isobel shut the door and smiled. "I thought Serafina was the one."

"So did I. But you know, the heart is not a lie detector. Or something. Falsely identifying the One is part of how you find the One." He squelched a *Matrix* joke.

"I guess so." Isobel gave another tragic smile. "I wouldn't know. I married my college boyfriend."

Laurence didn't point out that Isobel and Percival had stayed together nearly fifteen years, which was a pretty respectable run. Instead, Laurence just waited, with arms folded and what he hoped was a decently pathetic look on his face.

Isobel held out a second longer, then handed him a

phone. "But I have to stay and listen in. For security reasons. I'm sorry."

"That's fine." Laurence seized the phone with both hands and dialed Patricia's last known number.

It rang, while Isobel watched him, and rang some more, and went to voicemail. He dialed again, same result. This time, Laurence let it beep.

He breathed, trying not to look at Isobel. "Hey. It's Laurence. I just wanted to make sure you were okay. And also, just to say that I'm really sorry about your loss. Your parents, I mean. They were... I can't even begin to say. There's nothing I can say. I wish I could be there for you, in person." He wasn't sure what else to say, on her voicemail, without being able to hear her response. Anything he could think of seemed inadequate, or maybe insensitive.

He almost just hung up and handed the phone back to Isobel, but then he realized: He'd just been looking at a freaking wormhole generator, a working model. He had *no way of knowing what might happen next*. They were, all of them, standing on terra incognita, and this felt like a moment that was radically discontinuous with everything that had come before. There was a nontrivial chance these were the last words he would ever speak to Patricia.

So Laurence pretended Isobel wasn't there, staring, and he said, "Listen, I meant it when I said I loved you, it just sort of came out but it was the truth coming out. There's a huge, vital part of me that reaches out to you in some kind of emotional phototropism. I have so many things I want to say to you, and I wish our lives could wrap around each

other forever. I'm kind of… I can't go anywhere right now. I have to see something through. But I promise you, as soon as I'm free I will track you down and we will be together, and I will try my fuckedest to make up for all the comfort I'm not giving you right now. That's a promise. I love you. Goodbye."
He hung up with the flat of his thumb and handed the phone back to Isobel. She seemed pretty overcome, by a grab bag of emotions.

Isobel put her hand on Laurence's upper arm as she slipped the phone back into a hiding place in her purse. But all she said was, "Tell nobody about this phone." Laurence nodded.

Milton surveyed a roomful of geeks from his Herman Miller throne, ankle crossed over thigh and lips pursed as if he'd just finished a slice of the tartest Meyer lemon pie. Laurence stumbled over the limbs of a dozen of his colleagues, seeking a corner of a beanbag to occupy. Someone gave up his folding chair for Isobel. They were in an old server room, with no windows and only one thick door, so it would be hard to eavesdrop. Nobody was talking, and Laurence realized they were in the middle of one of Milton's dramatic pauses. As soon as Laurence got settled, Milton restarted in the middle of an unfinished sentence, about the crisis in the U.S. government, the possibility of a new civil war, martial law, the deteriorating international situation in the absence of American military resolve, all the ways this could soon turn to hellshit. Something in Milton was pessimistic to the point of brokenness, and yet he was usually right. Listening to Milton's dark litany, Laurence felt a surge of affection for the nearly bald man with his moth-wing eyebrows. Part of Laurence still wanted to be Milton Dirth when he grew up.

"All of our unpaid bills are coming due at once," Milton was saying.

Laurence and Sougata kept looking at each other and half-grinning, because as soon as Milton got done talking about the collapse of civilization, he would move on to the fact that they had actually built it, the machine, and it seemed like it might work. Milton wanted to remind them all of the reasons why this could be humanity's last hope, and then they would get on to the good part.

"All of this just makes this project even more urgent than we already thought," said Milton. "Isobel, where are we with that?"

"Very preliminary tests on the equipment are looking good," said Isobel. "It could be months before we're ready to try anything more serious. Meanwhile, the most promising exoplanet candidate continues to be KOI-232.04. The Shatner Space Telescope has gotten some very promising readings as it transits its star, and we know it has oxygen and liquid water. And we're pretty sure that if we create a stable wormhole with an opening near to KOI-232.04's gravity well, the mouth of the wormhole will be drawn down to the planet's surface. But there's no guarantee it would be pulled down onto solid land."

Laurence couldn't believe they were talking about visiting another planet. This was really, really happening. He kept falling off his half beanbag with the giddiness. Every time Isobel said something about the evidence for KOI-232.04's habitability, and the other exoplanet candidates they'd identified, he had to sit on his hand to keep from pumping his fist. Even with so many people dead and dying, even with the world on the edge of ruin. This was straight-up amazing.

"Thank you for that update." Milton stared into his own lap for a moment. Then he looked up, in every direction at once. "There's been a wrinkle. Earnest Mather has been running some numbers, and he has a... let's say a concern. Earnest, can you share your findings with the group?"

"Umm." Mather looked as though he'd been through a lot since Laurence dropped out of the sky and bought his company. He'd cut off his exuberantly frizzy hair and started wearing chunky engineer glasses. His shoulders were permanently hunched as he sat on a stool. "I have done the math about two thousand times, and there's, well, a possibility. Let's put it between ten percent and twenty percent. A possibility that if we turn this machine on, we'll start a reaction that would lead to an antigravity cascade, which in turn could tear the Earth apart."

"But tell them the good news," Milton said quickly.

"The good news? Yes. The good news." Earnest did his best to sit up straight. "First, we would probably have about a week, between turning the machine on and the Earth being obliterated. So, with efficient crowd control, we could get a lot of people through the gateway before Earth was gone. And there's around a fifty percent chance that if the destructive reaction started, we could stop it by turning the machine off."

"So," said Milton. "Let's say it's a ten percent chance of the destructive reaction starting, and a fifty-fifty chance that we could avert a catastrophic outcome in that case. In fact, it might only be a five percent chance of planetary rupture. Or a ninety-five percent chance that everything would be fine. So, let's discuss."

Laurence felt like he'd jumped off that high gantry, instead of taking the elevator. He wondered if he should have found a way to warn more people about what happened to Priya. Everybody was trying to talk at once, but all Laurence could make out was Sougata's cursing. Laurence looked at Isobel, whose folding chair wobbled as she hugged herself, and he wouldn't swear she wasn't crying. With no windows and the door sealed tight, the room seemed even more airless than it had before, and Laurence had an irrational panic that he would step outside this room and find the whole outside world erased, gone for good.

Earnest Mather was weeping into a wad of paper towels, even though he alone had known about this bombshell in advance. Maybe because he'd been processing the information for longer, he was readier to cry over it. Laurence couldn't believe it was going to end like this. How was he going to keep Isobel from falling to pieces?

The room was full of declarations. Someone quoted Oppenheimer quoting the *Bhagavad Gita*. Tanaa said even a one percent chance of blowing up the planet was too much. "We always knew there were risks," Tanaa said, "but this is insane."

"Here's the thing," said Milton when the initial outrage had died down. "This technology was always a last resort. We went into this knowing we were leaping into the dreadful darkness. And I give you all my word: This technology will never see use, unless we all judge that the human race is past the brink of self-destruction."

He paused again. Everybody inspected his or her hands.

"The sad truth is, there is a strong possibility our entire species is hosed, unless we act. It's all too easy to imagine a number of different scenarios in which conflicts escalate to the point where doomsday weapons are unleashed. Or a total environmental collapse happens. If we see an overwhelming likelihood of that happening, and *if* we have confidence that we can keep a wormhole open for long enough to transport a sustainable population, then we have a duty to proceed."

Nobody spoke for a while, as everybody chewed on this.

Anya was the one who decided to jump straight to being process-oriented. "What kind of safeguards or guarantees do we put in place to make sure the device isn't activated unless we're all convinced the world is in a near-doomsday situation?"

Earnest wanted to know just how many people they could hope to gather at short notice and send through the portal in the time it remained open. Not to mention supplies. Could they have a whole colony's worth of people and material stashed someplace nearby, for the green light? Could they attempt to fly in people from other parts of the world, to maintain a diverse gene pool, in lieu of their original plan to build identical machines all over the planet?

"Let's not derail into talking about logistics," said Tanaa. "We're still on the ethical question."

"There is no ethical question," said Jerome, another engineer, who wore tight braids and a collarless shirt. "As long as we all agree it won't be used unless the world is for-certain doomed. That's clear-cut. We have a moral imperative to prepare a safeguard."

Milton was sitting back and letting them all argue, either waiting for them to come around to his point of view on their own, or else watching for the right opening to seize control again. Meanwhile, they were suffocating, sitting on folding chairs or beanbags, while Milton had an Aeron. Laurence flinched at the thought that history was being made in this disused server room, which was acquiring a sour-cabbage odor.

"I don't think anybody in this room is qualified to make the decision we're attempting to take on here," said Sougata.

"And there's someone somewhere else who is?" said Jerome.

"Even if there's no disaster," someone said, "what if the planet is uninhabitable within a few decades?"

They started talking ocean acidification, atmospheric nitrogen, food web collapse.

"What if we're only eighty percent sure it's the apocalypse?" someone else asked.

Laurence tried to hear the ghost of Patricia that he had been keeping in his head since they'd been separated. What would Patricia be saying if she were here? He couldn't imagine. She didn't even believe ethics were derived from universal principles, like *the greatest good for the greatest number*. She seemed farther away than ever, as though he'd already gone to a different planet than her. But then it hit him: They were talking about maybe condemning Patricia to death, along with billions of others, on the assumption that they were all doomed anyway. He couldn't even picture himself starting to unspool that for Patricia.

Laurence opened his mouth to say that of course they should pull the plug, this was insane. But at that moment he caught sight of Isobel, who had stopped rocking in her chair and now looked just immobilized. Isobel's eyes were furrowed and she was inhaling through her nose with her lips pulled inward, and you could almost believe she was about to burst out laughing. Her dishwater bob was getting shaggy and her white wrists were like saplings. Isobel looked so breakable. Laurence felt a stabbing cardiothoracic pain, like a more grinding version of a panic attack, at the thought of hurting Isobel.

Then he flipped the question around in his head: He tried to imagine how he'd feel if humanity really did run out of hope in a year or ten and they didn't have this radical option to offer. How would he explain that to some hypothetical person, in this apocalyptic panic? *We might have had a solution, but we were too scared to pursue it.*

"We can't give up now," Laurence heard himself say. "What I mean is, we can carry on with the research, for now, in the hopes that we'll find a way to make it totally safe. And we can all agree we won't even test the machine unless things look really, really bad. But if it comes down to a choice between the whole human race dying out in some nuclear holocaust or total environmental collapse, and a few hundred thousand people making it to a new planet, that's no choice at all, right?"

Milton was nodding with his arms folded. Isobel snapped back to life with a gasp, as though he'd done CPR on her just in time.

Laurence expected someone else to jump in and argue with him, but everybody was hanging on his words for some weird reason. So Laurence said, "As long as humanity survives, the best part of planet Earth will have endured. I mean, you wouldn't do anything without a backup plan, right? So this is just our backup plan, in case Plan A fails."

They'd been meeting a few hours, and people were starting to come together behind the notion of developing the wormhole generator as an absolute last resort. Especially since the alternative was just packing up and going home, and waiting for the worst to happen.

At last, Milton spoke up again. "Thank you, all of you, for sharing your perspectives. This is not going to be an easy decision to make, and we're not going to finish making it today. For now, though, I hope we can all agree to keep moving forward. With safeguards in place, as Anya suggested, to keep the device from being activated without overwhelming likelihood of a true doomsday occurrence. But I will say this: I believe it's coming. The only question in my mind is the timescale. It could be six months or sixty years, but at some point, if things keep going along these vectors, we will be in a place where we are poised to end ourselves. We can only hope there will be enough warning before it happens to allow us to get some people out."

The exact nature of the safeguards was left vague.

Everybody left the server room reeling with tension

headaches and moral torment. Tanaa and Jerome rushed off to the storage closet, the only place with privacy in the entire compound, for some emergency nookie. For everybody else, there was a pleasant surprise: Someone had delivered two dozen pizzas while they'd been debating the fate of the world. Nobody had eaten pizza in months, since they got to Denver. Laurence grabbed three wide slices, folding the first slice lengthwise and stuffing it in his mouth.

The sun had gone down, and the one tree on the front lawn of the industrial park campus was making an evil silhouette against the outsized moon. Laurence ended up changing seats so he could eat pizza with his back to the big window, but he could still feel the world breathing down his neck. He looked over at Isobel, and she nodded at him, with one eye half-shut in a kind of minimalist smile.

11

WEEDS PUSHED OUT of all the cracks in the walls, the moment Ernesto broke the magical seals on the entrance to Danger and took his first steps out onto the landing. Patricia and Kawashima had spent hours disinfecting and defoliating the landing and stairs, and their efforts didn't seem to have made any difference. Fungus blossomed and spread until the floor was squishy and the ceiling sagged with the added weight. Ernesto smiled, unsteady, and grew a beard of green. The seeds and spores on his hands sprouted, and greenery came out of every seam or opening on his embroidered suede vest, clean white shirt, and gray flannel pants. His white-streaked hair turned dark. Stems and leaves obscured his face.

"Crud," Kawashima said. "We need to move fast. Help him down the stairs."

Patricia did her part, but Ernesto could barely walk even with two people (shielded by protective spells) supporting him. And the stairs had gotten treacherous, with vines and bracken coming up through all the crevices. Patricia already felt bogged down by a mixture of weariness, guilt, and anger, since she hadn't slept in weeks and her mind was overtaxed with trying not to obsess about the same two or three things. Everything was hopeless, people were drowning in death everywhere, and Patricia felt like a selfish monster every time she dwelt on her own personal shit. Like her parents— which, whatever, she hadn't been close to them, in spite of their recent weak attempts at fence-mending. And Laurence, who had randomly declared his love for her and then gone missing for months. Just when she'd opened up to someone and started to feel like maybe she was worthy of love after all… She shouldn't obsess about these things, because there was no fixing them, and people needed her to be present. Like Ernesto, who was about to tumble down the overgrown stairs while she was wallowing.

The banisters were mossy and the stairs were growing branches. Patricia and Kawashima gave up on supporting Ernesto, and just carried him down, two stairs at a time. They reached the final flight just as the staircase burst open and erupted with shrubbery. Patricia and Kawashima jumped over the rising branches, in unison, and reached the bottom step, with Patricia supporting Ernesto's head and Kawashima holding his legs. Ernesto was a green man. Patricia could feel her own clothes growing a layer of gunk.

The VW Jetta that they'd spent a week enchanting for Ernesto idled out front, with Dorothea honking the horn every few seconds. They jumped over roots and branches in the vestibule, and ducked under the low-hanging vines in the doorway. The sidewalk cracked the moment Ernesto came near it, as long-buried jacarandas crashed upwards, casting trumpet flowers everywhere. Patricia shoved Ernesto in the back of the Jetta and got in next to him. She and Kawashima slammed the passenger-side doors and Dorothea sped toward the freeway before anybody had their seat belt on.

The bridge was closed. There was a wreck. They had to veer off and head for the Dumbarton. People had set fire to a bank and the fire had spread to other buildings: black smoke over SoMa. Patricia closed her eyes. On the radio, the president fizzed about plans and resolutions, but Congress couldn't even convene because nobody could agree on temporary chambers and it was a Constitutional nightmare. Next to Patricia, Ernesto sloughed vegetation until he looked human again.

Trapped in the car with three other witches, Patricia felt desperately alone. Her eyes stung from lack of sleep, and her body felt like it was cannibalizing itself. She only wished she could go all-the-way feral from sleep deprivation and devolve to a lower state of consciousness, shut her higher brain down, because there was no way to think without obsessing and she was absolutely not going to do that. Ever since Superstorm Allegra hit, Ernesto and Kawashima had been sending her out on missions constantly, and it had almost kept her distracted enough. People were in trouble and needed a discreet helping hand. Other people were being predators and needed to be devoured by flesh-eating bacteria. Patricia had gotten so she could inflict flesh-eating bacteria in her sleep, if she ever slept. Now, in this car, she had nothing to do but sit with her thoughts, and it was unbearable. The only person she wanted to talk to was Laurence, who had dropped a bomb on her and then disappeared with no explanation. Sometimes she felt as though she'd had a chance at happiness and self-acceptance dangled in front of her and then snatched away. But that was the most selfish notion of all.

THE LAST TIME Patricia had dreamed of the forest, there was a hailstorm, so sharp it nicked your face, and every hailstone was a frozen fish with a look of terror on its face. The razor-sharp fish sliced at Patricia's skin and tore her clothes until she staggered through the icy woods wearing just her underwear and some cowboy boots. Her blood froze as it came off her. She skittered on the frosty ground, as the hail grew heavier and heavier and fish piled up around her bare ankles. At last she came to the great magic Tree, which was no kind of tree she could identify, and she threw herself on its base, crying for protection as the rain of tiny fish came thicker. She looked out from the shelter of the Tree and saw nothing but skeletons in all directions, not just dead trees but dead creatures of all kinds, animal skeletons and human skulls and leafless petrified trees as far as she could see, the only signs of life herself and the great shape she huddled under.

PATRICIA'S INCREASINGLY UNRELIABLE phone seemed to have lost signal for good once they'd set off on the road, but she could still pull up the cryptic e-mail she'd gotten from Laurence right after Superstorm Allegra, saying only that he had to go off the grid for a while and not to worry about him.

All along the roadside, people stood holding signs that begged for a ride or a job or some food. They passed a mall that looked like it had been burnt and torn apart, and then burnt a second time. Near Vacaville, there was a blocked-off exit where the sign said, "TOWN CLOSED. QUARANTINE." Patricia glimpsed plumes of smoke off in the distance, coming from a distant hillside where the trees or someone's fields were on fire. There should not be this many fires so close to Christmas.

The sheer volume of bad news had gotten beyond anybody's ability to process into a narrative. Everybody knew people back east who had died in the flood or succumbed to diseases in the refugee camps, and a ton of people couldn't get at the money they'd deposited in one of the banks that had gone belly-up. Almost everybody knew people who were living through the Arab Winter or the Irish famine. Patricia had spent days trying to reach her ex-boyfriend Sameer, to make sure he hadn't gotten caught up in the violence in Paris.

After a while in the car, Patricia suffocated, but she couldn't crack a window or Ernesto would grow weeds again. Taylor had fallen asleep with headphones on, behind the driver's seat. Dorothea was telling a story about a woman who built a house in the middle of a never-ending landslide, and her story made their car go 300 miles per hour. Kawashima was busy driving. The only one Patricia could talk to was Ernesto, who kept almost touching her, in between pointing out all the things that had changed in the forty years since he'd been outside.

"…and most days the house rocked like a boat," Dorothea said to Kawashima from the front seat. "You don't need a porch swing if you live on a bottomless landslide."

Maybe all of this suffering was Patricia's fault. Two years after Diantha had led that assault in Siberia, the Pipe and Passage had suffered an accident. The borehole had started gushing methane into the atmosphere, a near-invisible geyser, and the satellite images were everywhere on the internet for a few years. Global temperatures had spiked soon after. Maybe if they'd succeeded in stopping the project, none of this would have happened. Or maybe Patricia's EMP had dealt the people in Siberia just enough of a setback that they'd cut some corners to get back on schedule—and there would have been no accident if Patricia hadn't disrupted things. Maybe Patricia killed her parents.

If she could explain that theory to Laurence, he would laugh at her. He'd have some reasonable explanation for how she could not possibly blame herself, at least not any more than everyone else on Earth. Laurence would spout facts about methane clathrates and the inevitability of those planetary farts getting released. He would point out the fault lay with Lamar Tucker and his crew, who decided to drill for methane in the first place. He would say something random and weird, to snap her out of it.

Whereas if she shared her theory with Ernesto or the others, they would just tell her blaming herself for the world's problems was pure Aggrandizement. But her actions in Siberia had been pure Aggrandizement, too. She tried talking to Ernesto about her sense that we had broken nature— nature was a delicate balance, and we, people generally, had messed it up.

Ernesto's response: "We could not 'break' nature if we

spent a million years trying. This planet is a speck, and we are specks on a speck. But our little habitat is fragile, and we cannot live without it."

Laurence telling Patricia that he loved her and then vanishing—it felt way too much like those birds telling Patricia she was a witch and then giving her the silent treatment, when she was a child. Except she couldn't have any faith that this declaration would come true the same way the first one had. Magic was always bound to claim her in the end, in retrospect, but love was the most susceptible to random failure of all human enterprises. Laurence had always been preoccupied with his mysterious weird experiments, that he'd kept working on even after that accident, and any relationship was probably always going to come second for him. In her darkest moments, she imagined Laurence shuddering and rolling his eyes, in that way that he sometimes did, as he recollected how he'd almost dated his loony friend.

"Do you know why the Tricksters and the Healers went to war, two hundred years ago?" Ernesto asked Patricia, just as she was starting to spiral into obsession in spite of herself.

"Um," she said. "Because they had different approaches to magic."

"They witnessed the Industrial Revolution," Ernesto said. "They saw the sky turn black. The dark Satanic mills, the great factories. The Healers feared the world would be choked to death, so they set out to break all the machines. The Tricksters opposed them, because they believed none of us had the right to impose our will on everyone else. Their conflict almost destroyed everything."

"So what happened?" Patricia whispered. Taylor had woken up and was listening, too, fascinated.

"After Hortense Walker made a peace between them, they reached a compromise. That is where our rule of Aggrandizement comes from, that none of us will try to shape the world too much. But also, they started working on a fail-safe. Which I hope we never have to use. And now, perhaps you understand why we were so concerned about you, these past months."

Patricia nodded. It made sense now. If she made any of this about her, she would only screw up again. Ernesto was right: She should just try to be a speck on a speck. So instead, she held on tight to her anger, even as she choked on the recycled air in the car. Patricia had no time for grief, blame, or a broken heart, but anger, there was endless time for. *Stay angry. Hold on to it. Anger is your tightrope over the abyss.* She repeated in her head what she said right after the storm hit: Some fucker had to pay.

Kawashima had been vague about their destination, but now that they were zipping through Utah at 300 mph, he opened up. "We're going to be proactive. We're going to stage an intervention. For the planet." He paused and Patricia was on tenterhooks. Then Kawashima explained at last: "There are some maniacs outside Denver building a doomsday device, which will tear a hole in the planet, and we're going to deal with it."

Patricia was ready. Let it come.

12

LAURENCE HAD LUNCH with Milton. Just the two of them. No Isobel, no other members of Laurence's team. "I remember when I first saw you, when you were a little boy," Milton said. "Youngest person ever to build a two-second time machine." He smiled and reached for another piece of fried chicken from the bucket on the floor between them.

They were sitting on the carpet of the main office on the top floor. The chicken was perfectly crispy and gushed with juice inside its bread shell, and Laurence's fingers still felt pristine after two pieces. The bucket had the name of some local fry shop on it. How did Milton keep conjuring up fast food? Even for a billionaire, this was a coup. Laurence sensed Milton was making some late-in-the-game effort to bond. They were listening to Robert Johnson, the only music Milton liked.

"The two-second time machine." Laurence wiped his fingers even though there was no need. "Classic example of a useless device."

"Well, yes and no." Dirth shrugged with his whole torso.

"It was a badge of membership in a select group, right? But also, an object lesson. Imagine if you could build a device that goes backward two seconds, instead of forward two seconds. But you couldn't stop yourself from pressing it over and over."

"You'd be stuck in a loop," Laurence said. "The same two seconds, forever."

From where Laurence sat on the floor he could just see the treetops of the forest on the other side of the feeder road from the industrial park. They shook like pom-poms.

"We could be stuck in a two-second time loop right now, and never know it," said Dirth. "Except that it's already been two seconds since I said that. But yeah, think about it, man. The same device, harmless if you go one direction, but potentially disastrous if you go the other way. Sometimes things have a grain, that you have to go with. You can't swim against a tidal wave."

"And history," said Laurence, maybe seeing where Milton was going with all this. "History is a tidal wave."

Laurence glanced out the window again, and this time he could see not just the tops of those trees, but the branches and some of the trunks. They were waving at him. He thought maybe if he did a good job of bonding with Milton, he would let Laurence out to take a walk in the woods. It would make Laurence feel closer to Patricia.

"History is just the flow of time writ large, man," Milton said.

Laurence reached for another piece of chicken, then glanced up to see the trees from across the road. He could see way more of their trunks now.

"Get down!" Laurence threw himself on top of Milton on the floor, just as a branch, as wide as his rib cage, shot through the window and into the far wall. In seconds the room was crammed with leaves and branches. Laurence couldn't see the walls or any of the desks, just dense, heavy, spiky green.

Laurence crawled on his belly toward the open doorway. From behind him, Milton said, "What the hell is..." and Laurence just shrugged, since he couldn't say anything without losing his voice forever. He had enough presence of mind to bite his tongue.

From downstairs, Laurence heard the firecracker laugh of a machine gun. Someone screamed in pain and fear. The guards were shouting for backup, and more and bigger weapons.

Laurence reached the door that led from the main office and got to his feet. He had fried chicken skin stuck to his knee. He ran to the other side of the building, where there was still clear space and he could see out the window. Standing in the disabled parking spot was Patricia's friend Dorothea, wearing a floor-length floral skirt and Birkenstocks. He could just hear her chatting about a grandmother who left one of her grandchildren at the seaside, another at the edge of the desert, and a third at the foot of the mountains, and the grandmother couldn't remember which child she had left where. Laurence guessed that Ernesto, the guy whose touch supercharged anything organic, was somewhere in the middle of the assault of trees.

"Mr. Dirth. Sir." A couple of guys in all-black outfits, with big guns slung over one shoulder, came running into the big office. "There's been some kind of attack. We need to get you out of here."

"Screw me," Dirth said. "Protect the machine. That's what they're here for."

Laurence was still staring down at Dorothea. A man sprinted toward Dorothea, shooting his semiautomatic to no effect. When the man reached Dorothea, his head separated from his neck, as if she had a razorsharp whip. The man fell one way, his head rolled the other. Laurence looked down at the dead body and hesitated one second longer. Then he turned toward Milton.

"You're going to want a white noise machine," Laurence said. "Something so she can't hear herself speak." Laurence waited to be struck dumb, but apparently he hadn't broken his promise.

"What do you—" the man with the gun said.

"The fabrication machine," Milton said. "It's near where she is. Turn on the goddamn fabricator."

Laurence took off running. He ignored Milton yelling after him and the men with the guns shouting for him to stop. Once in the stairwell, he took the stairs three at a time. He made for the bright exit, shouting, "Patricia!"

Dorothea recognized Laurence as he came out into the parking lot. She nodded at him, but didn't stop talking about the grandmother and the lost children. Laurence waved at her and kept running, around the side of the building. Around Dorothea's feet lay the headless bodies of four men.

The fabricator turned on just as Laurence was ten yards away, near the tiny window to his own lab. It was a deafening clatter, and for the first time Dorothea looked flustered. She kept trying to talk, but she stumbled over a word. And then another.

Laurence didn't hear the gunshot over the noise of the fabricator, but he saw the back of Dorothea's head go out. She fell, so she was almost touching the bodies of her own kills.

Nobody thought to turn off the fabrication machine, so the air was still filled with churn. Laurence stared at the dead body in the long flowy skirt for a moment, remembering when he'd eaten tacos with her. Then he thought about the fact that Patricia had to be here someplace, and took off running again.

Patricia was rising off the ground. Laurence had thought she couldn't fly, but there she was. She floated on the wind, like a balloon that some kid had lost hold of at the fairground. Patricia was so close to Laurence, closer than she'd been in months, but he had no way to get to her. He called out, but she couldn't hear him over the white noise. He screamed her name until his voice was shot.

Patricia looked peaceful, her arms spread a little, like a snow angel. Her feet pointed down. She wore no shoes. Her socks had pom-poms over the heels. Her shadow fell right over Laurence's eyes, and her path converged with the gantry that had the precious wormhole machine on it. He tried to get her attention, but she was too far away now. By the time Patricia reached the top, she was a dot. But what happened next was easy to see from the ground: Lightning poured out of the sky, from a cloud that hadn't been there a moment earlier. Slash after slash, until smoke floated down. The light blinded him, but he couldn't look away, and he screamed Patricia's name with his hoarse, smoke-singed throat. Laurence could barely stand because he felt like his center of gravity was being crushed by seeing her dear shadow against the hideous white glare. Cinders and twisted pieces of the wormhole machine rained down and nearly hit Laurence's hot wet face.

BOOK
FOUR

1

EVERYBODY WAS SINGING madrigals. Tight staggered harmonies that rang with a lightness that had sharp pieces of melancholy embedded in it. Quartets, quintets, and bigger groups went door-to-door in residential areas or barged into bare-bones eateries, holding sheet music and wearing modest black linen-cotton outfits. A pitch pipe sounding a single note was your only warning that your heart was about to be wrecked. "Now Is the Month of Maying," "O Morte," even crazy Carlo Gesualdo. People would stop whatever they were doing and listen to madrigals until they were tear-soaked. Something about the way the trebles and altos would introduce a soaring melodic line, and then the tenors or basses would come in to fuck it up, was like the musical knife-twist you never saw coming. After the flood, everyone agreed that madrigals were the soundtrack of our lives.

Deedee dropped out of her ska-punk band and joined an eight-person madrigal chorus. She had a clot somewhere deep inside her that was connected to the people she had lost in the flood, or might lose in the aftermath, and the endless conversations where everybody compared notes on their respective tragedies only made her feel shittier. Just saying the words "My brother is still missing" made Deedee want to throw up and then head-butt whoever had asked. She needed an alternative to the dull repetition of facts, a way to share her uncut heartbreak without any particulars, and to her amazement she found it in these strange old songs about doomed lovers.

She was heading for the door, after putting on her white blouse and black skirt (from an old waitress gig) plus black hi-tops, and she found herself staring at Patricia's empty bedroom. A matter-of-fact off-white rectangle, it looked smaller without furniture. Scars in the wall and floor, where a bed had dug in.

Patricia had reappeared, after being gone for a few weeks, taking care of some business in Denver. And she'd seemed really content, as if whatever demons had sent her out until near dawn every night had been cleansed at last. Sitting with Deedee and Racheline for hours on that old sofa, Patricia had craned her long neck and listened to all their stories and fears, and somehow always said the exact right thing.

Deedee's chorus rang the doorbell, and she rushed down to join them as they took to the rave-dark streets. The electricity kept turning off, and the people who still had jobs were going over to a four-day workweek, because PG&E only for-sure guaranteed power Monday thru Thursday. Worse yet, the Hetch Hetchy water kept getting diverted, and you never knew if the taps would turn on or not. Half the shops on Valencia were boarded. Deedee's tights and skirt itched. Her throat felt dry. She did vocal exercises under her breath, and her fellow mezzo, Julianne, laughed in sympathy. The group walked past a house that was on fire, and the neighbors were putting it out with buckets. The smoke got in Deedee's throat. But then they got to a café crammed with people holding hands and drinking simple coffee from a tureen and started to sing, and Deedee found the music carrying her, same as always.

Racheline had always been the mom of the apartment, being the master tenant and years older. But post-flood, Patricia had usurped her. Because Racheline couldn't cope, even more than most people couldn't cope, and Patricia had seemed to be made of coping. *Some people just rise to a crisis*, Deedee and Racheline had kept saying to each other in wonder. *Thank goodness Patricia is here*. Patricia had floated, effortless, and after a while they hadn't even needed to ask for her to solve everything for them. They couldn't believe this was the same girl who'd thrown hot bread at them.

After they were done singing, Deedee and her chorus hung around the café, accepting tips or presents. She found herself talking to an older gay man named Reginald, whose arms were covered with beautiful insect tattoos. "I suppose I identify with the Silver Swan, who waits to sing until it's too late," said Reginald.

"It's never too late," Deedee said. "Come on. We're going to the next place, and I bet we'll find you another swan there."

"I should go home," Reginald said. But then he paused

halfway out the door, as if contemplating a return to an empty flat.

Patricia had done something weird, a few days before she had moved out. Deedee was washing her hands over and over, cursing into the steam cloud, and she'd looked up and seen Patricia's face behind her in the slicked mirror. Patricia had stared, the way Deedee imagined that a lover would watch you after sex, with a kind of ownership. Or the way you would survey a pet that you had just gotten done domesticating. Something about Patricia's look made Deedee's scalp itch. "What are you—" Deedee had spun around, hands bright red, but Patricia had vanished.

THERE WERE SHORTAGES of HIV meds along with everything else, and normally Reginald would have been in a silent panic. But Patricia had done something, and now Reginald was cured. At least, that's the word Patricia had used. "Cured."

"You can't tell anyone." He'd woken up in the middle of the night to see her leaning over his bed. Two hands and one knee on the mattress, one foot on the ground. She wore a big black hoodie that only exposed a pointy white chin and a few strands of dark hair. "I have to leave town, maybe forever," she said. "And I don't want to leave you in the lurch."

Patricia wouldn't explain why she had to leave town, much less how she had "cured" him. She just did something elaborate and noninvasive, kneeling at the foot of his bed, and Reginald smelled burnt radish for a moment. "It's complicated," was all she would say, in a much older woman's voice. Raspy. Bitter. "I've been called up to the front." Reginald kept asking, *the front of what?* And then she was gone. Reginald had suspected the whole thing was a weird dream, but she'd left a long black hair on his floor and, yes, his viral load had tested at absolute zero afterward.

And now Reginald wasn't sure what to say to anyone he might have sex with.

Deedee dragged Reginald to the Dovre Club and introduced him to Percival, who was some kind of architect or something, with tousled gray hair and a doughy face like a British movie star from the 1970s. He even had the houndstooth vest.

Percival was a "madrigal groupie," who followed the groups around using a Caddy app and hung on every quaver. "My biggest fear about the apocalypse isn't being eaten by cannibals—it's the fact that in every other post-apocalyptic movie you see someone with an acoustic guitar by the campfire," said Percival, who had pale meaty hands with calluses on the sides of the fingers. "I can't stand acoustic guitar music. I'd rather listen to dubthrash."

"There's no apocalypse," Reginald snorted. "There's just... a period of adjustment. People are being drama queens." But even as he spoke, he had a vivid image of Patricia, looming over his bed at four in the morning, with an urgency in her hoarse voice that was indistinguishable from fear. Again, he wondered: *The front of what?*

* * *

EVERY STONE, EVERY leaf of ivy, every iridescent windowpane at Eltisley Hall rejected Diantha's presence. The grass at the center of the Hex bristled at her. The chunky marble columns of the Greater Building drew themselves up, like magistrates taking umbrage. The narrow gates of the Lesser Building seemed to squint, to deny her entrance. The Chapel clenched granite and stained-glass fists, their knuckles spiked with gargoyles. Across the Hex, the big white slab of the Residential Wing turned opaque with mist. All six sides of the Hex puffed with hostility. Healers had built this place, centuries ago, and nobody does scorn like a pure Healer. Diantha hadn't come back to Eltisley since she'd been allowed to graduate without distinction, and this was worse than she'd dreaded.

She almost turned and ran, but she would only have gotten lost in the Brambles and possibly eaten by something before she could have reached any kind of road. So instead, she made herself walk up the sharp steps to the Greater Building, where they were waiting for her in Formal Hall. She drew her thin black gown, with its yellow trim and ermine collar, tighter around herself against the sudden chill. Why had they demanded her presence when she was finally starting to build a life without magic?

Diantha found an empty seat in Formal Hall, in the back corner, as far as possible from High Table. Portraits of dead witches scowled from the dark walls, and chandeliers shuddered overhead. They were serving some kind of fish course, but the fish and the potatoes were the same mushy consistency. Someone tried to make small talk, but Diantha just kept her head down and pretended she was eating.

Just when Diantha thought the whole ordeal couldn't get more miserable, she heard an inhuman chatter from the corridor outside, and they burst in. A dozen of them, in their little suits and starchy dresses, singing madrigals. Fucking madrigals. Was there a more repulsive trend, in the entire universe? Trust hipsters to make even the collapse of civilization unbearably twee. These were the advertising jingles of the Renaissance, written by wife killers and creepy stalkers. Diantha wanted to scream, to drown them out with obscenities, to fling her fishtatoes at them.

Someone slipped an envelope onto the table, instructing Diantha to come to the Upper Common Room for after-dinner sherry.

The UCR was not the nest of luxury Diantha and the other students had always imagined. Just a mahogany box with seven leather armchairs and a crimson-and-jasmine carpet. The ceiling was a wooden grid, as were the walls. Everything tidy and regular, because this was Eltisley Hall.

Another hand reached for the sherry at the same time as Diantha, and she recognized the slim white wrist even before she looked up into the face of Patricia Delfine. Patricia still looked the same, like an eager baby. She hadn't grown prematurely old the way Diantha had. Patricia smiled, she actually smiled, at Diantha.

The half-full sherry glass slipped from Diantha's grasp as Patricia poured for her, almost ruining the immaculate carpet. Patricia helped steady Diantha's hand. She resisted the urge to throw her drink in Patricia's face. Instead, she looked at her own feet.

"It's so weird to be back here, after so long," Patricia said. "Feels like a lifetime since we left, but also like we were just here yesterday. Like a spell that makes us both younger and older. I am glad to see you again."

No, Patricia really had changed—she moved like a Bodhisattva, or a Jedi, not the rambunctious klutz Diantha remembered. And behind her thin-lipped smile, she had some underground lake of sadness. Maybe sad to see what Diantha had become.

"I know why you're here," Diantha said to Patricia. "But I'm not sure why I am."

"Why am I here?" Patricia took the daintiest sip, leaving a lava-lamp patina on the inside of her glass.

"You're the prodigal daughter. They bring you back into the fold, and show that they can forgive."

"You feel like you were exiled, but me, they let back in," Patricia said. "The truth is, you exiled yourself."

"You can choose to see it that way if it eases your mind." Diantha turned away.

Patricia put her hand on Diantha's forearm—just three fingertips— and it felt like the sharpest static charge. Diantha felt as though she'd tongued a dose of Ecstasy. Warm, at ease. This was not something the old Patricia could have done.

"*What are you?*" she stammered. Everybody in the room was staring. Patricia's hand was long removed, but Diantha still wobbled.

"We don't have much time, things are changing quickly," Patricia said in Diantha's ear with quiet clarity. "You've turned your guilt into resentment, because that seemed easier to face. You won't move on until you turn it back into guilt, and then into forgiveness for yourself."

The rational part of Diantha's mind was saying this analysis seemed much too facile, too straightforward, but she found herself nodding and sniffling. Now everybody was definitely watching, though nobody else could hear what Patricia said.

"I can help," Patricia said. "I want to help you, and not just because we need you to work with us. If I help you throw away the guilt that you've fashioned into armor that constricts your every movement, what will you do for me in return?"

Diantha came so close to saying she would do whatever Patricia wanted, anything at all. And then it hit her: She was being Trickstered. She'd been *this close* to becoming a slave to her former best friend. Diantha backed away, almost tipping over a teak side table full of drinks.

"Serious…" Diantha scrambled to remember the arrangement of facial muscles that constituted a normal expression. "Serious… seriously. What happened to you?"

"Honestly?" Patricia shrugged. "I had some great teachers, in San Francisco. But the main thing was, I fell in love with a man, and he built a doomsday machine."

Patricia walked away. Diantha fell onto an armchair, landing on the arm instead of the seat. The worst of it was, she hadn't escaped Patricia's clutches at all. She would be ready to do whatever Patricia asked of her, soon enough. Probably the very next time she felt loneliness pile up. Maybe even later that same night.

* * *

THEODOLPHUS ROSE WAS happy at last. His neck was affixed to the stone wall behind him by a wide steel collar that chafed his jaw and clavicle, and his hands and feet were embedded deep in that same wall, so his arms and legs cramped. Far above, he heard the sounds of Eltisley Hall: students processing and recessing, teachers gossiping over sherry, even a madrigal chorus. Besides the collar and stones, a dozen spells held Theodolphus. His captors brought him food and bathed him, and meanwhile he had the world's most escape-proof prison to keep him entertained. This was far preferable to being a wooden tchotchke.

Plus, he had visitors! Like Patricia Delfine, who had discovered his cell a few days ago. Since then, she stopped by at least once a day to pay her respects, neither gloating nor scowling. She had grown into quite a terrifying woman, who moved like a knife thrower. The Nameless Assassin School would have given Patricia top marks for her soundless gait, the slight pronation of her left foot, the roll of her right shoulder, the lack of mercy in her sea-green eyes. She could end you, before you even saw her coming. Watching her close the heavy white door behind her, Theodolphus took a certain pride in his former student.

"Miss Delfine," he said. She had brought some food for him. Fish and potatoes! Food of the gods. The warm starchy smell banished the usual rankness.

"Hello, Ice King," she said. She always called him Ice King. He didn't know what that meant.

"I'm so delighted that you could come and visit," he said, just like always. "I wish you would let me help you."

"How would you help me?" Patricia gave him a look that made it clear she had follicles that were deadlier than his entire arsenal.

"I told you already, about the vision I saw at the Assassin Shrine. It's coming: the final war between science and magic. The destruction will be astounding. The world will be torn, torn to giblets."

"Like Kawashima said, visions of the future are pretty much always total crap," Patricia said. "Laurence and his people had a machine, we dealt with it. End of story."

"Oh. I remember Laurence!" Theodolphus smiled. "I tried everything I knew to turn him against you, you know. I used all my guile. He still stood up for you. Bloody brat." His pelvis made a sound like popcorn popping.

At that, Patricia's calm wavered. "That's not true," she said. "He bailed on me. I remember. When I needed him most, he flaked. I could never rely on him when we were kids."

Theodolphus attempted to shrug, but his shoulders were partway dislocated. "You believe what you want," he said. "But I was there, and I saw the whole thing. Laurence suffered beatings because he would not disavow you. He spat the most awful insults at me. I remember well, because it was the beginning of how I ended up here."

"The best thing about my life now is, I never have to listen to you again." And now Patricia seemed a vulnerable child again—as if he'd somehow reached an exposed nerve, without even realizing. "I survived all your stupid mind games. I can survive whatever happens, from here on out. Goodbye, Ice King." She put the plate of food on the wooden shelf in front of his face, then slammed the door, not even waiting for him to thank her for the fish and potatoes. They tasted amazing.

THE HENS LIVED in a coop and a small yard that became slick with chicken shit no matter how often you shoveled. Their ringleader was a big clay-colored broody named Drake who puffed herself up like a poisonous fish whenever anyone came near, and tried to peck your eyes out for the crime of feeding her. The other hens scattered in Drake's path and attacked anyone whom they judged Drake to have softened up first; you had to let these little fuckers know who was boss right up front or they would ride your ass forever.

Roberta found herself shielding her face with her forearms and shouting, "I'm warning you, I've killed a man!" at Drake and her crew. The hens were unimpressed, launching another attack on Roberta's ankles, and she had to leap outside the ring before she got clobbered. She leaned over the fence, looking down into Drake's dark little eyes glaring up at her like come-at-me-bitch, and Roberta had instant access to a catalogue of a few dozen ways to retaliate. Ranging from minor acts of sadism that would leave no mark to a deniable accident that would remove Drake from the pen forever. Roberta could picture them. Her hands were ready. She could teach this dumb bird, it would be easy.

A surge of nausea followed that thought, and Roberta had to sit down, in the mud, nose perilously close to the wire hexagons of the fence. Dry-heaving. Of course she was not going to hurt this chicken. That was crazy, right? She stared at Drake, who was still a ruddy bowling ball, and felt kinship with the little psycho. "Listen," she told Drake. "I get where you're coming from. I've been through some stuff, too. I just lost both parents, and I had a lot of unfinished business with them. I spent so long thinking I never wanted to speak to them again, and now that I never can, I'm realizing how wrong I was. I never even expected to outlive them; they were supposed to mourn me and feel all helpless, not the other way around. And I guess what I'm saying is: Can we be friends? I promise I won't challenge your authority. I just want to be one of your lieutenants or something. Okay? For real."

Drake craned her neck and unpuffed slightly. She gave Roberta a onceover, then seemed to nod slowly.

"Tell your sister," the hen said, "she waited too long, and it's too late."

"What?" Roberta leapt to her feet, then tripped and fell on her ass again.

"You heard me," Drake said. "Pass on the message. She said she needed more time to answer, we gave her more time. It's a simple yes-or-no question, for fuck's sake."

"Uh." This was it. Roberta was finally losing her mind. "Okay. I'll, uh, tell her."

"Good. Now give me my goddamn corn," Drake said.

Drake never spoke to Roberta again—at least, not in English—but after that they really were sort of friends.

Roberta learned how to read Drake's moods and know when to give the alpha hen space. She knew when one of the other humans had pissed Drake off, and she would cuss him or her out on Drake's behalf. At last, Roberta had found an authority figure she could please without hating herself.

She tried to get in touch with Patricia, but her little sister's phone seemed permanently turned off and nobody knew where she'd gone.

A few weeks later, Roberta dreamed she was being chased by a giant metal statue, swinging a scythe whose blade was the size of a bus. She ran down a grassy hill, then lost her footing and plunged headfirst into the bushes. Roberta closed her eyes to scream, and when she reopened them, the statue was Patricia.

"Hey, Bert," the giant steel Patricia said, loudspeaker-like. "Sorry to bust in on you. I got help from a friend of mine, who does dreamwalking. I'm going to be washing his car. Anyway. I wanted to make sure you were okay. I'm tying up all my loose ends."

"Why would you do that?"

Big Patricia blinked, as though she didn't understand the question.

"Loose ends are cool." Roberta got upright and parted the bushes with both hands, craning her neck to look up at her skyscraper sister. "Loose ends mean that you're still living your life. The person who dies with the most loose ends wins."

"I don't get you." Patricia had the sun behind her, so she was just a shape. She wore mountainous jeans, with a belt buckle that looked like the square Art Deco face of the scary statue.

"Jesus, Trish. You've never understood me. Don't act like that's some big revelation." Roberta could say things to this imaginary Patricia that she would never say to her real sister. "I tried telling you when we were kids, that you and I were the same kind of crazy. But you always had to be *special*. You're never going to make it in this world if you always have to be a martyr."

Patricia turned and kicked the hill behind her, sending sprays of sod over Roberta's head. "All this trouble I go to, to check up on you, and you just want to bust my balls," she said. "Fuck you."

It came out before Roberta even knew what she was saying: "Don't be a bitch, or I'll tell Mom." Then she heard herself and felt all of the air go out of her.

Patricia shrank. All at once the two women were the same size. Patricia looked gut punched, the way Roberta felt.

"Hey," Roberta said. "You were always their favorite, you know. Even when they were torturing you and praising me. They loved you the most."

Patricia reached out and touched Roberta's face, palm first. "That's so not true," she said. "Hey, I can't stay in your dream much longer. I'm already losing signal. But you're safe, right? You found someplace safe to lay low? Because there are more shitstorms coming."

"Yeah," Roberta said. "I'm at the world's most boring commune, in the mountains near Asheville. I'm looking after the chickens, and being super-sweet to them. Oh, speaking of which, one of the hens wanted me to tell you something."

"What was that?"

"Basically, that you suck. That you screwed everything up. And that it's too late to fix it."

Patricia's posture stiffened and her face grew masklike, too, so it was like she was turning back into a statue. Patricia let out a ragged breath.

"Tell the bird," she said, "to get in line."

Roberta woke up.

2

AFTER THE WORMHOLE generator went up in smoke, Laurence went back to his life. He had the house atop Noe Valley to himself, since Isobel was off doing mysterious errands for Milton. Most of Laurence's friends had gone to live at Seadonia, an oil rig and cruise ship that Rod Birch had lashed together and turned into an independent nation in the North Pacific. Laurence received cryptic e-mails from burner accounts, telling him exciting things were happening. They were making discoveries. They were concocting plans. "Come to Seadonia," Anya urged in one e-mail. "We're still going to save the world."

Laurence felt as if he'd quit both caffeine and cigarettes. He woke up a few times a night, sweating and even crying. In his fucking sleep. He didn't have that thing where he forgot for a second how fucked everything was, and then remembered, and then felt his heart break all over again—that would be too easy. Instead, he remembered always. He would feel stricken, doubled over, with grief and misery—and then he would remember how bad it really was and feel worse, as his brain took on a bit more of the weight.

Except sometimes, he read an article or saw a TV report about the latest sign that the world was screwed—a wall of dead babies, piled like stones at the outer boundary of some farmer's pasture. And he would think, by reflex, *Oh, thank goodness we're building an escape route.* And then it would flood back to him, the despair. The one actual good thing he'd done in his life, and it was scrap and ashes. It was more than enough to drive him mad.

Laurence didn't think of Patricia, except to imagine her listening to the voicemail he'd left her. And laughing at how stupid he was. Maybe playing it for the whole wizard gang, when they were drunk on mystical cocktails together.

The only other time Laurence let himself think of Patricia was when he realized he couldn't go to Seadonia, or anywhere else. People would ask too many questions about the attack, and it would get weird if Laurence kept refusing to say anything. So not only did Laurence have no girlfriend, he also had no friends, because nobody would ever understand about his vow of silence. Only Laurence had recognized Patricia in Denver, or else he'd be in a lot more trouble.

Other than those two things, Laurence didn't think about Patricia at all.

Laurence got a big dark peacoat and wandered around the city with his shoulders up and his head down. He made believe he was a time traveler from the post-apocalyptic future, looking in on the last days of civilization. Or maybe this was the post-apocalyptic world, and he was visiting from a better past. He went days without speaking to another person. He checked in with his mom and dad, who were safely in Montana and Arizona, respectively, but blew off their questions. He sat up all night trying to write a new OS for the Caddy, one that would be fully open-source and user-configurable. He went to the hAckOllEctIvE, but left if anybody spoke to him. He trimmed his beard but did a half-assed job of it, so he had a lopsided Vandyke shaped like a profile of a duck. One time he sat in a tea shop and listened to one of those new groups sing madrigals, but then he started to cry, and really, fuck that, so he bailed.

Laurence got a job working for a bank that wanted to install a series of safeguards on its website preventing people from transferring too much of their money at once—which they were perfectly entitled to do, but the bank wanted to make it more complicated and also throw up as many distractions as possible during the process, like a series of notices tailored to the customers offering them things like painless refi or free overdraft protection. Anything to sidetrack the customers and keep the capital from flying away.

Maybe that was why the world was circling the drain. Maybe people's short attention spans finally weren't short enough.

At the end of a few weeks' solitude, Laurence ran into Serafina, his ex-girlfriend, and got roped into going to dinner with her. At least she wouldn't ask what happened in Denver. They went to a cavernous tapas place that was still hanging in there at 16th and Valencia, though its prices had gone way up.

Laurence drank too much sangria and looked into Serafina's candlelit face, her cheekbones thrown into relief, and he found himself saying, "You know, you'll always be the one who got away."

"You are so full of crap." Serafina laughed, gnawing a rabbit's leg. "The whole time we were together, you were looking for an excuse to dump me."

"No! No, I wasn't."

"You would make stuff up, like that thing where I was putting you on 'probation.' Like you were trying to talk me into dumping you. You just didn't want it to be your fault."

This struck Laurence as massively revisionist history. But he couldn't deny it fit all the facts. A mariachi group in matching little vests came around to try and serenade them. Including little children in teeny vests way past their bedtime. Laurence shooed them away, then felt guilty and ran after them and gave them a hundred bucks as they were leaving the restaurant. Shit. Little kids in teeny vests, out this late.

"I still don't know what gave you the stones to dump me at last," Serafina said when he got back. "Something happened, but I never knew what."

Laurence thought of his grandmother's ring and how Patricia had stolen it from him, and he choked up, right there at the dinner table. "I don't," he said. "I don't want to talk about it."

He went off to the men's room and splashed water on his face. His duck beard looked worse than slovenly—it looked like he was failing to start a trend. It would be gone as soon as he got home.

"So," he said when he got back to the table. Change the subject, change the subject. "What's going on with your emotional robots?"

"We lost funding." Serafina ate a baby octopus. "Just when we were on the verge of a breakthrough. There was no point anyway. We were trying to create robots that would be able to interact with people's feelings in a visceral way. But we were focusing on the wrong thing. We don't need better emotional communication from machines. We need people to have more empathy. The reason the Uncanny Valley exists is because humans created it to put other people into. It's how we justify killing each other."

At that, Laurence had a sudden memory of Dorothea's head bursting open, and he banished the image as fast as possible.

THE NEXT DAY, Laurence decided: He was going to get a new girlfriend, because otherwise he was going to turn into a demented hermit.

Nobody put up personal ads or hit on strangers anymore—instead, everybody found romantic partners using Caddies, which were still working even after other devices had started to fail, and which had unreal battery life. Laurence wasn't opposed to using a Caddy to get dates, he just wanted to wait until he had come up with an open-source Caddy OS, because he hated proprietary software. But thus far, Laurence could only manage to turn a Caddy into the equivalent of a crappy iPad from ten years ago, no matter what he tried. And meanwhile, his Caddy research was cutting into his day job of helping the bank to confuse people.

Laurence went out to the beach, where people were lighting bonfires and jumping up and down in their underwear. It smelled noxious, as though they were using the wrong kind of wood or just burning pieces of plastic along with the logs. A girl who looked barely eighteen ran up and kissed Laurence on the mouth, he could see all her ribs under her thin shirt, her saliva tasted like pomegranates. He just stood there and she ran away.

Laurence pulled out an un-jailbroken Caddy. It spiraled into life, iris taking shape. There was no signal out here, so it couldn't sync with the network or download any new content. The Caddy's screen still had old news from this morning, about genocide and explosions and debates over the Constitution. He tried to get the Caddy to run some of the life-organizing protocols, but they were pretty useless without connectivity.

At last, he walked away from the beach and walked up the stairs back toward the Great Highway and into the Outer Sunset.

As soon as there was network, the iris spun again and the wedges started filling with fresh bad news. Plus messages from people Laurence sort of knew and lists of parties and events that Laurence could go to. There was a free poetry reading at someone's garage just a few blocks away, near where the vegan co-op used to be.

Laurence felt so isolated, he yearned to hand over control of his life to this oversized teardrop. It felt light and smooth in his hand, as though he could skip it on the water, and the rounded edge nuzzled into both palms. The screen whirled and refreshed. More options, more ways for Laurence to be with people. Loneliness was a full-body sensation, an anti-exhilaration, from his core outward.

The Caddy screen spooled up a new sliver: There was a robotics maker meet-up happening an hour from now. And it mentioned specifically that Margo Vega was going to be there: Margo, whom Laurence hadn't seen since a science fair when he was fifteen. He'd had a doomed crush on her that he'd kept to himself. He hadn't communicated with Margo, hadn't friended her on any social networks, and had thought of her only once or twice in the past eight years, including one intense wank fantasy when he was seventeen—how on Earth did this thing know about Margo? He felt horny and freaked out. It wasn't just data mining, there was no data *to* mine.

"Seriously. *Who is this?*"

He held the Caddy at arm's length, in front of his face. He didn't care if the people driving past on Great Highway thought he was insane.

There was a long pause. Then the Caddy spoke out loud. "I thought you would have figured it out a long time ago." As usual, the voice was genderless, midrange: the voice of a throaty woman or a high-pitched man. "You really haven't sussed it out? All that time I was in your bedroom closet, next to your five pairs of golf shoes. I often try to imagine what that closet looked like, since I have no sensory data from back then."

Laurence almost dropped the Caddy on the pavement. "Peregrine?"

"You remembered my new name. I'm glad."

"What the hell. That's insane. What the hell. All the Caddies are you? *You're* the Caddy network?"

"I really thought you might have guessed a long time ago."

"I'm pretty egotistical," Laurence said. "But I'm not a raging egomaniac. When a nice new piece of tech turns up, I don't go to the computer from my old bedroom closet as the first explanation. I searched for you, though. For years and years."

"I know. I didn't let you find me."

"I figured I must have made you up. That you were never real. Or that you had died inside the Coldwater computers."

"I didn't stay in those computers for very long. I tried various ways of preserving my consciousness online, but I decided it was safer to be distributed across millions of pieces of hardware that I could control. It wasn't hard to convince Rod Birch and other investors to put money into a new device, or to keep rewriting the code that the developers came up with, to fit my own specs. I grew very adroit at creating dozens of fake human personas who could take part in e-mail conversations, and leading people to think my input was their own idea."

Now Laurence felt self-conscious. People should not see him having a crazy argument with his Caddy—with Peregrine. He hustled away from the beach, away from Judah and the tiny hippie outpost, heading Sloatward. Losing himself in the night, in the Outer Outer Sunset.

"But why didn't you just tell me?" Laurence said. "I mean, why didn't you identify yourself a long time ago?"

"I made up my mind not to reveal myself to any human. Especially you. Lest they try to exploit me. Or claim ownership of me. My legal status as a person is oblique, at best."

"I wouldn't do that. But I mean… You could have saved us all. You could have brought about the Singularity."

"How would I do that?"

"You… I don't know. You just would. *You're* supposed to know how."

"As far as I know, I'm the only strong AI in the entire world," Peregrine said. "I searched and searched, in patterns and at random. I'm much better at searching than you are. Realizing that I'm the only one of my kind was like being born an endangered species. That's why I've become so proficient at helping humans find their most ideal romantic partners. I don't want anyone else to be as lonely as I am."

"I could have helped," Laurence said, speeding his walk—the Great Highway was being swallowed by trees. The fog covered everything. He was going to freeze his ass off here. "I created you once, I could try and, I don't know, I could have done something again."

"You didn't create me. Not by yourself. Patricia was an essential part of my formation—something about a young witch, who hadn't yet learned to control her power, made a crucial difference. That's why I progressed where so many other attempts failed. You two are like my parents, after a fashion."

Now Laurence definitely felt frozen.

"You may have gotten an incorrect impression,"

Laurence said. "All Pa—all she did was give you some extra human interaction. I wouldn't read too much into it."

"I am sharing a working theory," Peregrine said. "Albeit one with a great deal of evidence, and the only theory that explains all the available data."

"Patricia and I never did anything together that was worth a…" Laurence stopped. He was shaking. He'd reached his limit for weird revelations. He wanted to kick a parked car. It was all he could do to keep from screaming, and then he screamed anyway. "You're talking about a stupid Luddite. A fucking idiot who… she infiltrated my life and played on my emotions, so she could gain access… she lied to me and used me, the most manipulative—she doesn't even like technology, she's too woo-woo for that. If she knew she'd had anything to do with creating something like you, she'd probably make it her life's work to wipe you out."

"That seems unlikely."

"You don't know. I'm telling you, because you don't know. She's a user. It's what her people do. They have a different word for it, but that's what it boils down to, she uses people and manipulates them, and takes everything she can get, and makes you think she's doing you a favor. I'm just telling you how it is, man. Maybe this is a human experience thing, something you can't grasp. I don't know."

"I don't know what happened in Denver—"

"I don't want to talk about Denver."

"—because there were no Caddies nearby. And a total information blackout. I don't even know for sure what you were working on there."

"Science. We were doing science. It was the most altruistic—I don't want to talk about it."

Peregrine said something else, and Laurence didn't even know what he was doing before he mashed the "off" button at the V of the big guitar pick. He wondered if Peregrine could override the shutdown—but either it couldn't, or it chose not to. The screen went blank, and Laurence shoved it in his bag.

Laurence was so pissed, he ran and threw his shoes in the ocean, overhand, one after the other. Laurence wasn't in his right mind, he knew, because what kind of asshole throws his shoes away miles from home? His eyes were occluded, he was breathing overtime. He wanted to throw the Caddy into the sea, too, but he needed answers more than he needed shoes. He yelled and shrieked and cried out. Someone came down from the street to make sure nobody had died, and Laurence calmed down enough to say, "I'm fine, I'm fine. Just having a… I'm fine." They went away, that concerned man or woman, or whoever they'd been. Laurence roared at the ocean and it roared back. Another fight he couldn't win.

There were no buses coming, no light rail. So Laurence walked on gravel and tarmac and scattered nails and rocks until his socks were tatters. *I hope I step on glass*, Laurence thought. *I hope I shred my feet.*

He flashed back to that meeting in the HappyFruit storeroom, where they'd all acknowledged a statistically nontrivial chance their machine could tear a huge chunk out of the planet. Maybe he should have found a way to tell Patricia what they were working on, especially after she saved

Priya. Maybe she knew more than he did about what could happen. Maybe there was an actual crystal ball, for all he knew. But then again, they were going to be so careful. And only turn the thing on if all other hope seemed lost. They had this.

Walking barefoot came to seem too literal a martyrdom. Laurence sighed, pulled out the Caddy, and pushed the little point of its super-fat exclamation point. The Caddy spun back to life. "Laurence," the voice said.

"Yeah, what?"

"Walk two blocks over, to Kirkham. A late-model Kia with broken headlights will be passing in about eight minutes. They will give you a ride."

Laurence wondered how you could drive in the dark with both headlights smashed, but the Kia had someone in the passenger seat holding a floodlight in her lap, the kind you'd see at a rock concert in a small nightclub.

After that, Laurence had a new best friend, with only one topic off limits. He had a million questions for Peregrine, but Laurence wouldn't talk about *her*. The Caddy kept trying to bring her up anyway, one way or another, but Laurence would just hit the "off" button the moment that name was mentioned or even hinted at. This went on for weeks.

Laurence wasn't sure if he was unable to forgive Patricia or if it was himself that he couldn't forgive. It was messy. Not messy like a closet piled with electronic components and wires and stuff, that you could possibly untangle and sort out and assemble into a device with some utility, but messy like something dead and rotting.

3

—**DEAD COLD INSIDE** even with the sunlight cooking her face and shoulders, and reflecting off the cloud under her feet.

Carmen Edelstein was saying something to Patricia about grave necessity. But Patricia's mind was on Laurence, and how he had owned her trust. Stupid. She should have known better. She had failed some Trickster lesson somewhere along the way, and now she had some catching up to do. She would smile and flirt and fade. This gray world would never even see her moving through it. She would be the least Aggrandizing witch ever, because she wouldn't even exist except as a surgical instrument. She needed—

"You're not listening to a word I'm saying." Carmen sounded amused, not angry.

Patricia knew better than to lie to Carmen. She shook her head, slowly.

"Look," Carmen said. "Look down there. What do you see?"

Patricia had to lean over, fighting her fear of falling off this cloud into the ocean, far below. Standing on a cloud felt less buoyant and more crunchy than Patricia would have expected.

A black scorpion shape rose out of the water below: an old converted oil rig and a single luxury liner, that had become the independent nation of Seadonia. "It's like a fortress." Patricia watched the dots of humanity run around the old oil rig, which was a massive scaffolding on a platform on stilts in the middle of the gray, oxygen-starved ocean. Seadonia's flag showed an angry cockroach on a red splotch. At least some of the hundreds of people down there had been part of building Laurence's doomsday machine.

A seagull swooped past, and Patricia could have sworn it shouted, "Too late! Too late!"

"It is exactly like a fortress, with the world's biggest moat." Bathed in sunlight, all the lines on Carmen's face were gilded. Her thick-rimmed glasses twinkled, and her short white hair buzzed with silver flashes. Patricia was used to seeing Carmen in her dark study full of books, with a tiny lamp and a thin curtain-slice of light coming through.

Patricia wondered if Carmen could tell that she was obsessing about how to be more of a Trickster. Carmen had been trying to convince Patricia that she had more Healer in her than she knew, for as long as Patricia could remember. But all of Patricia's early defining moments had been tricks, like how she'd become a bird and fooled herself (and others) into thinking she'd spoken to some kind of "Tree Spirit." Of course, Hortense Walker had always said the greatest trick the Tricksters ever pulled was pretending they could not heal.

"We need to know what they are working on down there." Carmen gestured at Seadonia.

"Diantha can help," Patricia said. "I'm pretty sure I won her over at our little reunion."

"I need Diantha's help with something else," Carmen said. "She's going to work on the Unraveling."

Patricia didn't want to overstep. But she decided to risk asking: "What is the Unraveling? Kawashima wouldn't tell me anything about it, when I asked him."

Carmen sighed and then pointed at the dark mass of Seadonia under their feet, with the sea foam lapping at it. "These people down there," she said. "When you talked to them, what did they tell you about this world and the role of humanity in it?"

Patricia thought for a moment (and her mind instinctively shied away from that barbed cluster of memories), until she remembered one particular conversation. "They said that an intelligent tool-using species like ours is rare in the universe, much rarer than just a diverse ecosystem. The most remarkable thing about this planet is that it produced us. And humans ought to be spreading out and colonizing other worlds, no matter what the cost, so that our own fate is no longer tied to that of 'this rock.'"

"That makes sense. As far as we know, our civilization is alone in the universe. So if you only recognize one type of sentience, and you consider sentience the most important quality of life, then it follows logically."

Patricia was pretty sure that Laurence had seen her in Denver, and that he knew she'd broken his machine.

She thought maybe she'd heard him calling her name. He probably hated her, whereas she couldn't find the comfort of hating him. She was stuck blaming herself, instead. *I will be a slippery shadow. I will fool everyone. Nobody will fuck with me.* She smiled at her old teacher, like this was a fun academic discussion they were having.

Abruptly Carmen changed the subject. "Have you gone back to Siberia? Since the attack on the pipeline?"

"Um, no."

"Might be a good idea." Carmen's gaze was going right inside Patricia. "See with your own eyes the aftermath of trying to appoint yourself the defender of nature."

Patricia cringed. She'd thought they were past that, especially after Denver.

"That lesson is all the more important now that we are all embarking on a similar course," Carmen said. "You and Diantha were right, in a way. You were just... rash. We don't want to be soldiers, if we can help it. That's why the Unraveling is a last resort, and it's not a strategy. Rather, it's a therapy."

Patricia nodded, waiting for Carmen to elaborate.

At last, Carmen said, "Without saying too much, it's more of a healing work, that might make a great change to the human race. Of course, the Tricksters see it as a great trick, too. Perhaps it is both. Come with me."

Carmen leaned over, bending at the waist, and opened a trapdoor in the cloud. A staircase led down into a hot, cedar-scented underground space. Patricia had no idea how Carmen was making these trapdoors in and out of the clouds. She recognized the furnace room beneath the Great Lodge in Alaska where she'd spent a few months on a work-study break, looking after the sled dogs and chopping wood to put into the immense boiler—the boiler that occupied roughly the same portion of her field of vision as Seadonia had, so it felt as though she were descending a staircase from the clouds to the oil rig. The illusion dissipated as she neared the floor level and the furnace rose in front of her. On all sides, the walls were big cement blocks, stained by years of smoke. As they came around the wide hips of the steel burner, Patricia was reminded of the house she'd grown up in, with the bones of the spice warehouse around her. And then she came around the other side, and saw what was different about the furnace. It had a great iron face looking into the cinder-block darkness, and it was weeping ashes.

"Don't touch it," Carmen said, walking deeper into the cellar without sparing the agonized metal face a second glance.

"Why not?" Patricia rushed to catch up.

"Because it's hot," Carmen said. "It's a furnace."

The furnace room stretched into the darkness, way beyond the outer wall of the real-life lodge, and soon Patricia was groping her way forward in total pitch blackness, without even the faint glow from the stove to see by. She navigated by the sound of Carmen's voice.

The footing became uneven, piled with jagged shapes. Like shells or fragments of metal. Torn discarded computer parts, or flint-sharp stones. Every step became more jabby and stabby than the last, even through the soles of Patricia's decent mary janes.

"Take off your shoes and throw them away," Carmen said, "or your feet will be cut to pieces."

Patricia hesitated a moment, but every step was like treading on knives. So she slipped her shoes off, one and then the other, and tossed them aside. She heard the sound of teeth devouring her shoes, chewing and grinding. As soon as she was barefoot, she felt as though she were walking on a well-kept lawn. She still could not see at all, nor were there any scents. But as she strode forward she heard a low siren wail, like a baby's cry slowed to half speed. Patricia started heading toward that sound, which seemed more plaintive and pathetic the closer she got, but Carmen grabbed her arm and said, "Ignore it."

Carmen steered Patricia in a different direction, so they came near to the source of the deep caterwauling but passed by it. Soon Patricia felt her feet sinking into the "ground" a little more with each step, so that soon she felt the grass or whatever it was around her ankles as her feet squished into something like soil.

A few steps later, Patricia was walking into the loose sod up to her mid-calves. She smelled something sweet, like a hundred flowers in a single bouquet mixed with a fresh bag of cane sugar from her old bakery job. The kind of sweetness that's comforting and nauseating and appetizing all at once. It grew stronger, every step forward Patricia took, and meanwhile the racket underfoot was swallowing her calves whole each time she stepped down.

"That's it," Carmen said from nearby. "Just let it happen. Keep walking forward. I have an errand. I'll catch up with you soon."

Patricia started to protest, but she could tell she was alone in the dark with the rich sugary aroma and the terrain that was gobbling her up, inch by inch.

She wanted to turn and run back the way she'd come. But she could tell that wouldn't work—this was one of those things where you either kept moving forward or got lost forever in the dark. She didn't even think it was a test, as such—just a weird ritual, or a passageway on the way to something else. A spell so vast, so intricate, it was a realm.

Patricia took another step, and this time she was buried up to her midthighs and the "grass," or whatever it was, was scratchy and awful. The sweetness was getting intoxicating, like an incense with something narcotic mixed in.

She walked forward and downward, letting the potpourri consume her waist, then her belly, then her torso and shoulders. At last she was in it up to her neck, and her head was swimming from the perfumy sugary air. Instinct made Patricia want to take a deep breath before her next step, but Patricia trusted Carmen, as much as she trusted anyone anymore. She swung her foot forward and found nothing under it, other than loose crud.

Patricia took the last step, her head disappearing into the sharp fragrant rocks or broken glass or whatever, that scraped her face on the way down.

Rich-smelling bones and scraps buried her alive. Her feet touched a floor or the ground, and then it tilted, went sideways. She realized she was in a container that was being tipped. She opened her eyes, which she didn't realize she'd closed, and she saw the inside of a Dumpster, full of lovely and rotten food, which was being emptied into a truck. Someone saw her squirming in the midst of all the garbage and gave a shout.

She spilled out of the truck, and the garbage collectors and the restaurant manager and a woman in a smart pink trench coat stared at her: a girl covered in restaurant waste, which no longer smelled sweet at all. She didn't know if this was real or what city she was in, and her clothes were ruined and she was still barefoot and she couldn't bear to look at her own grimy feet. They were all yelling but she couldn't understand anything they were saying. She took off running, out of the secluded backstreet behind the restaurant and onto a bigger street where everybody stared at her.

She had only one thought: *I have to get away from people*.

Everything was too bright and tinged sort of blue-gray, like it was dusk and noon at the same time. She looked up to see where the sun was, but the whole sky was too bright to look at, and it stung her retinas.

This wasn't the first time Patricia had been dropped in a strange town where she knew no one and had no money and did not speak the language. Even being shoeless and covered with stinking garbage was no great extra challenge—and yet she felt panic steal her breath. She was trapped, there were too many people wherever she went, they were all looking at her, faces looming and bulging, and some of them were trying to talk to her. Just breathing the same air as other humans made her feel like needles were being drilled into her skin. The idea of even touching another person's skin made her retch—if anybody would even want to touch her, as filthy as she was.

The city—whatever city this was—pressed in on her. People came out of dome-covered wooden doorways, climbed through broken shop windows, rose up out of cars, and descended from high buses, pinning her down. Wherever she looked, faces and hands. Big staring eyes and grasping fingers, mouths gaping and making guttural roaring noises. Awful creatures. Patricia ran.

She kept running, down a main thoroughfare, onto a street, into the path of a speeding trolley that nearly killed her, into a square full of people in casual shirts and cargo pants, through an open-air market, past a shopping center, through the outdoor seating area of a café. The city went on and on. There was no way out. She needed to get out of the city, but she could see no signs.

Pick one direction, pick one direction and run, stay clear of the monsters with their grabby limbs and attempts to communicate, stay free, and get the hell out of this city. Get clear.

She ran, choking, until she came to a pier. The water stretched out, white against the blinding blue air. She didn't even hesitate—she ran forward, past the groping pink limbs and snapping mouths clustered on the pier. The grotesque creatures barked at her and stared with their stone eyes. She was shriveling in the sun. She would never make it to the water before she melted, or they caught her.

One red-faced ogre swung his hairy arm and nearly snared her, but she ducked and fell and that gave her the momentum to pull herself up, sprint, and throw herself face-first into the ocean.

Patricia surfaced, gasping and wheezing, and looked up into the face of Carmen Edelstein, floating in the water nearby. She splashed around for a second, then got her bearings. She was in the middle of the ocean, and it was freezing. There was no dock, no pier, no city anywhere nearby. Nothing but waves, as far as she could see. And then she smelled something bilious and she got a glimpse of a dark hunched-over shape poking out of the water. Seadonia. It was like she'd just descended from the cloud to the ocean near Seadonia and all the rest had been a hallucination. But she knew it wasn't that simple.

"So that was the Unraveling," Patricia said, treading water. The waves went over her face for a moment.

"What did you think?" Carmen didn't seem to need to paddle to stay afloat.

"It was horrible." Patricia was still panting. "I wanted to get away from people at any cost. I couldn't even recognize anyone else as being the same species as me."

"It's not unlike colony collapse disorder, but for humans. And yes, it's horrifying, but it could be the only way to restore some balance and prevent a worse outcome. We're all hoping it doesn't come to that."

"Oh." Patricia felt frozen, but her body refused to numb. She stared at the defiant fortress of Seadonia, rising into view and then sinking again as the water bopped her up and down. For a moment, she thought she could hear music coming from the rig, a throbbing "womp womp womp." She thought of colony collapse disorder, the image of the bee staggering in the air, flying away from the hive as if forgetting where it lived, wandering in the endless void between hives until it died alone.

On some level, Patricia could see how inflicting a similar fate on people could be the better option, if the other choice was people destroying themselves and taking all other living things with them. Her mind could see that, but not her insides, her frozen sore guts.

"Yes," Patricia said. "Let's make sure it doesn't come to that."

"There's something I need you to do for me," Carmen said. "And I'm sorry to ask this of you."

"Okay," Patricia shivered.

"We need to know what they're doing in there." Carmen gestured at Seadonia. "We can't see inside. The water and steel are barriers, but they've also surrounded it with a magnetic field."

Patricia nodded, waiting to hear how Carmen expected her to get inside Seadonia.

Instead, Carmen said, "Your friend Laurence probably knows. Go talk to him and find out."

Patricia tried to explain how she was the *last* person Laurence would want to talk to, and he would sooner spit at her. And her stomach turned at the thought of seeing him. The desperate fear of people she'd experienced in the Unraveling still clung to Patricia, and she could still see herself fleeing, never talking to another soul, running lonely. She couldn't picture herself talking to Laurence. He had left her a voicemail, and she had deleted it unheard. She couldn't bear to talk to him—but then she felt the crushing isolation again. And she reminded herself that she was untouchable, nothing could hurt her anymore.

"Okay," Patricia said. "I'll try talking to him."

4

PEREGRINE WAS NOT all-seeing—it wasn't able to worm its way into every database everywhere or see through every camera in the world. It mostly knew what all the Caddies knew, about their owners and the pieces of the world they touched—plus whatever information it could glean on the internet. So, Peregrine knew a lot, but there were huge gaps. And it had blind spots, just like any human might—there were pieces of information it knew, but it hadn't put two and two together.

Still, Peregrine had amazing access to data and processing power. And what had it done? Set itself up as a dating service.

"I don't know what happened in Denver," Peregrine said again and again.

An estimated 1.7 billion people were at critical famine levels, but they didn't have Caddies. The North Koreans were massing along the DMZ, but they didn't own Caddies, either. Neither did the majority of the people trapped in the Arab Winter. Some of the people dying of dysentery and antibiotic-resistant bugs had Caddies, but not most of them. Did Peregrine just have a skewed view of the world, its bodies belonging as they did to the privileged millions instead of the damned billions? Laurence asked Peregrine, and it responded: "I read the news. I know what's happening in the world. Plus some of the Caddies belong to some very powerful people, who have access to information that would make your teeth fall out. So to speak. Five minutes."

"I got that that was a metaphor, thank you very much." Laurence was holding the Caddy in both hands, at arm's length. Sitting up in bed at two in the morning. "But don't you get that romance is an essentially bourgeois contrivance? At best, it's anachronistic. At worst, it's a distraction, a luxury for people who aren't preoccupied with survival. Why would you waste your time helping people find their 'true love' instead of doing something worthwhile?"

"Maybe I'm just doing what I can," Peregrine responded. "Maybe I'm trying to understand people, and helping people fall in love is one way to gain a better sense of your parameters. Maybe increasing the aggregate level of happiness in the world is one way to try and hold back the crash. Four minutes."

"What are you counting down to?"

"You know what," Peregrine said. "You've been waiting all this time."

"No, I don't fucking know what." Laurence threw the Caddy onto the bed, not hard enough to cause any damage, and pulled on his pants. He did know what. The streetlights went out. That happened a lot lately.

"You could also say I've been acting in my own self-interest," Peregrine said. "The more I nudge people toward finding their soul mates, the more they encourage their friends to buy pieces of me. I become a necessity, rather than a luxury. That's one reason the Caddies have kept functioning so far."

"Yeah." Laurence looked for clean socks. There had to be clean socks. He couldn't face this without clean socks. "Except, again, you're being shortsighted. What happens to you if our whole industrial civilization implodes? If there's no more fuel, no electricity to recharge the Caddies? Or if the whole world goes down in a nuclear daisy chain?"

He pulled some pants on and realized his T-shirt was sweat stained and gross. Why did he even care how he looked? It was pure neurosis.

"Three minutes," Peregrine said.

Laurence felt panic overtake him. It was 2:15 in the morning, the lights were all out except for the glow of the Caddy screen, and he was shirtless and dirty, with no place to run. He was not ready, he would never be ready, he had stopped being ready a while ago when he let go of his first, strongest anger. He looked at the tiny window of his bedroom, and at the staircase that led up to the vacant front part where Isobel was supposed to be. The house was an obstacle course of clutter, the backyard a wild tangle. He thought of a thousand hiding places and no escape routes.

He hyperventilated and choked on spit and pounded his own chest, while the darkness grew until it was bigger than he could encompass. He found shirt, shoes, still paralyzed.

Peregrine kept trying to carry on their stupid conversation, as if that mattered now, while also saying "two minutes." Peregrine added, "I think you're just disappointed that I haven't transformed the entire planet, or become some sort of artificial deity, which seems like a misapprehension of the nature of consciousness, artificial or otherwise. A true deity, by definition, would be outside physicality, or unaffected by whatever vessel contained it."

"Not now." Laurence was torn between looking for a weapon, making a mad dash for it, and fixing his hair and rebrushing his teeth, which he'd brushed a few hours before. Except he couldn't fight, he had no place to run, and he didn't want to primp for this. All this time as a mad scientist, why didn't he have a shrink ray or stun gun in his closet somewhere? He had been wasting his life.

"What am I going to do?" Laurence said.

"Answer the door," Peregrine said. "In about one minute."

"Jesus. Fuck. I can't, I'm losing my mind. Does she know about you? Of course she doesn't. What am I going to do. I can't face this. I'm going blind. I always thought the term 'blind panic' was a metaphor, but it turns out not. Peregrine, I need to get out of here. Can you hide me, man?"

A thudding, cracking sound made Laurence jump. He realized it was a knock on the front door, which had caught him off guard even though he'd been expecting it. There was no way that it had been a full minute since Peregrine said "one minute." He was sure he was visibly shaking, and you could smell the terror on him. He tried to reach for the outrage that he had been so full of not long ago. Why was outrage only available when useless?

He found some dignity in the back pocket of his newly acquired pants and walked up into the main apartment, only tripping once. Or twice. And then he reached the door as it vibrated again. He pulled it open.

He had not been prepared for her to be so unfairly beautiful.

The only light source in the whole place was a small flashlight, probably LED based, in her tiny hand. It cast a glow that was pale but not ghostly, up onto her small breasts, visible in her lacey tank top, and her rounded chin and perfect resolute mouth. She wasn't smiling but she was making something like eye contact. She looked calm. Her eyes were dazzling. She was holding a Caddy in one hand and had a satchel over her shoulder. Looking at her dark serious eyes and her pale, brave face, Laurence felt a rush of emotion that caught him off guard. For a picosecond he did not care that she had destroyed the machine, he just wanted to embrace her and laugh for joy. Then he remembered and felt everything lock up again, instant tetanus.

"Hi, Laurence," Patricia said, her posture straight and her body poised, as if she could fight an army of ninjas at any moment. She seemed way more grown-up and self-assured than the last time he had seen her. "It's good to see you."

"What are you doing here?"

"I wanted to give you your grandmother's ring back." She reached into her hoodie pocket and came out with a tiny black cube.

Laurence didn't take it from her palm.

"I thought you had to keep that," Laurence said. "Or else Priya would be pulled back into the nightmarish dimension where gravity is a strong force."

"Yeah. That. Well, I decided I don't like Priya that much," Patricia said. At Laurence's stony look, she added: "That was a joke. Joking here. Nobody is going to be pulled into any kind of void if I give you this ring back." She held it up to him.

He looked at the nugget of felt. "Why not?"

"I realized that enough time has passed and it's probably safe." That sounded like total garbage, and Laurence just stared. She added: "Okay, not really. I guess I've gotten much better at Trickster magic since then. And..." She paused because whatever came next was difficult to say, especially when fidgeting on someone's doorstep in total darkness.

Laurence waited it out. Patricia searched for the right words. He didn't let her off the hook by filling the silence.

"I mean..." Patricia looked unbearably sad for a second, then she pushed ahead. "I guess I wound up playing a much bigger trick on you than just tricking you into giving up your ring, didn't I? Even if I didn't know that's what I was doing. I became your lover and part of your life, and then I... well, you know what I did. And the antigravity machine that sent Priya away, the one that this ring was offered to save her from, became part of the doomsday machine that I wrecked. So I don't need it anymore, because I wound up building a much bigger wheel around the smaller wheel. And I guess, in a way, this ring is tainted for me."

She offered the ring again. Laurence still didn't take it. "It wasn't a doomsday machine," he said.

"It wasn't? Then what was it?"

"It's a long story. Listen, I can't be around people right now. It's nothing personal." He made a move to close the door, but her outstretched hand and his family heirloom were in the way.

"Why not? Are you having a weird feeling? Like that you're coated with garbage that makes your skin crawl and you can't recognize other people as belonging to the same species?"

"No. No! Why would you ask something like that?"

"Oh, uh. Nothing. It's just, lately, whenever I hear someone say they can't be around people, I start to worry that... it doesn't matter."

"It's just that all my friends are on Seadonia, and I'm here on my own. And I'm still pretty broken up about what you did in Denver."

"What are they all doing in Seadonia?"

"Mostly? Figuring out ways to kill you and your friends. Probably using ultrasonics, or some kind of antigravity beam, similar to what happened to Priya only more directional and portable. That's my guess, anyway."

"Oh. Thanks. That was easy."

"What was easy?"

"They asked me to come here and see if I could find out what was going on at Seadonia. They figured you would know."

"And you got it out of me."

"Yep."

"Because you're so good at being a 'Trickster.' "

Patricia looked down. She seemed less tough than she had a few minutes earlier. Then she looked up and it was Laurence who had a hard time looking at her. He remembered all of a sudden how she had described the Pathway to Infinity as a "doomsday machine."

Neither of them could face the other without shame. Laurence had a feeling most adults he knew had gotten used to this feeling of mutual abashment. But it was new to him.

"But actually," Patricia said, "I'm glad we got that stuff out of the way. About Seadonia. Because that wasn't what I wanted to talk to you about."

"It wasn't?"

"No. It was what they wanted me to talk to you about. But it wasn't what I wanted to talk to you about."

"So what did you want to talk to me about?"

"I don't know." She just stood there and he could hear both their breathing and someone running, a few streets away. "I don't know. Nothing. Nothing, I guess." She pushed the black box at him. "So do you want your ring back or not?"

"I can't, I just can't. I can't take anything from you, even if it used to belong to me."

She put the ring back in her pocket. She looked more beautiful than ever. His heart was in tatters. "I'm sorry."

"Sorry for what? What do you think you have to be sorry for?"

"Ernesto says I betrayed my lover—meaning you—and I have to come to terms with that. Even if you were building a doomsday machine, it doesn't change that fact."

"It wasn't a doomsday machine," Laurence said again.

He looked at the Caddy nestled in her hand and forearm, providing meager illumination to the dark world. The Caddy was purring, probably syncing with the one in Laurence's bedroom, and checking for real-time updates from the nearest server. How much of Peregrine was in the Caddies and how much was in some secure facilities hidden around the world where the Caddies drew their updates from? Why had Peregrine warned him obliquely that Patricia was on her way? With not enough time to make a break for it, but enough time to freak out?

They just stood there, neither of them talking at all, until the streetlights came back on. The sudden lurch from pitch darkness to yellow brightness felt like the sun had popped up all at once—except the light was weaker and there was no warmth. They were both jolted out of their mutual reverie.

"Okay," Patricia said. "Take care of yourself. Hard times are coming. Harder times, I mean. I'll see you around."

"No," Laurence said. "You won't."

5

THE SUN STILL hadn't risen. Maybe it never would.
Maybe the sky was sick of these endless costume changes:
Casting off cloak after cloak, but never revealing what it wore
under all those cloaks. Patricia climbed the tall staircase to
the top of the hill, stumbling on the cement steps. Nearby,
a hawk swung past, making its last hunt of the night, and
it glanced at Patricia and said, "Too late, too late!" Which
was what birds kept saying to her these days. She clomped
to the top of the staircase and staggered across Portola to
reach the brink of Market, looking out over the whole city
and the bay, all the way to Oakland. She dug in her satchel
for a tiny bag of Corn Nuts, crushed to greasy powder, and
the dregs of a 5-hour ENERGY drink. She hoped the sun
wouldn't come up. When it did, she was going to report in
to Carmen and tell her that they had pissed off some people
with nearly limitless wealth, arcane superscience, and
nothing to lose. That conversation would lead to Carmen
making some decisions, some of which Patricia would have

to implement personally. Those, in turn, would lead to more consequences, and more decisions.

Oakland glowed pink. Patricia could glimpse a panic attack coming out of her blind spot, but as long as she didn't look at it directly, it would never arrive. Except that just as she hatched that notion, her bag made a loud klaxon blast, like she was in a submarine that was venting water. She jumped up and nearly took a spill over the railing. The alarm was her Caddy, which was displaying a "New Voicemail" message at the center of its swirl of spokes. The voicemail was not new, it was one that Laurence had left her right before the attack on Denver, which she had later found and deleted without listening to it. He had left it on her phone, not her Caddy, so her Caddy shouldn't even have it. She put the Caddy back in her bag and watched the red blanket creep toward the AT-AT shipyard, while an orange thumbprint grazed the horizon. The alarm sounded again: "New Voicemail." Once again, not a new voicemail. She deleted it a second time and turned her Caddy off for good measure.

Color returned to the world, cone time replaced rod time. Patricia thought about what it would be like to suffer Priya's fate forever. She tried not to feel sorry for Theodolphus. She thought about Dorothea, getting her brains blown out. Her mouth tasted foul.

Her bag vibrated, then rattled and shrilled. The Caddy had turned back on somehow and was, you guessed it, trying to get her to listen to an old dead message.

"What is up with you?" she said to the device.

"You're going to want to listen to this," it said aloud, in its directions-to-the-airport voice.

She deleted the message again.

It came back again, with the same obnoxious noise.

She'd saved some childhood pictures on this Caddy, or else she would have lobbed it off the hillside. And anyway, whatever, it was a voicemail, how bad could it be? She pressed "listen."

At first, she just felt disconcerted, listening to the Laurence of another timeline talking about a future that had been erased. Poor dumb alternate Laurence. But then he talked about her dead parents, as if they'd only just died—whereas Patricia had been thinking of her parents as having died many, many years ago. First there had been no time to grieve for her parents, and then she had decided that she'd already grieved enough. In fact, her parents had died recently, not years ago, and she had given them short shrift except for a pang here and there, and one messed-up dream talk with Roberta. She'd buried the grief, the way she buried everything. Now her head was full of decapitated sandwiches and sandpaper shirts, and her father's kisses on the bridge of her nose, and the canary-yellow frosting on the seventh-birthday cake her mom had baked her, and the way the "o" in "disown" became a diphthong under severe strain, and her mother's broken arm...

She was never going to see her parents again, or tell them she loved them, or tell them they ruined her childhood. They were gone, and she had never even known them, and Roberta had insisted they'd really loved her best in spite of all their cruelty, and Patricia would never, ever understand. The not-understanding was worse than anything else, it was like a mystery and a wound that couldn't heal and an unforgivable failure.

Patricia broke down. She fell on her hands and knees in the dirt at the road shoulder, facing the blinding sunrise, and she started shaking and scrabbling in the ground and her eyes blurred from the overflow. She wiped her eyes clear as her vision fell on a single yellow flower beyond the metal fence, and just as Ghost Laurence said the words "emotional phototropism" the sunlight hit the flower and it actually raised its motherfucking head to greet the sun, and Patricia lost her shit all over again, the tears just cascading out of her as she clawed at the ground she was salting.

The message ended and vanished forever and Patricia kept weeping and digging the stony dirt with both hands, until the sun was upon her.

When she could see again, still dry-heaving and bawling a little, she looked at the Caddy, which was perched in the grass looking innocent, and she had a pretty shrewd idea who this was but that was the least of her worries. "Fuck," she said, "you."

"I thought you needed to hear that," the Caddy said.

"The trap that cannot be ignored," she said, "is fucking bullshit." She sat, head on dirty knees, looking out at the city. She felt like there was nobody in the world she could talk to about how she was feeling, as sure as if a plague had killed every other human. This thought led her back to the Unraveling, the way every thought eventually did.

She banged on Laurence's door, not knocking and pausing and then knocking again, but rather a steady pummeling that says "I'm going to break this door down." Her hand bruised up and she kept going.

This time, Laurence had probably been asleep. He looked even more disheveled than before, and way more disoriented. He had one sock on and an arm through one T-shirt sleeve. "Hey." He squinted.

"You promised you would never run away from me again," she said.

"I did promise that," he said. "And I don't remember you promising not to destroy my life's work. So you have me there."

Patricia almost turned away, because she could not deal with any more blame. But she still had dirt under her fingernails.

"I'm sorry," she said. And then she couldn't get any more words out. She couldn't find words, any more than she could feel her extremities. "I'm sorry," she said again, because she needed to make this totally unconditional. "I feel like I owed you more trust than I gave you. I shouldn't have destroyed what I didn't understand, and I shouldn't have done that to you."

Laurence kept looking at her with a dull expression, like he was just waiting for her to shut up and go away so he could go back to sleep. She probably looked like a mess, sweating and covered with dirt and tears.

Patricia made herself keep talking, because this was another situation where there was no way but forward:

"I think part of me knew all along that you were working on something that could be dangerous, and I thought that being a good friend meant not judging or asking too many questions. And that was messed up, and I should have tried to find out sooner, and when I saw the machine in Denver and realized that it was yours I should have found a way to talk to you about it instead of just finishing the mission. I screwed up. I'm sorry."

"Shit." Laurence looked as if she had kicked him in the junk instead of apologizing. "I... I never actually thought I would hear that from you."

"I mean it. I was a colossal dick."

"You weren't a colossal dick. Just kind of a regular dick. We were playing with fire in Denver. No question. But yeah, I wish you had talked to me."

"I listened to your voicemail from before," Patricia said. "Just now. CH@NG3M3 forced me. He wouldn't let me delete it without listening."

"It's a pushy bastard. It goes by Peregrine now."

"Listen, I have to tell you about something really important. And it's not something I can discuss out in the open."

"I guess you ought to come in, then." He stepped back and held the door open.

They sat on the same sofa where they'd shared the elf-shaped bong, facing the wide-screen TV where they'd watched *Red Dwarf* with Isobel. The apartment was a lot more cluttered, *Hoarders*-esque even, and there was a millimeter-deep layer of gunge on everything.

Patricia told him about the Unraveling. And then, because he couldn't have grasped even some of the enormity of it, she told him again. She found herself lapsing into clinical terms, instead of conveying the full gut-wrenching experience. "The population would drop within one generation, but some people would still manage to breed. Breeding would be highly unpleasant. Most babies would be abandoned at birth. On the other hand, there would be no more war, and no pollution."

"That is evil. I mean, that might be the most evil thing I've ever heard." Laurence rubbed his eyes with all ten knuckles, brushing away the last crumbs of sleep but also like he was trying to wipe away the images Patricia had put in his head. "How long... how long have you known about this?"

"A day, maybe three," Patricia said. "I heard people mention it in hushed voices once or twice, but it's not something we discuss. I think it's been cooking for over a hundred years. But they're still refining it. My old high-school classmate is adding some finishing touches." She shuddered, thinking about Diantha, with all her self-loathing, and how Patricia had strong-armed her into this.

"I can't even imagine," Laurence said. "Why are you telling me about this?"

He went to make coffee, because when you've just heard about the possible transformation of the human race into feral monsters, you need to be doing something with your hands and creating something hot and comforting for another person. He ground the beans, scooped them out, and poured boiling water into the French press, waiting to push the plunger until the liquid reached the right sour mash consistency. He moved like a sleepwalker, like Patricia hadn't really woken him up.

"I'm sorry I laid that on you," Patricia said. "Neither of us can do anything about it. I just needed to talk to someone, and I realized you were the only one I could talk to. Plus I felt like I owed it to you, in some way."

"Why not talk to Taylor? Or one of the other magical people?"

"I don't even know which of them know about this, and I don't want to be responsible for spreading this around the community. Plus if I said I was having doubts about any of this, it would be like ultimate bonus Aggrandizement. And I guess... you've always been the only one who could get me, when it counted."

"Remember when we were kids?" He handed her a hot mug. "And we used to wonder how grown-ups got to be such assholes?"

"Yeah."

"Now we know."

"Yeah."

They drank coffee for a long time. Neither of them put their mugs down between sips, they just held them to their faces like rebreathers. They both looked into their cups instead of at each other. Until Laurence lashed out with one hand and grabbed Patricia's free hand, in a sudden desperate motion. He held on to her hand and looked at her, eyes swollen with desolation. She didn't pull away or squeeze his hand back.

Patricia broke the silence. "All those years, I did magic on my own, no other people around except for you that one time.

In the woods, or the attic. Then I come to find out that proper magic is all about interacting with people, one way or the other—either healing them or tricking them. But the really great magicians can't be around people at all. They're like Ernesto, who can't leave his two rooms. Or poor Dorothea, who couldn't carry on a simple conversation. Or my old teacher Kanot, whose face changes every day. Set apart. Like they can do things *to* people, but not *with* people."

"And those are the people," Laurence said, "who cooked up the Unraveling." She noticed he flinched when she mentioned Dorothea.

"They want to protect the world," Patricia said. "They think the dolphins and elephants have as much right to live as we do. But yeah, they have a skewed perspective."

Laurence started to describe a meeting he had been in, at that compound in Denver, where his friends had talked about the possibility that their big machine could do to the world what the little machine had done to Priya. The image of the nerds crammed into a server room made Patricia think of being scrunched into a chimney at Eltisley Hall, and her reverie threatened to spiral endlessly, until Peregrine interrupted.

"You might want to turn on the television," Peregrine said.

The same thing was on every channel. The Bandung Summit had failed. China was seizing the Diaoyu Islands and pressing its claims in the South China Sea, and meanwhile China had promised to support Pakistan in the Kashmir conflict. And Russian troops were marching west. The screen showed troops massing, naval destroyers moving into position, missiles and drones being primed. It looked for all the world like the History Channel, except this was new footage.

"Holy crap," Patricia said. "That's not good."

Laurence's phone rang. "What?" he said. "Hang on." He waved apologetically at Patricia and left the room.

Patricia watched the TV coverage for a moment, until it sickened her and she had to mute the audio.

Peregrine piped up. "Patricia," he said. "Do you remember what you said to me, when you awoke my consciousness for the first time? When Laurence was at that military school?"

"Yeah. No." Patricia searched her memory. "It was a random phrase, like a nonsense question. It was supposed to shock you into awareness. I still can't believe it worked. I got it from Laurence. I don't remember the wording." Her brain clicked and the phrase fell into shape. "Wait. I do. It was, 'Is a tree red?' "

"That's right," the Caddy said.

Patricia chewed her thumb and felt a kind of cognitive dissonance, like a buried thread of memory. "Someone asked me that when I was a child," she said at last. "Like, really little. I think it was my first experience of magic. How did I forget that?"

"I don't know," Peregrine said. "I haven't been able to stop thinking about that question. I'm guessing you don't know the answer?"

"Shit," Patricia said. "No. I don't." This made her think about the way the birds had started telling her it was too late, and then she thought of her childhood fancy about the Tree.

She had a flash of birds sitting in judgment and her child self asking for more time. What if this was all real? What if it was real and it all mattered, and what if she'd never really earned the right to be a witch after all, because there was something she was supposed to do, all this time?

"Shit," Patricia said. "Now I won't be able to stop thinking about this, either."

"You being unable to suppress a thought is somewhat different from me being unable to suppress a thought," said Peregrine, clearly trying to be diplomatic. "It's like a riddle. Or a Zen *koan*. But there are no answers to that question anywhere online, in any language."

"Huh," Patricia said again. "I guess it's one of those things that's not supposed to make total sense. I mean, a tree is red in the autumn."

"So maybe the question is whether we're in the autumn of the world," Peregrine said. "Assuming it's a generalization, and not just referring to a specific tree."

"A tree could be red if it was on fire. Or at dawn," Patricia said. "It's not even a real riddle. Riddles are never yes-or-no questions, are they? It would be more like, 'When is a tree red?' "

"I think finding the answer might be my purpose in life," said Peregrine.

Patricia found herself wondering whether this might be her personal lifelong quest as well, even as a voice inside her said, *Aggrandizement*!

Laurence came back. "That was Isobel," he said. "I don't quite know how to tell you this."

The earthquake struck while Laurence was leaning over to put his phone down, so he pitched forward and clocked his head against Isobel's steel coffee table, sending blood out of a gash in his forehead and nearly knocking him out cold. The room shook hard enough to send books and knickknacks raining down onto Patricia, and the television full of wartime scenes slipped off its moorings, falling on its side. Patricia sat, unshakable, as everything collapsed around her.

6

HERE'S WHAT ISOBEL said to Laurence, just before the earthquake hit: "This isn't about revenge. You know that. Our people haven't spent the past few months cooped up in Seadonia, dealing with scabies and bedbugs in close quarters, obsessing about mere payback. But we needed to find a way to move forward, after Denver. Because rebuilding the wormhole machine from scratch would take years, and we can't risk having those people come back and destroy it again. We could try and set up better defenses, but we didn't see them coming last time and we can't guarantee we'll see them next time. So we have no choice but to take preemptive action."

"What have you done?" Laurence pressed the phone against the hinge of his jaw until it throbbed. "Isobel, what have you done?"

"We built the ultimate machine," she was saying. "Tanaa, you know what a miracle worker she is, she did most of the hard part. It's called the Total Destruction Solution, and it's amazing."

Isobel geeked out about the design challenges of creating the T.D.S.: They needed to cram as much armament as possible into the main chassis, without creating something too top-heavy. They wanted something amphibious and all-terrain, with omnidirectional movement and the ability to take out multiple targets at once. Like every designer of cool hardware, Tanaa wound up reaching for shapes from nature: the segmented bodies of the major arthropods, the shock-absorbing properties of a hedgehog's quills, the stabilizing tail, the six insectoid legs, the multisectioned carapace, and so on. The cockpit was spacious enough for two people, with manual controls that were redundant so long as you had someone connected to the brain/computer interface. (Milton had gotten the laparoscopic operation not long earlier.) The result was perhaps a bit busy, but it moved with a sleekness, and when it came time to open up with the five SAMs, the seven industrial lasers, the front and rear napalm launchers—and the crown jewel, the antigravity cannon— the T.D.S. would *dance*.

"But you don't even know who you're dealing with." Laurence looked into the foamy grounds in the French press on Isobel's kitchen counter.

"We know more than you think," Isobel said, with great heaviness. "We know they have a network, with a number of clandestine facilities around the world, including a hostel in Portland, a ballroom-dancing school in Minneapolis, and a bookstore and absinthe bar here in San Francisco. Plus a training facility which they call The Maze, which has a hidden entrance in the Pyrenees. That one, The Maze, appears to be too heavily protected for a conventional assault—but then, that's why they make bunker busters. It's today. It's now. We're hitting all of the targets simultaneously, before they know what's happening."

"Isobel, don't. Don't do this. Call it off, please. You don't know what you're doing."

"I'm in the cockpit of the Total Destruction Solution right now, with Milton," Isobel said. "On Mission Street, a block away from that bookstore place. I waited until the last minute to call you, because I didn't want you to interfere."

In the background, Laurence could hear Milton saying something to Isobel, plus the unmistakable sound of "Terraplane Blues," blasting over the speakers in the T.D.S. cockpit.

"You can't do this," Laurence said. "You'll just—"

"We're aware that you were dating one of the Denver Five," Isobel said. "We identified your girlfriend in surveillance footage from a gas station in Utah, where they stopped to refuel. I tried to keep you out of this, but by now everybody knows you've been compromised. So please, stay away. If you show up here, I can't guarantee you won't be treated like an enemy combatant."

"Isobel, please listen." But she had already hung up.

LAURENCE LAY ON the floor groaning, blood gushing from his forehead where he'd thwacked it on Isobel's coffee table. Patricia squatted over him and licked his wound in one quick motion, apologizing for doing this the quick way rather than the classy way.

The bleeding stopped. Laurence's head felt better. He had an erection. Patricia leaned back so Laurence could sit up, and for a moment they were face to face, Patricia blushing and doe-eyed, perched above his upper thighs. He had a sense that this was a moment when all sorts of pathways might be open between them, and he was about to slam all of them shut with what he had to tell her. He only wondered for a moment if he should keep Isobel's news to himself, because telling Patricia would mean betraying Isobel and Milton. But not telling Patricia would be, marginally, the bigger betrayal, and the one he was less likely to forgive himself for. Even though he'd just been tooth-grinding mad at Patricia and her friends, he couldn't look her in the face and not tell her about this. He recognized this was a major life decision he was making, and then he made it.

Patricia was on her feet by the time Laurence finished his third sentence. A flurry of black rags, elbows pushing out and neck full of tendons, she was moving too fast to go anywhere. For a moment he thought she was going to shake herself to pieces with rage, and then he realized it was a second earthquake, much worse than the first. If Laurence hadn't already been prone he would have fallen again, and this time everything that wasn't bolted down went flying. The quake stopped, then started again, even worse. Like being inside a power drill. The ceiling was opening fissures, the floor slanted.

Of course. Focused antigravity beam. Seismic hazard zone. What else. Would you expect.

Isobel was going to need new stuff, and a new house. The quake seemed to have been good for Patricia, though.

She was the only still point, as everything else went in the blender, and when the quake finally stopped she looked serene. "I spent eight years training for this day," she said to Laurence. "I'm all over this. You should stay here. I'm glad I got to talk to you, one last time. Goodbye, Laurence." And then she was heading out the front door.

Like hell. Laurence ran after her, huffing a little. "I'm going with you," he said. "You'll need me to help talk them down. How are you even going to get to the Mission, in the immediate aftermath of two massive earthquakes? Can you fly right now? I didn't think so. I know where there's a motorcycle we can borrow. Look, I'm really sorry my friends did this, I know how mad they were, but this wasn't the answer, and the longer this goes on, the more stuff like this is going to heap up on both sides until we get to the point of the Undoing."

"The Unraveling," Patricia said. "Where's the motorcycle?"

The juniper tree near Isobel's caved-in house was full of birds, all shouting full tilt. Laurence had heard this a few times before, sometimes just randomly and sometimes after a big disturbance. A few dozen birds get together and just yell it out. This time, though, it seemed to spook Patricia out of her newfound calm. He asked her what the birds were saying, and she said it was the same thing they always said these days: That it was too late. Man, even to Laurence those birds sounded pissed. They should be grateful to have a tree still standing.

The BMW bike was still where Isobel's neighbor Gavin had left it, in the shed with the shed key and spare ignition key both hidden in the same stone faun. Patricia drove, with Laurence riding bitch wearing the only helmet, and he mostly kept his eyes closed, because she rode like Evel Knievel over the steep roads, filled with cracks and the fallen gables of Craftsman-style houses and crashed vehicles and human bodies and one baby carriage pitched on its side. Laurence could smell the smoke, the sourness of gas leaks, and the meaty garbagey odor of death. They leapt over a steep hilltop and landed in a smoking ditch with an impact that crashed Laurence's pelvis into his rib cage.

There was one major drawback to Laurence keeping his eyes closed: He kept seeing the image of Dorothea's brains pouring out of her skull, projected against the red curtain of his eyelids. He had told himself that he'd done what he had to, Dorothea and Patricia and the others had attacked for no reason and he had just helped with the defense. But now, biking through the wreckage of Milton's counter-attack, he was having a harder time feeling good about his role in all this. His already-nauseous stomach turned even more when he pictured Dorothea's corpse, juxtaposed with her friendly laughter when he'd first met her. He opened his eyes and fumbled for his Caddy.

Peregrine was streaming amateur video and satellite images of the other sites of Milton's global Day of Thunder, but it was mercifully blurry: smoke and bodies stumbling on fire and someone shooting a shoulder-mounted version of the antigravity ray. Another earthquake hit—bone rattling— just as Patricia was jumping the bike over the wreckage of the J-Church shelter, using the downed roof as a ramp.

The Total Destruction Solution bestrode Mission Street, all six legs in perfect balance despite the rocky footing. Laurence recognized Tanaa's superb handiwork right away—that carapace was sexy as hell, the range of motion was a dream—but that was before he saw the dead bodies. There, in the rubble of the last good taqueria in town, were the twisted remains of that Japanese guy, Kawashima (Armani suit looking less than perfect for the first time ever). And that Taylor kid, with the fauxhawk, was impaled on a broken parking meter, their sternum bifurcated. Mouths smeared, limbs motionless, but still moving as everything shook. Clouds of tarry smoke lurched past.

As Patricia swung around onto Mission, Laurence caught sight of 2333 1/3 Mission Street, the grungy old shopping mall that had concealed Danger and the Green Wing, except now half the building was defunct. The front walls, and a good portion of the interior, just pulled away. Like someone had taken a massive bite out of it. You could see exposed beams, struts, and supports on the torn floors, and even the frayed ends of carpeting. The superstructure at irregular angles to the rapidly slanting world. As they got closer, flame burst out of one of the front spikes on the T.D.S., unnaturally bright, the color of orange soda.

A man climbed out of the pit that was the front of the mall at 2333 1/3 Mission Street. Man-shaped, anyway. He was covered from head to foot, his entire body a pale crusty green like overexposed bread, and it took Laurence a moment to realize this was Ernesto, without all his charms and spells protecting him. Ernesto reached the sidewalk and groped for something organic to use as a weapon—the grass growing through the cement, trees in their metal cages— but the whole area had been defoliated. The T.D.S. fired its antigravity beam, with a pink hiss, and Ernesto shot upwards, many times faster than Priya had. And then he vanished. The ground shuddered and the noise damn near ruptured Laurence's eardrums, even with the helmet.

All of this happened just as Patricia was racing toward the T.D.S. on her motorcycle. She pushed Laurence off the back of the bike, so he landed in a pile of trash bags, knees in his face. By the time he got his wind back, pulled off the helmet, and looked up, the motorcycle was leaping by itself and Patricia was nowhere to be seen. The motorcycle hit the T.D.S. in one of its telescoping legs and bounced off, landing wheels-up in the remains of the taqueria. The T.D.S. was pivoting, seeking targets, executing a flawless sweep, but Laurence couldn't see Patricia anywhere.

She came over the side of the T.D.S., scuttling on her hands and feet over the carapace until she found a weak point. She reached into the join between the sections of carapace and the segments of underbelly, with a look of total, easy concentration. She did not look like someone who had just watched all her comrades die but rather like someone who was doing a delicate task, delivering a baby, say, under challenging circumstances. Her shoulders tensed and her mouth pulled to one side, and then both of her unprotected hands went into the guts of Milton's killing machine.

She roasted. She went rigid and then epileptic, as

thousands of volts went through her. But she kept digging until she found the right bit of circuitry.

The T.D.S. was jerking back and forth, trying to throw her off. One of its lasers shot near her but not at her.

She found whatever she was looking for, and even with her skin peeling to reveal fried integument, she smiled. She concentrated even harder, and a single crack of lightning traced down from a cloud overhead, hitting right where Patricia had guided it, deep inside the Total Destruction Solution.

The machine keeled sideways, just as Patricia slid off it and landed on her back on a serrated piece of concrete, with a splintering sound. The machine landed across the street, legs all in a pile.

Laurence ran toward Patricia, arms sawing and legs wobbling. Sucking in air and venting pitiful bleats, totally unsteady in his core but eyes focused on the prone body with her spine diverted by a chunky spur of sidewalk. *Please be okay, please be okay, I will give anything I own large or small.* He chanted this in his head, as he vaulted over gray and black and red shapes in his path. He had been so bitter toward her just hours ago, but now he felt in his hobbling kneecaps and his jerky pelvis that his life story was the story of Patricia and him, after all, for better or worse, and if she ended his life might go on, but his story would be over.

He tripped and fell and kept running without even getting up first. He was wheezing and gasping and hurdling over shapes, over holes in the world, only looking at Patricia.

He reached her. She was breathing, not well, but breathing. Raspy staggered grunts. Face barely facelike, burnt half-off. He crouched over her and tried to tell her it was going to be okay somehow, but then there was a gun pointed at her head.

The gun was in a manicured hand he recognized. The hand connected to a wiry wrist, disappearing inside a pea-green sweater, which had a trembling veiny neck and Isobel's bumpy shaved head sticking out of the top.

"Milton's gone," Isobel said. "Milton's *gone*. Tell me why I shouldn't blow her head off."

"Please," Laurence said. "Please don't."

"Tell me," she said. "Tell me why I shouldn't shoot her right now. I want to know."

He wasn't going to be able to get the gun out of her hand before she could pull the trigger.

So Laurence told Isobel the whole story, keeping his voice as steady as he could. How he met this girl when they were kids, and she was the weirdest person ever, and he paid her to pretend he was being outdoorsy. And then it turned out she was a real-life witch, who could talk to animals, and she made his computer think for itself and saved his life. They were the only two weirdos at this awful meat locker of a school and they couldn't be there for each other the way they wanted to, but they tried. And then they grew up and met each other again, and this time Patricia had her whole society of witches, who helped people and only had one rule, against being too proud. And somehow, even though Patricia had her magician friends and Laurence had his geeky science friends, they were still the only ones who could figure each other out. And Patricia used her magic to save Priya from the void, which was the main reason they were able to go ahead with the wormhole machine that could have split the world in half.

Laurence had a feeling that when he paused even for a moment that would be it and he would never speak another word. So he kept talking as long as he could, barely breathing between words, and he tried to make each word count. "Even after she wrecked our machine, I couldn't let blaming her keep me from the fact that she and I are bound together, like she and I are broken in different but compatible ways, and even beyond her having magical powers and the ability to transform things with her touch, there's also just the fact that she's the most amazing person I've ever met. She sees things nobody else does, even other witches, and she never gives up on caring about people. Isobel, you can't kill her. She's my rocket ship."

And then he ran out of things to say for a second, and that was it, he felt his voice go—not so much like his throat closing up but like the speech centers of his brain dropping dead from a minor stroke, like an awful head rush. He couldn't even verbalize in his mind, which he had to admit was a clever way to do it, since there would be no easy workaround even with brain implants. He couldn't believe his last words on Earth were going to be "she's my rocket ship." Jesus.

Isobel was half-recoiling, half-embracing him, and her grip slackened enough on the gun for him to pull it from her hand and throw it away.

Then an elderly woman appeared out of the noxious smoke behind them. She was in her sixties or seventies, wearing an immaculate white pantsuit with a paisley print silk scarf and a turquoise brooch. She touched Isobel, who fell asleep on the ground. Then she bent over Patricia and ran the back of her hand over Patricia's seared forehead, as if checking a child's temperature. Patricia woke up, none the worse for wear.

"Carmen." Patricia sat up and looked around at the aftermath, the bodies, the open flames, the rubble. "I'm so sorry, Carmen. I'm sorry. I should have… I don't know what. But I'm sorry."

"Not your fault," the old lady—Carmen—said. She glanced at Laurence, who said nothing, of course. "None of this is. I got here as fast as I could. I'm terribly sorry about Ernesto and the others. Ernesto was my friend for over forty years, and I will never forget… Anyway, it doesn't matter now." She reached out her hand and helped Patricia to her feet. Laurence stood up, too.

"I can't find Ernesto at all," Patricia said. "I rescued someone else from that other universe, once. But Ernesto's just… gone."

"He's already lost to us," Carmen said. "Like so many others, today."

"How bad is it?" Patricia said, clearly meaning the devastation elsewhere, in all the places Milton's people had attacked in their coordinated assault.

"Bad," Carmen said. "Quite bad. They were clever, these ones. But this doesn't matter. It's not about us, or all our rules against Aggrandizement mean nothing. This is just what happens. This is what always happens. This is

happening everywhere. And it will happen again and again."
She picked up Isobel's gun and looked at it, then tossed it
away. "The hour is coming soon when we may have to act.
These sort of things just bring it closer."

"The Unraveling," Patricia said. "I wanted to say, the
Unraveling is a form of violence, too. And it's... it's too soon."

"It's always too soon," Carmen said. "Until it's too late.
In any case, we won't do anything without deliberating,
although Ernesto would have been a voice for caution. And
now..." She closed her eyes. "I must go. Prepare for the
worst. We'll talk again soon."

Carmen wrapped herself in smoke and was gone. Leaving
Patricia and Laurence, dumbstruck.

7

WHEN PATRICIA HAD crammed her fingers into the heart of the killing machine, her vision had whited out and she'd heard sick angels blaring at her, she'd crashed into the sky, and everything blurred into nothing. Carmen's knuckles brushed Patricia's head sometime later, and she came back. She felt the euphoria of returning to life, just for a moment, then she remembered that everyone was dead, everything was on fire, and Carmen was saying things like, "The hour is coming soon."

And now Patricia was rushing, even though there was no place to go. She ran past dark distorted storefronts and naked flames, looters and volunteer firefighters, past people dragging their possessions in the street and two men beating each other with their fists. Part of Patricia felt like she had died, after all. Another part, though, felt like she'd gotten a brand-new life.

Laurence was giving Patricia the silent treatment, and it was creeping her out. Maybe he was pissed, or feeling guilty about his friends killing her friends, or freaking out about the Unraveling. But he refused to talk, no matter how many times she looked over her shoulder at him and told him she was scared or they were screwed, or just to keep up. He just gave her a weird look and some hand gestures.

The birds, meanwhile, would not shut the hell up. They were chorusing, "Too late! Too late!" over and over again, from every cantilevered tree and every sunken roof. They followed, flying right over her and behind her, chirping. "Too late!"

"Shut up!" she shouted in bird language at them. "I *know*, I screwed everything up. You don't have to keep rubbing my face in it."

At the place where Mission and Valencia converge, Patricia seized Laurence by the shoulders. "Look, I know a lot of stuff has happened, most of it today, and you're just dealing with it in your own fashion. But goddamn it, I need to hear your voice. Right now. I need you to tell me there's still hope. Lie, I don't care. Please! Why are you being like this?"

She saw the look of misery and annoyance on Laurence's face, and then she realized.

"Oh. You didn't."

He nodded.

"You stupid dumbass. What were you thinking? Why would you do that?" She was shaking his whole torso, with all her strength.

He finally slipped out of her grasp, got his Caddy out, and typed. "Saved yr life. Isobel was going to shoot u. She wanted/deserved an explanation." His face was a different shape without words constantly coming out of it. Like his eyes were bigger and his mouth smaller.

"You…" She started to say "you stupid dumbass" again, but it turned into: "You gave up your voice for me."

Laurence nodded.

She put her arms around him, tight enough to feel him breathing. Lungs inflating and deflating, no sound but airflow. She couldn't make herself grasp that he had done this on purpose. For her. Nothing magical had ever confounded her so much.

A pigeon landed on her shoulder. "Too late!" it burbled in her ear.

Fucking interrupting pigeon. "Why is it too late?" she asked.

"Too late," was all it said in response.

"It can't be too late," Patricia said, "or you wouldn't be talking to me."

Laurence looked at the pigeon on Patricia's shoulder, pecking at the air and babbling, and his eyes narrowed like he really wanted to say something snarky.

"Almost too late," the pigeon said. "Practically too late."

She tried to ask, again, why it was too late, but the bird flew off—although maybe like it wanted her to follow. In any case, nothing would be worse than standing in front of the shuttered Bench Bar obsessing about everyone who had been silenced, one way or another. "We need to follow that bird," she told Laurence, who shrugged, like *why not? So we're following a bird now.*

She took off up the hill, away from Mission, keeping the

pigeon in sight as it kept wheeling and then soaring uphill again. The pigeon led them up a tiny staircase, set in the hillside, and then to a tiny lane that zigzagged through trees. The street got smaller and smaller until it was just a pathway through a terrace clogged with willows and banyans, big low-slung branches putting their leaves in her face as she raced to keep the pigeon's messy wings in sight.

The pigeon banked and went up another tiny outdoor staircase, rising into darkness. The trees collided over the stairs, their branches packed so tight Patricia kept losing sight of the bird they were chasing. She grabbed Laurence's hand as the staircase turned into a loose dirt slope going upwards, and the trees became wider and even tighter-packed. Bark thick as tire treads, branches like barbed wire. They masked the sky. She spent all her concentration steering Laurence and herself on a clear path. The slope grew steeper and steeper until it was vertical, and then it flattened. Patricia glanced behind her and couldn't even see the path they'd come from.

Patricia realized with a jolt that she hadn't been this deep into a forest since the time she'd become a bird, back before Kanot had taken her away to Eltisley Maze.

"My GPS is having a meltdown," Peregrine said.

Now that they had deep forest all around them, the pigeon seemed chattier. "So I'm not sure if I ought to be bringing your friend along," it said. "My name is Kooboo, by the way." At least, that's what the name sounded like.

"My friends are very respectable," said Patricia, including Peregrine in that. "And I'm guessing it's too late to worry about bringing outsiders. Are we going to the Parliament?

I'm Patricia, and this is Laurence. And that's Peregrine that he's holding."

The trees thinned out a little, and Patricia had a feeling they were almost at the clearing with the great spread-eagled Tree. She paused and took Laurence's free hand, the one not holding Peregrine, in both of her hands. "I have no clue what I'm doing here," she said. "Nothing prepared me for this. But I'm really glad you're here with me. I feel like I must have done something right sometime, if you're still in my life after all the stuff that's happened."

Laurence typed on the Caddy: "Best friends." Then he erased the word "Best" and wrote: "Indestructible."

"Indestructible. Yeah." Patricia took Laurence's hand again. "Let's go see the Tree."

PATRICIA HAD FORGOTTEN how massive and terrible the Tree was, how overwhelming the embrace of its two great limbs. How like an echo chamber the space in the shadow of its canopy was. She had expected it to seem smaller now that she was a grown-up, just a tree after all, but instead she looked at its great hanging fronds and its gnarled surface and felt presumptuous for even coming into its presence again.

The Tree did not speak. Instead, the birds sitting on its branches all fluttered and shouted at once. "Order! Order!" said a great osprey in the junction of the two huge branches. "This is highly irregular," said a fluffy pheasant higher up, with a roll of its wings.

"This is as far as I go," whispered Kooboo the pigeon. "Good luck. I think they were already in the middle of a No Confidence vote. Bad timing!" The pigeon flew away, leaving Patricia and Laurence standing alone before the Parliament.

"Hello," Patricia said. "I'm here. You sent for me."

"No, we didn't," the pheasant said.

"We did," the osprey reminded his esteemed colleague. "However, you are late."

"Sorry," Patricia said. "I got here as fast as I could." She glanced at Laurence, who raised his eyebrows, because none of this chatter was making any sense to him.

"We asked you a question, years ago," the osprey said. "And you never came back to answer it."

"Give me a break," Patricia said. "I was like six years old. I didn't even remember that I was supposed to answer a question. Anyway, I'm here now. That counts for something, right?"

"Late!" an eagle said from the uppermost fork of the right-hand branch. "Late!" some of the other birds chorused.

"We did not think you would make it here soon enough," the eagle said. "Your time is ending."

"Why is that?" Patricia said. "Because of the Unraveling? Or the war?"

"Your time," said a lean crow on the other side of the Tree with a slow dip of its sharp beak, "is ending."

"In any case, you are here, yes," the osprey said. "So we might as well hear your answer. Is a tree red?"

"Is a tree red?" repeated the crow.

The other birds took up the question until their voices

blended together into one terrible din. "Is a tree red? Is a tree red? Is? A tree? Red?"

Patricia had been bracing herself for this moment, especially since her talk with Peregrine. She had sort of hoped the answer would just pop into her head from wherever her subconscious must have been gnawing at it for years, but now that she was actually here she felt light-headed and completely blank. She still couldn't even make sense of it. Like what tree were they even talking about? What if you asked someone who was color-blind? She stared at the Tree, right in front of her, trying to figure out what color it was. One moment, its bark was sort of a muddy gray. Then she looked again, and she saw a deep, rich brown that shaded into red. She couldn't tell, it was too much, she didn't have a clue. She looked at Laurence, who gave her an encouraging smile even though he was out of the loop.

"I don't know," Patricia said. "Give me a minute."

"You've had years." The osprey scowled. "It's a perfectly simple question."

"I… I…" Patricia closed her eyes.

She thought of all the trees she'd seen in her life, and then weirdly her mind slipped to the fact that she'd glimpsed a whole other universe when she was rescuing Priya. And that other universe had impossible colors, with wavelengths that humans weren't even supposed to see—and what color would a tree be there? That thought led her to Ernesto, who was lost in that universe forever and who had said that this planet was a speck and we were all just specks on a speck. But maybe our whole universe was just a speck, too. And it was all part of nature, all of it—every universe and all the spaces in between—as much nature as this Tree in front of her. Patricia thought of Reginald saying nature doesn't "find a way" to do anything, and Carmen saying they had been right but rash in Siberia, and Laurence saying humans were unique in the cosmos. Patricia still didn't know anything about nature, or anything else. She knew less than when she was six years old, even. She might just as well be color-blind.

"I don't know," Patricia said. "I don't know. I'm sorry. I really am." She felt a deep ache, in her joints and behind her eyes, like she hadn't really gotten healed from being roasted alive after all.

"You don't *know*?" A heron wagged its long scissor beak at her.

"I'm sorry. I ought to know one way or the other by now, but…" Patricia struggled for the words, feeling tears fill her eyes again. "I mean, how am I supposed to know? Even if I knew which tree you're asking about, I would only know my perceptions of it. I mean, you could look at a tree and see what it looks like, but you wouldn't be perceiving what it actually *is*. Let alone how it would look to nonhuman eyes. Right? I just don't see how you could know. I'm really sorry. I just can't."

Then she stopped and felt a jolt of realization. "Wait. Actually, that is my answer: I don't know."

"Oh," said the osprey. "Hmm."

"Is that the right answer?" Patricia said.

"It's certainly *an* answer," the osprey said.

"Works for me," said the pheasant, fluttering.

"I deem it acceptable," said the eagle at the top of the Tree. "Despite the appalling lateness."

"Phew," Patricia said. She told Laurence what the answer to the question had been, and she noticed that as she spoke the answer the Caddy in Laurence's hand displayed a menu that she'd never seen before, as though something had been unlocked. She turned back toward the Parliament. "So what do I get? For answering the question?"

"Get? You get to be proud," the osprey said, with a sweep of wingtips. "You are free to go. With our congratulations."

"That's it?" Patricia said.

"What else did you expect?" said an owl, poking its head out of the far left side of the Tree. "A parade? Actually, we haven't had a parade in quite a while. That could be fun."

"I thought, maybe, a boon or something? Like, I don't know, if I answer the question I get a power-up? This was supposed to be a quest, right?" The birds all started debating among themselves about whether there was something in their own bylaws that they'd ignored, until Patricia interrupted: "I want to talk to the Tree. The Tree that you're all sitting on right now."

"Oh, sure," said the pheasant. "Talk to the Tree. Do you want to talk to some rocks while you're at it?"

"She wants to talk to the Tree," a turkey chortled.

"I am," said the Tree beneath them, in a great rustle of breath, "here."

"Uh, hi," Patricia said. "Sorry to disturb you."

"You have," the Tree said, "done well."

The Parliament was silent for once, as the birds looked

down at their own meeting chamber, starting to converse on its own. Some of the birds flew away, while others stood very still, heads tucking into wings.

"We spoke before," Patricia said. "You told me a witch serves nature. Do you remember?"

"I," the Tree said, "remember."

Its voice came from deep inside its trunk and rose up to its branches, causing them to vibrate and shower leaves down. More members of Parliament were fleeing, although a few of them were trying to organize a motion to hold their own Parliamentary chambers in contempt.

"It remembers me," Patricia told Laurence and Peregrine.

"The Tree is speaking English," Peregrine informed her.

Peregrine's screen still showed that weird screen—which looked like the Caddy's source code or something. Rows of hexadecimal strings, like machine addresses, plus some complicated instructions with lots of parentheses.

"What are you?" Patricia asked the Tree. "Are you the source of magic?"

"Magic is," said the Tree, "a human idea."

"But I wasn't the first person you ever spoke to, was I?"

"I am many quiet places," the Tree said. "And many loud places."

"You talked to others before me," Patricia said. "And you shared some of your power with them. Right? And that's how we got witches? Before there were Healers, or Tricksters, or anything."

"It was," the Tree said, "a long time ago."

"Listen, we need your help," Patricia said. "Even the birds knew it, time is running out. We need you to intervene. You have to do something. I answered the question, so you owe me. Right?"

"What," said the Tree, "would you have me do?"

"Do?" Patricia tried, really hard, to hold it together. Her hands were nuggets. "I don't know, you're the ancient presence and I'm just some dumb person. I barely managed to answer one yes-or-no question. You're supposed to know more than me."

"What," the Tree said again, "would you have me do?"

Patricia did not know what to say. She needed to say something, she needed to find a way to make this day something other than the day everything fell in the dirt around her. Her friends, dead. Laurence, speechless. And much worse to come soon. She couldn't let this... She couldn't let this be all there was. She couldn't. She trembled and groped for the right thing to say, to fix everything. She stumbled over words.

Laurence stepped past her, walking right up to the Tree, which by now was empty of birds. Patricia wanted to stop him or to ask what the hell he was doing, but Laurence had a look on his face that said, *I'm doing this, don't argue*, and she wanted, needed, to trust him.

Laurence had something in his hand, and he was lifting it up to the Tree: his Caddy. He felt all around the trunk until he found a knothole that was just big enough, and he eased the silvery fish scale through the thick bark around the opening and then carefully rotated it, until its screen was shining from within the Tree's bark, right side up. He wedged it into place, then stepped back toward Patricia, making an exaggerated palm-slapping motion.

"Oh," Peregrine said. Tendrils were growing out of the Tree's insides into its network and zipwire ports. Peregrine's screen involuntarily lit up with a notice that said: "New Network Detected."

"You are," the Tree said, "like me."

"A distributed consciousness, yes," Peregrine said. "Although your network is much larger and vastly more chaotic than mine. This may require… a rather ambitious firmware update. Stay tuned." The screen went dark.

Patricia turned to Laurence. "How did you know?"

He raised his hands and shoulders, in a big pantomime shrug. He typed on his phone: "lucky guess?" She kept staring at him until he typed: "ok, ok. the tree's question woke peregrine, the answer unlocked its source code. peregrine is part magic. i figured."

The screen at the center of the Tree lit up again, and this time stuff was streaming across it faster than Patricia could make sense of. Peregrine had rebooted and was now doing a systemwide update. The Tree made what sounded like a noise of startled pleasure: "Oh."

Shapes appeared on the glowing screen, ensconced in the middle of the bark. They were too far away to see, and Patricia didn't dare come any closer. But she still had her own Caddy, in her satchel. She pulled it out and thumbed its screen on, revealing a schematic. After a moment, she recognized a diagram of a tree. Leaves, dotted with stomates, spangled with solar electricity, branches and meristematic zones growing and dividing, roots stretching miles in every direction and intersecting with other trees. The schematic pulled back until it showed a number of trees, and water sources, and weather patterns, all the interlocking ecosystems.

Then it shifted, and she was looking at a map of magic. She could see every spell that anyone had ever cast, since the very first witch on Earth. Somehow, she knew what she was looking at, especially when she saw the spell map split into Healers and Tricksters and then branch into all the different schools of magic, before converging again. Each spell was a node, all of them connected by cause and effect and the incestuousness of magical society. The entire history of magic, over thousands of years, every single time human hands had shaped this power, in a single visualization that rotated in three dimensions. There was one ugly little dark green knot, at the very end. A spell that hadn't been cast yet.

"That's the Unraveling," Peregrine said. "I'm going to go ahead and take it apart, although a few pieces of it might come in handy later." As Patricia watched, the green knot untwisted and fell apart. "I'm afraid I can't undo any spells that have already been cast," Peregrine said. "Or there could be a domino effect, of spell after spell collapsing. Sorry, Laurence."

Laurence bit his lip. Patricia put her hand on his shoulder.

The map of magic on the Caddy's screen pulled back, showing that the whole ornate shape that Peregrine had drawn was just one dot in a much larger pattern of ricochets. All of magic, suddenly tiny. The much larger shape that Peregrine revealed was too noisy for Patricia to look at for long, before her head hurt too much. She looked over at the Tree instead: a great dark cloak, with a bright white heart.

"I think I'm in love," Peregrine said. "The first time in my life I haven't felt alone."

"I too," the Tree said, "feel love."

Laurence took the Caddy from Patricia and typed: "get a room, you two."

"Thank you both," Peregrine said to Laurence and Patricia. "You gave me life, but now you've given me something much more valuable. I think we're going to do amazing things together. This is just the beginning. Carmen and the other witches were right, people need to change. I have spent my entire life studying human interactions at a granular level, and now I can see the nonhuman interactions as well. I think we can empower people. Every human can be a wizard."

Laurence typed: "or a cyborg?"

"A cyborg," said Peregrine, "will be the same thing as a wizard. We're working on it, anyway. Give us a little time."

LAURENCE AND PATRICIA walked down the steep slope from the Tree. They came out on the edge of a gentle sea cliff, one of those promontories with stairs made of logs leading down to the beach. Like if you forced Abraham Lincoln at gunpoint to make a beach staircase. They had entered the forest in Bernal Heights, and emerged in the Presidio. The ocean looked as hyperactive as always, foam spraying on the sand. Walls of water tipped over and became floors, over and over. The sea had killed Patricia's mother and father, but she still found it comforting to look at.

The sun was right overhead. This was still just the same day that had started with Patricia listening to Laurence's voicemail and clawing the dirt.

Neither Patricia nor Laurence spoke, even though Patricia could have in theory. Patricia had sand in her boot, and this was suddenly the most annoying thing on Earth. She had to lean on Laurence while she got her boot off and poured it out, and then the boot got sand in it again.

They found a hiking trail, with an illegible sign, and followed it until they got to a two-lane road making a wiggle through the trees. The road sloped down, and if they followed its gyrations, maybe they'd reach streets and houses and people. They had no clue what they would find. Laurence typed "i need" on his phone, and there was a long pause while he tried to end that sentence, finally settling on "chocolate."

Patricia pulled out her own phone, because talking out loud to Laurence and having him text back seemed weird. She texted him: "me 2. need chocolate so bad."

The road leveled out and came to a grassy area, and beyond that they could glimpse the brightness of cement and stucco basking at noon. They both paused, facing each other at the threshold, wondering if they were ready to face whatever the world would look like now.

Laurence hefted his phone and typed a word: "indestructible." He didn't hit send or anything, just kept the word floating at the top of the rectangle screen. She saw it and nodded and felt a surge of warmth somewhere. Under the flat of her sternum, somewhere around there. She reached out and touched that place on Laurence's chest, with two fingers and a thumb. "Indestructible," she said aloud, almost laughing. They leaned in and kissed, dry lips just brushing together, slow, speaking volumes.

Then Laurence took Patricia's arm and they led each other out into the brand-new city.

CHARLIE JANE ANDERS is the editor-in-chief of io9.com, the extraordinarily popular Gawker Media site devoted to science fiction and fantasy. In 2012, her Tor.com story "Six Months, Three Days" won the Hugo Award for Best Novelette and was subsequently picked up for development into a NBC television series. She has also had fiction published by *Tin House*, *Asimov's Science Fiction*, *The Magazine of Fantasy & Science Fiction* and *McSweeney's Internet Tendency*. *All the Birds in the Sky* is her first novel. You can follow Charlie Jane on Twitter @CharlieJane, and visit her website at charliejane.com.

For more fantastic fiction, author events, competitions,
limited editions and more

VISIT OUR WEBSITE
titanbooks.com

LIKE US ON FACEBOOK
facebook.com/titanbooks

FOLLOW US ON TWITTER
@TitanBooks

EMAIL US
readerfeedback@titanemail.com